Jim

Best Wishes

Ava, Nathan, Lola,

Read On ! :)

The Collin Chronicles

Book 1:

Magic, Bones, and Catacombs

By

T.K. Garrison

The Collin Chronicles—Book 1: Magic, Bones, and Catacombs

By T. K. Garrison

Feedback to the author: timg@constructioncalc.com or by mail: ConstructionCalc, Inc, 18579 W. Lakeview Lane, Mount Vernon, WA 98274

Cover by Angi Shearstone, copyright © 2005.
All other illustrations copyright © 2006 by the author.
The photograph of Collin and Ramey in Chapter 1 is actually of the author's sons: Connor and Corey Garrison, ages 12 and 10. Photo copyright © 2006 by Kurt Garrison, the author's brother.
The sketches of Collin and Ramey are also tracings of the author's sons, Connor and Corey Garrison.
Sketches of gold mining equipment are tracings from *The Mining Camps Speak*, by Beth and Bill Sagstetter, Benchmark Publishing of Colorado, 1998, benchmarkcolo@worldnet.att.net, by permission.
The sketch of Peter Kringle is a tracing of the author's good friend and architect, Allen Elliott.

This book is available through Amazon.com, Borders.com, and at other online bookstores.

ISBN 1-4196-5887-5

This book is dedicated to my family.

No aspiring author will ever be understood
by those not shackled to the necessity to write. My wife,
Cindy, and kids, Connor and Corey, are no exception.

In the end, however, a truly loving family like mine will come
to understand the unextinguishable need for its resident author
(or author-in-training) to spend ridiculous amounts of time in
front of a glowing liquid crystal display. Cindy calls mine "my
girlfriend." No, hon, you are the one and only. Thanks for
your patience and understanding.

Connor and Corey, though you are too young to know it, you
are my inspiration. This book is for you—this book is *about*
you.

CONTENTS

FOREWARD

This is a work of fiction.

Some names herein are based on people I've known and places I've been, though the events and situations are one-hundred-percent fabricated. Well, let me qualify that: a few of the scenes involving country life on a farm are based on my own childhood.

Lest this book spark the prospect of a real gold mine existing somewhere in the mountains of Washington State, rest assured, no such place exists, at least not to my knowledge. But, nevertheless, hunting for gold can be a lot of fun and I heartily recommend Beth and Bill Sagstetter's book, *The Mining Camps Speak*, BenchMark Publishing of Colorado, 1998, as an excellent resource if you're so inclined.

Thank you for picking up this book. I hope you have as much fun reading it as I did writing it.

T. K. Garrison

Chapter One
Magic?

I didn't used to believe in magic; that is, until I learned to fly. And become invisible. And time travel. A lot has happened to me, Collin Miller, in my lifetime—things you wouldn't believe.

When this whole crazy business started, I was twelve years old. My kid brother, Ramey, was ten. The year was 1972. As I write this now, in 2002, I am forty-two.

Because of the events you are about to read, my life today is a fairy-tale. I travel the world exploring fantastic, exotic places. I dine in the fanciest restaurants, sail on the most luxurious yachts, drive the fastest cars. Any sporting event I want to attend—the Superbowl, World Series, Olympics, Wimbledon, you name it—I simply go there. How? Magic, that's how.

Sometimes I wonder, why me? Why did this fabulous, treacherous, set of circumstances happen to me, Collin Miller? I mean, I was nobody. I lived in a nowhere town and had a bunch of nobody friends. Why does anything happen to anybody? Why was Babe Ruth the greatest of all time? Heck, I don't know, sometimes it just works out that way.

Did I say treacherous? You can't imagine the hazards Ramey and I faced in our pursuit of a little gold. This is how dangerous it was: because of us, a lot of people, my dad included, got badly injured, and someone even died. You can see the dead person wasn't me, and I don't want to ruin the story, so I can't tell you who the unlucky soul was. But rest assured, someone does not make it through the final chapter.

Just before my fateful decision to search for Dark Quartz Gold, Ramey's and my lives were pretty good. Okay, we had too many chores, but what country boy doesn't? It's like my dad always said: "Ain't nothin' good ever comes easy." Now that I've been through heck and back, I can tell you, my dad was right.

Anyway, so there we were, Ramey, our parents, and me, living up on that mountainside near Furry-Pine, Washington. Dad had mortgaged everything to buy our acreage. It came with a humble log cabin, a large old hay barn, a livestock barn, a chicken coop and an equipment shed. Dad named our spread "The Stump and Gorge" for obvious reasons.

We were so poor that… well, you'll find out just how poor we were.

What did I look like back then? I was average for a scrawny twelve-year-old. People said I favored my father, with wavy brown hair and green eyes. I wasn't the fastest kid in my class, either in sports or scholastics. But what I lacked in those attributes, I more than made up for in tenacity. When I set my mind to something, I didn't quit.

Ramey favored my mom with his straight blond hair and blue eyes. He was lean and tough, fairly tall for his age. Because he was two years younger than me, he had to work harder at everything to keep up. As a result, he was scrappy and advanced, both mentally and physically, for his age. As far as he was concerned he was equal to me in every way, and if someone didn't believe it, he would be happy to prove it to them.

I recently scrounged through a bunch of dusty shoe boxes and found this old photo of Ramey and me. It was taken during the summer of 1972—the very summer that my my mom got sick.

I'm on the right—the one with the fish, of course. Ramey is on the left (his fish fell out of his kreel while bicycling up the hill).

The story you are embarking on is a full accounting, to the best of my recollection, of how I discovered magic, found some gold, saved a few lives, and…well, had the best time of my entire life.

Chapter Two

The Hay Barn

<u>June, 1972</u>

Sometimes my kid brother, Ramey, can be a real pain. Then again, sometimes he's pretty darned funny.

Like for instance, the other day. We were up in the rafters of the hay barn having a pigeon egg fight when my dad came looking for us.

"Collin!" dad hollered through the big barn doors. "Son— where're you at?!"

"Here, dad," I replied. "Over at…um, by the pig pen!"

"I'm standing by the pig pen, boy—and I don't see you nowheres. *Where* by the pig pen?"

"Up here, dad, *above* the pig pen."

Dad tilted his head back. Then he saw me, about twenty-five feet off the ground, one arm wrapped around a cobwebbed post, the other hidden in a shadowy place among the rafter heels and knee-braces.

"Collin, what in tarrr-nation are you doin' up there? I thought you had chores to tend to! How're you gonna' get anything done dancing around in them rafters?"

See, my dad is a logger. He doesn't always speak properly. It used to really upset my mom, but after fifteen years she's pretty much given up on him.

"Um, well dad, y'see, Ramey, he and I were just about finished, then he, Ramey, got this idea…"

Before I could finish my sentence, from somewhere in Ramey's proximity came a loud slipping noise then a "*Whoops!*", then a "*Whoooaaaaaa!*", then a scraping sound followed by a *thud!*

"Ramey! You okay?" I shouted, creeping my way along the roofline to where he was moments before. I knew what had happened: Ramey lost his grip and took the express route down the steep corrugated metal roof to land – *splat!* – a colossal belly flop in the pig pen below.

My dad knew, too, and shot off like a rocket to check on his youngest son. In a few great strides he was standing boot-deep in squishy pig manure looking over Ramey. A couple of curious piglets came nosing over to investigate. They were rooting and grunting at the side of Ramey's head. There was something yellow splattered there and the pigs smelled it.

Dad sent the piglets squealing away with a flail of his boot then reached down with one giant paw and in a great swooping motion plucked Ramey from the mire. He came free with a *schhhhh-pock!* Dad set him on his feet. Ramey stood there, grime-coated from hair to toe, blinking hard and trying his best to look innocent. He was all right—the yellow on his head was pigeon egg, not brain.

"Thanks—thanks dad," he sputtered, spitting out a few

chunks of nasty black stuff. "I was, um…kinda' having trouble breathing down there."

"Ramey, I swear to Swamie!" dad exclaimed, crossing his arms over his chest. "You've got to be the most accident-prone kid to ever walk the face of the earth! Now, son, that was a ten-foot fall. Are you sure you're all right?"

"Oh, yeah, dad, I'm fine. Manure broke my fall. Lucky thing for pig poop."

I tried not to laugh, but a giggle squeaked out anyway.

"Lucky ain't the word for you, Ramey," dad said, shooting me a glare. "Now, what's that yellow stuff smeared over the back of your head them pigs were after?"

"Oh, that—yeah, um, well, that's the reason I—uh, we were up there in the first place. See, Collin and I, um, we were having a pigeon egg fight, dad. Collin, he spackled me good when I wasn't looking. Nailed the back of my head."

Now I could tell dad was straining not to laugh, too. He grinned. "Okay, okay. Well, I reckon there's no harm in that. Now look here. I'm heading off to town for a few supplies. You boys need to finish up your chores. I don't mind a little slacking-off time, but only *after* your chores are done. Understand?"

"Yes, dad, we'll finish," Ramey and I answered in unison.

"Good. Make sure you do." He turned and strode for his faded blue International Harvester pickup. After a few grinds on the starter, the engine popped and backfired to life. Dad clicked it into gear and down the dusty gravel driveway he sputtered.

"Man, we sure were lucky just now," I said. "Good thing dad's in a happy mood."

Ramey didn't answer. He was consumed with removing more black matter from the inside of his mouth.

"Ramey!" I exclaimed. "I just remembered something. Now that dad's gone, let's hang up our new rope swing here in the hay barn!"

Ramey, one filthy hand gripping the end of his tongue and stretching it, the other scraping away at the topside, replied, "Moway! Yar woo crzy? Woo herd dad. Weoo thuppothed to finith owa chorths."

"Tell you what, Ramey. You finish the chores and I'll tie the rope to the beam. Deal?"

Ramey scraped away at his tongue a bit longer until he was satisfied that he'd elevated his mouth to an acceptably sanitary condition. Then he occupied himself with removing egg shells from his hair and scalp. "Yeah, sure," he finally said.

I shot off, leaving Ramey to his shell picking. The rope I was after was a logger's castoff I'd spotted at one of dad's abandoned log landings. He'd said it was okay for me to keep, so I put it in a five-gallon bucket in the tack room next to the chicken coop.

I opened the tack room door and a great gust of billowing dust poofed out. My mom was in there cleaning.

"Oh, hi—*cough, cough*—mom," I said, trying to dodge below the dust.

"Hi, hon," she replied from somewhere in the gray-brown depths. "I—*cough, cough*—can't tell you how much I despise this job… all the dust, and debris, and—*hack*—especially, the mouse droppings. There must be ten thousand of those darned rodents living in here."

I didn't stick around for conversation. I knew where the bucket was, held my breath, snatched it and bolted. "See ya," I shouted behind me.

I had no idea, but that very instant in time—my mom in that awful, dusty, enclosed tack room—would cause my life to change forever. No one in Washington State had ever heard of Hantavirus—the deadly disease transmitted through contact with deer mice excrement— in 1972. But for some unexplainable reason, it chose our little farm as its first place to surface west of the Mississippi River.

Back into the hay barn's rafters I went, tugging my rope behind me. To position the rope, I had to shimmy out a large, unfinished beam some forty feet up. I did it by straddling the beam and scooching across. Man, did that beam have a lot of splinters.

After the rope was in place, I clambered down, then tied a stick-handle through the low end. Just about that time Ramey came racing up, eyes fixed on our new toy.

"You got all the chores done, right?" I asked.

"Yep."

"Well, I got the swing hung. Guess I'll give 'er a test." I jumped up a foot or so and grabbed the handle then hung there like a chub of salami. Nothing happened so I dropped to the floor then proclaimed enthusiastically, "She's safe all right! Strong as a bull. Now, Ramey, you give 'er the first run, from that post over there."

Ramey turned in the direction I was pointing, a look of suspicion on his face.

"See Ramey," I instructed. "What you do is climb up the post, grab the handle in both hands, then jump off toward the barn doors. You swing back and forth through the doors. Got it? Simple. Now, you give 'er the ol' acid test, the real McCoy."

Ramey looked up the forty-foot rope, its proximity to the jambs of the big barn doors and its potential return path. "Um—I dunno Collin," he said. "I was just thinking, *you* set it up—prolly it ought to be *you* who gets first run."

"Nope," I replied firmly. "You get honors, Ramey."

Ramey again eyeballed the probable reverse trajectory. "Uuuuhh—yeah," he stammered. "'Course I'll go, but are you double-duck sure you don't want to be the first one to try out this *cool new swing*? Just think, ten years from now, Collin, you'll be able to say *I was first!*"

I stood firm, hands folded across my chest. I'd used that same psychology on Ramey too many times to be suckered by it. "Nope. It's okay with me if you're the one who says that in ten years."

End of discussion. Torn between the thrill of the ride and the peril of the post, Ramey grabbed the rope and climbed to a suitable jumping-off point. But being Ramey, he reasoned if you're gonna' do it, you might as well do it right, and so found the highest knee-brace he could climb... then fearlessly leaped.

Everything went well at first: a smooth, swift downward fall through the big doors, a graceful upward arc over the barnyard, awe-inspiring views of the grounds, then a backward returning sweep.

But just as he reached the pinnacle of his backward arc, the jumping-off post did a dastardly thing. It suddenly and silently crept sideways a foot. Because he was now traveling backward, blindly, Ramey never saw it coming.

Whack! It was a glancing blow—the post striking his right shoulder blade. This quite unbalanced him, spinning him madly, like a wounded helicopter, back downward. But now his path for the open doors was compromised and instead of flying through them, the rope pulled him straight into the door jamb. *Slam!* He hit the 12x12 post squarely. If there was anything good about the collision, it was that he was near the bottom of the arc, so when his fingers went limp and he dropped, it was only a foot and a half to the dirt.

I rushed over. "Ramey! Are you all right? Ramey—what happened? Ramey!"

He was lying flat on his back, eyes wide open but focused on nothing. As I hovered there, wondering whether or not he was dead, I was surprised to hear the voice...of my father.

"What in the sam hill is going on here?!" he bellowed as he came stomping up. "Mama said something about you fetching a rope. Now look what you've did! Is he all right? He ain't moving."

I was quick to answer, "Well Dad, y'see, Ramey—he was trying out our new rope swing, and—well, he jumped wrong, and somehow the post got in his way, and—*it wasn't my fault, Dad!* I didn't do a thing! Ramey did it all by himself! He hit the jamb post with his side, and now..."

I stopped my sentence short because just then Ramey moved slightly. He'd apparently been listening and was determined to debunk the load of horse manure suddenly spewing from my mouth. He raised up a little, staring blankly at the two blurry shapes over him.

"Oh look, he's fine, dad!" I shouted. "See—he's not even dead! Right, Ramey? Isn't that right, Ramey—you're alive—and...and you're fine! Not one broken bone, right?"

"Collin!" dad rebuked sternly. "Why'nt you quit your blabberin' for half a minute and let me see if your brother's gonna' live or die here. Looks to me like he's got a dent in the side of his head the size of a sweet potata and his eyes ain't right. Now, Ramey, can you hear me, son? Son, are you all right?"

"Yeah, dad—I'm...okay," he replied woozily, scratching around in the dirt for traction to stand. "If you'd just step back a little and let me up—uh...I'll be...fine."

Dad and I backed away and slowly Ramey regained his feet. Wobbling, he dusted himself off and rubbed the right side of his head. "Darn, that post sure is hard," he said crossly.

Dad closely observed him for a few more moments just to be sure there was no serious damage. Then he turned his attention to the swing now hanging statically a few feet away. "Well, well," he exclaimed with mock surprise. "Looks to me like someone or another went and hung themselves up a little rope swing. Collin, I don't suppose you know anything about how this swing got here, do you?"

I gulped hard. I knew better than to tell a lie. "Yes, dad—I do know about it."

"Hmmm, and I don't suppose you asked your mama or me if you could tie that rope onto that beam, waaaayyy up in them rafters, did you?"

"Um—no, dad."

"I see. And I don't suppose Ramey had to beat you up to be first on the swing, did he?"

"Nn—no." It always amazed me how dad never failed to ask the exact questions necessary to extract the maximum possible guilt in any situation.

"Well then, son, do you figure you made a pack o' good choices about this rope swing? Or were your choices of the other kind, you know, the BAD kind?"

I could feel my face flushing with heat. "Um—well…you didn't say we *couldn't* hang up a rope swing—and, and you let us go on the one down at the lake—and I didn't…"

"Collin!" dad interrupted angrily. "You're not answering my question, son! Were your choices the *good* kind or the BAD kind? I need a straight answer, son!"

"Uh—the bad kind—I guess."

"All right then. What do you reckon your punishment ought to be?"

"Um—well, I don't know. How about extra chores for a week?"

"Extra chores?" he roared. "What kind of limp noodle, wet rag answer is that? I've got half a mind to send *you* up on the swing just like you done your brother and make *you* jump off! But…"

And as he said "but," to my tremendous surprise, he turned, cracked a slight smile, and eased the tension in his forehead.

"But…I'm in a good mood today. Not only that, there was a time when even I had a rope swing. And fact of the matter is, I had a couple of brothers, too. Now, I'm not saying what you done here is tolerable, nosir. But on the other hand, I understand boys, and you happened to catch me at a weak moment. So I'm gonna' let you off the hook easy this time."

As he glanced back and forth at Ramey and me, noting our sudden expressions of profound stupefaction, he let his smile broaden to a full-fledged beaming grin. And that grin was contagious so within a second I found I was smiling, too.

Dad continued, "I think what I'm gonna do, Collin, is instead of making you jump off the swing, I'll do it myself just to be sure she's safe. Last thing we need around here is bunged up, busted and broken boys. Them kind of boys can't get no chores done. So, if there's any bungin' gonna be done, it's gonna be on me."

I could feel my face light up like a Christmas tree. Ramey's wooziness amazingly cleared and he smiled. What a rare treat! Not only did dad spare me the rod, he actually volunteered to sport around with us a bit; well, in a roundabout sort of way.

Dad grabbed the swing and strode off for the post.

"Hey, dad! Wait a minute!" I hollered after him. "You better be careful—uh, I think there's a certain way you should jump off. You don't want to wind up like…"

Without turning, dad cut my sentence short, yelling over his shoulder, "Son, don't forget—I've been jumping off rope swings longer'n you've been alive."

Ramey and I stared in amazement as dad, fully outfitted in his logging gear, climbed the post just as nimbly as an alley cat. Once there, he paused and stared back and forth at the top of the rope, the doorway, and the barnyard beyond. It was like he was calculating something in his mind. Then suddenly, he jumped. And as he did, he let out a whoop and holler that filled the entire barn and rolled out into the orchards beyond.

"YYEEeeee… HHAAAaaaaaa!"

It was the loudest sound I had ever heard come from his mouth. We riveted our eyes on him as he swung downward. Would he hit the jamb? Would his fingers slip off? The rope stretched under his weight and the beam overhead bowed dangerously.

Suddenly, I wasn't breathing and every hair on the back of my neck was standing straight up. Would dad blame me when he wiped out? How bad would the collision be? Broken bones? An emergency trip to the doctor's office?

He swung down through the bottom of the arc. To keep his long legs from dragging he heisted them up then let out another whoop. I started laughing. This was downright comical! At that moment, my dad looked like a grinning rodeo cowboy clamped tightly to a twirling bull. Ramey was laughing, too.

Dad rode the swing through the doors, then up, up to the top of the arc. His eyes grew to the size of silver dollars as he glanced about, taking in the view. Then down he came, backwards. Now he was laughing, too—a great, big belly laugh that shook his whole body. Back through the doors, legs hiked, then up, up, up—blindly toward the post.

The post!

I swallowed my laugh. Would the dastardly fir pole be as cruel to dad as it had been to Ramey?

Whoosh! Up he flew, missing it by a good foot, then back down again. Ramey heaved a great sigh, as did I.

Another colossal *"YEEE-HHhaaaa!"* and back out the doors he zoomed. Ramey and I burst into peals of laughter again as he rode the bucking rope-bronco back and forth, ultimately taming it to submission.

Finally, he dropped lightly to the barn floor then strode on over.

"Therenow!" he boomed, still smiling. "Did you fellers take note o' that? *That's* how you ride a rope swing! I do believe it's safe enough for you two boys, so go ahead and give 'er a run. But, just be careful. And don't be ashamed to start out on the lower rung until you get the *hang* of 'er. Ahem, get it? *Hang*? Ha ha! Now, I know mama's got some chores lined up for you, but I reckon it won't hurt nothin' if you play on your swing for a little while anyways."

Then, to my great surprise, rather than turn heel and walk back to the house, he knelt down, put a big, callused paw on the top of my head and ruffled my hair a bit then did the same to Ramey. He looked us squarely in the eye and said, "Every now an' then, boys, you've gotta' stop and smell the roses. Cut loose a little, if you know what I mean. I know I don't do enough of that around here. Seems like there's too much work nagging after me all the time. But maybe you can learn something from your old dad about how *not* to do certain things. And maybe when you're grown up you'll be better at them than me. Now, g'wan and have yourself some fun."

I could feel my smile reaching each ear. It was true; my dad was frugal at showing outward affection, but just the same, there was never the smallest shred of doubt in Ramey's or my mind that he loved us tremendously.

I watched him stride away, thinking, *Boy-o-boy, there's no way I could ever be better than my dad—at anything.*

Chapter Three

Tall Tales

The next day Ramey and I were outdoors early, intent on finishing our chores so we would have plenty of time to visit our friends, Larry and David Aimwell, that afternoon.

At about eleven o'clock, our log cabin's screen door opened and mom emerged. "Boooooys!" she called. "Guess what I've got for yoouuuuu!"

That was all the invitation we needed to interrupt our duties and come racing for the door. The wonderful scent of something baking hit my nostrils at the front porch. "Ramey," I gasped, "I think its cookies!"

"Yeah, and I bet I can tell what kind from here—*snuff, sniff*—yep, my favorite, chocolate chip coconut!"

Stepping into the house, the rich aroma of mom's baked treat washed over us. I inhaled deeply, tilting my head back in ecstasy.

"My, you boys sure got here in a hurry," mom said with a smile. "It's like you were on your way to a fire or something. Now, I just happen to have some cookies, fresh out of the oven, and two frosty glasses of milk for two particularly handsome boys, if they happen to be hungry. But, it'll cost you. Mama needs a hug and kiss from each boy first. Any takers?"

Her question was about as necessary as asking a wolf whether or not he'd be interested in a T-bone steak. First, Ramey and I were always hungry. And second, we loved our mom so much, a great big hug and kiss was something we actually looked forward to. She was so pretty—always smiling and laughing, gleeful blue eyes that sparkled with fun.

Today it was cookies. Tomorrow it might be freshly-baked bread with tangy, homemade raspberry jam. The next day, blueberry muffins. It seemed every day mom did something special for Ramey and me.

"Mom, it's Sa'rday," I muffled around a gigantic chomp of cookie. "We're still going over to the Aimwells t'night, right?"

"Of course, Collin," she replied with a reproachful smile. "That is, if you don't choke on that cookie first! My goodness! Slow down or your taste buds won't even know there was something sweet flying past them. It's all arranged. I'll take you there at four and pick you up after supper."

"Mom," Ramey said, slurping down a last gulp of milk and wiping his face with a shirt sleeve. "Will you please finish reading *Charlotte's Web* to us tonight? I've been thinking. Even though Wilbur won the blue ribbon at the fair, I still don't see how Charlotte and Templeton can keep him from winding up bacon and sausage. Shoot, if one of our pigs ever won at the fair, we'd still butcher 'em an' eat 'em, wouldn't we, mom?"

"Ramey!" she responded, half-scolding. "That kind of talk is not appropriate at our eating table! There is a time and place for discussing farming activities and this is neither. Now, you boys go back out and see if there's anything you can do to help your father. I'll have lunch ready in a little while."

Four o'clock finally rolled around and Mom shuttled us to the Aimwells, who lived five miles away on a small piece of land on the banks of the Tigaks River.

After a rousing game of four-boy sandlot baseball, we retreated to Larry and David's tree fort. It was a crude conglomeration of planks and rusted tin siding haphazardly nailed within the bough of a gnarly old maple tree. Access was via a number of railroad spike-rungs driven into the central trunk.

Once convened in the tree fort, the fibbing began. It was practically a contest—to see who could spin the tallest, most flabbergasting tale. We took our seats around an apple-box table on raspberry crate chairs. As usual, the topic ultimately came around to the Dark Quartz Mine.

All the local kids knew about it. Supposedly, the Dark Quartz was the richest gold mine in the state, maybe the entire world. Nobody was exactly sure where its entrance was, though Furry-Pine was thought to be the closest town. Even if the location was known, few souls, if any, would be brave enough to go in. Kids who purported to know said the Dark Quartz carried with it a terrible curse, a curse originated and perpetuated by the mine's owner—a wicked, stingy man known only as Malcrook.

"'Course, anyone who goes in—they never come back out," Larry Aimwell, the gap-toothed, freckle-faced thirteen-year-old, remarked with an air of supreme knowledge. "That place is one gargantuan danger. First off, there's only one entrance tunnel and it's so well hidden bloodhounds couldn't find it. But if somehow you did and were stupid enough to go in, the first thing you'd come to would be a giant pool, about fifty-feet across and thirty-feet deep, filled to the brim with acid. You'd think it was a huge witch's pot, bubbling and boiling with this…this evil brew. Just smelling the vapors could melt your brain. And if you fell in! Bones! A skeleton is all there'd be left. The acid would eat the flesh right off you quicker than a pack of piranhas."

"Yeah," said David, Larry's dark-haired, brown-eyed, eleven-year-old brother. "But, if you somehow got past the acid, you know what'd be waiting on the other side don't you? Dogs! Doberman Pinschers. Savage man-eaters! See, ol' Malcrook, he never feeds 'em, so they have to roam around in the mine's spider web of tunnels until they find their own food. Rats, kids, grown-ups, you name it. If it moves, they eat it. Bones and all—that's how hungry those dogs are."

"Bones?" I exclaimed, taking exception. "Dogs can't chew through bones, David. That's stupid."

"Oh, yeah? These dogs can. Malcrook…well, just to make sure his dogs have the sharpest, toughest teeth in the world, when each one is still a puppy he makes a set of false teeth—dentures— out of stainless steel. He sharpens the steel like buzz-saw blades and then permanently attaches them to the dog's choppers. There's nothing they can't bite through. Like your leg, f'rinstance, Collin. One chomp—take it clean off, all the way up to your thigh."

"Okay, maybe so," I said. "But, you think that's bad? Hunh—that's nothing. You're forgetting about the vault and the booby traps. You guys know Malcrook uses children, about our age, to run his mine, right? Kidnaps 'em. Well, those kids don't do anything all day but dig and blast for gold—been doing it for maybe a hundred years. Deep, deep in dark tunnels they work. And over the years, they've gotten a huge ol' hoard of it—pure, sparkling gold! Malcrook keeps it in this vault, see? It's an underground room, about as big as our whole house. And it's full to the ceiling! In fact, it's so bright in there, you have to wear special welder's goggles or the glare can blind you. Anyway, it's kept safe by this giant metal door. About two feet thick, solid steel, it is. Swings on these massive hinges set right into the rock. You couldn't blow through it with a hundred tons of dynamite.

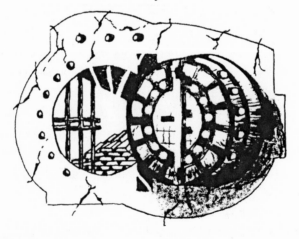

The only way in is by knowing the combination. See, right in the middle of the door is a combination dial, kind of like the one on your bike-lock. But this one's different. There's not just one dial, there's three! And each one is big—the size of a grapefruit. You gotta' get the combination exactly right on each one within sixty seconds, or…or…"

At this juncture, I paused. The other kids were on the edge of their seats, leaning toward me, their eyes wider than headlights. I really had them going. Finally Ramey could stand it no longer. "Or what, Collin?!"

"Booby traps, that's what!" I replied smugly. "And I don't mean just one booby trap, either. There's five, at least—all sprung the instant you mess up the combination. First, you'd be harpooned through the back by spears shot from holes in the wall. Then, a giant steel plate would drop from the ceiling—smash you like a bug. Then poison gas comes shooting out from each of the three combination dials—dissolves your lungs. At the same time, a giant wave of acid gushes up from tiny holes in the floor. And if all that didn't get you, the machine guns would. Buried right in the door, there's twenty, fully-automatic, fifty-caliber machine guns. In two seconds, you'd be so full of holes, you'd look like a colander."

"Yeah, well, all that stuff doesn't mean a thing," Ramey quipped, making sure to take his shot at the fibbing competition. "Let's say somehow you found the mine's entrance and made it past the acid and the dogs. The problem is, you'd never even make it to the vault. Sure, the vault's where all the gold is stored, but it wouldn't do you a scoshe of good because you'd never find it. See, the Dark Quartz Mine is actually this huge underground maze. A catacomb. There's tunnels in every direction: up, down, and sideways. None of 'em are straight, so in a second you'd be turned around and lost. And every tunnel branches off the other. Let's say you were lucky enough to remember a flashlight. Well, you better hope you filled your pockets with batteries because once you got lost you'd just wander for miles, in circles—until your batteries died. Then…then, the trouble really starts. You guys know how dark it is underground? Lemme tell you—it's so dark, you can't see your hand two inches in front of your face! You'd wander around, bumping into walls and ceilings with your head. Pretty soon you'd be covered in blood and scabs. But way, way worse than that are the rats. They'd smell you—sense your panic and come running. The fastest ones, they'd leap on you first—run up a pant leg. Then the others… In a minute, your body would be covered with 'em, but remember, you can't see a thing! No matter how many you managed to throw off, there'd be ten more—every one taking a hunk of hide with 'em. Fifteen minutes—that's all it'd take until you were a…a…bone pile."

Such were the tales we spun, though any actual proof of the mine or Malcrook was in exceedingly short supply.

In later years I would be astonished at how close our tall tales came to truly describing the horrors of that place. And little did I know, fate was already bending and twisting my future directly to the core of it.

Chapter Four

Beaver Lake

"Chores! Seems like all we ever do around here," I complained loudly (as if anyone would care), dragging a hay bale across the enormous stack in our hay barn.

"Yeah, tell me about it," Ramey agreed, stabbing an obstinate bale with his own hay hooks.

"And it's so darned hot today," I continued, wiping a layer of grimy sweat from my forehead.

"Especially here in the hay barn," Ramey said. "Did'ja ever notice it can be nice and cool outside, but in here it's like an oven? A smelly, dusty oven."

"Smelly?" I tilted my face upward and sniffed. "I *like* the smell in here. The hay, the tractors, heck, even the animal pens—all smells kind of good to me."

Ramey raised his nose and gave a mighty snuff, then remarked, "Collin, you're crazy. All I smell is—*snuffff*—your bad breath!" This comment was designed to start a tussle, and Ramey knew it.

I was more than happy to oblige. Even half an excuse to waylay our chores could not be ignored. "You little booger! I'll show you some bad breath!" I put my head down, took a running start, and buried it like a battering ram into my brother's gut. Ramey flew backward, landing precariously close to the haystack's edge and a twenty-foot free-fall to the wooden stanchions below. The object of this familiar grappling game was to be the first to get a good firm headlock on the other, thus gaining position to breathe purposefully and directly into his face.

Swiftly recovering from the wrecking-ball head to the gut,

Ramey twisted around, threw me off, regained his feet, and as fast as a leopard, grabbed me by the shirt and slammed me down. "So— you wanna scrap? Well you came to the right place, mister stinky-breath. Take this!" Diving head first, he shot an arm around my neck to get face-to-face for a brutal exchange of point-blank lung-blowing.

We rolled to the very edge of the stack, but somehow stopped before toppling off. Finding myself in a bad way, I gathered my strength and using arms and legs, pushed my clinging brother away. Ramey spun off in a wildly exaggerated manner, flailing like he'd just taken a shotgun blast to the stomach. "Now, you take that!" I shouted, then immediately gave chase. "And a little more of this!" I dove, taking Ramey down like a linebacker.

After several more minutes of hay-wrestling, I, who at the moment was belly-down on the stack with my cheek pinned to a prickly bale and my arm in a semi-painful hammer lock, managed to grunt, "Unh...hey Ramey, uh, let's finish our chores...then maybe mom will let us...ungh...go to the lake, to our rope swing."

"Hey, that's a good idea!," Ramey said loosening his grip and climbing off. "Probably the best one you've ever had, Weakio."

"Well, I had to come up with something quick. Had to save you from the major romping I was just about to lay on your scrawny bee-hind."

"Yeah, right. The amount of hay I was making you eat just now—I'm surprised you're not walking on four feet, mooing. Since it was *me* just putting the whuppin' on *you*, you've got to be the one to ask mom."

"Oh, I'll ask, alright. But only because you're not smart enough to figure out how."

We tore back into our chores, using our brotherly bicker as fuel to finish quickly. In no time we polished off the last task and left the barn at a sprint. Across the barnyard we ran, practically hurdling the corral fence. Ramey skidded to a stop on the front porch. I continued on inside.

"Mom—mom!" I blurted, exploding into the kitchen. "Mom, Ramey and I have all our chores done, and, well, it's real hot out today. We were wondering if—maybe, we could go to the lake—to our rope swing."

Mom looked up from her steam-shrouded stovetop. Her face was red and beaded with perspiration. "You say it's hot today? Imagine that!" Smiling, she turned and faced me squarely, one hand on her hip. "So, you want to goof off at the lake, do you? Are you sure you'd rather not help me can this mess of green beans instead?"

"Ummm—well if you really need…"

"I'm just kidding, hon," she said, smiling and walking over to encircle my shoulders with an arm. "You boys do plenty around here—you don't need to help me in the kitchen, at least not today. And no, I don't mind if you go. However, that rope swing scares me a little. Just be careful. I'd hate you to crash into a tree or let go too soon and…"

Mom didn't bother to finish. I was out the door, with a hurried "Thanks mom!"

Down the long gravel driveway Ramey and I hurtled on our bicycles, dodging potholes as if they were land mines. The forest's trees and undergrowth whizzed by in a blur. Shortly, we skidded to a dusty stop at a secluded cove along Beaver Lake's tree-dotted southern shore.

"You first, Ramey," I said, peeling off all my clothes except for a tattered pair of shorts. "I had to ask mom, so you've got to go first."

Going first wasn't so bad, except it meant you had to be the one to retrieve the swing. This particular swing consisted of a thick rope with a bulky, multiple knot at the bottom. I had risked my life jerry-rigging it to an upper bough of an ancient leaning alder tree a couple years ago.

"Aaahhh…all right, I'll go first—this time," Ramey carped.

"But sure as shootin', you have to go first next time." Arms folded across his skinny chest, he tiptoed to the water's edge then dipped in a toe. "Brrrrrr." But then, with one mighty leap, he was in—a swan dive over a knot of gnarled roots where water met bank. He swam and retrieved the rope from its stationary position over the deep part of the lagoon. Then he hauled it up, slipping and sliding among the exposed roots and clay of the lake's steep bank to an irregular slab of sandstone that jutted skyward at a crazy angle. The sandstone formed something of a platform on which he stood for a moment, shivering, gathering his courage, looking down on the riffled surface many feet below.

"Watch this, Collin!" he yelled. "This is gonna be a two-and-a-half with eight twists!"

He gripped the rope as tightly as he could then jumped into mid-air. It was a free fall for the first few feet, then, just as the wind became quick in his hair and the goose bumps on his arms raised to the size of thumbtacks, the knot at the rope's lower end tightened under his clutching feet. Up, up, up, to the top of the arc he zoomed. Then, release. He tucked and spun wildly. He looked like a smoking war plane auguring earthward with one of its wings shot off. Ramey untucked just a moment too soon and was laid out flat as a board when his back slapped the water—*smack!*

I doubled over laughing. That had to hurt. But Ramey resurfaced victoriously, pumping a fist, hollering, "Yeah! Yeah, did you see that!" as if he'd just won a gold medal at the Olympics.

After an hour or so at the swing, I noted the lengthening shadows and said, "Ramey, we'd better get back home. Dad'll be looking for us. We're supposed to hoe five rows each in the garden today. And you know dad, he won't care if it takes till midnight to get it done."

Back to our bikes and up the hill we charged. Little did we know, the rope swing we left behind, now swaying gently in the breeze, would one day provide refuge from a dark peril lurking in the depths of our very swimming hole.

Dad happened to be mowing the lawn as we came straggling up the hill. "You boys have a good swim?" he asked, letting his tired old lawnmower come to a wheezing stop.

We were walking our bikes—it was too steep to pedal them. "Yeah, but we sure are pooped," I replied, making sure to sound plenty pathetic.

Dad didn't fall for it for one second. "Well, that's *good* news! Because I've got just the remedy for tired boys. Work! That'll wake you up quicker'n a cold hosin' at midnight. Now, I don't know who gave you permission to go bullygagging down to the lake, but it sure wasn't me. Where I come from, there wasn't no playing until the work was all done. And if my memory serves right,

25

you fellers still owe five rows of hoeing each today. Now, go get your clothes changed and come on back out here. Mama's already in the garden and we need to help her."

"But, dad," I protested, hoping to buy a few more minutes of leisure, "*Mom said* we could go for a swim."

Dad paused for a moment. I could see the conflict on his face. He didn't like it when mom let us goof off if there were chores to be done. They were so different, my mom and dad. She came from a rich family, and his was dirt poor. She was college-educated, he didn't even finish high school. How they ever connected in the first place, I'll never know.

"Well, what're you waiting for?" he finally barked. "The cows to come home? Crack to! We don't allow any blaggards here at The Stump and Gorge, no matter what mama says."

Away we plodded. We knew better than to question dad.

Chapter Five

Furry-Pine

"Yep, those were the days," dad exclaimed aloud after supper that evening, settling into our threadbare sofa. "This summertime heat reminds me of when I used to work down at the lumber mill. You wanna talk about heat! Working summertimes there—it was enough to make a feller feel like a spit wad on a skillet! But it sure was innerestin'. Did I ever tell you fellers about my time at the Janicki-Pacific Mill?"

It was a rare treat when dad would tell us a story. Not hesitating a second, Ramey and I hurled ourselves onto the couch and snuggled up to him, a boy on each side. All the cabin's windows were flung wide in a desperate attempt to trap a little breeze. Mom's rocking chair creaked softly as she watched us, over a knitting project, with a pleasant smile. Wide-eyed, I said, "Yes, I mean, no—I mean, yes you have, but please, dad, tell us again!"

"All right then, I will. Now, you fellers know the closest town to us is Furry-Pine, right? And these days it's small—darned near a ghost town. Well, it wasn't always that way. Not so long ago Furry-Pine was a pretty good-sized bustling frontier city. Built on logging, it was. There were two lumber mills in town, see. I worked at the Janicki-Pacific—the biggest in world, once upon a time. Those grounds had maybe fifty buildings spattered over forty acres. Did you fellers know that?"

"Yep," Ramey replied, "And it was dangerous, too! Right, dad?"

"Ohhh, you betcha! Dangerous ain't hardly a powerful enough word for the hazards a feller could step into there. There'd be trucks buzzin' all over the place, hauling in loads of hemlock and

27

cedar." (Dad swooped his arms in a spaghetti-like motion to illustrate.) "At the same time, there'd be a train docked up with a hundred flatcars of fir logs from up the Tigaks Canyon. And maybe there'd be a fifty-car train heading out too, with fresh sawn lumber—bound for Oregon, or California, or Timbuktu—who knows. You had loading tractors and forklifts zoomin' around all over the place—rigs with tires bigger than two of you, Ramey. And better stay out of their way! They're not stopping for nothin'— nosir. Splat!" (He smacked his hands together crisply.) "Boy, they'd squish you like a bug and not even notice. The driver would probably figure he ran over a pebble or something."

"What about the saws, dad?" I asked. "You ran a buzz-saw, right?"

"Yep, that's exactly what I run—a six-foot buzz on a motorized swing-arm. The logs, they'd come shootin' down this conveyer, see, and it was my job to drop that blade in just the right place at the right time. Sixty-foot log'd leave my station looking more like mincemeat than a tree. Lemme tell you something—you wanna talk about powerful! That saw could cut spang-through a three-foot fir and not even lug. Buzz through it just like a spoon in runny pancake batter. Why, if a small boy was goofing around and accidentally came down that conveyor! I don't even want to think about that."

"Did you ever have any boys come down your conveyor, dad?" Ramey asked with eyes big as baseballs, his imagination running wild.

"Nosir, I didn't, and it's a good thing too," he replied, stifling a grin. "That big ol' six-foot blade—sometimes she plumb went haywire! Just dropped for no good reason. And it didn't care what's coming along under it neither. Boy, log, someone's lunch pail...*schloop!* One dip o' the blade and that's all she wrote!"

"What about the rest of the town," I inquired, anxious to change the subject. "Tell us about when the mill went down—what happened to Furry-Pine."

"Yeah, that was a sad day, that," dad said, his expression turning grim. "See, Furry-Pine—it run on logging. But when there's no more logging, there's hardly any more Furry-Pine. One day, the mills, they up and shut down. Closed their doors, both of 'em, one right after the other. The newspapers ran headlines how logs from Russia and Latin America and Canada could be processed and shipped here cheaper'n we could harvest and process our own. Some folks blamed the environmentalists for inventing up a bunch of cock-and-bull stories about spotted owls and speckled horny toads and who-knows-what other endangered critters. Me? I don't know about any of that. All's I know is at exactly 3:30, the last shift at the Janicki-Pacific let out and then the doors closed. *Bang!* Like a gunshot, it was. Even the clock tower in town square stopped ticking—never made it to 3:31.

"Used to be, no matter where you was in town, you could

hear the saws a-buzzin' and smell the sawdust a-flyin'. Those were good sounds and smells, yessir. And there were people! All kinds of folks milling around town square: loggers, moms pushing baby carriages, businessmen, pretty girls working at the shops, you name it. Nowadays, though, it's all gone for the most part. Businesses busted, people broke—heck, there isn't even enough money to fix potholes in the streets."

"What about the toyshop, dad—tell us about Kringle's," I exclaimed. It was my favorite topic of all time.

"Well, now," dad responded, wrinkling his forehead. "That there was surely the most curious one o' the batch. Lots of businesses went belly up, no doubt. But when a business goes under, usually they clear out their stuff and leave the building empty. Not Kringle's though, nosir. You fellers know where his store is on the corner of Whitworth and Metcalf? Well, on the inside it's exactly the same today as it was when I was a kid—and when my daddy was a kid—and his daddy before him."

"Tell us about that, dad—when you were a kid and went in there," Ramey begged.

"Hmmm, well, let's see how good my memory is. When I was your age, I remember walking down the sidewalk, coming up on that building. Ahhh, yes—I can see it now. Red brick with bright green trim, and a candy-striped awning. And there's a sign over the door, about yay big…" (he put his hands out four feet apart) "…made from a knotty ol' cedar plank that read,

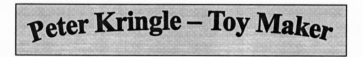

"I recall walking through those big glass doors. I wouldn't go but two feet and I'd have to stop. Because if I didn't, my eyes would bug clean out of my skull and I'd have to pick 'em up off the

floor and stuff 'em back in again. You've never seen such a collection of toys! There were airplanes: silver, black, and red; fighter planes, jets, double-deckers—had to be twenty different kinds hanging from the ceiling. Then there was this overhead train, y'see. A huge model railroad winding its way amongst all those airplanes. At the front was a steam engine, belching out real steam! And boxcars, and flatcars with logs, and cattle cars, and a bright red caboose pulling up the rear. There were wooden trestles, and wee little buildings, a miniature forest, a brick roundhouse, and even a lake with running water! Ol' Kringle, he was so clever, there were probably even bitty little trout in that lake!

"But that's not all. That's just what was hanging from the ceiling. On the floor there were shelves and oak tables all over the place with more stuff than you can imagine. There were carved wooden castles with drawbridges that'd go up and down, with toy soldiers standing guard. And rocking horses, for the smallest tot, to even grown-ups. And there were dolls and tops, toy trucks, nutcrackers, boats, chess sets, wagons, and on and on. Every single one painted just right with bright, thick colors. Makes me dizzy just thinking about it!"

"What about Kringle, dad—tell us about Peter Kringle!" Ramey and I were fairly slavering at this point.

"You wanna know about the old boy himself? Well, right in the middle of the place, next to a shiny iron and brass potbelly stove, was his workbench. Purt'neer any day you walked in, there he'd be, gray beard hanging down, bent over chipping, whittling, or sanding away. Hardly ever looked up or said anything. Not that he was bad-mannered; he was just focused, if you know what I'm saying. Then there was that young feller, Evon, bustling around in the background. Nice man, Evon. Always racing here and there— filling orders, straightening shelves, stoking the potbelly, fetching tools, whatever. He was the one that'd slip you a cookie, if you were nice, and lucky."

31

"What about a toy, dad? Did you ever get a Kringle toy?" I asked.

"Nope—never owned a one. No kid in town did, except maybe one of the rich kids. Y'see, his toys were so special, so sought after, most were sold before the paint had time to dry. Orders came in from all over the world, from every corner of the globe. Requests for more toys than Kringle could make in a lifetime came in the span of a single month. He'd make as many as he could, then, out they'd go—on trucks and ships and trains, headed for some far-flung corner of the earth. Darned few stayed in Washington State, let alone Furry-Pine."

"And it's been how long since Mister Kringle closed up his shop?" Ramey quizzed. "I know you've told us before, but tell what happened to him again—please."

Dad shot a cocked eye at Ramey, paused, then responded with an air of mystery. "Now, that topic…that's a peculiar one. It was a little more than five years ago—when you two fellers were just little shavers. One day some folks saw Kringle and Evon walking south down Metcalf Street to the edge of town. Wellsir, they kept right on a-walking, past the old warehouse, the train depot, and the bowling alley. Right out into the wilds of the Tigaks Flats. The next day there wasn't no one in the toyshop. Nor the day after, nor the day after that. So, the man who owns the building next door, ol' lawyer Hawkwelts, he up and locked the doors. Ain't no one seen nor heard of Kringle or Evon since.

"After a few years, the shop's storefront fell to looking kind of dingy, just like the other buildings in town, so it blended right in. Other than some small talk around the bar at the Button Ram Tavern, nobody investigated or said a thing. Now, some folks think maybe Kringle went on some exotic, long-winded vacation. But I don't see it that a-way. Looks to me like the toy business hit the same brick wall as the rest of the businesses in town. Plain went belly-up."

And so dad's tale ended. But with regard to the fate of Peter Kringle and Evon, neither the townsfolk nor dad had it right. As Ramey and I would soon find out, the truth was much more complicated—and much darker.

Chapter Six

A Not-So-Tall Tale

So many things in my life would have turned out differently, the most noteworthy being that I would likely have died a premature and agonizing death, were it not for Torry.

Torry was the lynchpin of my entire adventure with magic, flying, and the Dark Quartz Mine. She was the reason that Peter Kringle and Evon visited Malcrook in the first place. Were it not for her, the magical Red Rocket Wagon would have never been created. Were it not for her, when I ultimately went seeking the Dark Quartz Mine, I would have led my kid brother straight into horrors so awful I hesitate to even mention them (don't worry, though, I will mention them—all in good time. Oh, yes, I'll tell you all about those terrors soon enough).

Following is how it all started—what *really* happened to Peter Kringle and his young, ruddy-faced apprentice, Evon, on that fateful day the townsfolk last saw them walking south on Metcalf Street.

Peter Kringle had been operating his toyshop as usual. Both of Furry-Pine's lumber mills were recently closed and local companies were beginning to feel the pinch. Kringle's toy business, however, didn't seem to be affected. Orders kept coming faster than ever and Peter Kringle did his best to fill them.

There was a little girl who would come to Kringle's regularly and stare at the colorful medley of toys through the big plate-glass storefront. She looked to be about ten. Her face was always dirty and her clothes ragged.

Peter paid little attention to the kids who came to gawk, this little girl being no exception. Evon, however, noticed the particular neglect that this girl bore and took a special liking to her. But every time he tried to approach—to offer a cookie or other treat, she would dash off. He wondered whether this girl had a decent home— or a home at all. If she did, it was obvious she was not getting the care and attention she needed. Evon would occasionally see her hanging around town with the rough gang of boys, though she never quite fit in. Oh, she was tough enough, that wasn't the issue—she wouldn't take guff from any of them. But she was standoffish. She didn't find it necessary to show off at every opportunity like the boys did. Evon always admired her pluck and her moxie.

Evon came to learn the little girl's name, Torry, from the other kids. Sometimes she would show up at the window looking especially thin and bedraggled. The sorrow and neglect in her green eyes and stringy brown hair tugged at his heart. Did she have a mom—or a dad? Where did she sleep at night? How many days in a row did she wear the same clothes? Most of the kids who came to stare into the shop window were of meager means, some were downright poor. But of them all, this little girl probably had it the toughest.

Oh how I wish I could help her—even if only to give her a toy, Evon often thought. *A Kringle toy! Wouldn't that brighten her day—brighten her whole year!*

But, alas, he could not. Peter had a strict rule against giving away his toys. He knew it would start an onslaught of panhandling and begging among the kids who did not get one. Or worse, it might cause a fight spawned of jealousy. That would certainly never do. But Peter didn't have any rules against giving a bit of food or little treats to the more needy children, so Evon would occasionally leave a small plate or some cookies for Torry. As long as he kept his distance, she would take the food.

One day as Torry was looking in through the window, a man approached her. Evon happened to be stocking shelves near the front and noticed the man extend his hand, showing her something glittering and shiny. Rather than run away, she stared, awestruck. Evon secretly positioned himself for a better view. He noticed immediately one of the man's hands was disfigured, missing the ring finger and pinky. Torry didn't seem to mind. She was spellbound by his other hand, for in it was gold—pure gleaming gold. Evon could see the man speaking softly, and Torry was listening. With every word, her eyes grew brighter and bigger. Then he gestured to follow him. He turned and walked away. Torry followed, keeping her distance. Down Metcalf Street and out of town they walked.

Evon knew this man was up to no good. He quickly related what had happened to Peter, who guessed the man was Malcrook— the owner of The Dark Quartz Mine. The very same Malcrook rumored to enslave children for the running of his operation. Peter and Evon decided to follow—to see if there was anything they could do to help their little friend.

Creeping out the back door, they snuck their way down Metcalf Street, keeping out of Malcrook's view. They followed past the buildings, through the flats, into the woods, and up the mountainside. The man followed a creek which led to a box canyon containing a magnificent waterfall.

At one point Torry sensed that she was trapped and being lured into something dangerous. She tried to escape; run away up a crude set of old stairs cut into the side of the box canyon. But Malcrook was too wily and quick. He caught her at the top of the stairs and pulled her back down, kicking and screaming.

Evon and Peter could do nothing, watching from a distant cluster of vine maples, as Malcrook drug Torry through the canyon, over some rocks, and behind the waterfall's curtain of cascading water, disappearing forever.

They didn't dare follow; they'd heard the horror stories concerning Malcrook and his mine. So, feeling awful indeed, they returned to their toyshop.

Both men tried to resume their work, but the memory of Torry haunted them. They knew that if they did nothing they would never see her bright green eyes in the shop window again. For two more days they brooded, their brains in turmoil as to what they should do—if anything.

Finally, after four days, and against every grain of common sense in his head, Peter could stand it no longer. He had to help Torry—or at least try. The thought of that bright-eyed, freckle-faced, ten-year-old spending the rest of her life a slave at the hands of the wretched Malcrook was too much for his kind heart to bear. He had no trouble convincing Evon they must attempt a rescue.

But Peter knew they couldn't simply walk into the mine, grab Torry and walk back out. They would need something special—a tool or weapon to give them a chance against Malcrook and his multiple defenses. Yet Peter was a toymaker, not a warrior. What weapon could he invent?

After a little thought, it came to him. He would not create a weapon; no, rather, he would create a vehicle. Something to allow entry into the mine without detection. Something that could fly and become invisible. Something deeply and richly embedded with magic.

Of course, magic, for Peter Kringle, was not an obstacle. Though no one other than Evon knew it, he'd had the unexplainable gift of enchantment for many years. But he avoided its use. His magic, though powerful, could sometimes be unpredictable and dangerous. But his need now was urgent and he would have to risk embedding a tremendous dose of sorcery in this new vehicle. Torry's life depended on it.

He went to work hammering and forging. Into the wee hours he toiled, keeping his head down, intent on his task. Slowly his creation took shape.

By sunrise the next day, the Red Rocket wagon was born. It

was a masterpiece: red, of course, with green lettering and silver shooting stars, comets, and moons.

Peter took little time testing the wagon or learning to fly it. The longer he waited, the more torture Torry would endure. He took the Red Rocket into the back alley for a trial flight only twice.

The first time all went well until the landing. He banked around, meaning to set it down by the arbor, but he came in too low and caught the front wheels on the lip of the concrete curb. The wagon stopped instantly, but Peter didn't. He was ejected over the front, sprawling, arms flapping wildly, and landed belly-first on the sidewalk—*thud!* Evon watched the whole affair. At first it was comical—a grown man flying around in a toy wagon—wind whistling through his tousled hair, a nervous grin on his face. But Peter's collision was of sufficient magnitude that Evon's mirth quickly dissipated and he came charging up to offer assistance and first aid.

Fortunately, no major harm was done to Peter (save a skinned nose and bruised belly) or the wagon. Peter straightened the front wheels and unkinked the diagonal struts then tried again. This time the flight went perfectly—except for the Rocket's tendency to unexplainably speed up. Peter conveniently neglected to inform

Evon of this "trivial nuisance." Upon landing, Peter proclaimed victoriously that they were ready for the mines!

Evon, always the worrier, still had his doubts. It was indeed a good thing to posses this vehicle—this magic wagon. But the actual rescuing was another matter entirely, a task they would have to accomplish using only their wits and what strength they possessed naturally. Would the two of them truly be enough, pitted against Malcrook and his diabolical fortifications?

Evon was quite aware that performing a risky rescue mission was well beyond Peter's area of expertise. Had he ever done—or even considered—anything like this? And he was in such a rush. Evon kept waiting for an intelligent plan—a specific method of entering the mine, finding Torry, grabbing her, avoiding Malcrook, and escaping. And what would their bailout plan be, should they run into trouble? But no plan of any kind was mentioned. Apparently, Peter figured they would simply fly in undetected, load Torry in the wagon and fly back out before anyone was any the wiser. There was no provision for problems of any kind.

But maybe Peter wasn't truly as confident as he portrayed because just before leaving, Evon noticed he paid a quick visit to their neighbor, the attorney, Artimus Hawkwelts. Through an open window Evon overheard the hushed conversation.

"Artimus," Peter queried, a nervous edge to his voice, "Um, Evon and I will be out of the shop today. We should be back soon…tonight at the latest. But, in case we're waylaid, would you mind looking after things?"

"Waylaid?" the lawyer replied, narrowing his eyes. "Waylaid for how long? Are we talking a day, a week, months?"

"Oh, I shouldn't imagine any more than a day or two. But…this small errand involves a flight, and you know how unpredictable those can be."

Of course, Peter did not disclose that his *flight* would be in a magic wagon rather than an airplane. He continued, "We're not going far, mind you. Anyway, just in case we're not back in a, eh, reasonable amount of time, if you would be so kind as to pay the bills. You know, look after my affairs. Of course I'm good for the repayment."

"Pay the bills? So, you're expecting it may be *months* before you return? What about my time? I don't work for free, Kringle."

"I should hope we're not away any longer than a day, let alone months. And, yes, of course, I'll pay for your time. Goodness knows your time is valuable and I wouldn't dream of swindling you. Thank you, thanks so much and will see you again soon."

"What about your building?" Artimus blurted as Peter turned to leave. "I mean, flights can be hazardous. What if you're not back in a *year*? It's no secret that I consider your building to be in an excellent location, and I've had in mind expanding my business...you know, if something unfortunate happened to you or you were to ever consider selling..."

"You'll have first opportunity, Artimus, should either of those events come about. Must go now. Sorry for the rush. Again, thank you."

Later that afternoon, Peter climbed into the wagon and gestured for Evon to hop in behind him. Two seconds later Peter uttered the command, "shrink." In a heartbeat Evon, Peter, and the wagon shrunk to the approximate size of a bumblebee. Peter spoke another command and off they hurtled to the Dark Quartz Mine.

Flying through the wide-open spaces between the toyshop and the waterfall was simple, and within ten minutes the pair crested the lip of the box canyon and headed for the edge of the waterfall. But as their flight path narrowed, Evon discovered Peter's command of the dicey wagon left something to be desired. Minute adjustments of the handle had rather large consequences on their trajectory.

Approaching the waterfall, droplets of water began pelting

them. But the droplets didn't seem like harmless bits of mist to them. In their miniature form, each droplet was like a water balloon fired from a cannon. One particularly large droplet caught Evon squarely in the side of the head, and nearly tore him from his seat. He redoubled his grip on the sides. Peter struggled mightily through the pounding mist, the wagon bobbing and dipping treacherously in the wild air currents. Somehow they made it, flying close along the moss-draped canyon wall.

When they finally rested, levitating in the calm, hollowed out area behind the waterfall, they found that they were completely drenched. Water sloshed about in the bottom of the wagon, disturbing its tenuous state of balance. Now Peter was wishing he'd spent a little more time practicing.

But there was no turning back. Peter quickly located the hollowed-out area's only tunnel entrance, swiveled around and proceeded as slowly as he could. This exposed another problem he hadn't fully considered. The wagon needed substantial forward velocity or it would lose altitude. It would only go or stop—there wasn't much in between. But in-between was what Peter needed most because they'd never been here before and had no idea where they were going. Peter did his best using "lift" and "down" commands intermittently to modulate their speed. All this acceleration–deceleration left Evon's neck feeling whiplashed, like he'd been in a car with a first-time teenage driver.

After fifty or so feet, the tunnel opened abruptly into a gigantic cavern. Both passengers were cold, wet, and very tired. They'd expended a lot of adrenaline and energy simply navigating and holding on.

Now what? Neither had the slightest idea where they were or where to go next. Peter set the wagon down, and between chattering teeth, uttered the command, "grow." They popped back to normal size and decided to explore on foot for awhile, thinking the exercise would help warm them.

Discussing their next move, their voices richoched around the cavern like an echo chamber. They could not have known that a tunnel branched off in the black shadows of the far end; that their voices carried like sirens screaming into that tunnel; and that a four-legged sentry happened to be patrolling at that precise moment in time. The sentry, one of Malcrook's infamous Doberman Pinschers, pricked up his ears, growled, and took off at a run to alert others.

Peter and Evon soon found a tunnel—not the one at the cavern's far end—but another one much nearer the entrance, between a pair of gigantic stalactites which reminded Evon of rattlesnake's fangs. They entered, towing the wagon with them.

Evon lit the small kerosene miner's lantern he'd brought and handed it to Peter, who began a fearful traverse into undefined darkness. Both men were utterly out of their element in this cold, rocky world. Every nerve was on edge.

Suddenly a noise jarred Evon's eardrums.

"Psst…Peter, did you hear that?" he whispered, alarm edging his voice. "I—I thought I heard something. Kind of a shuffling sound—from back in the cave."

Peter froze in his tracks and cocked his head sideways, straining to listen. Now he turned, the lantern's small flame dancing shadows across his face. "Yes, I hear it, too. Quickly, Evon, here, dowse the lantern. Pull the wagon a little further into the tunnel and stow it. Then take cover while I investigate. If someone wants to ruin our rescue, they'll have to deal with me first."

Through the lantern's last flickering light, Evon glanced at his master. Although Peter Kringle was old—ancient, in fact—just now he didn't look it. His deep-set blue eyes flashed dangerously and his normally kind face was dour and grim. There was powerful magic in him, but as far as Evon knew, that magic was only useful in the creation of toys. Would it have any effect in fighting evil?

The thought of Peter facing their foe alone sent ice-chills through Evon's body. "I'll go with…" he started to protest, but was cut off by his master.

"No, I need you here. Go quickly now, Evon!"

Evon quietly and swiftly obeyed. Heart hammering in his chest, he tugged the brilliant Red Rocket as silently as he could further into the tunnel's blackness.

More scuffling and grinding, this time louder than before. *Malcrook!* Evon thought. *That's probably him. If he were to capture us, get his lousy grubs on the Rocket—oh my stars. What then?* He shuddered at the prospect.

Smack! Out of nowhere, something struck Evon's forehead.

I'm being attacked! He recoiled. Visions of subterranean ghouls pouring from invisible side openings flared in his mind. He put up his fists anticipating the next blow. But none came. Extending a hand cautiously, he realized he'd come, most unexpectedly, to the tunnel's end. *Whew! That's a relief. Well, no escaping this way. No choice—I'll stow the Rocket here.*

He carefully set the handle on the rock floor, turned and hustled back to rejoin his master. Now he could hear it clearly: the unmistakable sound of tramping feet. There was definitely someone or something in the cave beyond.

"Peter—psst, Peter!" he whispered as loudly as he dared. "Are you sure I can't go with…"

Too late. Peter had already crept around the corner and into the vast cave beyond. Suddenly, there was a loud hiss and a brilliant illumination as if someone had set off a flare. From his hiding place in the shadows, Evon flinched and blinked hard. Then he heard a voice, low and gravelly, like that of a very old man, but robust and vigorous—and wicked.

"So, you've come to rescue your little girlfriend, have you? Aha ha ha ha ha!!!… I thought I might wind up luring you here! Just can't stand to see children WORK for a living, can you? Well, mister goody-two-shoes toymaker, you'll see them work all right. You'll see just how productive an eleven-year-old can be! But that's about all you'll see, because after that, it's to the dungeons with you! I've no use for toymakers or old people. No—too feisty, too heroic. Always wanting to steal away my precious children. Toys! Bah! What a *pathetic* waste of time! No productive work ever got done while playing—PLAYING with toys! Capturing you will be good riddance indeed. You shall make an excellent supper for my little friends. Yessss, my small, wicked friends, the Tommyknockers!"

Malcrook, Evon affirmed, cursing under his breath. Then he heard another sound that chilled him to the bone. Barking—and panting. Dogs! Malcrook's notorious Doberman Pinschers.

Suddenly Evon felt very strange. Something was happening inside him. He was shrinking, and at the same time—sprouting hair! Tufts and tufts of thick brown hair were suddenly springing up all over his arms and legs. Pain, sharp and intense, penetrated every bone. He opened his mouth to shout, but nothing came. He watched in horror as his fingers crackled, twisted, and shrank. At the same time his fingernails grew, transforming into small claws. His arms and legs shortened, turning brown with thick fur. He could feel his face compressing, nose sharpening, ears flattening. Something was growing from his backside—something long and bushy. Was it a tail? He was turning—changing—morphing into something else, not human. *What the…?!* In the next instant, he found himself standing on the rock floor on all fours, small, brown, and furry.

He was no longer Evon the toymaker's apprentice. Through some unexplainable sorcery, he had now been reduced to…a common gray squirrel.

Terror mounted in his heart. The realization that he was suddenly but six inches tall in this huge underground world hit him like an anvil. *What… what now?!* He began noticing things—many things he'd never paid attention to before. Every rock and irregularity in the floor and walls came into sharp focus. His mind visualized bounding over them, where each paw would fall, how he'd spring from landing to landing. The sound of the dogs was now acute and abrasive to his ears. It made him flinch and quiver. Panic shot through his veins and the hair along his back stood up straight. He'd always been nervous about large dogs, but now that fear escalated to absolute terror. He twitched and shuddered uncontrollably with only one thought—*escape!*

He inched forward and chanced a peek around the corner into the enormous cave beyond. Peter was crouched face-to-face with a horde of slavering Dobermans—all pawing the ground, teeth bared, yellow eyes glaring. A hideously ugly, fattish man was standing behind the dogs, a wicked leer on his face.

Evon quickly jerked back, his little heart pounding like drums. He wanted desperately to rush out and help his master, but the dogs were simply too strong and vicious. In a moment Peter would be overwhelmed, and a squirrel would not have a prayer.

The next sound to reach Evon's ears was the single most horrifying thing he'd ever heard. In a guttural voice, Malcrook shouted "Cleaver, Scimitar, Cutlass, Switchblade, Scythe, Pegleg—SIC'EM!"

Responding like a wall of fury the dogs leaped forward, jaws snapping as they came. With the cold efficiency of a tidal wave, they knocked Peter to the ground.

Suddenly, Evon's mind switched to autopilot. The next thing he knew, he was bolting—bounding and scampering like the wind—directly for the cave's entrance and freedom. *Will the dogs notice me?* He half-hoped they would—maybe deflect the assault on his master.

Keeping to the wall, Evon glanced right. What he saw would cause him nightmares for years to come. The Dobermans, six in all, were tearing and grabbing at Peter's clothing, arms and legs. Poor Peter was petrified, the whites of his eyes bulging in their sockets. Yet he was fighting valiantly, pushing fangs and dog faces away with the quickness of a madman. But to no avail. In an instant they had him pinned, immobile. Now he could do nothing but endure their gnashing, razor-white teeth.

Malcrook made his way across the cave, rubbing his hands together and cackling with glee. "Easy, now, easy there, boys," he spoke to the dogs. "Let's not take too much flesh. We wouldn't want to spoil the treat for the Tommyknockers. They like their meals fresh…still quivering. Yes. Oh yes! Ah, ha, ha!"

Evon darted from the cave, unnoticed, and didn't stop running until he was halfway back to Furry-Pine. He collapsed next to a softly gurgling stream as sorrow overcame him. In a moment he was sobbing uncontrollably. *Will I see Peter again? Is Peter even alive?* His mind toiled against the unthinkable. Their plan to rescue the dirty-faced little girl who used to gaze into their toyshop window had gone bad—disastrously bad.

At that moment, back in the cave, emptiness once again filled the huge, dank space. The last sounds of Malcrook's exiting procession echoed and rattled off the haunting rock formations like a fading funeral chant. Sunlight stabbed timelessly through five holes in the cave's ceiling creating ghostly sabers from the swirling dust the awful commotion had stirred. Most satisfied with his prize, Malcrook fortunately did not go snooping for other treasures. For in the blackness of the side tunnel where Evon had been hiding, the Red Rocket wagon still sat, its shiny red body and brilliant green lettering invisible in the inky gloom. It would stay in precisely that location, collecting dust, for nearly six years.

Chapter Seven

Froghair

A month passed at the Stump and Gorge. Summer's heat gave way to fall's colors. Unbeknownst to the residents of Tigaks County, a particularly miserable northwest winter was brewing far, far out in the Pacific Ocean. But more worrisome to my family was the trouble festering right in our own back yard. My mom got sick.

Mom's probably just got the flu or a bad cold, I thought that particular October evening as I watched her shamble about the kitchen. Her normal springy step and cheery smile were absent, replaced by dogged shuffling and a strained horizontal line across her lips.

Several days went by, then a week, then two weeks, and she did not get better. In fact, she got worse. It started slowly at first—a dry cough and being extra tired in the evenings. As her sickness progressed, the cough didn't go away and her exhaustion became more pronounced. It was as if something inside was sapping her energy.

After a month, the toll of her illness became grievous. The more she tried to keep up, it seemed, the farther behind she got. "If I could just sit for a moment…," she would say weakly. "Maybe I'll get my second wind…" But her second wind never came. Instead, if she sat for more than two minutes, her head would slump over and she would be breathing coarsely, drifting in and out of fitful sleep.

October's reds and yellows faded to November's grays. I awoke one Saturday to a hazy sunrise, but by the time breakfast was finished and I headed outdoors, dark clouds had gathered. A few chilly drops of rain spit from the sky. I stood in the barnyard,

47

leaning on the middle rail of the corral fence, watching an unusually small red, whitefaced calf in the pasture beyond. Dad and Ramey were next to me doing the same.

"That calf yonder," dad said very seriously, motioning. "There's something wrong with him, otherwise his mama wouldn't have abandoned him."

"What do you mean?" I questioned.

"What I mean is, do you see how there's no other cows around? And how he just stands there with his head hung low? Cows are sociable creatures, boys. If one gets off by itself, either it's gone blind or it's got a bad disease. That calf there, I can tell you, it ain't blind."

"So, you're saying he's sick?" Ramey said.

"Worse than that. What I'm saying is he's got a disease, a sickness to his core. He's probably gonna die and his mama knows it. Cows aren't so dumb as folks think. Sometimes they just know things."

"But dad, we can't just stand back and let him…" (gulp) "die," I said.

"Son, if there was anything we could do for that little feller, we would. But I've seen this before. All the doctoring in the world won't help him. We humans need to just let nature take its course."

After a few days it became too painful to watch. The poor little fellow had lain down in the pasture midway between the barn and the cabin. Every time someone walked past, he would watch, his big brown eyes following—as if to say, *Can't someone help me, please?*

By the third day, I could stand it no longer. I pleaded with my parents. "Please let me keep it. I'll doctor it, feed it, take care of it. Maybe the problem is with the calf's mother, not the calf."

"Collin," dad responded, looking down at my long face. "Now, you shouldn't go meddlin' in the affairs of no barn animals."

I hung my head. But much to my surprise dad kept speaking. "However, there may be a lesson to be learned here somewheres, so I'm prepared to let you keep that runt calf."

I brightened immediately, looking up, a shaky smile on my lips.

"Now don't go getting all starry-eyed on me, son," he said. "This is serious business. You can keep him, but only under two conditions. First, you gotta' take care of him—feed him morning and night; and second, you can't go getting all caved in if he dies. And chances are pretty darn good he's gonna die."

I named the small orphan Froghair because he'd come so close, within a frog's hair, of dying. Much to my delight, after a few feedings, Froghair seemed to rally. He put on some weight and actually spunked around his pen a few times, butting heads with the other calves. But then, for no apparent reason, my little guy spiraled downward. He lost his appetite and got skinny. After a few weeks, he didn't want to even stand up. So he just laid there. I now had to force feed him, shovel away his manure, and manually work his legs to keep them from binding up. It was agonizing.

But an even worse tragedy was playing out at the same time. Through some mean trick of fate, mom's deterioration exactly paralleled Froghair's—they seemed to be going down together.

A week later I was tending to my chores. A moist, depressing fog had rolled up the hill and engulfed our weathered old barn buildings in gray. I arrived at the small tin shed which was home to our laying hens, unlatched the makeshift door and ducked through the squatty opening. Stooping to collect a light-brown egg from each of the ten smelly wooden cubbies, I noted that the chickens were extra talkative today. Squawking and clucking away, as if there wasn't a problem in the world, they watched me with jerky head motions from their galvanized-pipe roost a few feet away.

Lucky buggers, I thought. *Sometimes I wish I could be a farm animal. Heck, they don't have a worry in the world. Get up when you want, get fed twice a day, sit around and do nothing— yeah, that would be the life. Just about anything would be better than what I've got. Why couldn't it be someone else's mom who got sick? No other kid in the world needs a healthy mom more than Ramey and me. What if she can't keep up? Who'll do the cooking and laundry? Who'll tend the gardens and do the canning? And that's just the main stuff. But there's more, a lot more, like going to our ballgames and taking us to our friend's houses, and baking. It's been a month since she's baked anything at all. Oh man, do I miss those muffins, and pies, and cookies.*

Finishing up in the chicken coop, I pressed on to the calves' pens. I entered by climbing through the hay barn's worn stanchions located on the side opposite the pig pens. Immediately five black, red, and white faces appeared through the fly-speckled boards with tongues flapping and lolling expectantly. "Oh, I see you," I said with zero enthusiasm. "But you've already been fed. I'm not here for you, I'm here for Froghair."

The calves didn't flinch, instead they pressed harder at the boards and a couple bleated eagerly. They didn't care about

Froghair or having already been fed. They wanted more. They always wanted more.

"Forget it," I said. "You know what would happen if I fed you more? Scours, that's what. Your poop would turn yellow and go squirting out everywhere like a fire hose. Yeah, it'd be just like a poop-bazooka—spacklins shooting all over the place, even on each other. Yucch!"

I walked to the corner of the first pen, Froghair's. He didn't even lift his head when I entered. He just laid there curled up—big brown eyes open, watching.

"Wassa' matter fella?" I asked softly, kneeling down. "Are you hungry yet? I sure hope so because I've got to feed you anyway."

Gently, I exercised Froghair's stiff, bony legs, then force-fed him his bottle, all the time thinking how cruelly similar my mom's situation was.

I finished then left the barn, the gray fog at once swallowing me whole.

Chapter Eight

Tough Choices

As time rolled on, and mom did not get better, I became awfully worried. She was now dangerously thin. Her once robust body was withering. Her arms were bony, her sparkling blue eyes, sunken and pale. Her once silken blond hair was stringy and dull. When she smiled, which was rare, the skin of her face stretched over her cheek bones in a ghoulish way. A terrible thought began to fester in my mind. *What if she didn't get better—couldn't beat this illness? What then? Might Ramey and I have to live the rest of our lives without a mom?* The unimaginable prospect of her actually dying seeped into my brain.

One night, after everyone had gone to bed, I took council with Ramey.

"Ramey – psst, Ramey, you still awake?" I whispered as loudly as I dared.

"Yeah, but I don't wanna be," came the whispered reply. "You better go to sleep before dad hears. You know how grouchy he's been lately."

"I know, but this is important. I'm worried about mom. She's getting…so skinny. Never seems to have any energy."

Ramey knew exactly what I was talking about, yet it was a topic his ten-year-old mind preferred not to confront. His reply was brusque. "You probably wouldn't have any energy either if you did all the stuff she does. Maybe she wouldn't be so tired if you helped out a little more."

"Ramey, you know we both do all we can. But with school and helping dad with his logging business there's not much time left. I'm not bringing this up because I want to argue. It's just, well,

I'm real worried about mom. And not only that, have you thought about what will happen if she can't keep up? The cows and goats will get sick or dry up; weeds'll take over the garden; we'll have to wear dirty clothes; eat off dirty plates—if there's any food to be eaten."

Ramey didn't reply. My words had thrown him into a spin. Dread was taking over.

I continued. "It wouldn't be a problem if we had money, but that's exactly the problem. Ramey, you know as well as me, we're poor. We've got just enough to buy the things we can't grow ourselves: clothes, electricity, gasoline, chainsaw parts, stuff like that. We need our gardens and our livestock to live. Mom needs to go to the doctor, but I don't think dad can afford it. He's a logger, it's all he knows. But with the logging industry in such a mess, he says he has to work twice as hard as he used to for half the pay. Ramey, our family is in trouble. I feel like I should do something but I don't know what."

Ramey pulled his pillow over his head.

Through the dim light, I saw his reaction and stopped talking. I pulled my own covers up, rolled over and continued wrestling with my thoughts. After a while a fitful sleep stole me away.

As mom's condition became more critical, dad scraped together his extra pennies and took her to the hospital. Tests were run, samples were taken and analyzed. Finally, two weeks later, dad was called in to discuss the results. Ramey and I went along. Mom didn't. She had come down with the flu and was in bed with a high fever and violent cough.

"Hmm…" fretted Doctor Hobbs rubbing his chin.

Doctor Hobbs looked exactly like you'd expect a small town doctor to look: tall and slender, sixty-something, bald, garbed in a white lab coat with several pens sticking out from the upper left pocket. Ramey, dad, and I anxiously stared up at him from our uncomfortable orange plastic chairs.

"I understand you are dreadfully concerned about Marge," Doctor Hobbs finally said with a frustrated look. "But I'm afraid my news is not good. On the other hand, it's not all bad either. The truth is I don't exactly know what the problem is. We've done all the testing we can at our little facility here. But the results don't show anything alarming. Other than a slightly high white blood count, which would be standard for any sick person, she seems normal in every way."

"Well, doc, then, what do I gotta do?" dad questioned, a heavy expression on his brow.

"First and foremost, make sure she gets plenty to eat and lots of fluids. But beyond that, the only thing I can recommend is more tests, at a larger facility. She needs to go to the university hospital in Seattle and undergo a full battery there."

"Hmmm... I see," dad muttered, looking down. "The food

and drink—that ain't no problem. But the other part… I hate to ask, doc. I mean, it's not like I'm trying to put a price on my wife's health or anything, but what does something like that cost?"

I felt my face heating up—embarrassed at my dad's question, at our family's poverty.

Doctor Hobbs didn't say anything for a long time. Arms folded across his chest, he stared back down at the big, strapping man, and his two wide-eyed sons. "I don't know…" he finally said evenly. "But I can tell you it's not going to be cheap. Maybe there's a welfare program or something you could enroll in."

There was no hesitation in dad's reply. "No, thanks, doc. I ain't no charity case. No offense, but I pay my own way. Appreciate it." He stood, spun and walked out, Ramey and I hustling to keep up.

Inconclusive. The doctor's prognosis could not have been worse. Dad, Ramey and I piled into our International Harvester pickup and rattled off for home. I sat by the passenger's door looking out, saying nothing. Ramey sat in the middle, absently fiddling with the worn gearshift knob. Dad, one hand on the big black steering wheel, the other hanging out the window, wrestled with an impossible, gut-wrenching dilemma.

Our faded-blue pickup sputtered and popped its way along, slowly approaching the shores of Beaver Lake. Evening was deepening and the water was now in shadow. I noted how dark and spooky the lake appeared in this dim light. It didn't help my mood much.

Days and weeks crawled by. Mom tried her best to eat extra but it didn't seem to help much. To compensate for his inability to help his flagging wife, dad did the only thing he knew—he worked harder. He was gone before Ramey and I woke up. And he didn't return until dark. Most evenings he came home exhausted—literally dragging himself through the front door. After doggedly taking off his boots and leather chaps, he would sit at the supper table like a zombie and mechanically eat, saying nothing. The only sounds around our normally chatty, cheery table were the hollow clinking of silverware and the chewing of bland food. I would glance nervously at Ramey, afraid to speak, worried at what dad might do next. It seemed he could snap at any minute. His patience was paper-thin. He'd shout at us for the smallest thing. He actually punched our milk cow in the nose a few weeks back when she kicked over the bucket shooing a horsefly. Nearly broke his hand.

Finally I could stand it no longer. I decided I had to do something. Again, I took bedtime council with my brother.

"Psst, Ramey... Ramey, you're not sleeping yet are you?"

"No, but I'm not in the mood for talking if that's what you wanna know."

"Yeah, I know. But we can't just go on ignoring things, hoping it'll all work out by itself. I've got a bad feeling it won't. In case you haven't noticed, our family is in real trouble. Mom is sick, dad is always angry, our gardens aren't producing right. And to make it worse, Froghair died two day's ago."

"Yeah, that was sad about Froghair, Collin. Sorry. But if you're thinking there's something we can do to help mom and dad, in case you forgot, we're just a couple of kids. How're we gonna do something grown-ups can't?"

"Well, that's exactly what I've been thinking about. I'm starting to hatch a plan. The one thing we need is money. Think about it Ramey, money would get mom to the doctor, the best in the state. Buy all the tests and medicine she needs. And it would help dad, too. Make it so he doesn't have to work so hard all the time. Then he'd have more time to spend with us, hunting and fishing. We might even get him to play a little football or baseball."

"Okay, and where're we gonna get all this money? Go rob a bank? Dig up some pirate's treasure? Collin, you don't have to be a spaceship scientist to figure out there's no money for us to get."

"You mean rocket scientist? Whatever. Anyway, I know it

sounds obvious that we've got to find some money, but that's the part I've been working on. *Gold*, Ramey. The answer is gold. You know as well as me there's a mountainful of it somewhere around here. The Dark Quartz Mine. All we have to do is find it, sneak in and take a little, and our troubles will be over. Just a pound or two, the amount we could carry in our pockets. We'd be rich!"

"Yeah, and how're you gonna spend all that money when you're dead? Collin, that's got to be the stupidest idea to ever spout from your melon. You think ol' Malcrook will just invite us in with wide open arms; maybe toss us a few cookies while we're filling our pockets? And what makes you think we can even find the mine in the first place? As far as we know, no one has seen or heard of the Dark Quartz in fifty years."

"Yes, I know. But, Ramey, if we don't do something, I'm afraid mama's…well, you know, you've seen her, how skinny she's gotten. I'll be darned if I'm going to sit back and do nothing. I want to hug her again and feel her body soft, like it used to be. I can't even remember the last time she baked us treats. I've made my decision, Ramey. You can help me or not. But either way, I'm trying it."

Ramey said nothing more. His mind must have felt like it was tearing in two: one half burning to help me and our family; the other reluctant to do anything—fearful of the unspeakable dangers involved with the Dark Quartz Mine. And also fearful of his own father should he discover what we were up to.

I rolled over and waited restlessly for sleep to come. What I did not know was that my decision placed me on a collision course with someone else, an ally actually, equally desperate to infiltrate the Dark Quartz Mine.

Chapter Nine

Squirrel Hunt

Over the course of the next week Ramey came to the same conclusion as me—that we had to do something to help our mom, and an attempt at the Dark Quartz Mine was our best option. Saturday was our first chance to launch a decent search. Dad had rumbled off to town for supplies.

"Mom?" I asked tentatively. She looked up blearily from her seat at the kitchen table. She had been clearing the morning's dishes, but had fatigued and nodded off.

"Yes, Collin," she said forcing a thin smile.

I measured my next words carefully, not wanting to divulge the true nature of my request. Any mention of the word "mine" would snuff out the excursion before it even started.

"Um, would it be okay if Ramey and I, uh, went exploring this afternoon—after our chores are done, of course."

My ploy worked brilliantly. "Certainly, hon," she replied without hesitation. "You boys work so hard around here. I don't mind if you take a little time for yourselves."

About mid-morning Ramey and I departed. With no supplies whatever, we headed westward on a brush-choked, abandoned logging trail.

After I was sure we were out of mom's earshot, I paused and explained our mission. "Ramey, here's what we need to do. We're looking for the Dark Quartz Mine, right?"

"Yeah," came the sober reply. Normally, Ramey would have had a sarcastic response to this obvious question. But with the stakes so high, plus the fact that he was a little nervous about venturing forth into the wilderness without so much as a map or compass, he was willing to cooperate.

"Right," I continued. "What we're looking for is evidence of anything old and manmade that could lead us to the mine. Stuff like rusty tin cans, half-buried coils of cable, old bottles, old tools, wood or tin siding from an old building, anything like that. Got it?

"Yep, got it."

"All right then, let's go."

I turned and launched into the thicket.

After three fruitless hours of braving house-sized briar patches, climbing up and down near-vertical ravines, and jumping over fallen logs, we both were hot and sweaty, a little frustrated, and more than ready for a break. We halted in a grassy clearing, the first decent-sized one we'd encountered.

"So, whose stoooopid idea was it to go searching for the Dark Quartz Mine?" Ramey asked loudly, arching his back like a hobbled old man.

"Mine. Wanna make something of it?" I replied.

"I might if you weren't such…such a thribble!" Ramey said, throwing me the evil-eye. "But I'm afraid if I touched you, you'd probably start crying like a spanked baby and we'd have to call the waaahhmbulance!"

That was invitation enough for me. With a mighty war cry, I lit into my brother. The wrestling match was on.

What neither of us knew was that my war cry had attracted the attention of someone else. Someone who was not at all expecting two trespassing boys. Noiselessly, he crept closer. Ramey and I could not have been more oblivious. Our lives were on the brink of a dramatic turn, yet we had no clue.

Ramey took an early command of the bout. Catching me slightly off-balance, he threw all his weight into my chest, pushing me backward at full speed. I backpedaled furiously, trying to keep my balance, but my legs lost their coordination and down I went, *boom,* a backflop. My head smacked the ground with a thump, and instantly Ramey was on me, an elbow thrust painfully into my adam's apple.

"Say uncle!" he crowed triumphantly.

"No way, you…you little snothead! I'll get you…"
Mustering my strength, I reared back and heaved my hips skyward. Ramey went flying.

I quickly regained my feet, dusted myself off and prepared for another assault. But just then I noticed something out the corner of my eye.

"Hey Ramey, hold it a sec," I said between deep breaths. "D'you see that?" I was pointing at something small and brown a few feet away.

Breathing hard, Ramey paused, turned and looked. It was a squirrel sitting on a small granite boulder. It was almost as if it had come down from the trees to grab a ringside seat.

"Yeah, I see it, Collin," Ramey coarsely whispered. "That's got to be the biggest, fattest squirrel of all time. I don't know about you, but I'm thinking he'd look mighty good on our supper table!"

"Oh, yeah!" I agreed.

Immediately, we scrambled around, hands groping among the grass and leaves for a rock or other projectile to hurl at the potential meal.

Upon hearing the words "supper table!" the squirrel jumped two feet vertically, then scampered off westward through the forest.

I took the lead; the chase was on. Wouldn't dad be proud if we brought home a fresh, plump gray squirrel for dinner!

I could not believe our good luck. The squirrel ran straight to a well-used deer trail and stayed on it. Not only that, it never got so far ahead as to lose us, though it did stay far enough away to elude our projectiles. Amazingly, rather than scamper up a tall cedar or maple, a sure escape, the squirrel stayed on the ground, always following the deer trail, tending steadily westward.

Ramey and I became completely absorbed in the hunt. We lost track of time, distance, and direction. It was like a bizarre game of cat and mouse. We—the cats—of course were having a grand old time at the chase but, weirdly, the "mouse" seemed only too happy to oblige, as well.

After several hundred yards of jumping over fallen logs, racing around and through thickets, and scaling the occasional granite boulder, Ramey tripped on something. It was sharp, catching the toe of his boot and ripping it wide open. With a shout, he fell head first to the ground—*slam!* I heard the commotion, stopped and turned.

"What're you doing laying there on the ground?" I panted. "No way we'll ever get that squirrel with you bullygagging around like that."

"I...I think I just ruined my boot," He was now sitting cross-legged examining the tear in the boot's leather toe. A small stain of red saturated the tip of his white sock. He hastily untied the boot and yanked it off, taking the sock and all.

"Phew!" he exclaimed after a moment of examination. "Just caught the tip of my big toe. Nothing major." He quickly checked his arms, hands, and legs for further damage then said, "And everything else seems okay too."

I came over and investigated. "Wow, that's a nasty rip. Sure you're okay?"

"Yeah, I'm fine. I think my toe has just about stopped bleeding already. What'd I trip on anyway?"

I turned and searched for the culprit. It wasn't hard to find. There, suspended about six inches off the ground was a taut, rusty strand of the most vicious barbed wire I'd ever seen. The barbs were arranged in clusters of four, each protruding a good inch. Somehow, flying by so quickly, my eyes glued on the squirrel, I'd missed it myself. Looking right and left, though, now I saw it plainly. Sure enough, fence posts—rotting, decayed, and listing—formed a crooked line stretching away through the woods as far as I could see in either direction. Ramey had tripped on the bottom strand of what was once a four- or five-strand fence. The upper strands were long gone, rusted or otherwise dislodged from the crumbling posts.

"It's an old barbed wire fence," I declared. "But that's weird. I didn't know there were any fences around here. Kind of strange, barbed wire in the middle of the forest. I thought these were only on farms and ranches to keep cows and stuff in."

"Yeah," Ramey replied hoisting himself up and reinstalling his sock and boot. Already he was looking around, his mind switching back to the hunt. "Weird. Now, where's that durned squirrel?"

We scanned the area. Within a few seconds we'd forgotten the barbed wire and the torn boot. Little did we know, however, the fence was designed not to keep livestock in, but rather to keep people out. Had we investigated just a little further up the zigzagging fence line, we would have found a rusted, round steel plate about sixteen-inches across. It was half buried, but with enough exposed to read what had been crudely painted on it many, many years ago:

Although the sign's author had erred in his spelling, it was a forewarning just as applicable today as it was the day he painted it. And it was a small piece of precisely what we had been searching for all morning.

Suddenly, the squirrel's unmistakable shrill chirp ripped through the air. I pointed westward and exclaimed, "There he is, let's go!"

We raced up a short grade paralleling the old fence. Nearing the top of a small rise, I heard a sound I did not like. It was a muffled roar coming from over the lip of the next ravine some fifty yards ahead.

Ramey heard it too and stopped dead in his tracks. "Do you hear that?" he whispered between ragged breaths.

"Yeah. I sure hope that stupid squirrel hasn't led us into a bear's den."

Ramey cocked his head sideways and held his breath, listening intently. "Collin," he finally gasped. "Remember the list of dangerous things in the woods dad is always warning us about? You know: cougars, bears, blind cliffs, hornets, waterfalls? Well, that sound, it's no bear. I bech'a there's a creek in the next draw, and I bet that sound is a waterfall."

As I considered whether or not to advance further to investigate my brother's theory, the squirrel reappeared on a great cedar stump at the ravine's edge, staring back as if to say, *come on boys, just a little further.*

If there was any doubt as to whether or not to proceed, the squirrel cast the deciding vote.

Chapter Ten

Waterfall

"Get 'im!" I shouted, leaping forward with blind courage and renewed vigor.

Away scampered the squirrel again, disappearing into the ravine. Ramey and I crested the rim, and stopped, our eyes popping from our skulls and our jaws dropping in stark amazement.

Before us was a raging torrent, a swollen creek, tearing down the mountain from high up to the south. It crashed and tumbled among jumbled boulders like a tormented demon. Immediately in front of us the creek bed leveled to a short, flat shelf, a launching pad of sorts, swept clean of any rock or other obstruction. Beyond this was nothing but sky. It was the end of the creek bed, the top of a tremendous waterfall. At that point the mountainside receded abruptly straight down, some two hundred feet or more. The tortured water hit the shelf with fantastic velocity, then, like a cannon, shot straight outward. It arced gracefully until gathering itself for a silent free-fall plunge into a bubbling, mist-shrouded pool. The termination was so furious, a steady fog mounted from the splash pool, slapping us in the face like a cold shower.

"Whoa!" I yelled over the roar, teetering on the edge. "This is exactly what dad warned us about. A kid could fall off here and die in less than a second!" I grabbed Ramey by the arm and jerked backward.

When we were safely a few paces back, Ramey shouted, pointing to the bottom of the canyon, "Hey, there's that stupid squirrel again!"

Sure enough, the squirrel was there, several yards from the edge of the dark blue splash pool. It was in the same stance as when we first saw it; on its back legs, twitching front paws, staring directly back up at us. The squirrel was poised on an irregular chunk of canyon wall near a jagged pile of rocks.

Looking more closely, I could see how the squirrel had descended into the canyon.

"Hey Ramey, see that? It's a trail…I think. Look, you can just make out steps carved into the rock."

Ramey followed my pointing finger. He saw it too. A trail. Or rather, a crude gouge winding in a semi-circular arc down the canyon's sheer rock wall.

"Oh, yeah, I see it," he replied. "Maybe a long time ago it was steps. Think we can climb down them without falling? I don't see any other way into this thing."

I turned left and right, scanning the remainder of the canyon's walls. Nothing but vertical rock. This gouge appeared the only way down. Studying it more closely I noted thick, saturated moss concealing each step. A stiff breeze gusted upward and sideways from the fragmented water as it hammered into the splash pool. "I don't think we should go down there," I half-yelled. "It looks too dangerous. One slip and it's two hundred feet straight into that rock pile."

Ramey sized up the situation. He had a different opinion as usual. "Wassa matter, you chicken? Come on. If we're careful, this'll be a cinch."

I wrinkled my brow and shook my head slowly. "Nope, too risky. There's no squirrel worth dying over."

Ramey eyeballed me then studied the gouge again. Then he blurted, flapping his arms, "BAWK BAWWWWK, what a sissy!" And without warning, before I could even react, he bolted forward… right over the edge of the cliff!

My heart just about shot right out of my chest. "NOOO, Ramey!" But it was too late. The blond mop of my brother's hair had already disappeared over the edge. Forgetting caution, I charged forward. If my brother was going to die on this mountain, the least I could do was try to save him.

Looking into the jaws of the rock pile far below, I felt my head swim as a wave of dizziness washed over my brain. But there was my kid brother, ten feet below, scrambling down the cliff, grappling and scraping for foot and handholds. "Ramey, wait!" I yelled, "I'm coming with you!"

The moss was so thick, I was surprised to find it actually wasn't that slippery. It tore in long slabs cleanly from the rock. Only in a rare few thin places did its sliminess cause my feet and hands to lose traction. Now I could tell for sure that the gouge was indeed a set of crudely crafted stairs. The moss, ferns, and stunted cedar trees growing from the brown-gray cliff walls were just concealing it.

Someone had gone to great toil to create this stairway—to carve it right into the rock of the canyon walls. Clearly, however, it hadn't been used, at least by humans, in many years.

When we finally reached the bottom, the squirrel was gone. But where? Surveying my surroundings, I confirmed that this was a box canyon. Other than the stairs, the only outlet was where the river exited. One quick inspection told me it would be impossible for anything on foot to leave that way. Even the water, in order to escape the canyon, had to boil up from the depths then squeeze through a narrow gap. There were no ledges or walkways, only vertical rock face. From where I was standing, the canyon exit looked like two butcher knives poised to chop anything that tried to pass.

Where was the squirrel? My eyes caught a slightly unnatural movement in the direction of the waterfall itself. I squinted, straining to see through the mist. *The squirrel? What?* The thing I saw was either directly in the waterfall, or behind it, I couldn't tell which.

"Hey Ramey, I think I see 'im."

"Where?"

"Right over there, behind the waterfall." I pointed but Ramey still could not see the obscured shape. I took his head in the palms of my hands and twisted it in the correct direction.

"Look there, *behind* the waterfall."

"Ow! Stop it, you…ohhh, oh yeah, I think I see 'im now. Yeah! Let's go!"

Again, the chase was on. Ramey and I picked our way among the jagged boulders littering the canyon floor. The shore was fairly wide where we started but as it wound around the cliff, back toward the waterfall, it became narrower and narrower. I skirted the cliff edge, staying as far from the restless, dark water as possible. Shortly, however, the shore narrowed to a shelf little wider than my shoulders. To my left was the base of the vertical wall and to my right was frigid, turbulent water. Under me was a jumble of jagged, slippery rocks.

The mist was now peppering me ferociously. I was completely drenched, the small droplets stinging like horseflies biting. And the thunderous racket of crashing water was so deafening it would have been difficult to hear Ramey even if he'd been shouting. I had to squint to keep the sideways spray from pelting my eyeballs. My soaked hair hung over my face like a wet rag. It was tricky just determining where the next foothold would be. I was having serious second thoughts about this squirrel hunt. It had become too dangerous. It was time to reverse course and bail out. "Ramey! Ramey" I hollered. "Let's get out of here! It's too…"

But Ramey was in the lead, a few steps ahead, and he couldn't hear me. He was teetering precariously—stepping over this rock, balancing tenuously on the next.

Suddenly his right foot slipped and he went down.

His right arm instinctively reached for something to grab, but there was nothing. *Slam!* His waist hit the edge of a boulder, ricocheting him to the right, *directly into the pool.* I watched in horror, too far away to do anything.

In an instant Ramey was gone, submerged under the roiling water. But two seconds later he bobbed back to the surface flailing his arms like a madman, gasping for air. He was struggling supremely to keep his head above the surface.

Normally, he would have had no trouble paddling back to shore, but not in this pool. The waterfall was pulling him in with its powerful undercurrent. In two more seconds he would be gone—sucked under the tons of water raging ceaselessly from above.

I could see Ramey didn't have a chance. Either I did something right now or my brother…was a dead boy.

Chapter Eleven

Out of Breath

Suddenly, I was flying through the air, arms outstretched. The water hit me like a sledgehammer. It was ice-cold and was pulling me violently inward. Did I dive? Or had something thrown me in? There was no time to think about it now. I swam madly toward my brother, knowing I was his only chance.

Just before Ramey disappeared for good under the outer fringes of the crashing water, I threw a groping hand in his direction. My fingers hit something and clenched. A shirtsleeve! Yes! I had Ramey just below the left shoulder.

The water froze my skin and my drenched clothes clung like a straightjacket. My boots pulled downward like anchors. Even though I'd only swum a few feet, I was already laboring—breathing hard and getting tired.

Thrashing arms and legs as fast as my muscles could flex, I began to slowly pull Ramey back away from the thundering, hammering water storm. The undercurrent was so powerful, and having only the use of one paddling arm, I barely kept ahead of it. Gravity tugged relentlessly at my boots. My left arm ached at the exertion. Waves splashed into my mouth as I gasped for air. Coldness penetrated my bones. I could feel my limbs quickly approaching the limit of their endurance. Another inch, and another.

Ramey was trying to help, swimming as best he could, but his arms were clumsily slapping the surface and his legs couldn't overcome his boot's waterlogged weight. His torso had just about gone vertical.

I swam doggedly but my progress was painfully slow. Now Ramey began to feel heavy, very heavy. He started to sink. Through the blinding mist, I shouted at him, "Swim, dangit—swim! You're too heavy, you've got to help!" But Ramey was overwhelmed. He was utterly spent, the frigid pool had sucked the swim out of him. Face half submerged, he stared blankly back at me through drenched strands of hair as if to say, *Sorry, brother, I'm done.* In the next instant, he became lifeless and waterlogged—his wet clothes and boots pulling him down like a brick. He disappeared under the surface. Again, I shouted to swim. But Ramey couldn't hear, his head was completely under.

The seconds ticked by. We were a good ten feet from the bank and moving an inch every few seconds. I tried to reach the bottom with my outstretched feet. No good, too deep. And I was wearing out. I began to seriously worry that we would not make it. But still I kept a death-grip on Ramey's shirt. It was all or nothing; either I would be successful hauling him in or I was going down too.

Now I was struggling to keep my own head above the surface. A wave blindsided me and I inhaled a big slug of water. I went under. Expending what might have been my last reservoir of energy, I surged upward, coughing and sputtering.

The undercurrent kept tugging. Down I went again. What was desperate had become grave.

Suddenly, everything was green. I was completely under, eyes open, mouth shut tight, breath held. Now I, too, was spent. My brain screamed at my arm and leg muscles to move, to tread water, to swim, but they simply refused. It was as if the current and the bitter cold had paralyzed them.

Ramey had been under for nearly a minute and he was showing no signs of life. Through the greenish, bubble-laced water, I could see him. His hair was standing up, waving in the current like seaweed. His eyes and mouth were wide open, locked in a gape of horror. Could he see me—or was it too late?

Neither Ramey or I could resurface. There was not a thing

we could do…but sink.

So, this is what it's like to drown, I thought. *Who would have believed a squirrel would be the death of us?* Rays of light filtered through the churning water from above creating stabbing vanes of emerald. A kind of calm came over me as my body aligned itself for the slow trip to the bottom. *Well, at least I tried all I could to save my brother.*

Everything had switched to a kind of weird slow motion. My hand still had a vulture's grip on Ramey as he sank a foot, then two. Pressure began to build on my eardrums. I continued holding my breath, out of instinct more than anything. It was just a matter of time before I had to open my mouth and suck in. *How will that feel? Water shooting into my windpipe and down into my lungs? Will it hurt? Will I cough? Will I barf?*

Three feet…four. *Had Ramey already experienced it?*

Oddly, my panic was gone. I resigned myself to whatever fate lay ahead.

A minor commotion and a big burst of bubbles on the surface caused me to look up. I watched calmly as a big cedar log bobbed along the surface above me. *Oh, that's nice, a log. Probably just took the express route over the waterfall.*

A LOG!!! A floating log! One last chance at surviving!

Maybe I wasn't finished after all—not yet. If I could somehow grab the log and pull myself up. An adrenaline shot slammed me like a bolt of electricity. Mustering everything I had, I surged toward the surface, kicking my legs frantically. The spent air in my lungs burned like fire. I had to breathe, couldn't hold it any longer. My mouth flew open and I sucked in.

Just at that moment, my outstretched arm caught a downturned branch of the floating log and I yanked with all my might. *Sssccchhhh!* came the sound from my mouth and nostrils as they crested the surface and sucked in…

Air! Sweet, fresh air!

My other hand jerked as hard as it could, and up popped Ramey, eyes wide open, but completely lifeless. I levered myself against the log, regripped Ramey's shirt collar, and shoved his arms and head over it. I banged on Ramey's back trying to dislodge the water from his lungs and kick-start his breathing again.

Nothing. He was as lifeless as a dishrag. I banged harder. "Breathe, darnit! Breathe!"

Suddenly, Ramey gave a gasp, coughed up a gout of green fluid then sucked raggedly for oxygen. *Yes! He was still alive!* He continued a turmoil of spasmodic coughing, wheezing, and gagging—his will to live still burned within him.

Fortunately, the waterfall, rather than towing us backward into its eternal tempest, spit us like a beach ball into the placid water toward the center of the pool. We floated lazily, aimlessly. I had no energy to propel or guide us. It was all I could do just to cling and hope our course did not reverse itself. Soon, we found ourselves washing toward shore, near the place we started from—the foot of the abandoned stairs.

My dangling boots scraped the bottom. Wobbly, I stood. A weak smile came to my face at the feeling of my weight being supported by my legs. Like a shipwreck, I dragged my brother and myself onto the rocks. I draped Ramey over a large, smooth boulder, and gave his back a few more whacks, hoping to get more of the water out. Then I fell, exhausted, onto the pebbly beach and sucked air—I could not get enough. The sun beat down on me, its warming rays penetrating deep into my body, and it felt good.

Ramey was unconscious but breathing, sort of. I watched, unable to help now, praying silently he would be okay. He'd been completely submerged for some time. Had it been two minutes? Three? Four? Ten? Had it been too long to recover? Would he be brain-damaged from the lack of oxygen? How much trouble would I be in when our parents found out?

Every few breaths, Ramey convulsed into a coughing spasm, expelling more green fluid.

After what seemed like an hour, his breathing finally stabilized. He stopped coughing. I lay on the pebbly shore, my face turned toward him, watching, waiting with reserved hope.

He stirred slightly. Slowly one of his eyelids drifted open, then the other. He blinked wearily, wanly shook his head a couple of times, then gradually levered himself up on his elbows.

I interrupted a silent prayer. "Ramey, can you hear me? Ramey…you all right?"

He did not answer. There was a thick line of greenish ooze trailing from his mouth. His gaze was distant, like a school kid daydreaming out the classroom window. Now I was convinced of it; Ramey had sustained brain damage.

I spoke again, slowly. "Ramey…answer – me – are – you - okay?"

Finally he spoke in a groggy tone. "Hey, I giddn't brown. Unhhh…I mean—I didn't drown."

I jerked myself up, holding my breath.

Ramey, giving his head another dazed shake or two and smearing the spittle across his chin with a wet shirtsleeve, continued, "I fought—I mean, thought, for sure I…we…were goners."

He looked over at me and then at the log beyond gently grating at the pebbles of the shore. The realization of what had just happened registered in his brain and a faint smile came to his lips. "Collin, fanks for thescuing me."

I stared back as a stupid grin spread over my face. I felt my eyes moisten with tears, knowing I had indeed just saved my brother's life. I wanted to say something, but no words came.

Seeing that I was at a loss for words and feeling the life return to him by the second, Ramey added with a slight chuckle, "But, you didn't have to keep…uh, whacking me on the back. What were you trying to do, pick a fight?"

"You little!…" Now I knew my kid brother was fine. I felt like pouncing on him but thought better of it and replied, "Yeah, well, you're welcome. But you better watch your lip or I might just up and toss you right back in!"

We both laughed, feeling grateful to be alive, and grateful in knowing everything appeared back to normal.

Presently, I turned toward the location the squirrel had been previously. I blinked hard and looked again, unable to believe what I was seeing.

The squirrel was still there, except now instead of behind the waterfall, it was very near where Ramey went in, sitting on its hind legs as usual. But astonishingly, it was sitting *on top of the water*. At that location the rocky shore diminished into the vertical sandstone wall, leaving nothing to support weight but agitated, dark water.

Chapter Twelve

Walking on Water

I could see a nine- or ten-foot open span of water separating the triangular point of the rocky shore with another ledge or trail of some sort beyond. It was between these two patches of terra firma that the squirrel was poised, watching.

"Hey Ramey," I said. "Can squirrels walk on water?"

"No, I don't think they can even swim. Why?"

"Well, there's that squirrel and he's sitting *right on top of the water*, over there by where you went in. What the...?"

Ramey twisted his head around to see for himself. "No way...," he breathed. "Think he's magic or something?"

I was spellbound. "Uh, I don't believe in magic," I said. "But if that squirrel's not sitting on water, then I'm a pig in a waller. We've got to check this out."

"Um, I don't know, Collin. I'd sooner believe the part about you being a pig than worry about that squirrel any more. I think I've just about had enough chasing him for one day."

"Ramey," I said, trying to sound firm, yet compassionate, "we've come this far, we can't let it get away that easy. Besides, nothing worse could happen than already has, right? And if we're—you're—real careful, we ought to be able to crawl on those rocks real slow and not fall in. We'll just go over to where he's sitting and then we'll turn around. We've *got* to check this out."

Ramey was looking at the squirrel, wanting like mad to investigate. But he still felt waterlogged and weak, and although he wouldn't admit it, the waterfall and splash pool had him spooked. There was almost an evil feel to it: the throbbing roar, the deadly undercurrent, the icy cold, the shadowy blackness. He shook his head, furrowed his brow and said, "I—I think it's time we head for home. I'm sure mom and dad are looking for us by now. We better get going, Collin."

I sized up my brother and considered our options. *Nope,* I thought, *this'll only take another ten minutes. Can't go back now. Ramey's slip happened because he was being reckless—going too fast. We'll be safe if we just go slow—crawl over the rocks. Hmm, looks like I'll have to bring out the heavy artillery.* I blurted my retort, "BAAAWWWK, BawwWWKkk, now who's the, BAWWWK, chicken? If you won't go with… bk.. bbbkk... bawwwkkk, me, then… beegaWWWKKk… I'll just go by myself!"

The hairs on the back of Ramey's neck stood straight up. I could see blood churning in his face. Nobody called him a chicken, nobody. "I'm no CHICKEN!" he shot back. "You, Mister Big Brave Man, want to go back to the waterfall—awright then, lets go!"

I smiled privately, knowing my little reverse-psychology ploy had worked perfectly. Within seconds we were again picking our way, though much more carefully this time, among the rocks toward the squirrel and the waterfall.

As we traversed the narrowing ledge, again the spray stung our faces and the noise escalated. I was in the lead, edging my way among the jumbled rocks on all fours, kind of like a crab. Ramey followed in a similar fashion. With each inch, fear clenched its grip, especially on Ramey, a little tighter.

I kept an eagle eye on the squirrel, which did not move, but just watched us, twitching. Closer and closer I crept until I reached the point of the triangle, the end of the ledge. My heart quickened at being so close to our prey. I could almost reach out and grab him. Why wasn't he fleeing? And how did he manage not to sink? Through squinting eyes, I could see him clearly now. He was a plain old gray squirrel, a very large one to be sure, just sitting there on the water.

Then I noticed something unusual about his face. I'd seen

many a squirrel; dad hunted them and our family had them routinely for supper. This one, though, was different. Its face appeared to have almost…almost humanlike features. The eyes were not exactly round and not dark brown like normal. They were instead slightly elongated with a grayish tint. The nose was not long and pointy either, but was more blunt and upturned. Even its front teeth did not protrude. And it seemed to be showing an expression, a humanlike expression, of…of sadness. *What the… ?*

But, it was just beyond my reach.

A new thought entered my mind. *What's really going on with this squirrel? Something's not right—something is weird. Is this really a regular old gray squirrel or something different? And who is chasing who? Who really is the cat, and who the mouse?*

As the blasting mist continued its assault on my wincing face, I had yet another thought. *And just what will I do if we catch this squirrel? Kill it, or not?*

I squinted and looked down. The dark water riffled and lapped restlessly against the cliff wall at my left. There was no telling the depth by looking and I wasn't about to dip in to find out. Was this the end of our hunt?

Suddenly, the squirrel chirped several times then sprang away. It hopped on top of the water away from me five or so feet to the far bank. From there it scampered a few feet more then turned and sat back up, again watching.

I scratched the top of my sopping-wet head. Had the squirrel just hopped on water? And where did the ledge on the other side lead to? It appeared to be a walkway of sorts to a hollowed-out area behind the waterfall. *Verrry interesting.*

I thought of Ramey and that he undoubtedly wanted to turn back. But we couldn't give up now. There was something going on with this squirrel and I meant to find out what it was.

My mind raced. *So, how to cross this ten-foot stretch of water? There's no way to jump it, especially since a running start is out of the question. And we can't walk on water, either. Or can we? Wait a minute. What if there's a bridge or something just under the surface I'm not seeing?*

Carefully I dabbed my boot into the black water. *Thunk.* It hit something. I reached a little farther and dabbed again. *Thunk.* My pulse quickened.

Ah-ha! There is something down there all right, just under the surface. But what? And will it hold any weight?

"Ramey, hold on to my hand! There's something just under the surface. Steady me."

Great, Ramey thought as he blinked the drizzling water from his eyes. *Here we go again.*

I thrust an arm sideways for him to grab. Ramey cleared the driving mist from his face with a couple of sharp shakes of his head, then wedged himself between two very large, angular boulders. Gritting his teeth, he took hold. There was no way he was letting me pull him in. One near-death experience in a day was enough.

I knelt down, and with my free hand scraped and knocked at the submerged thing. It was a ledge or a walkway of some sort. But it was not hard like I expected. It was soft and spongy, certainly not rock. I stood up, still grasping Ramey's hand, and with my other reached for my pocketknife.

Bending back down, my hand unexpectedly slipped from Ramey's! Suddenly, the pounding of the waterfall amplified like shotgun blasts in my ears. Adrenaline slammed my heart as I teetered, but then steadied myself. *Whoa! That was close.* I regripped, and lowered to one knee. Blinking furiously, I scraped a layer of moss and slime from the thing. Wood! With my blade I gouged out a sliver, brought it to my face and sniffed. An unmistakable scent filled my nostrils: cedar.

So, it's a cedar bridge. Wonder how wide? Reaching as far as I could to the right, following the submerged boards with my nearly-numb fingers, I quickly found the jagged ends; about a foot and a half from the cliff wall. I could also feel the wood's thickness; some two or three inches. A light went on in my mind.

I know what these are...of course! After all, my dad is a logger. These are spring boards, just like the old-time loggers used to stand on while they felled a tree. But these are jammed into gouges in the face of this cliff-wall instead of a big ol' stump. This is too weird. Someone went to a lot of trouble and risk building this secret bridge. Who? And how long ago? And why? There's got to be something behind that waterfall. And the squirrel is leading us to it. Or is the squirrel leading us at all? I was more determined than ever to get some answers.

For all I knew, the spring boards could have been a hundred years old and could have been completely rotten. I leaned out and pressed down. The boards flexed and moss squished up between my fingers, but they seemed to hold. To apply more weight, I'd have to lean a little farther. Ramey was holding tight, but his ten-year-old arm was extended as far as it could go. *Just a little further. We've got to be sure these boards are strong enough...need to lean just a bit furth...*

Suddenly, with absolutely no warning, our hands flew apart. My arm recoiled like a cable snapping. Instantly, I fell forward into the pool. There was not a thing in the world I could do to stop myself. The eerie scene of the dark emerald world below—not being able to come back up, fast-forwarded through my brain.

Splash! My face and body slammed the water.

Thunk. I stopped.

Not daring to breath or move, I laid there for a moment. The waterfall ripped at my eardrums a few feet to my right, but otherwise nothing happened. I had fallen forward, directly onto the spring boards, and now was laying on them, face down. They'd held!

"Collin, you all right?!" Ramey hollered with a panicked voice. "Sss—sorry, my hand slipped!"

"Yeah, yeah, I'm fine. Whew! It looks like these boards might hold after all."

Cautiously, I gathered myself, raised to my feet, and slowly, slowly crept across. I scarcely reached the other side, when I heard a splashing commotion from behind. Here came Ramey, at a full sprint!

In three quick strides he was across. "I didn't want to give 'er time to even think of breaking," he said, dousing me with a wet-dog spray from his blond mop.

"Thanks for the bath. Nice to see you're your old self again."

We were now standing on a smooth, narrow rock ledge which led to some sort of open space behind the waterfall. This was unbelievable! Was it a secret passage? To where? When was the last time a human stood where Ramey and I now were? *Whoa*...

I cautiously stepped forward. After ten feet, we were standing in a shelter of sorts, directly behind the waterfall. We faced it, pale blue and flat. It looked like a perpetually rolling translucent curtain, like something out of Disneyland. I could have easily stuck a hand into the coursing water; it was only two feet away.

The rock face was hollowed out backward, creating a pocket with enough room for both of us, plus three more, easily. Oddly, in the middle of the space, a lone, smooth rock pillar protruded up waist-high from the floor. This must have been the pedestal the squirrel was perched on when I first saw it.

For some reason, it wasn't nearly as noisy where we now stood. And the spray from the pounding water was only a very slight mist swirling at our feet. We looked around in wonderment. I had never been in such a place. Water drip-drip-dripped from mossy protrusions over our heads. The rock wall was heavily fractured and angular, but smooth, too, as if eons of churning had rounded the edges. We were in a place secret to nearly every other human on earth.

Chapter Thirteen

Pitch Black

Our gaping amazement was dashed suddenly by a shrill, repetitive whistle. Something was behind us! We wheeled. In the shadows just beyond our grasp... was the squirrel. Ramey jumped at it, but just that quickly, it was gone.

"Did you see that, Collin?" He said in amazement. "That squirrel just disappeared into thin air! This is getting a little spooky. I...I'm beginning to wonder if maybe you were right—about that squirrel being magic or something."

"It's about time you admit my superior intelligence," I remarked, trying to look brainy. "But, I'm not convinced the squirrel is magic, yet. Look at this, where it just was. The wall—it splits back here. Looks like some sort of giant grabbed the rock and pulled; so hard, it ripped. And inside—boy, it's dark back here."

"Yeah," Ramey whispered, poking his head around the corner. "You're not kidding it's dark. Seems like that rip is sucking in all the light and none escapes. What do you make of it? Think maybe it's a cave or something?"

I didn't answer for a second as my eyes strained to see through the blackness. Then I whispered, "Yeah—yeah, I think that's exactly what it is. This must be where the squirrel went. I'm going in."

"But, but," Ramey stammered. "It's so dark in there. I can't see the back. I can't even see the walls after the first couple of feet."

"C'mon Ramey," I replied. "What's wrong, you afraid of the dark?" Bock, Bawwwkkk!"

"NO!" he replied indignantly, only half-telling the truth. Actually, shadowy visions were already playing across his mind.

Scenes of swooping bats and sudden drop-offs to sunken chambers with no exit—and of other things undefined, groping and grabbing with long bony fingers. Just to reassure himself of his resolve, again he said, "No, I'm not even a little afraid. But you, Mister Big Brave Man, you go first."

I crept slowly into the entrance. A chill went up my spine. Within three paces, I was blind, utterly. There was no light at all. I put my arms out and felt for the rock walls. Even though my hands were only a foot from my eyes, they were invisible. The naked rock was rough, cool, and moist to the touch. My own imagination started up. Visions of ghouls and monsters silently approaching, grabbing, clutching, filled my head. *Don't be stupid*, I thought. *There's no such thing as monsters.* After a few more steps, though, I began to wonder whether or not it was time to call this squirrel hunt quits and head back to the safety of our sunny log home and mountainside farm.

I felt something touching my back—Ramey no doubt.

Hesitant to admit fear, I took a few more steps then just to be sure, I whispered, "Ramey, that you?"

No answer.

"Ramey? Is that you touching my shirt?"

Still no answer. But whoever it was, was still there, touching me ever so lightly. I could hear heavy breathing. What if Ramey had been nabbed and I was next?

"Ramey!" Stop playing games! That better be you." I spun around...

"BOO!" Ramey shouted. "Scared you didn't I?"

"Ramey! Darn you! No...no you didn't scare me, it's just, well I wanted to be sure it was you, that's all."

"Who else would it be, you big scaredy-cat. The boogie-man?"

I harrumphed, turned and continued my slow travail.

Thump! Without warning, something clubbed me squarely

in the forehead. I recoiled, holding my breath, bracing for an attack. I could feel the pounding of my heart and the rushing of blood in my ears. But nothing else happened. "Ouch!" I finally managed. "Something just whacked me in the head, Ramey. It better not have been you again."

"Nnno..." he stammered. "I'm still *behind* you."

After a few tense moments, Ramey said, "Collin, are you sure something whacked you or could you have just bumped your head on the ceiling?"

"Well, it felt like I got hit, but maybe in the darkness I just banked my head on a low spot." I reached up and tentatively felt for the ceiling. Sure enough the rock was lower now.

"Yep, Ramey," I said with palpable relief, "looks like you're right, for once in your life."

We stooped and continued into the darkness. The tunnel was getting steadily smaller. Soon we were on our hands and knees.

"*Hey,*" I whispered loudly. "I see light up ahead! Keep going."

The light got brighter as the tunnel got smaller. After ten more yards of crawling, we exited through an opening just large enough for a full-sized man on his hands and knees.

Now we were able to stand again. We had just stumbled into an enormous underground cavern! My eyes nearly popped from their sockets taking in the magnificence of the place. It was oval-shaped, maybe sixty feet in one direction and eighty in the other. I guessed the distance from floor to the highest part of the jagged, domed ceiling was at least a hundred feet. I blinked hard, scanning upward toward the source of light.

Sunlight stabbed in from five roundish holes in the ceiling, varying in diameter from about six-inches to a foot-and-a-half. Each thrust down diagonal shafts like searchlights. Apparently, we weren't all that far underground.

The walls were a mix-mash of angular rock, protruding and

bulging like ghoulish masks in places, receding into shadowy cavities in others. The floor was surprisingly level, irregular to be sure, but even enough to walk across easily in any direction.

What I found most astounding, though, were the multitudinous daggers of white rock jutting straight down from the ceiling and also thrusting up from the floor. Some were fat at their base and irregularly shaped, like crazy tornadoes. Others were narrow, long, and straight, something like gigantic dinosaur teeth. Water dripped from the tip of those on the ceiling, and landed directly on the tip of those on the floor. It was so quiet, each drip reverberated in the huge space like the beating of distant drums. I could hear my own heart over the wheeze of air entering and leaving my lungs.

"Whhooooaaa…" I breathed as excitement tingled through me. "This place is awesome! Ramey, check out those stalactites."

"Stalacwhats?" Ramey questioned blankly. He was too absorbed, gawking, dumbfounded, to really hear my words.

"Stalactites. They're the ones pointing down from the ceiling. Stalagmites are the ones coming up from the floor. You'll learn about them in sixth grade."

"Yeah, they're cool alright," Ramey replied. "But what I really like is all the gold, over there."

I turned to the wall at which Ramey was pointing. One shaft of sunlight struck it squarely, shattering into a thousand sparkles. Sure enough, there, in bright yellow splotches, plastered over nearly the entire wall was… *gold!*

Chapter Fourteen

Gold!

"GOLD!" we both shouted, ripping the silence of the place. Immediately we forgot everything else. Visions of wealth beyond comprehension zipped through our brains. Like steel to a magnet, we took off at a sprint across the broken floor, eyes fixed on the gleaming yellow.

"*Oof!*" I yelled out suddenly as my foot slammed into something. I stumbled, lost balance, and in a great cloud of dust, fell to the ground. Fortunately, save a banged elbow and skinned knee, I didn't sustain any serious damage. My eyes had instinctively closed as I fell, but when I reopened them I got the shock of my life.

There, laying amid the dust and pebbles, staring directly back into my face—was a skull. A human skull.

"Whaaatttt the…!" I shouted. "Raaayyymmmeeyyyyy!"

Ramey had not stopped at my fall. Indeed, he had continued running, grinning that my little misfortune would ensure he'd get to the gold first. But my scream did stop him. He turned and now he saw it, too.

It was a human skeleton.

I had plowed into its ribcage, sending bones flying. The skull had skidded a few feet, coming to rest scant inches from my own face. Its jaw was slightly detached and agape, as if locked in an eternal shout of frozen horror.

I hastily lifted myself, stepped back nervously, and stared at the scattered bones. I then did what I always did when nervous: reached into my back pocket, grabbed my comb and, trembling slightly, mechanically ran it through my hair.

"Collin," Ramey breathed. "You… you just kicked a dead

guy."

"Yeah, I know," I answered in monotone, my eyes still riveted on the skull. "Looks like someone got here before us. But...but they didn't make it back out. I...I'm starting to get a little scared."

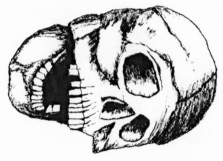

"Yeah, m-m-me too," Ramey said. Then, changing his tone, he continued. "Hey, wait a minute, look at this." He knelt down and pointed to some dusty sticks on floor. He brushed the gray powder off one of them, held it up, and said, "Look at this stick. See what's on the tip of it?" Ramey was running his finger along the sharp edge of a small rock tied crudely to the end of the shaft. "Collin, this is an arrowhead! And these sticks...they're arrows. And look at that curved stick over there. It's the bow! This is a bow and a set of arrows, and there's the quiver over there by his other arm. Know what? I becha' this guy was an Indian."

My fear began to dissolve. If this was indeed an Indian, then he probably died many hundreds of years ago by some natural occurrence rather than by foul play. Somehow this notion made the situation considerably less scary. "I wonder what killed him?" I said.

Ramey was already working on the answer. "Collin, look where he's laying."

I looked about, searching for some clue. Not seeing anything obvious, I replied, "On the floor, ninny, anyone can see that."

"No, no you schtoopnagul. That's not what I mean. Look where he is in relation to that hole in the ceiling."

I followed my brother's pointing finger straight up to the largest hole in the roof. Indeed, the skeleton was exactly, directly below the only hole large enough for a person to fit through. "Oh...I get it," I finally said. "You're thinking this guy was hunting along up above, not watching where he was going then he stepped into that hole—*schloop*—a hundred-foot swan dive to the rock floor."

"Yep, that's 'zactly what I was thinking." Ramey said.

"You know, Ramey, sometimes you're not as dumb as you look," I said, neatly fitting the comb back into my pocket.

But the insult fell on deaf ears. Ramey was already, again, sprinting for the wall of gold.

"Hey, wait for me!"

By the time we reached the sparkling wall, greed had firmly entrenched itself. We gouged frantically at the valuable mineral with our fingernails. Not having immediate success, I took my pocketknife and pried like a lunatic at the rock. Ramey, seeing that I was now having more success than he was, followed suit with his own pocketknife. Suddenly, from the tip of my blade, out popped a small chunk the size of a pea. It landed in my hand, glimmering.

"Ramey," I sputtered, "see this chunk here. Just this small piece is probably worth five hundred dollars! And it's only the tip of the iceberg! There's so much—we'll be rich! Now we can get mom to the doctor. And dad won't have to work so hard all the time. Yes! We've found it. This has to be the Dark Quartz Mine! *The Dark Quartz Mine, Ramey!* We're rich, we're rich!"

Ramey and I, feeling ebullient indeed, were not aware that our noisy celebration was carrying, clear as a bell, across the floor and beyond. We were not the only ones to ever have set foot in the cave, not by a long shot. In our haste to get to the gold, we failed to notice a shadowy hole in the gloom of the far wall. We could not have guessed that the hole was an entrance to another tunnel; a tunnel which sprawled deep into the mountain, running on for miles—with more tangled and twisted branches and offshoots than a black widow's web.

One of those branches had been traveled some five-and-a-half years ago by an evil man and his dogs. They had just been party to a capture and were dragging their wounded prisoner to other tunnels where he would be left to rot. But perhaps even more menacing was the threat lurking in yet other branches—the deepest, darkest tunnels. Someone lived down there. Actually lots of someones, and they were not nice. At that moment a small band of them were running, hustling to investigate the noisy disturbance in their entrance cave. To see what or who was inviting them so carelessly to…to a little party, perchance. And they were coming with wicked intentions.

Ignorant of the danger rapidly approaching, Ramey and I continued celebrating our find.

"After we take care of mom, I'm gonna buy me a brand new bike!" Ramey crowed. "And it's gonna have big knobby tires, and hand brakes, and shocks front and back. A bike for jumping, that's what I'm gonna get!"

"Yeah, well, you go ahead and get your stupid bike," I responded. "I'm buying a motorcycle! A dirt bike, maybe a 125 or a 250, with so much power I'll be able to climb any hill. A trials bike, that's what I want, so I can ride over fallen logs and boulders. I'll be able to go anywhere on the mountain I want to."

"Hey wait a minute," Ramey protested. "If you're getting a motorcycle, then I want one too, just 'zackly like yours!"

"Oh, no…" I said, trying to sound authoritarian. "You're too little. Dad would never let you have a motorcycle, not until you're at least twelve."

"Oh, yes he would! You're just saying that because you want to be the only one with a motorcycle! This gold is half mine and I can buy whatever I want!"

It had only been five minutes and already the power of gold was working its perilous spell. But far worse were the small, malicious denizens of the sprawling tunnels who were now running at full sprint, only about sixty seconds from the cave.

"We'll just see about that," I said, again trying to sound important. "Wait 'til we get home and dad tells you exactly what I'm telling you now. Then you'll see I'm right and you're wrong!"

Suddenly, something hard, like a small rock, hit me in the back of the head.

"Ouch! Ramey, did you just hit me in the back of the head?"

"No. How could I hit you in the *back* of the head when I'm standing right here in *front* of you?"

"What the...?" I said, turning around. There, not ten feet away, was the squirrel. It squeaked a terrific "chechecheeeee!" then turned and dashed away.

"You little...!" I shouted, giving chase. The squirrel made a bee-line for the entrance and in a blink was gone. I closed in behind him. I had the gold nugget in my pocket and was more or less ready to leave anyway.

Ramey hot-footed it after us both.

And just in the nick of time! Just as Ramey's bottom squiggled through the narrow entrance tunnel, a host of dirty, snarling faces filled the other tunnel opening. A murmur of disappointed grunts and slaverings followed us, though unheard, out the tunnel, over the submerged spring boards, across the slippery, jagged rocks, and up the rough-hewn stairs. Six thwarted Tommyknockers frowned menacingly, turned and retreated, muttering curses into the darkness. We had escaped, this time.

Chapter Fifteen

Of Fools and Decisions

Back home we ran. The squirrel easily eluded us up a tall maple tree. I wondered where it had gone but didn't slow down to find out. I had a very important discovery to share with my parents.

It was a little after 6:00 when Ramey and I finally burst through the screen door. Mom was struggling to prepare a simple meal of leftover goat meat, steamed green beans and rice. She looked like a shipwreck, ragged with exhaustion. Dad busied himself setting the table. His brow was furrowed and his broad shoulders bowed as if he was carrying the weight of the world. When the door opened, he looked up, frowned and spoke harshly, "Boys, where you been? You should've been home two hours ago. Your mother was worried sick for you. I can't tolerate that kind of behavior, you know that."

We bustled to take off our boots. Before either of us could rattle off an explanation, dad was already preparing corrective measures. "Now come on over here and get your medicine."

He meant to deliver a swift spank to each of us, but, instead, I caught him off guard. Racing over, all out of breath, extending my hand and blurting almost too fast to be comprehensible, "Dad, DAD, mom! Look, look what we found! It's gold, GOLD! Ramey and I found the Dark Quartz Mine! Dad, the *Dark Quartz Mine!* It's hidden behind a waterfall. There was this squirrel, see, and he led us there, and we fell in the water, but I grabbed a log. Then the cave, behind the waterfall—the whole wall, nothing but GOLD! Pure GOLD. Now we can buy…get the medicine mom needs, and, and she can go to the doctor. Can you believe it, dad? Look for yourself…"

Dad's scowl gave way to puzzlement. Mom lifted her head, turned from the stovetop, and felt her face flush with the first color it had displayed in weeks. Sure enough, there in the palm of my shaking hand was a sparkling nugget of yellow.

"Now slow down, son," dad said, retracting his anger. "You're talking so fast, you're just making gibberish. Slow down, and tell me what you've got there and where it come from."

Ramey and I spent the next five minutes dueling to tell the story. We conveniently glossed over the part about Ramey's near-drowning. No need to overly worry our parents.

Mom and dad, not yet fully comprehending the magnitude of what was transpiring, listened patiently, interrupting occasionally to dispense a scold or warning. When the story finally wound to its conclusion, dad, suspicious of the source of the nugget asked, "So, this gold here, you boys sure you found it in the wall of a cave and not in someone's house?"

I answered earnestly, "Oh, yes, dad, I mean no—I mean if we took the gold from someone's house, that would be stealing. We wouldn't ever steal, if that's what you're asking. You taught us never to take what's not ours. The cave, it doesn't belong to anyone. I mean, well, there was the dead Indian, but no one else, dad. I promise."

Satisfied that I was telling the truth, that the nugget had in fact been found by us rather than misappropriated or otherwise absconded, he plucked it from my hand and examined it carefully under the end table lamp.

Mom looked on with the first real hope she'd had in a year. The room fell completely silent.

After what seemed like an hour, dad finally looked up with a faint smile, a sad faint smile.

"Boys," he said. "I hate to tell you this, but your nugget ain't…it's not gold at all. It's fool's gold—iron pyrite. It's worthless."

His words were like a gust of wind that sucked the hopes
and dreams from everyone and left us standing there like frozen
stones. Suddenly, our fantastic future crashed back to the oppressive
present. Dad looked over at mom, whose expression of hope fell to
a blank gape. Tears welled up in her sunken eyes. "I'm sorry, boys,"
he said. "Sorry, mama."

I was shell-shocked. My mouth hung half open and my eyes
glazed over. *Fool's gold?* I thought. *How could that be possible?
Why would there be a secret cave with secret stairs, secret spring
boards, and a secret tunnel, just to be filled with fool's gold? No
one in their right mind would go to so much trouble and danger to
get to that cave if all it contained was fool's gold. This can't be true.
And what about mom? She needs it to be real gold—needs it. Her
very life depends on it being the real thing. Ramey and I risked our
lives and nearly died for this? It can't be happening...*

But my profound disappointment took yet another blow
with dad's next sentence.

"Boys, I never want you goin' back to that cave again. First
of all, it sounds like you nearly died getting there once—I surely

94

don't want none of them happenings again. But there's other things, too. You don't know it, but caves can be mighty dangerous places. Sometimes the air in 'em is poisonous. You wouldn't even notice until it's too late. You'd just fall asleep and never wake up. Carbon monoxide. Can't see it. Can't smell it, but it's deadly poison. Not only that, cave and tunnel roofs can fall in and trap you. You'd die of thirst or starvation; that is, if one of the falling boulders didn't smash you first. But maybe worst of all, and I hate to even mention the word, are the Tommyknockers."

I took a hard gulp. Suddenly my throat and tongue had gone dry. *Tommyknockers…what are those? Poisonous gases?* It all seemed alien and impossible. *But, I've… we've been there—to the cave already. It's safe inside. There was no poisonous gas. I didn't get even a little sleepy. The worst danger by far is on the outside.*

Nobody said anything. Silence hung in the room like an oil slick. Finally, Ramey could stand the tension no longer and spoke. "Dad? What's a Tommyknocker?"

"Well Ramey," dad replied sternly, but in a compassionate tone, "you boys come on over here and I'll tell you."

Heads down, we obediently followed him into the living room, to the beat-up sofa, and sat, one boy on each side. As we plopped down, a depressing dust puffed from the cushions.

Dad looked down at us, forced a smile, and began. "See, fellers, it's like this. Tommyknockers are mysterious little men who live underground, especially in mines. As far as I know, they've been around as long as humans. In fact, from what I understand, they used to roam the earth, side-by-side, with us. But a long, long time ago, before my grampa's grampa's grampa, some of us big folk, that's what they call us, decided they was no count, being small and all—that they weren't as good as us. So some big folks started treating 'em bad. Turned 'em into slaves and left them do all the dirty work. Well, you can guess how well they liked them apples. So to escape the mean treatment, they went underground.

Pert'neer disappeared from the face o' the earth. But they surely didn't disappear from the guts o' the earth, nosir. And I'll tell you another thing; down through the years, they remembered all that bad treatment our ancestors dished out, and it sticks in their craw. That's exactly why, to this day, they ain't nice to us big folk. Fact is, they're downright mean little buggers. Whenever they get even half a chance, they reckon it's time to extract a little revengance."

Dad paused, looking from side to side to be sure we were listening. Listening? We were sitting bolt-upright, staring wide eyed into the distance. He definitely had our attention, so he continued. "Nowadays, miners are the ones who have to bear the brunt of that revenge, because they're the ones alltime underground. F'rinstance, whenever some worker in a mine turns up missing, or a blasting cap misfires, or a winch cable snaps, or the lights go out without warning—the miners blame the Tommyknockers. But the Tommyknockers, they're crafty devils. No one ever sees 'em or hears 'em. But most folk who've worked in mines for any amount of time swear they're real. No seasoned miner would ever go anyplace in a mine alone, or leastwise without a trustworthy lamp, for fear of gettin ambushed. You know, Tommyknockers can see better in the dark than the light. They ain't big enough to take on two or more men, but if they were desperate or hungry enough, a gaggle of 'em might up and take a single man. And I can tell you this much for sure, a boy or even two boys, they'd be Tommyknocker stew faster'n a beagle runnin' a rabbit."

Ramey and I sat there, galvanized. This was the most we'd heard dad speak in a month, cumulatively. For that, we were happy. But as his story unfolded, a nervous, worried look overcame us and by the time he finished, our eyes were more white than colored. *Were there Tommyknockers in our cave? And were we just lucky to avoid them?*

Again, Ramey questioned, "Tommyknocker stew? Dad, do you mean the Tommyknockers…actually eat…kids?"

96

Dad looked down at his fidgeting son, smiled ever so slightly, and replied in a softer tone, "Well, Ramey, I can't say for sure if they do or if they don't. I can't even say for sure if they're real. All I can tell you is what I learned from the folks I've knowed who did a little mining. Every one of 'em talks about the Tommyknockers, and what they say ain't good. But enough about that. I don't want you going and inventing up a bunch of nightmares worrying about no Tommyknockers. You're going to do like your pa says and not go back to that cave, nohow. Now, your mama's made us a nice supper and we better get on up to the table before it turns to ice."

That night as I lay in bed, struggling with visions of caves, gold, waterfalls, and small evil underground men, I tossed for a while then whispered, "Ramey, you still awake?"

"Yeah," came the reply. "I keep thinking about the cave, and all the fool's gold, and mama, and...."

"I know," I interrupted. "Me, too. I don't care what dad says about fool's gold or Tommyknockers. I just know *that* cave is the entrance to the Dark Quartz Mine. It's got to be. And whether there's such a thing as Tommyknockers or not—we've got to go back and explore some more. Maybe there's some other tunnels we missed, leading off to the *real* parts of the mine, where the *real* gold is."

"But, Collin," Ramey hissed almost too loudly. "You heard dad. We aren't supposed to go near that cave again. I don't want to even think of how much trouble we'll be in if we do and we get caught."

"I know, I know," I replied. "But we've got to risk it. Mama's dying. She'll probably be gone by Christmas if something good doesn't happen. Ramey, it's up to us. If we don't find the Dark Quartz ourselves, mama won't get to the doctor and, well..."

There was a long, dead-quiet pause. The grownups had

gone to bed and the entire cabin was stone-still. Ramey didn't bother to respond. He was too busy tuggling with a brain full of impossible dilemmas and the slow infusion of sleep.

A glowing full moon shone its brilliance through our lone bedroom window, illuminating a humble lamp table which separated our two small beds. I lay on my side facing the table, eyes wide open, staring at my favorite toy—a miniature carved wooden wagon with a wooden boy sitting therein, hands grasping the handle. The wagon was bright red and the boy was dressed in royal blue trousers with a cheerful yellow shirt. His face was painted with a big, broad smile. It was a present from six birthdays ago. Of course it wasn't a Kringle toy, our family could never afford that. But it was, nonetheless, sturdy and gaily painted, and the wheels would actually spin when you pushed it. I wanted desperately to be happy and carefree, like the boy in my wooden wagon. But with my mother's illness and my dad's gloomy work situation, I hadn't felt that way since...well, I couldn't remember when.

As sleep began weaving its way through my consciousness, I made up my mind that I was going back to the cave, with or without Ramey. I *had* to find the Dark Quartz Mine. My last thoughts before drifting off concerned the possibility of being captured in some dark tunnel. *Well,* I thought, *at least I will have tried...*

Chapter Sixteen

Search

A week went by quietly. The only item worthy of note was mom's decline ever deeper into her sickness' steel grip. She continued striving valiantly to get things done—hold up her end of the workload. But her efforts more often than not were in vain. If she had to trudge more than ten paces at a time, she was looking for a place to sit, be it a chair, table edge, or even the floor. There was never a smile on her lips, nor a twinkle in her eyes. It almost seemed that she was someone else, not even my own mom.

I could tell that she, especially, had been let down by the fool's gold hoax. If somehow I could have bottled the hope in her eyes as Ramey and I told of the cave and the wall of gold. But alas, that hope was fleeting and it was false. In the end, our bogus claim exacted a greater toll on her than if we hadn't brought back anything that day except a hearty appetite.

Mom's decline that week greatly troubled Ramey. Until then his ten-year-old mind assumed that she just had a real bad cold or the flu and would be turning the corner any day. Either that, or somehow dad would do something to make it better. Dad always came through when things got tough. But now Ramey saw that she was nearing a critical condition. The spark of life that once burst forth within her was slowly extinguishing. Her days were numbered and no one, not even dad, could help. The thought of being without a mom sunk in. I continued haranguing him about going back to the cave, but Ramey, fearful of dad's warnings, resisted. By the time the next Saturday rolled around, however, Ramey could see that we *had* to go back. We were running out of time.

After breakfast, I told our parents that we were going

hunting, which wasn't exactly a lie—we were indeed hunting: for gold. We mowed through our chores, then struck out at about ten o'clock. Forty-five minutes later, without incident, we approached the rim of the box canyon. Hiking up the abandoned logging road, Ramey noticed a movement in the briars to his left. Not 20 feet away was...the squirrel. It was scampering along beside us, slipping in and out among the maples, alders, and salmonberries, and more or less staying out of rock-throwing range.

"Collin," Ramey called, pointing, "There's that squirrel. Wanna bean 'im?"

Ramey was a little surprised by my response. "No. I don't think we should throw any more rocks at that squirrel. For some strange reason, I think he's on our side. I mean, I don't understand exactly what's going on, but I think that squirrel knows something we don't, and it aims to show us. Think about it, Ramey. If it wasn't for the squirrel, we would never have found the cave. I think he lead us there, and maybe, if we leave him alone, he'll lead us to the gold."

"Have you lost your marbles?" Ramey retorted. "Since when do squirrels lead anything more than a wild goose chase away from their winter stock of nuts? Oh, he'll lead us all right, straight into a pack of cougars or hornets or something. Next thing you're gonna tell me is that squirrel can talk, or ride a bike, or do magic tricks."

"Ramey, I'm not saying anything about bikes or magic tricks or anything else. All I'm saying is that squirrel led us to the cave and I think it knew exactly what it was doing. I say we let it alone and see what happens. There really isn't any reason to hunt him anyway. We've got all the meat we need in the freezer."

"But, we're supposed to be *hunting*," Ramey protested. "If we actually bring back a fat ol' squirrel, dad will know for sure we really were hunting and I don't mean for gold."

We continued this discussion for several more minutes

while the squirrel watched, twitching its front paws. Finally, Ramey gave in. "Okay," he said, "I'll let it alone. But, hear me now. If that four-legged, overstuffed rodent doesn't produce something, he's meat. Dead meat."

"Fine."

We scrambled down the box canyon's moss-carpeted stairs, over the jagged rocks, across the spring boards, through the tunnel, and soon found ourselves, once again, standing in the cave. Just like before, we were awestruck with the magnitude of it all. There was something exciting about just being there.

But we were on a mission: to find new tunnels or shafts. After absorbing the ambiance we began scanning the shadowed recesses for openings. We started at the cave entrance and worked around to our left.

Suddenly a slight shuffling sound and quick movement caught my attention. My imagination engaged. *Tommyknockers! We're being ambushed!*

Memories of dad's fearful descriptions came flooding back. *What now? How will we defend ourselves? Do I have time to dig out and open my pocketknife? Will a puny little pocketknife actually do any good? What if there's a hundred of them?*

I whipped around and crouched into an attack position expecting the worst.

The squirrel.

It's only that stupid squirrel. Whew! What a relief.

Ramey, reacting to my sudden movement, wrenched his head around too. Upon seeing it was a false alarm, he chided, "It's just your good buddy: Mister Soon-to-be-Supper-Squirrel, Collin. The way you whipped your head around, I was afraid maybe you'd seen a Tommyknocker or something. Yeah, I bet that's what you were thinking, that we were being ambushed. Ha ha ha. Boy, if you could've seen the look on your face just now. What a bock-bock-bock—chick... ick... icken!"

My voice was a little shaky, responding with fake confidence, "Naw, I d-don't believe in them. I think dad was just making that up to try and scare us."

The squirrel scampered to the other side of the cave and took a perch on one of the rocky high points, whereupon it assumed its familiar position and fixed its stare on us. We turned and resumed our search of the cave walls. The perimeter zigged and jagged in and out, the ceiling rising and falling with the ever-changing Martian floor.

Each shadowy indentation was a black hole that had to be explored. We cautiously poked our heads and hands into each, straining to see through the blackness. None went any deeper than a foot or two. We found several piles of small bones—rats we reckoned, hidden in the depths, but nothing more. It soon became amply apparent that we should have remembered a flashlight, but in our haste to mislead our parents, we took off so fast we were lucky to remember our trousers.

After thirty painstaking minutes of searching, we came upon a very smooth rock projecting slightly from the cave wall. It was located opposite the entrance tunnel. Compared to what we had seen thus far, it was unusual. All the other rocks were sharp and angular yet this one was smooth, as if worn that way from someone having climbed over it many, many times. I walked from one side to the other examining as I went. As I did, my skin prickled with a definite cooling. A chill seemed to emanate from the rock. And I noticed an odor too. It was stale, like a dry must, but with a wisp of something rotten.

I ran my hands across the chilly surface searching for something, anything indicative of past human activity. Maybe this was some sort of trap door, and maybe there was a knob or handle concealed in a secret pocket or compartment.

Suddenly the squirrel began chattering, but differently than ever before. It was not his normal obnoxious squeak. No, this was a string of chatters, rising and falling, pausing, undulating with almost humanlike patterns. Ramey and I looked at each other, then at the squirrel. *Was he trying to speak to us? What in the world?*

But just as soon as the squirrel's chatter started, it stopped. Then it went back to its silent, incessant twitching. I spoke up, "Ramey, this rock must mean something. Do you feel the coldness coming from it? And did you hear that crazy squirrel? You'll probably think I'm bonkers, but I think he was trying to say something. I almost could understand it."

"Yeah, me too—I mean, not the bonkers part. I hate to think he's worth anything more than a meal, but his squeaks *did* sound funny, and he was awful excited. Maybe there's something about this smooth rock."

Forgetting the squirrel for a moment, we searched all around the base of the rock. Nothing. Then it occurred to Ramey: the coolness, there was a slight motion to it, a faint draft. His skin and the hairs on his arms told him it was moving from high to low. He looked up.

"Collin!" he exclaimed, pointing. "Look up there. An opening. A tunnel!"

Sure enough, at the top of the rock the rough walls receded backward into blackness. The opening was roundish, some four feet across. What little light there was in this part of the cave seemed to be swallowed greedily by the jet darkness of the hole. I thought I could almost see odorous vapors tumbling out, trailing down the rock's face like fog rolling across a murky swamp.

Just then the squirrel let out another string of chatters, this time more rapid and excited than the first.

"Ramey!" I exclaimed, "We must be on to something."

"Yeah. Unless I'm nuts-er than you, I could've sworn the squirrel just said something like 'mine,' and 'tunnel' and 'Peter.'"

"I know. That's what I thought too."

I looked over at the squirrel hoping for some more prattling, but again, it had gone stone-silent except for the barely audible rubbing of its front paws.

"So, it's another tunnel," I continued. "But how will we get up there? It's a good six feet to the bottom of the opening and there's no other rocks or anything else to grab onto."

Cursing ourselves for not bringing either a flashlight or a ladder, we tried to boost each other, scrambling as best we could on the smooth rock. No use. We would have to bring a ladder or a rope next time.

But this little discovery had buoyed our spirits. "If there's two tunnels, Collin, maybe there's three," Ramey suggested, unquenchably. "We're only about halfway around."

We resumed our search, picking our way slowly among the projections and recesses, climbing the stalagmites, dodging the stalactites, following the cave wall further to the right.

Just as we were about to give up, having gone nearly all the way around, I noticed a narrow gap between two stalactites only ten feet from the cave entrance. The formation resembled the bared fangs of a huge rattlesnake and was just wide enough for a person to squeeze through. Beyond it, the cave wall darkened in shadow. As I approached, from behind me the squirrel burst forth with a string of excited chatter. It hopped off its rocky perch and bounded toward me, stopping short some ten yards away.

Ramey had been searching in another direction but turned toward the commotion.

"Hey, Ramey," I said, pointing. "I think I might've found something. See these stalactites, look behind them to that dark place."

Ramey scrambled over, shoving his way in front of me. "Oh, yeah! I see it," he exclaimed, poking his head between the fangs. "There's definitely something here and we don't need a ladder to get to it. I'm going in!"

"Watch out for Tommykno..... I mean, be careful. I'm right

behind you!"

Ramey squeezed through the gap and disappeared into the blackness before I could catch up.

Suddenly a blood-curdling scream came from the tunnel's depths. It was Ramey!

Chapter Seventeen

Discovery

"RAMEY!" I shouted, thrusting my body blindly into the ink. "What happened? Are you all right? Where are you? I can't see a thing!"

I put my arms out and inched forward. I could hear breathing ahead, but could see nothing. Then, out of the darkness, the glowing of two eyes became visible. They were low to the ground—gleaming directly into my face. Then a low, evil-sounding voice broke the silence, "I am a TOMMYKNOCKER! I have just made stew of your brother, and I'm coming for you next!"

In a flash, I snatched my pocketknife, whipped open the blade and prepared to launch myself at the eyes. Then, just as I was ready to spring forward, a peal of laughter, my brother's laughter, filled the tunnel. "Scared you, didn't I?" he blurted between chuckles.

"RAMEY! Darn YOU!" I exploded. "Don't EVER do that

again. I was just about to stab you with my pocketknife! You, you
SCHTOOPNAGUL!"

Ramey recoiled a little, realizing maybe he should be more
careful with his pranks. "Okay, okay… I won't do that anymore.
Sorry. But I thought you didn't believe in Tommyknockers."

"Well, maybe I don't and maybe I do. How am I supposed
to know anyway? Just don't play those kinds of tricks on me."

"Okay."

The racket of Ramey's scream and my rebuke reverberated
crisply through the cave and well into the other tunnel. From deep
within the mountain, in a tiny, filthy chamber, with a ceiling no
higher than four feet, a dirty face pricked up. A sinister smile slowly
spread across the Tommyknocker's lips. *They're back*, he thought
with malicious glee. *The two child-visitors have returned—and still
acting careless and stupid! Oh, this is good, yesss…very good! This
time, perhaps they'll stick around long enough for a little fun.
Yessss, some nasssty fun and games!*

He sprang from the crude wooden table where he'd been
preparing a meal of boiled rat.

Already, four of his comrades had gathered in the darkness
outside his lair and were talking excitedly.

Ramey and I were completely oblivious to the danger
brewing deep below. Ramey's practical joke had disturbed me and I
wasn't in the mood for any more shenanigans. "Now, let's finish
exploring this tunnel," I commanded. "I'm going first this time."

I shuffled past him in the tunnel's narrow confines, put my
hands out and slowly inched forward. It was pitch black. A small
blast of adrenaline shot through my heart, quickening my pulse.
This must be how it feels to be a bat, I thought, taking another
cautious step. *But at least bats have sonar. I could step into a
bottomless pit and not even know it until I was airborne.*

After about ten painstaking yards, my feet unexpectedly
struck something—something odd, definitely not rock. I lost my

balance and tipped forward, but my outstretched hands hit the rock of the wall stopping me. *So, tunnel's end. That was short. But what did I hit with my boot?* Tentatively I kicked forward again. Whatever it was made a slight clanking sound, like it was metallic. Another shot of adrenaline raced in my veins. Instantly visions of gold, spilling from chests and thick cast iron pots, sprang up in my imagination. *Maybe this is the tunnel we're looking for and here is a small sampling of what fabulous riches await us!*

"Hey, Ramey," I whispered excitedly. "I just kicked something and I think it's made out of metal."

"Well, don't just stand there, nincompoop. Reach down and see what it is. Just be careful it's not some kind of Tommyknocker trap. Ha, ha!"

"I don't think that's even a little funny," I retorted, groping downward.

One touch told me it wasn't a chest or pot, or gold of any kind. Disappointment fizzled in my mind. I ran my hands over the thing trying to formulate a guess as to what it was. *Okay, so maybe this isn't the mother lode, but it is something—something verrry interesting. Something that must've been hidden here a long time.*

"Well?!" whispered Ramey urgently, "What is it?!"

"Um, it's – it's... well, I can't tell what it is, but it seems like it's made out of metal and wood. Smooth, square...hey, it has wheels...and a handle and it's not all that heavy. I've got hold of it now, I'm pulling it out."

Ramey backed slowly out, followed by me towing the object. It rolled along with incredible ease, bumping noisily on the rough rock floor. Soon we were back in the main cave under one of the holes in the roof, a thick cylinder of bright sunlight illuminating our find.

It was a wagon. A child's wagon—an exceptionally large one to be sure—covered completely with powdery gray dust. We excitedly brushed it off with our shirt sleeves.

Without warning, we were startled by a shuffling noise behind us.

My heart jumped and the hair on the back of my neck bristled. I wheeled around.

Once again it was only the squirrel, scampering directly toward us. It stopped a mere three feet away and began chattering up a storm.

I paused for a moment and stared at the squirrel in amazement. As it prattled on, this time I was sure I could understand a few human words amongst its squeaks and chitters.

"Do you hear that?" I asked my equally dumbfounded brother. "I'm sure I understood a few words that time. I'm positive he said, 'Peter' and 'dungeon,' and he keeps saying something like 'Malcrook'."

I crouched down and looked squarely at the squirrel. Save some quivering of its whiskers it did not move, but rather stared directly back. Again, I thought I recognized something distantly human in its face.

"Slow down, big fella," I said gently. "I can make out some of what you're trying to say, but you're going so fast I can't get it all. Just relax and slow down. We won't hurt you."

The squirrel chattered a response, "Ookaycheche…che…buthow'mI… che…supposedtobesure…sure aboutthat….che cheche… Youwere justthrowingrocks-che!sticks…atme aweekago… How'mI…how'mIsupposed… cheche… howm'Isupposed… tobesureanyway?"

My eyes bugged out. "Ramey, I could understand it! He said he's not sure we won't throw more rocks at him. Did you hear that?!"

"Yeah, I heard it! Mom and dad'll never believe this!"

I turned and spoke very slowly to the squirrel, adding emphasis to every word. "I…we…won't – throw – any – more – rocks—at – you, – we – promise."

The squirrel responded, "Thatsgreat... but... cheche... youdon'thaveto ... cheche... talksoslow... whatdoyouthinkIam... che... whatamI, stupid?"

I blinked hard, a little taken aback by the squirrel's surly remark. "No, – not – stupid, – it's – just – we're – not – used – to – talking – to - squirrels, - that's – all."

"Okayokayokay... nowthatyourused... toit... che... youcanspeaknormally... che... Iunderstandyou... cheche... perfectly."

"Okay, – all – right...I mean okay. I'll try to talk— normally. But it would be helpful if you could slow down a little yourself. I'm still having trouble understanding you."

"OkayI'lltry... too. Butyou... see... che... Ihaven'tspokento... anyone... innearlysix... sixlong... years. Oh, exceptfor Peter... ofcourse... yesexcept for Peter... a verysmall... che... amount. SoI'm... I'mnotused... to talkingto... che... people... to humansyet. That'swhy... Ikeepsaying... cheche... somuch. I'lltrytostop... dispensewith... the che-che's. You'llhaveto... pardonthem... theyjustseem... tocome... che... naturally."

"Oh, that's all right," I replied. "If you'll just talk slowly, you can say 'che che' as much as you like. I don't mind at all. But— Peter? You keep talking about this Peter. Who is that? And who are *you*?"

"Peter... Peter... ? Youdon'tknowPeter... ? I'msureyoudo... youknowPeter... cheche... PeterisPeter... Kringle... the toymaker... andthatwagonthere... thatwagonwasmade... che... ! wasmadebyPeter. And asforme... I'm... cheche... I'm... well... Ineedto... musttellyou... whoIam... butIbet... che... youwon'tbelieveit."

My eyes widened. I turned to Ramey. We looked at each other with blank expressions of sheer disbelief. Peter Kringle? *The* Peter Kringle? He hadn't been heard from in nearly six years. And *this* was a Kringle wagon? Any disappointment I felt earlier at our discovery not being gold vanished like a wisp of wind sucked out through one of the holes in the ceiling. If this was truly a Kringle toy, to a kid it was every bit as valuable as any pot of gold.

Now the squirrel took a deep breath as if to concentrate on what he wanted to say next.

"Youtwo... boys. Che! Youtwohave... havejust found... Peter Kringle's... mostmagnificent... and wonderfultoy... ofall... time. Youhavejust... found... checheche... themagical... Red Rocket!"

Chapter Eighteen

Evon

First a talking squirrel, now a magical wagon—a *Kringle* magic wagon! What would be next?! My excitement was nearly overflowing as Ramey and I faced each other with bulging eyes and gaping mouths.

But what would actually be next was not nearly so wonderful. From the dark depths many hundreds of feet below, serious trouble had marshaled and was heading rapidly our way. Already a half dozen Tommyknockers were hustling along twisting, craggy tunnels intent on spoiling the noisy celebration that had sprung up in their entrance cave above.

Completely ignorant of our peril, Ramey and I struggled to process this new, unbelievable information. Certainly, our family's meager financial situation fairly guaranteed we could never afford a Kringle toy. But now, here was one, a magnificent one at that, being literally dumped in our laps! Unbelievable! My mind raced, *Magical?! What kind of magic?*

But then a bullet of reality hit and my jubilation deflated. In my mind's eye I saw my dad's stern face looking down at Ramey and I and our new find, suspicion on his brow. His first comment would not be how happy he was that we now owned a Kringle toy. No, he would want to know who's it was and how we'd come to posses it. Ramey and I would be under the microscope of his scrutiny and we'd better have a good answer.

Whose is it, really? I thought. *Because Ramey and I found it, does that mean it's ours to keep? Or does it belong to someone else and we'll have to give it back?*

I pulled my hand away from the dusty toy and asked the

squirrel, "Magical wagon? You did say magical, didn't you? What did you mean by that? And who does it belong to?"

"ImeanwhatIsaid... magical... magicalwagon. It'smagic... Areyouhardof... deaf? Andasfor... whoit...belongsto... well, nowthatyou've... found it... cheche... Isuppose... it'sfinder's keepers... loser'sweepers... right?... itmustbe... well... belongstoyou."

A gigantic smile, a Christmas morning smile, spread across my face. My head was filling with visions of Ramey and me playing with our new Kringle toy: rambling down the driveway, wind in our hair, hauling each other around the barnyard. Or better yet, since it was magical, maybe no pushing or pulling was needed! Maybe this wagon went all by itself. Wow! Now that would be some terrific fun!

I fumbled a hand into my back pocket, pulled out my comb, and began running it through my hair. "Yes – I mean no, I mean – um, my hearing's fine," I stumbled. "I just wanted to be sure I heard what you said. *Ours*, right? Do you mean it's ours to keep?"

"WellIsuppose... so. Idon'tsee... anyone elsearound... heretotake... useit. Che! Don'twantto... leaveit... for *them*... anyhow... certainlynot... no, thatwouldnever... do! But... it'snot... noit'sdefinitelynot... made... forchildren... notforkids... oh no."

Not for kids? Suddenly, something was fishy. I fired back, "But you just said we could keep it. Aren't we kids? And by the way, if you've been able to talk all along, why didn't you say something when we first saw you. We could've killed you with those rocks we were throwing. And who exactly do you mean by 'them'?"

The squirrel pawed at his twitching whiskers and darted his eyes nervously. "Ican't... answeryourfirst question... aboutthewagon... soeasily. Itsjustnotthateasy... yousee. There's a longstorytoit... andIcan'ttellyou... about the wagon...

113

notthewagon… untilItellyou… about me… youmustknow… aboutmefirst. Thenyou'llunderstand… you'llknowwhy… Ididn't sayanything… rightaway… at first."

It was obvious the squirrel was edgy. There was something bothering him; something he was hesitant to bring up.

After a pause he continued, "Butwhateveryoudo… don'tthrowanymore… rocks!" His small voice squeaked violently as he pronounced the word "rocks." "I… Ineedyou… andyouneed… you'vegottohaveme. Ifyou'reworriedabout… whoowns… thewagon… don't. Nodon'tfretor… worryaboutthat… It's yoursandyou'llget… yourchance… to use it. Certainlyyes… you'll useitallright. Iwasjustsaying… itwasn't invented… Peterdidn'tmake itforuse… tobeusedas… a toy. That'sall… nota toy. I'msorry… ifIcameoff… a bit… surly… brusque... ifyouwill. MaybeIwas… stillangry… atall… thoserocks… youboys… werethrowingatme… or maybeit'sjust… beentoolong… sinceI've spoken… toanother human… I don'tknow. Butnonetheless… Iamsorry! NowthatI've… hadachance… tomeet… gettoknow… youalittle… Ishallbe… nice… mindmymanners! Anyway… regarding… *them.* Yes… certainlyyes… youdo… need… to worryabout… *them!* The Tommyknockers. Infact… youshouldbe… realworried… rightnow! Itwouldn'tsurprise… meonebit… onetinylittlesmidgeon… if they wereontheir… wayhere… atthisverymoment! Don'ttake… thiswrong… it'snothing… personal,boys, but you makemoreracket… than a pyro… pyromaniac inafirecracker… factory!"

Now I wasn't sure whether I felt any better or worse. It was at least comforting to think that we might be able to *use* the wagon. But, just what exactly did it mean to *use* the wagon? Would the squirrel put restrictions on it because it wasn't a toy? And also, what did he mean *we would need him*? But the most worrisome thing he'd said was about the Tommyknockers. Suddenly the prospect of them being real was too believable for comfort.

Ramey, who had been listening with his arms folded across his chest and a scowl of distrust on his face, spoke up. "I don't believe you, Mister Squirrel...Furmeister. I think this whole business is some fake story you made up to trick us. It looks to me like you're some messenger of Malcrook's! Somehow he taught you to talk and you're using this wagon to lure us into slaving for him. I'm thinking we should'a beaned you a long time ago—saved ourselves from nearly drowning and getting in so much trouble with our parents. Yeah, I'm thinking you'd still look mighty good— barbequed squirrel—on our supper table!"

At the sound of the word "barbequed," the squirrel visibly jumped, then struggled to gain control of his furiously twitching paws and tail. "Nononono... nobarbeque! Iknowit'sall... hard... toughto believe. But... youhaveto... trustme. It'strue... I'mnotlying. And... I'dtasteterrible anyway. Yousee, I'm not whatyouthink. I'm notreallya squirrel... no,notafurrysquirrel... at all. EventhoughIdon't look likeone, I'm a man. Justlikeyou... only... only oldermucholder... I'mreallyahuman...a human being."

A human being-squirrel? Now I didn't know what to think.

The squirrel was now twitching and looking about even more nervously than before, his agitation building by the second. He continued, talking so rapidly it was like he was trying to jam too many words into too small a space. "Myname... mynameis Evon. Evon Carpenter. I am... was... Peter'sPeter Kringle's... assistant. Iworkedforhim... in the toyshop. Butthatwassix.... nearlysix years ago. Somethingterrible... somethingreally... horrible happened. Torry usedto... likedto... lookinthe windows...oftheshop. ThenMalcrook came... andTorrywent... with him... to themines. Wehadtorescueher... PeterandI... withthewagon. Torryandthekids... lotsandlots... of kids... inthemines. Malcrookcaptured... seized Peter!Lockedhimaway. Butsomehow... Petermanaged... beforeMalcrooktook... him, toturn... transform meintoa... squirrel. IbringPeter... food... notmuchmindyou... as muchasI cancarry… but watch out! Havetokeep… stayawayfrom… theTommyknockers! They'llbeatyou… stealeverything… bewareofthem… verymean… theTommyknockers!"

Suddenly the cave was deathly quiet, except for the intermittent drum of the eternal water droplets. The squirrel stopped speaking and glanced around again as if expecting to be attacked from all sides at once.

But nothing happened. Ramey and I waited for him to continue—to further explain the twenty things he had just glossed over. But he sat there, twitching, watching, frittering.

"You see what I mean, Collin, he's a liar," Ramey sneered. It's all a pack of lies. He's just trying to scare us so we'll follow him some more. Yeah, right into Malcrook's open arms. Remember, you said we could bag him if he didn't prove out. Well, I've got all the proof I need."

Ramey bent down to grab some rocks.

"Hang on, Ramey," I said. "You might be right, but let's give him one more chance to explain". Folding my arms over my chest I addressed our new "friend". "Okay, Mister Evon Squirrel

Carpenter, if that really is your name. You heard my brother. Now prove to us what you're saying is true."

"Okayokayokay… Icando that. Butnotinhere… nonotwheretheylive… the Tommyknockers. We have to getoutofhthiscavefirst. Yesgetout… now… before they come. They'llripus… we'retoosmallandtoofew.Theyseethrough… intotheblackness… wecan't.They'lltakeustodarkplaces. Let'sgetout… getoutofhere. Now! Butwehavetotake… mustcarrythewagon… outtoo. Can'tletthem find it… they'lldestroy… wreckit. It'sdisturbed…. wemoveditnow. They'll findout… finditfor sure. Andiftheydothat… we'll neverget… neverrescuePeter. The wagonis… it'souronly… ouronly hope. Hurry… beforetheycome… the Tommyknockers. Saytheword… 'shrink'!"

I could see the fear etched in the whites of his little eyes. Tommyknockers—so were they real after all? And what our dad had said about them being evil was true? I looked around the cave with wide eyes, half expecting the very walls to erupt in a boiling mass of marauding attackers.

"Okay," I said, trying to stay calm. "Let's get out of here. But how will we fit the wagon through the tunnel?" I glanced back and forth between the cave entrance and the wagon, comparing their size. "I think it's too big to make it through. What did you say about *shrink*?"

"Yourright…" Evon answered quickly. "Itwon't…itistoobigto… fit. That'swhyItoldyoutosay…tosay theword 'shrink.'

Suddenly, Ramey blurted out, "Shrink!"

His voice echoed and bounced off the cave walls like a ping pong ball. Nothing happened.

"Shhh… notsoloud!" Evon hissed. "They'llhear… they'llhearusfor… sure!"

But it was too late.

117

Chapter Nineteen

Tommyknockers

Just then I heard the sound I'd been dreading—the shuffling and scratching of rocks and pebbles under the soles of hurrying shoes. I snapped my head toward the tunnel at the back of the cave.

A face, horrible and grimy, was framed in the dark opening. Then another face peeked from behind the first. Then another, and another…

"Tommyknockers!" shrieked the squirrel. "Touchthewagon…touchitandsay 'shrink'!"

Panic gripped me as I tried to obey. For a moment, time seemed to freeze. I stared, transfixed, at the Tommyknocker. He was short, no more than three feet tall, with a dirty, stubbly face and stringy, matted hair bulging unevenly from a rumpled, narrow-rimmed felt hat. He was dressed in coarse, filthy clothes, with a broad black belt connected at his bulging belly with a metallic buckle. His boots had decidedly pointed toes, and were laced up nearly to the knee. He smiled sinisterly, pointed a finger directly at my heart, let out a gravelly yell, and hopped down into the cave.

Nerves, from head to toe, fired in me like electricity. I grabbed the wagon by the handle and blurted the word "shrink." In a split second, the weight in my hand reduced from a couple of pounds to—nothing. The wagon had vanished! Or had it? I looked in astonishment at my outstretched hand. There, hanging from finger and thumb, no more than an inch long, was the wagon—the entire wagon. It had shrunk to one-hundredth its former size.

"Run!" screeched the squirrel.

It took me a second to process what had just happened. But in that stretch of time, the Tommyknockers, six of them, were now running straight at us. Across the uneven cave floor they came, hurtling over rocks and stalagmites, ducking and darting with astounding speed and agility.

Finally my legs engaged and I was fleeing—several feet behind my brother and the squirrel. Fortunately, we had been standing close to the exit tunnel and in five hurried strides were there. Ramey and the squirrel stuffed themselves through easily. Now only I was left. Had I been fast enough? Without looking back, I dove for the tunnel and began scrambling on hands and knees. So far so good, but the Tommyknockers would hardly have to duck to follow.

Then it happened. Disaster.

I felt a sharp tug at the back of my shirt and heard a low chuckle. My collar snapped backward around my neck. One of them had a grip on me! Scrambling as fast as my knees and hands could gyrate, I continued, desperately hoping the Tommyknocker would lose his handhold.

Instead, my collar tightened. Now the Tommyknocker was laughing and digging in his heels, pulling backward with tremendous force. My shirt cut into my windpipe. My tongue came out and I was gasping for breath. A foul stench like rotting onions filled the tunnel. I wrinkled my nose in disgust. Breathing had just become doubly hard.

"So… our little friends came back to play again!" a horrible voice hissed between panting breaths. "Well, young boys should know it's ruuude to have a party and not invite everyone! But we heard you, noisy, obnoxious boys, oh yes! We hear everything. Now, you will come back to *our* house—to playyy. Yes, and just in time for supper, too!"

I had no intention of going back to their house. Gruesome thoughts of what the supper menu might be, including myself, reeled across my mind. But my situation was getting worse by the second. Now, gagging and choking against the tightening collar, I felt a hand…fingers, gritty and calloused, grab my arm at the wrist. The hand jerked backward sharply, prying my arm nearly out of its socket. I tried to continue crawling but my momentum had stopped. I opened my mouth to yell for help, but the collar choked out my voice completely.

I didn't turn back, didn't want to see those dirty, ugly faces. *Got to keep… going… forward,* I thought, desperately digging and scratching at the rock for traction. Now I could hear many voices behind me. All gurgling and mean, with drool and spit spattering around their words. *Got… to… do something… now – or I'm… dead.*

What happened next, I didn't plan or consciously think about. It just happened. I felt myself being dragged backward. All of a sudden, I dug my boots into the floor and spun. And as my body twirled, I clenched my free fist, brought it back to my chest and just as my eyes connected with the surprised Tommyknocker's, let forth with all my might—a sledgehammer punch directly at his knobbly, wart-covered nose. *Splat!* My knuckles connected squarely. I felt bumpy rough skin smashing and turning to jelly between my fingers. The impact jarred the Tommyknocker's hands loose and sent him sprawling backward, right into the smelly pack of his comrades behind. Several went down like bowling pins. Luckily, they were still in the short, narrow part of the tunnel so none were able to get around those who had fallen. The Tommyknocker who'd just had his nose mashed let out a screech that made my hair stand on end. But I didn't care. By then I was scrabbling madly for daylight.

In a flash I was on my feet, running in a crouched position. I could hear the muffled sound of the waterfall ahead, and the hungry jabbers of the foiled Tommyknockers behind. Would I make it before they had time to regroup? Expecting to be cold-cocked at any instant, I sprinted as fast as I could past the rock pedestal, over the spring boards, across the rocks, and up the old stairs. When I got to the top I was so exhausted I couldn't run another step. If the Tommyknockers had followed and still wanted a piece of me, I was prepared to engage them again. Panting coarsely, I wheeled around, put up my dukes, and readied myself for battle.

"What're you doing?" a voice called out. "Getting ready to beat up some... air? Aha ha ha!"

No Tommyknocker had followed.

The chiding voice was Ramey's. He and the squirrel had arrived at the top half a minute ago and had no idea I'd just about been captured and hauled away to some evil Tommyknocker's lair. My face burned at the jibe.

"No!" I retorted. "No thanks to you, Mister-First-One-Out-of-the-Tunnel-Yellow-Streak! One of them had me! I'm lucky to even be standing here right now!"

Ramey recoiled a little and gaped at me with surprise. "Oh..." he stammered. "Geez, sorry about that, brother. I didn't know..."

"Yeah, it was close. One got a hold of my collar, but I managed to give 'em a whack—square in the nose. Powdered him good."

"Whoa… " Ramey replied, his voice suddenly shaky. "None of 'em followed you, di… did they?"

"I sure hope not," I said, scanning the box canyon for slinkers.

We were standing in a small clearing just beyond the canyon's rim. The squirrel spoke up, "Che! It'sallright… boys. Don'tworry, che che…we'resafe… wereokaynow… They don't theywon'tfollow… notintheday… inthesunlight. Hurtstheireyes. It'ssafenow. Yes… yes, you,Collin… we… were luckythat… time. Nexttime… youboysbetter… youbetter be… morequiet… or youmightwindup… justmightbecome… Tommyknocker stew! Say,Collin… you… I surehope… youmuststillhave… the RedRocket… you've gotthewagon… don't you?"

My heart jumped. *Did* I still have it? Where was it? I held out my hands displaying two empty palms. *Oh, no!* Had I dropped it in the tunnel? What if the Tommyknockers found it? I patted my pockets frantically. There was something hard and angular in my pant's right front. I thrust my hand in. The wagon! *Yes—whew!* Double relief!

I pulled out the diminutive treasure. For the first time, we got a good look at it. It was polished clean from its rough ride. Even in miniature, it was breathtaking—more a work of art than a toy. It was, of course, red. But not plain old red. It was the brightest, deepest fire engine red I'd ever seen. The handle and wheels were gloss black. There were bright chrome hubcaps covering the axle nuts that reflected like miniature suns. And painted in deep, forest green on both sides in italic, block letters amid silver shooting stars and comets were the words *Red Rocket*.

Ramey broke the silence. "Evon, I think I owe you an apology. Sorry about not trusting you and all that talk of a barbeque. It's just, well, so much bad has happened to Collin and me lately, I just couldn't believe…"

"Rameymyboy" he interrupted, "… mylad, thinknothing… of it. Idon'tfault… can'tsay… I blameyou… one bit. I'dhavea… tough… hardtimebelieving… atalking… squirrel too,if I didn'thappen… tobeone. Let'sput… allthatbehind… inthepast… behind us. Friends?"

He extended a furry little paw as if to shake. Ramey grinned, took the paw in his hand and gently shook it. "Yes, friends."

"Me, too," I said, also giving Evon's paw a dainty shake. "Now, Evon, I think we still have some time before our parents expect us home. Do you mind telling your story now—from the beginning?"

"No,no… notat all. AbsolutelyIwill."

I placed the wagon back in my pocket and Ramey and I seated ourselves on an old cedar stump at the clearing's edge.

Evon bounded over, leapt up and seated himself between us. This is the tale he told.…

Chapter Twenty

Peter Kringle

There was no way Ramey or I could have prepared ourselves for the story Evon told. It was unbelievable, fantastic—chock full of the very things grownups and school teachers instruct you not to believe.

Evon's tale begins many, many years ago in a quaint alpine village across the ocean, in another part of the world. There was a woodcrafter named Hitchner Kringle who lived with his wife, Mabel, in a small cottage toward the outskirts of town.

The cottage had a woodcrafting shop downstairs and a humble living quarters in the loft. Mr. Kringle was widely recognized as the finest woodcrafter in the land. However, because the village was so small, and it was tucked so far away in the mountains, the market for his wares was quite limited. This was a time when the fastest travel was by horse and buggy—well before the internal combustion engine or the automobile had even been conceived. So whatever Hitchner made, he sold locally. In any given month, he might sell a chair to one villager, a table to another, and a butcher's block to a third. He had just enough business to make a simple living.

His true passion, though, was making toys. There was no money in that, of course; the townsfolk could barely afford the essentials. Regardless, after working all day on furniture or other so-called useful items, Kringle could be found most evenings bent over his oaken workbench whittling and *tap-tap-tapping* away under lamplight at some magnificent toy. And when he finished carving and assembling it he would painstakingly paint it. He used only the brightest, most expensive paints and went about the task with the care and precision of a clockmaker. Then, because no one could afford to buy the toy, he would simply give it away!

But he would give it in a most unusual manner. The last thing Hitchner wanted was the gift of one of his toys to cause any parent feelings of guilt or shame—shame in that they were unable to afford it outright. So he would secretly deliver the toy in the night, creeping in through an open window or door left ajar. (This was also a time when doors and windows were made without locks or latches—nobody worried about burglars then.) He was very careful to not touch anything while in someone else's house for fear of upsetting what was not his or awakening the folks who lived there. After several years of practice, he became very good at it—never once got caught.

Alas, though, Hitchner and Mabel longed for children of

their own. To be sure, they gained tremendous satisfaction in gifting a shiny new toy to nearly every child in town, but through some cruel irony, no child was ever born unto them. Oh, how they wished to see the joy on their own girl or boy's face—riding a brightly painted maple rocking horse or flinging an ebony top. But year upon year slipped by, and sadly, no child came. As disheartening as this was, never did it diminish their happiness in creating and giving wonderful toys to other children.

Then one night, while laboring away at his workbench, Hitchner noticed a strange glow shining through his shopfront window. He rubbed his eyes and checked the clock. It was late, he must be imagining things. But the glow did not dim; rather, it got steadily brighter until the entire cottage was awash in a soft blue-white radiance. His wife woke with a start, hastily wrapped herself in a nightgown and hurried down the stairs. She could not believe her eyes. Standing in front of them, surrounded in a soft aura of light, was…a fairy.

"Hitchner Kringle," said the fairy. "You have brought so much joy to others in your lifetime, selflessly giving wonderful toys—the fruits of your own labor. And you, Mabel, have supported your husband in this endeavor and have given him inspiration. I know, however, that you are lacking the one thing you love most—a child you can call your own. Do not despair! I bring tidings of a miracle! Tomorrow, at exactly 12:00 noon, you will go into the woods with a picnic basket. Go to the large meadow at the foot of Andelwein Mountain where the River Multow slows to its widest spot. Find the gurgling spring at the cleft rock near a great gnarled oak tree. Fill your cups with water from that spring. Enjoy your picnic and each other's company. In a year's time you will be blessed."

The fairy then touched them both gently on the shoulder and disappeared, dissolving into wisps of tiny white and blue sparkles. Hitchner and Mabel looked at each other in amazement, wondering whether what had just happened was real or a dream.

The next day Mabel packed a lovely picnic and went with her husband into the woods at precisely 12:00 noon. It was a perfect summer day—deep blue sky, the fresh smell of pine and wildflowers lightly scenting the air. They found the wide spot in the river, the meadow, and the spring. Following the fairy's directions could not have been easier; it was as if their hearts knew instinctively what to do. They spent the entire afternoon lying in the grass, eating, visiting, laughing, relaxing, and drinking the sparkling cold spring water.

Exactly one year later, the Kringles were blessed…with twin boys! One they named Christopher and the other Peter. The proud parents doted over their children, teaching them everything they knew about woodcrafting and about life. The boys thrived in their loving environment.

All too soon, however, they grew up and decided they must venture into the world to make their own way.

The young men traveled to a large city many miles away and set up their own woodcrafting shop. They worked together, practicing the art their father had taught them. Very soon, their wares were in high demand and they prospered. And, like their father, they found particular pleasure in the creation of toys. Fortunately, in the bustling city where they lived, they were able to actually sell a few of them.

As word spread of the Kringle brother's excellence in woodcrafting, and especially in toy making, their business flourished. They began selling toys in places well beyond the limits of their own city. Their toys were being delivered as fast and as far as horses and wagons could carry them. Some even made it on sailing ships to exotic destinations overseas.

The more they sold, the more orders came in. Their success exploded like wildfire. Within a very few year's span, both of the young Kringle men were enjoying prosperity and had become wealthy indeed. They both found wives and moved into luxurious homes.

Suddenly their toys were in such demand they could no longer keep orders filled by themselves. Rather than disappoint even one child, they expanded their business. The shop grew to a factory and they hired many workers. Toys were now being manufactured and assembled by scores of busy dexterous hands on great assembly lines. There were workers who did nothing but lathe wooden toy wheels all day long. Others carved nutcracker arms from dawn to dusk. Another group hammered out metal axle spindles. And yet others painted: this man applying eyebrows and lips to dolls' faces, that man painting silver belt buckles. The factory had become very large, with billowing smokestacks and great, deafening machines.

While, certainly, the Kringles were now churning out vast numbers of toys to meet the ever-increasing orders, this fabulous success came at a cost. Gradually, Kringle toys lost much of their charm and warmth. They became objects—molded and manipulated pieces of wood and metal *chink, clink, chinking* from assembly lines. Decals took the place of hand-painting, stamped sheet metal was substituted for wood. To make matters worse, Peter and Christopher became mired in the business concerns that were required to make and sell the toys: taking orders, sending invoices, managing employees, and balancing ledger sheets. They rarely ever went into the woodworking parts of the factory any more, let alone ever handling a chisel or mallet.

One day Peter decided he was not happy with what his life had become. On one hand, it felt good to be successful and wealthy and to enjoy all that went along with it. But on the other, he was finding it difficult to be content with the pressures of running such a large operation. He was, after all, a woodcrafter first and foremost. He came to realize he truly missed whittling and shaping toys with his own hands, then painting them himself.

Peter took council with his brother, who was thinking

similar thoughts, and after surprisingly little discussion, they decided they must undo the very thing they had toiled so hard to create. Their plan was to simply close the factory doors, move to a different town, and start over. The next time, however, they would keep their business small and stick to the thing they loved—making toys.

But then something unexpected and most unfortunate happened. Upon announcing the new plan to his wife, JoDae, Peter was shocked to learn she had no desire whatsoever to close the factory and start over. JoDae had become accustomed to an abundant lifestyle, and did not want to give it up, regardless of the consequences to her husband. Peter pleaded with her, explaining that he and Christopher would have no trouble starting over and becoming successful again—perhaps not to the same degree, but they would most assuredly lead a comfortable lifestyle.

Comfortable, however, was not an option for her.

Now, Peter truly loved JoDae, but she made it clear: if he were to pursue this new plan, he must chose between her and the new business. Being a devoted husband, he chose her.

Christopher, meanwhile, made the same proposal to his wife, Olive, who preferred simply to be addressed as Mrs. Kringle. She was more than happy to go along with her husband's wishes. It was much more important to her that he be happy, doing what he loved, than any amount of wealth or affluence.

Peter and Christopher took council again. Christopher was greatly saddened to learn of his brother's news. He could see the true nature of JoDae, and asked Peter many times whether he truly felt it was the right choice to stay with her and thus keep the bloated old business. Alas, what could Peter do? He knew in his heart his brother was right, yet he had made a commitment to JoDae. He stood by his word to his wife.

With a heavy heart, Christopher honored his brother's wishes. He, however, wanted no part of a business in which JoDae was involved. Wishing Peter the best, Christopher gave up his share of the toy company and moved away—to the far north (but that is another story all together).

For several years, Peter continued running the business. Or rather, it ran him. Without his trusting brother, he had to depend on others to mind the books and the money. Many people took advantage of his honest nature and stole from him. His chief business manager, a short, balding man named Louhn Reekroth, was the worst offender. All he cared for was himself. He had no sense of fellowship or teamwork. To Peter's face, he smiled broadly and spoke sweetly, but when Peter turned away, he manipulated others and spent money solely to his own advantage.

Gradually, the quality of Peter Kringle's toys declined, and with it went his reputation. Soon the demand slowed, and after a few years, orders virtually stopped coming all together. Nobody wanted a nutcracker that would bend or break on its first use or a doll with sloppily painted lips and eyes. The Kringle toy company went broke. Peter had to sell everything to pay his debts, and within two months, he was utterly bankrupt.

All of this, of course, did not sit well with JoDae, and one day she packed her suitcase and left. To add insult, Peter saw her a week later, dining and having a jolly old time in the finest restaurant with none other than Reekroth. Could things get any worse?

Now Peter was left with nothing. His brother was long gone, JoDae had left him, and his business defunct. His very name was laughable. If, for example, someone had a faulty tool or defective devise, another person might ridicule them for being stuck with a "Kringle."

He was too ashamed to return home to his parents, and could not bear to stay where he was, so Peter packed his few belongings and what remaining woodworking tools he could carry and left town.

His disgrace weighed heavily upon him. He felt he had

nothing worthwhile to contribute to the world, so he straggled here and there, more or less waiting for old age to take him from the earth. He would wander into a village and find a menial job as a kitchen helper or errand boy—just to earn enough to get by.

In his spare time, though, he found he still enjoyed crafting toys. There was an instinct deep in his soul that drove him to create—to carve and whittle wood into beautiful shapes that boys and girls could not resist. But he had no interest in profiting from his creations, so, following in his father's footsteps, he secretly gave them away.

He kept to himself—the last thing he wanted was to trust anyone again. His remembered vividly what his ex-wife and people like Reekroth had taught him: chiefly, that a friend could be a very risky and, more likely than not, a hurtful proposition.

But his good nature and his magnificent toys drew people, irresistibly, to him. While he simply wanted to be left alone, to his dismay, people would approach, and sometimes… start a conversation! They wanted to be his friend. He avoided such advances, employing tactics like pretending to be deaf or mute. He made himself difficult to find, choosing to live in shady, out-of-the-way apartments or moldy, dank cellars. He even once tried being mean, but was so inept at it, the other person became confused with compassion and was only drawn closer.

As the years passed, something very strange happened—or rather, did not happen. Peter Kringle did not age. After his 58th birthday, he simply did not appear to get a day older. Peter traveled the countryside, visiting every town and berg. He roamed the boundaries of his home country first, then the entire continent. Then, when he ran out of continent, he boarded a sailing vessel and crossed the ocean. When he reached a strange, distant shore, he did the same thing all over again. Years and decades rolled by. He turned 70, then 80, then 90. Regardless of the passing time, he looked and felt exactly as he did at age 58! Not one additional grey hair, no wrinkly hands, no age spots, nothing. His life was becoming rich with adventures and strange exotic travels, but his simple desire to grow old and leave the earth was not being granted.

What in the world is going on? he thought. *Could my brother, Christopher, also be experiencing the same thing, wherever he is?*

Peter heard no news whatsoever of his brother. As far as he knew, Christopher could have been long dead, or perhaps was living in some remote corner of the earth still making toys. Wherever he went, Peter would ask the locals if they'd heard the name Christopher Kringle. A sympathetic sideways shake of the head was all he ever got.

His parents had told him the wondrous story of how he and his brother came to be—about the fairy and the magical picnic. They had often called him and Christopher "their little miracles." But, growing up a normal boy in a normal town, and with normal parents, Peter never gave it a second thought.

Now, at age 110, he had outlived everyone he ever knew. In his travels, he'd heard a rumor that his parents, content and happy well into their 80s, had passed on some 40 years previously. Naturally, he was greatly saddened to learn this, and thought surely he would soon be joining them in another dimension. But it did not happen, did not even come close.

However, something else *was* happening. As the decades rolled past, Peter began to notice he could, at times, do things which defied explanation. For example, he might reach for a shaker of salt, concentrate on it, and it would scoot across the table to his outstretched hand! Or he might ask his left shoe if it had seen his missing right sock, and on occasion, the shoe would levitate, fly across the room, and land in the exact place where the missing sock was hiding!

Peter had never believed in magic—he even avoided use of the word. At first, he dismissed these unusual events as tricks of the light or curious quirks of nature. But as they became more commonplace—as he became able to control them—it was apparent something else was at work. *Was it magic?*

In time he had no choice but to accept it as true. Yes, he, Peter Kringle, a dejected failure who wished only to grow old and die…was instead…a sorcerer! He was blessed with the uncanny gift of the supernatural.

As Peter became more and more comfortable with his new powers he began experimenting. What if he could embed magic in his toys? Imagine a little boy's excitement playing with a toy soldier that could march. Or a little girl's exhilaration riding a rocking horse that could walk and prance! Peter's mind whirred with wondrous possibilities. Why, he could create wagons that would go without pushing; gliders that could take off and fly from a standstill; tops that would never stop spinning; chess sets that played automatically; dolls that could talk and sip tea; sailing ships with cannons that fired real cannonballs! The possibilities were fantastic… limitless!

But Peter found that harnessing magic was considerably more tricky and unpredictable than he had imagined. Sometimes a spell worked and sometimes it fizzled. And sometimes a completely different thing would happen than he expected. For instance, he once extended his finger to magically start a fire in the fireplace, and just at that moment, a dish sprang from the cupboard and flew like a discus straight into the hearth, exploding into a firework of glass splinters. And on another occasion, while magically painting a doll's face, the paintbrush lost control and painted a finger where the nose should have been and switched the eyes with the ears. Once, the paintbrush mistook Peter's head for the block of wood, and began applying an additional set of bright red lips to his own!

Sometimes his magic was just plain dangerous. Once, Peter thought he'd embedded an automobility function into a tricycle. Instead, the tricycle burst into flames. Another time he was outdoors testing a self-guided wooden glider. Without warning it went haywire, turning itself into a dive bomber! Screaming madly through the air, it strafed the neighborhood dog, which was so astonished and frightened, it sprinted headlong into a patch of briars. The plane then spiraled out of control, smashing through the front window of his landlord's house, and crashed most violently—splintering into a thousand shards of wood—against the far wall.

But the worst calamity occurred several months after the glider incident when Peter was walking through his landlord's house and noticed a soiled cloth napkin on the floor. Rather than bending over and picking it up, he lazily pointed a finger at it expecting it to throw itself into the laundry hamper. Unfortunately, something very different happened. The napkin levitated and then began to float in a circular manner, slowly at first, but with every turn, gaining velocity. In a moment it was spinning rapidly, creating a vortex wind. Seconds later pieces of paper, from various places in the room, lifted themselves and joined the napkin in it's swirling eddy. With each new piece of paper the wind increased, ever building momentum on itself. Soon a miniature tornado had formed and began sucking larger objects such as books and a vase of flowers into its tempest.

Peter was aghast. He had inadvertently created a room-wrecking monster. He pointed his finger and spoke every incantation he could think of: "Stop", "Unspin", "No-Tornado", "Twist-Not", and others. But the whirlwind paid no attention.

Now, even larger objects scooted sideways and got sucked in: lamps, cups, saucers, and fireplace tools. The landlord's cat, which had been napping peaceably by the hearth, heard the commotion and sprung, startled out of its wits, to its feet only to be coldcocked in the head by the ash shovel as it cartwheeled past. The poor feline was rendered unconscious and it too slid across the floor then into the air, joining the rest of the swirling debris in the frightening maelstrom.

And with every new addition, the tornado gained strength.

Peter did not know what to do. In horror he observed now furniture: chairs, small tables, bookshelves, sliding inward, spinning as they went. In a panic, he, grabbed the curtains from the window and ripped them off. He flailed wildly at his evil creation as if he were dowsing a fire. But instead of quenching it, the tornado tore the curtains from his hands and deposited them, too, in the midst of the other gyrating junk.

Now, the whirlwind had become loud. It was groaning and howling, clanking and banging. And it had become too large to be contained in the room. Suddenly, as if it were a frenzied prisoner bent on escape, it hurled an end table through the large plate glass window (the very one that Peter had paid nearly a year's salary to replace when his disobedient glider slammed through it a few months earlier), which shattered in a mighty explosion.

Swoosh! Out through the window the whirlwind spun, taking large hunks of sill, jamb, and wall with it. It tore across the yard, ripping up sod like potato chips. Bushes and small trees were plucked up by their roots and added to the flailing jumble. Peter stood in the house, hands clasped to his cheeks, watching in horror as his tornado rampaged across the street and lifted the roof from a neighbor's house, sucking out furniture like soda up a straw.

Then, suddenly, as if someone had flicked its switch, the tornado stopped. All of the airborne detritus crashed back to the earth in a chaotic heap.

Fortunately no one got hurt. Even the cat, which became wedged in the corner of a gyroscopic bookshelf, was able to wobble away, struggling against an acute case of vertigo.

Certainly, such mistakes would not be tolerable if people, especially children, were involved. Practice as he might, experiment as he would, Peter was dismayed to learn that he could never be absolutely, one hundred percent sure that the magical thing he intended would indeed occur. So, over the years, he used magic less and less and never in a toy.

The decades rolled by and still Peter did not age. He came to accept that his lot in life was not what he'd expected. He simply would not get old and die like the rest of humanity. No, apparently he'd been placed on the earth for another purpose and he decided that purpose was to make toys just like his father before him. Ultimately, he found a permanent place to live that suited him just right and opened a toyshop. Of course, his business prospered, but this time he kept it at a level he could manage by himself. With a single exception: he took on one employee to assist with miscellaneous chores.

"And... thatis... theshort... condensed versionofhow... PeterKringlecame... tolivein... thesmall... logging town... ofFurryPine, Washington... onehundredand... fifty... orso... yearsago," Evon concluded.

I gaped blankly into the distance struggling to digest it all.

"Ofcouse... youboys... canguess... figureoutwho... theoneexception...was? Me! Itwasme... EvonCarpenter! Peterfound... rescuedme... from myhome... whichwas... a ramshackle... tinlean-to... underthe... ThirdStreetBridge. Best... luckiestdayof... mylife! Yousee... I don'tevenremember... my parents. Theyleft... abandonedme... whenIwas... verylittle... ayoungshaver. But, that'sneitherhere... northere. Peterbecame... mynew... well, parents... ifyouwill.

Andyouknow... whatelse? AfterI'dbeen... livingand... workingwithPeter... for twentyfour... years, I too... stoppedaging! Althoughyou... can't tellbylooking... atme now. I'm old... very oldindeed. Woulditsurprise... youtolearn... nextFebruary... willbemy... onehundred... seventy seventh... birthday?!"

Chapter Twenty-One

Running

Ramey and I sat there gawking into space, spellbound, as Evon finished his story. We had a trillion questions to ask, but before any words came out, Evon continued, "Whattime... whenwere you... youtwosupposedtobe... home? It'sgotto... be... certainlymustbe... at leastsix...o'clock."

This simple question smacked me like a yardstick across the knuckles. "Holy diapers!" I exclaimed. "Ramey, we've got to go—now!"

We jumped from the cedar stump and hit the ground running. I hollered over my shoulder, "We'll be back tomorrow, Evon! Meet us right here at ten o'clock."

Evon watched us disappear into the woods. He twitched his whiskers and jerkily brushed his nose, thinking, *You'd better be back tomorrow. I need you more than you can imagine.*

Ramey and I approached our cabin's front door at a dead-on sprint. We burst in, sweaty and out of breath. Mom and dad were sitting at the table quietly eating their supper. There were no place settings for Ramey or me.

"Collin Miller," dad said in a forced tone, not even turning his head to acknowledge us.

I immediately knew we were in deep trouble, not only from the tone of dad's voice, but also because he'd used my last name.

"You boys were supposed to be home at 4:00. It's now 6:30. I thought we had a unnerstandin' about this last week. 'Parently you boys ain't got no regard for what your daddy tells you. Now, I've been thinking about it and I'm not going to whup you even though you deserve a good one. No, you're gettin' too old for that, especially you, Collin. Instead, your punishment will be something that'll make you think twice about any more bad choices for a good long time. Tonight, you go to bed without supper. And starting Monday, you'll be with me, working all day long. I'm taking you out of school for a month. You'll stay home and work in the forest with me during the day and then at night you'll read and write and do your arithmetic all the way 'till bedtime. There'll be no desserts or treats and you'll have no friends over to play. You're grounded. If you think you can ignore your parents, I'm here to teach you, you can't. Now, you two boys strip down, take your showers and get off to bed. I don't want to see hide nor hair of you any more tonight."

We hung our heads—dad had spoken. There was no point in even offering an excuse. I knew when he was in this kind of mood anything I said could easily double our punishment. As we trudged down the hall I thought I heard mom whisper, "George, don't you think you're being a bit hard on them? A whole month?"

There was no answer except the clinking of silverware on porcelain. Our sentence was cast in stone.

After taking a shower, putting on pajamas, and climbing—very hungry indeed—into bed, I began to worry. Seriously worry. I did not have a month to spend being punished. Mom couldn't wait that long. It might be her *last* month. I had to think of something, a plan of some kind. We were supposed to be back at the waterfall tomorrow morning by 10:00 to meet Evon. But how? There would be no way I could do anything if I had to spend every waking minute with dad or doing homework.

My mind raced trying desperately to formulate a workable plan. But the more I thought about it, the fewer options came to me. "Ramey," I finally whispered. "What are we gonna do? How can we find the Dark Quartz Mine if we have to spend all day and all night with dad and mom? I'm telling you, we're in trouble, deep trouble. But it's really mom who's in the most trouble of all."

"My mind is so full of thoughts right now," Ramey whispered in reply, "I'm beginning to worry it might blow up. I don't know what we can do, except what dad says."

"I know. I'm in the same boat. But the more I think about it, the more I'm coming around to a certain thought. Except I don't like the sound of that thought, not one bit."

"What're you thinking?"

"I'm thinking we've only got one choice. And that choice is to... we're going to have to—run... run away from home."

The room fell silent. It was as if the words "run away from home" had sucked our lives right out the window. We both laid there staring at the ceiling, hardly breathing. Neither of us wanted to break the silence, and certainly neither wanted to agree with this horrifying option. But the alternative was worse. At least if we did run away, we'd be making an effort to save our mom's life.

"Collin," Ramey whispered, "I'm...I'm with you. Whatever choice you make, I'll go along with it."

"Okay," I replied after a long hesitation. Lying there, it felt as if the weight of the world was bearing down on my skinny shoulders. "Then here's what we'll do. Tomorrow is Sunday. Mom and dad won't be getting up until probably eight o'clock. We'll have to get up at six, pack our stuff and be out of here no later than seven. And, Ramey, I don't know when we'll be back. It might be a day or a week. I sure hope it's not longer than that but I can't guarantee anything. Are you sure you want to go through with this?"

No answer. I could tell Ramey had started to cry. Shortly, he gathered himself and said, "Yes, I'm sure. I don't want to go the rest of my life thinking I was the one who let mama... " Ramey couldn't finish his sentence. His tears got in the way.

"Okay little bro," I croaked around a big lump in my own throat. "Try not to worry. Let's get some sleep. I've got a feeling we'll be needing it."

I lay there for quite some time before sleep crept over me. My dreams that night were tortured, spooky things. I saw my mother, gaunt and pale in a dark dungeon cell next to Peter Kringle's. They both had their bony arms extended through the bars, pleading for help, but there was nothing I could do. Then along came a band of lurking Tommyknockers. They built a fire and hung a great kettle over it. "Hu-man stew. Hu-man stew," they chanted. I couldn't bear the thought of my mom and Peter being boiled for someone's supper, but I was so helpless. My arms and legs felt like leaden salamis hanging at my side. I had no strength at all. Finally, the Tommyknockers unlocked the cell doors. They plucked mom and Peter Kringle, horrified and cowering, from their corners. Suddenly, without a clear notion of what I was doing, I sprang from the shadows and made straight for the fire. If I could knock it out, maybe, somehow mom and Peter could be spared. I knew I would get burned—badly, but I didn't care. I gave a mighty war cry and leaped straight into the heart of the glowing embers....

KABOOM!

Ramey and I bolted upright in our beds as the remnants of a lightning flash dissolved away into the half-light of the dawning day. I was drenched in sweat. Outside it was raining—hard. The driving droplets sounded like bullets tearing through the corrugated tin roof overhead. Lightning and thunder flashed and boomed across the mountainside. What time was it?

"Ramey," I whispered urgently. "It's time. We've got to go—now."

We quickly and quietly climbed from our beds and went about the task of getting dressed and packing a spare change of clothes in our rucksacks. Ramey glanced at his unmade bed wondering if he would ever sleep in it again.

It only took five minutes to get ready. For perhaps the first time in our lives, we went about our business like soldiers. No bickering or goofing off this morning. We crept down the hall, grabbed some bread, cheese, and a half-empty jar of peanut butter. Before we knew it, we were out the door and walking down the old gravel logging road, backs turned on our home and our parents. Rain fell steadily from a lead-colored sky, quickly soaking us and our supplies. I looked over at Ramey, who turned away to hide his tears.

"Don't worry, little bro," I said softly. "It's gonna be okay. We'll be back before you know it—with the…gold… " I tried to sound encouraging but a knot in my throat made my voice trail away to a whisper.

"Yeah, I know," he replied between sniffs. "I'm just gonna miss mom and dad, that's all."

Nothing else was said for the forty-five minutes it took to get to the rim of the waterfall. Soaked to the skin, we took our seats on the wet cedar stump, stared blankly off into the gray drizzle, and waited. It was probably 7:00. Evon wasn't expecting us until ten.

"Hey, I'm hungry," I finally broke the silence, remembering it had been nearly 24 hours since our last meal. "How about something to eat?"

"Sure," Ramey replied.

I took out the bread, cheese and peanut butter, and trying to shelter our breakfast from the rain using my head and body, made a couple of sandwiches. By the time they were made, they were more like peanut butter and cheese dishrags. We gnawed at them expressionlessly and kept waiting. I was shocked to see that our breakfast had exactly cut the food supply in half. We had enough for one more meal, two if we scrimped. We'd better succeed—and fast—or we would be getting very hungry, very soon.

"Myyouboys…. youguys are early."

I stopped mid-chew and glanced upward. Evon was perched on the branch of a nearby hemlock, watching, twitching. He scampered down and hopped over to us. The look on our faces told him something was up, and it wasn't good.

Chapter Twenty-One

"Whythelong… whysosad… this bright cheerymorning?"
Neither of us even cracked a smile.

In the next five minutes I disclosed all that had happened
last night and this morning. I explained that we'd just eaten half our
food reserves and had no real idea where we would be staying.
Certainly, we couldn't stay in the cave. Nobody wanted to be
surprised in the night by a pillaging band of Tommyknockers.

"Wellwell… that's badgoodbad… news. Imeanbad
thatyouhad… to leavehome… butgoodthat youcameback…
verygood you came back." He paused and began twitching a little
more severely than usual. "Say… sayIhaveanidea… a
planthatmight… just mightworkfor… youwayward… boys.
Doyouhave… did you bringthewagon withyou… surely youhave…

thewagon?"

I reached into my pocket, pulled out the miniature treasure, and set it on the stump between Ramey and me. Yep, it's right here," I said glumly.

As I placed it on the stump, the rain seemed to slacken and the gray clouds parted a bit, hustling their way northward, making way for a few shafts of reluctant sunlight.

"Good... veryverygood," replied Evon. The first... mostimportant... thingtodo... isforyou... boys to learntofly... fly the wagon."

Ramey and I looked at each other, blinking our eyes in disbelief.

"Evon, did you just say we have to learn to—to *fly* the wagon?" I asked dumbfoundedly.

"Yes, yesthat'sjust... exactlywhat... I said... you mustlearnto... *fly* thewagon."

I was speechless. My mind struggled to absorb the magnitude of Evon's comment. For the first time in a very long time I completely forgot my troubles. Would Ramey and I really fly through the air in Kringle's magic wagon? This was the stuff of my wildest, most fantastic dreams. It was too amazing to be true. Of course, it was every kid's fantasy to fly—to spread your arms, take off running, jump into the air and not come down. And here was a chance, not exactly like that, but to fly nonetheless. It was happening to me. Nothing good ever happened to me.

Chapter Twenty-Two

A Rocky Takeoff

Evon could see the elation building in our faces and in our bright eyes. And this made him glad. It had been nearly six years since he'd had anything to be happy about himself. Memories of working side by side with Peter—the eager faces of boys and girls pressed against their shopfront window—came filtering back. He smiled (as best as a squirrel could), then spoke. "Yes, flythewagon… you must. Anditwill… nodoubtbe… fun! But alsoitmay be a littledangerous… Yousee, Idon'tknow… exactly... Peter nevershowedme precisely… howitworks. Notonlythat… Peter'smagicdoesn't always… isn'talwaysperfect. You'llhave to be… verycareful!"

We nodded eagerly and sat in rapt attention for instructions.

"Now, we mustfirst… enlarge… grow the wagon backtoitsnormal... its regularsize. Collin… touch thewagon… and saytheword…'grow.'"

I obeyed. "Grow."

Instantly, the wagon went from two inches to a full-sized, shiny red wagon. A slight problem occurred, however, in the transition. I had placed it on the cedar stump between myself and Ramey and as it popped back to its normal size it now occupied the entire stump. Having no regard for two boys also taking up stumptop space, like a punch in the ribs, it knocked us, most unexpectedly, onto the wet grass.

We collected ourselves, our pride being hurt far more than any other body part. Evon emitted a series of high-pitched squeaks. I misunderstood this outburst as a warning cry and immediately jerked my head toward the waterfall, fearful of Tommyknockers or some other evil.

Evon quickly allayed my fears. "Nonono… no… there'snothing… wrong. I'mjust… laughing… atyou two! That was… thefunniestthing… therootinest… tootenest thing… I've seen inalong… in quitesometime! But now… let'sgetdownto… get aboutthebusiness… at hand. Takedown… liftthewagon… fromthe stump, andthenget… in. Collininfront… Ramey, you sit… intheback. We'vegot… gotsomeflying… todoboys!"

I lifted the wagon from the stump, placed it on the grass, and climbed into the front. Ramey followed, sitting cross-legged in the back. There was room to spare.

"OkaynowCollin… grabthehandle… but don'tsayanything… notaword… yet."

I carefully obeyed. When my hand encircled the handle, the strangest sensation I'd ever felt surged from the metal into me. It was like an electric shock but without the electricity. A deep, magnificent tingle rushed through my fingers, radiated up my arm, and coursed along my torso downward to the very tips of my toes. Every hair on my body stood on end. A thrill welled up inside me. This was something very, very special!

"Okay, nowI'll tell youthecommands… at least… theonesIknow. ButI'm… afraidtheremaybe… just mightbemore… Idon'tknow. 'Shrink,' 'grow,' 'rollforward,' 'roll… back,' 'lift,' and… 'down,'" That's it… that's allIknow. Petertoldmethose… andsaidtherest… would… justcome naturally."

"Whoa," I said, "you said those so fast, Evon, I'm not sure I got them all. Could you please run through them again, only a little slower this time?"

But before Evon could respond, Ramey, from his position behind me, blurted, "Roll forward!"

"Whooooaaaa!… "

The wagon lurched forward. It worked! Suddenly we were rolling through the grass…by magic! The unexpected acceleration thrust both of us backward but I kept a grip on the handle. Between the jolt of the movement and the thrill of the ride I did not notice the handle give slightly backward. As it went back, our speed increased. I didn't know it yet but the handle was the throttle. Suddenly we were bumping and bouncing violently along the forest floor heading away from Evon and the stump—directly for the rim of the canyon.

My sudden glee turned to worry as the edge of the yawning free-fall rapidly approached. The shock of Ramey's command and the amazement of this wondrous magic had momentarily paralyzed me—left me wide-eyed, unable to move or speak. I was sitting as far back as I could, directly against Ramey's knees, holding onto the handle with all my might.

Bump, bump, bump...rattle, rattle. My head bounced and my teeth clattered as we accelerated across the uneven ground. The canyon rim was only twenty feet away. Now fear had a grip on me. Why couldn't I speak or steer? I glanced down and saw Ramey's white knuckles gripping the wagon sides. The canyon rim got closer and closer. I could hear Evon squeaking madly behind me, but I couldn't make out a word of it.

Then suddenly, we were airborne.

But we were *not* flying.

No, rather we had pitched off the edge and were hurtling down—straight for the jagged rock pile at the edge of the splash pool. Unless something changed right now, in less than two seconds we would be splattered on the rocks. I closed my eyes, held tight, and waited for the wagon to lift.

But it didn't.

With each passing microsecond, the nose of the wagon angled steeper and steeper downward. Wind whistled through my hair. It felt like we were in an airplane whose engine had quit. Now we were approaching vertical. I could feel my weight shifting forward—I would have slid out the front had my feet not been wedged against the wagon's wooden rim. It was a 200-foot free fall—we'd already gone 100. We were dead and I knew it. I braced myself for the life-extinguishing impact.

Just then, a voice from behind hollered, "LIFT!"

Suddenly, the wagon shifted under me and my bottom began to press hard against the floor of the contraption as the nose changed angle—from directly downward to level, then to upward. But our downward momentum was still carrying us toward the rocks! How much space did it take to turn this thing? Would we make it?

The jagged rocks aimed their hungry teeth directly at my heart. Now the nose of the wagon was pointing upward. I thought I could feel my weight being hoisted away from earth's gravity. The ravenous rocks were but a few feet away. Ramey had shouted "Lift" a split-second too late. We were not going to make it. "Hold on Ramey!" I shouted just before impact.

Smack!

The right rear wheel crashed into the razor's edge of the

highest rock as the wagon zoomed through the bottom of its arc. Ramey, being seated directly over the rear axle, was tossed vertically several feet and I jerked upward a few inches…but the wagon kept flying—upward! It was a glancing blow that set the right rear wheel spinning like a pinwheel but did not knock us from our climb. I opened my eyes and looked down. The rocks were behind us! The Red Rocket was now climbing with incredible speed over the splash pool. *Whew! We made it.*

"Hey, Ramey!" I finally managed. "We made it! We're not dead—we're flying! Ramey… Ramey…? RAMEY?!!!

No answer. And I could not feel the pressure of his legs on my back. I slid backward an inch or so to check for him. Nothing. Ramey was not there!

My heart sank. Thoughts of Ramey being tossed into the rocks, or worse, into the splash pool filled my brain. *Holy dynamite! Hitting that rock must've knocked Ramey out!* Just then I heard my name being screeched.

"COLLIN! Collin! I'm here…down here! Help me back in!"

The wagon whooshed upward like a rocket. Past the waterfall, past the other side of the canyon rim, and on into thin air. I chanced a quick glance backward hoping to see fingers gripping the wagon's back rim. Nothing. My brother's voice yelled at me again, more urgently than before. "COLLIN! I'M UNDERNEATH. SET THIS THING DOWN! I CAN'T HOLD ON MUCH LONGER!"

The tops of cedar trees were disappearing behind me as the wagon continued to climb. I arched my head over the side and looked beneath. There was Ramey, hanging on for dear life to the rear axle. Somehow, when we hit the rock it knocked him overboard, but he'd managed to catch hold of the axle. Now he was dangling 300 feet in the air, and climbing.

I knew I had to do something, and fast. Ramey hollered

again. "COLLIN, MY HANDS ARE SLIPPING! I'M GONNA FALL IN A SECOND!"

But what could I do? I didn't have the first clue how to drive this thing, let alone land it…let alone land it slowly enough to avoid smearing Ramey into the earth. *Darn it! I've got to do something…anything…and quick, or Ramey is a dead boy.*

There would be no way to reach under and grab him—it would probably just pull me out too; plus I'd have to let go of the handle. *The handle!* The only thing I could actually do was move the handle, there were no other working parts. If Kringle intended this thing to be maneuverable, the handle had to be the steering wheel and the accelerator.

But there was no time for flight school. If I could somehow just figure out the basics. I slid the handle to the left. Immediately the wagon banked slightly and entered a right turn. I slid it to the right—a left turn. So it turned in the air just like it would on the ground—following the direction of the wheels. Next, I lifted the handle up. The nose of the wagon declined and we dove. I pulled back and the nose inclined. With each maneuver, I could feel my brother's dangling weight sway one way or the other. At least Ramey was still hanging on. But how much longer could his straining fingers hold?

As it turned out, Ramey's fingers were already beyond the limit of their strength. All at once, I felt the wagon jerk upward as Ramey's fingers slipped…and he fell. "COLLLLlli.n..n..n.n..n…"

Chapter Twenty-Three

Flying

What happened next happened so fast and so instinctively, it surprised even me. I slammed the handle to the left and lifted it at the same time. Instantly the wagon went into a hard diving banked turn. For some reason, at that instant my mind became clear—crystal clear. My senses were sharp, my reflexes quick. The next few split-seconds seemed to unfold in slow motion. I swung the wagon around one hundred eighty degrees in a tight, gravity-defying downward dive. Now I could see my brother falling…in front of me. Ramey was still fully stretched out. His face was white frozen terror. The only things indicating he was moving at 120 miles per hour were his fluttering clothes and his hair—it was standing straight up.

I shot directly at him. I had to judge this perfectly; there would be only one chance. Either time it right, or Ramey died, it was that simple. I fixed my eyes on his and let my hands move the handle automatically. We were now below the level of the treetops. Two seconds to impact…one second…*Oooff!*

Ramey's feet hit the front-bottom of the wagon hard and slid backward along my hips. The wagon jerked downward, but quickly regained its momentum. Ramey's body slumped over mine. Suddenly, I had a limp body draped over me like a saddle blanket and I couldn't see. *But, the body was there!* I'd plucked my brother from thin air! *Yes!*

Now, must climb. Blindly, I jerked back on the handle. I hoped there weren't any trees or cliffs in front of us. The nose of the wagon pointed up, the pressure on my bottom increased, and we shot skyward. If we were going to collide with something it would be... now.

But nothing happened except altitude gain and louder wind in my ears. "Ramey!" I shouted, "Snap out of it! You're safe now, but you've got to get off me! I can't see where I'm driving!"

"Am I dead?" came his groggy response. "Are we going to heaven?"

"We may be going to heaven—someday, but not today. We're still in the wagon. Darn... you're heavy, though! You've got to move a little so I can see."

Ramey lifted himself and looked at me. I was furiously bobbing my head this way and that, straining to see around him. "Holy donuts... we're alive! You caught me out of mid-air! WOW!"

Ramey's words sounded good. For the second time in less than a month, I had saved my brother's life. A warm feeling filled me and a smile came to my face. "Yeah, but I'm not sure how I did it," I said. "And I wouldn't want to do it again. Now, can you slide around back, so I can see to drive this crazy contraption?"

Ramey scooted around, and after a good bit of tuggling and jostling made his way to his original position. "By the way, Collin," he said with a slight chuckle after he got settled. "Next time you take off, try not to aim for the rocks."

"You little snot!" I reached back and whacked him on the knee. "Next time, *you* better keep your yap shut and let *me* do the driving!"

I eased up on the handle and leveled out. We were now soaring at a good safe altitude. Wind blew stiffly over our faces, pulling our hair back in fluttery bursts. Treetops passed silently several hundred feet below. I saw a woodpecker flying in spurts from one hemlock to another. Thickets and meadows approached, then in a second fell away again. It was the most incredible feeling in the world. We were flying—just like in a dream! I slid the handle slightly and the wagon banked gently to the right. We streamed across the blue sky, making a wide arcing turn. In the distance I could see the waterfall. What a sight! From this angle, the drama and fury of the crashing tumult was breathtaking. There was a perfect rainbow over it like something out of a fairy tale. And to think, just a few days ago we were *that close* to being permanent fixtures, trout fodder, on the bottom of the pool!

"What do you say we find Evon and set this thing down," Ramey said, still a little unnerved.

"Okay, I'll circle the clearing. You keep your eyes peeled for Evon," I eased up on the handle and our speed decreased. As we slowed, we also lost altitude. Treetops quickly became larger. I slid the handle a little left and we began our approach. Now we were over the clearing, our eyes scouring the ground for Evon. Ramey spotted him.

"Collin, he's up in that tree—that fir there."

Sure enough, at the very top of the tallest fir tree on the perimeter of the clearing was Evon. He was standing on the highest branch, waving his little arms frantically and squeaking like a maniac. We couldn't hear a word he was saying; the wind was still too loud in our ears.

"Okay," I said. "I'm taking 'er in. I hope Evon's not trying to tell me how to land this thing—I can't hear him at all. Hang on tight."

Ramey, not wanting to chance another bounce from the wagon, encircled my waist with his arms, gripping with all he was worth.

"Not so hard!" I wheezed, "You're gonna' squeeze the peanut butter right out of me!"

Ramey slackened his grip, but not too much. Now I concentrated on the task at hand—landing. I circled the clearing, constantly losing altitude and slowing. *Now, what were those commands?* I racked my brain trying to remember Evon's rapid-fire recitation of them. *Let's see... 'shrink,' 'grow,' 'roll forward,' 'roll back,' 'lift'…and what was the last one? Was it 'land'? No, that doesn't sound right.*

We were now at the level of the treetops, turning ever tighter to stay in the clearing. The wagon's speed was still too fast for any kind of safe landing. But I noticed the more I eased up on the handle, the more precipitously we dropped. I had to keep our speed about where it was now or it seemed we would simply fall from the sky. We were flying in a large circle, maintaining about a hundred feet altitude—way too high for a mistake. A spill now and we'd be only slightly better off than a few minutes ago nose-diving for the rocks. I eased forward a bit more on the handle. Speed and altitude decreased. *Darnit! What was that last command!? 'Dive'?… no. 'Drop'?… not it…*

We were now at 50 feet, going what seemed like a hundred miles an hour. I could finally hear Evon's frantic squeaks but couldn't make out a single word. *What was that last command?!*

Now we were only 20 feet up, but still going way too fast. If I didn't think of the right word quickly, we'd be forest floor road rash. Ten feet. I gritted my teeth and braced for the impact.

Suddenly, from behind, Ramey blurted the magic word, "Down!"

All at once, as if the wagon applied air brakes, it slowed to a halt. I closed my eyes and held my breath, not moving the handle even a micron. I tensed for the impact. But we didn't crash. I opened my eyes and looked around. The ground was about seven feet below and we weren't moving. We were hovering three feet to the left of the cedar stump.

Evon came bounding up, squeaking and squealing like a stuck pig.

"Liftthehandle… Liftthehandle… slow… slow… slow… Liftit… liftitIsay!"

Now that there was no wind in my ears, I could at last understand him. Carefully I lifted the handle and the wagon responded, descending vertically. Down it came, settling softly into the grass. I released my grip. My fingers felt like they were welded to it—I hadn't relaxed them since I got in. Like rigormortised skeleton bones, they creaked and crackled as they straightened. Ramey climbed out—I followed.

"Phew! We made it!" I exclaimed.

"Goodwork… waytogo… boys! Forasecond…foraminutethere… I thoughtyouwere… surely… definitelygoners. Especiallyyou… Ramey! Thatwassure… thatwaswhatIcall… a close shave. Butnow… you must… havetoget… backin… we've gotsomeplace… somewhere to go… Now!"

Chapter Twenty-Four

Backward and Forward

Where did Evon want to take us? And what was his big rush?

I wondered these things as I climbed back into the wagon. Whatever plan Evon had up his sleeve was bound to be better than the one Ramey and I had, or rather, didn't have.

Ramey spoke up. "Hey, I want to drive this time."

"But…" I stammered. The thought of my life in my sometimes wacky kid brother's hands didn't much appeal to me.

"Yeah," he continued. "It's my turn. You can't even remember the right commands, Collin."

Struggle as I might, I could not think of a good reason *not* to let Ramey give it a try. Evon chimed in, "YouknowCollin… Ithink, yesRameyhas… a goodpoint… I'd say. Youbothshouldknow… howtofly this… thing. Wemightget… ourselvesina… pickle… a jam somewhere alongtheline… youknow… a bind… whenyou'reunableto… can'ttakethe controls."

"Ohhhkayyy… " I said. "If we have to."

Ramey grinned broadly and shimmied in, in front of me.

"Scootback… allthewaytotheback… youtwo… I'mgoing… comingalongtoo!" Evon bounded over and just like that, hopped in directly in front of Ramey, who recoiled a little, shocked to suddenly have a furry mammal in his lap.

Evon squiggled himself down and fixed his eyes straight ahead. He then sat motionless, waiting in anticipation like a dog expecting a treat.

"Um… Evon, where are we going?" Ramey asked.

"Where?… Oh yes!… yesyesyes… where? I haven'ttold

youwhere... wherewe'regoing... yet! Silly... sillyme! I gotsoexcited... flustered... I forgottosaywhere... wherewe're headed to! Why, we're headedto... directlyto... withoutstopping... Peter'stoyshop! Youboysneed... musthave... a placetocall... home... don'tyou? Otherwise... wherewouldyou... stay? You'rerunningaway... running... fromhome, right? Or... haveyouchanged... decidedagainst... it?"

Peter's Toyshop! I thought. *Wow! That would be incredible! To stay, even if only temporarily, in the legendary place where all those fabulous toys come from.* This new development not only solved a lot of logistical problems in my mind, it also made running away from home just a little easier to bear. I responded to Evon's question, "Yes...no...I mean we haven't changed our minds. We are going through with this—we've got no other choice. So let's crack!"

Draping his arms around the narrow shoulders of Evon, Ramey touched the handle.

"Waitwaitwait... a minute!" Evon squeaked. "There'sone... somethingwemust... be careful... verycareful about. We must'ntletpeople... nopeoplecan... seeusflying. Sowhenwetravel... we'vegotto... go incognito... wemust doitsmall. Ramey... yourememberthe... shrinkcommand... don't you?"

"Yes. But why can't we let people see us? That would be cool!"

"Cool?! Areyoucrazy... out... ofyourmind? No... itwouldbe... hot! Ordoesthat also... mean... cool toyouyoungsters... whippersnappers? Yourlingo... Itellyou... Ican't... scarcely can keeptrack ofwhatmeanswhat... bad or good... nowadays. Bad... adisaster... iswhatit... would be. Badbecause... because... canyouimagine? Thinkofthescandal! A flying wagon... withtworunaway... boys? Whyitwould... causesuch... a stir. Peoplewouldn'tbelieve...such a thing... butthey all... would wanttoinvestigate... pry... sticktheirnoses... in anyway.

Wewouldget… absolutelyno… peace… to go aboutourbusiness… nonewhatsoever!"

"Okay, yeah I guess you're right," Ramey admitted.

"Now," continued Evon, as he turned forward again, and gripped the front, "let's… let'sgetthis… jalopy… get thistrainmoving!"

Ramey gripped the handle firmly, cleared his throat and spoke, "Shrink!"

Nothing happened.

"What the… ?" he said. "Lift!" he spoke again, only louder this time.

Nothing.

"Evon, what's wrong with this thing? Am I not doing it right?"

"Uh… Ithinkso… Ithink. Butagain… Idon't, er, can'tsaylrightly… know, Ramey. Itshouldhave… wassupposedto… shrink and lift."

"Ramey," I interjected, "when you grabbed the handle, did you feel anything weird in your hand and arm?"

"Um, no, not that I remember. Here let me do it again." He unloosened his grip then grabbed the handle again, hard. "Lift! Shrink, I say!"

Nothing.

"Here, let me try," I said from behind him. "Shrink!"

Nothing.

"Lift!"

Again, nothing.

"Well that's strange," I said. "Maybe you broke it, Ramey."

"I did NOT! I didn't do anything! Here, Mister Sky Pilot, you think you're so *special*, you try!"

Ramey and I switched places. When Evon was back in too, nestled in my lap, I touched the handle. Immediately that same tingling sensation radiated from my fingertips to my toes. "Lift."

The wagon responded with a lurch, straight upward. It rose a few feet then hovered, vibrating slightly, as if eager for its next command.

"See, I didn't break anything," Ramey said, a certain amount of disgust in his voice. "I guess it just doesn't like me, that's all."

"Nownow,Ramey," Evon said. "Don'ttakeit... personally. SometimesPeter's creationscan... well, sometimesthey'rejustnot... allthatpredictable. Sometimestheyjust... go... haywire... docrazythings... forno... good reason."

"Yeah, Ramey," I said. "Maybe it just misfired on you. Remember earlier, *your* commands were the ones that saved our bacon, twice."

"Well, okay," he said. "That's true. So, what are we waiting for anyway, the cows to come home? Let's get this apple crate moving!"

Ramey probably didn't realize how much he sounded like our dad just then. Was he missing our parents as much as I was? An idea came to me.

"Shrink!" I said.

Suddenly an odd feeling zapped through me. A peculiar sensation started within, at the very core of my bones. The feeling was kind of a dull ache, but not painful in any way. It was as if ten thousand tiny hammers were unleashed on my skeleton—each *tap, tap, tapping* on every bone from every possible direction—reshaping, remolding me from the inside out. As my skeleton gave way, all the muscles, tendons, and ligaments attached thereto had no choice but to follow. And as my muscles shrank, they seemed to suck my skin inward too. The overall feeling reminded me of diving too deeply from our rope swing at Beaver Lake, except this intense pressure affected every square inch of my body, inside and out, not just my eardrums. In the blink of an eye I went from normal size to a little over an inch in height!

I turned around to check on Ramey. Sure enough, there he was sitting exactly as he'd been a minute ago, only now, he too, was barely an inch tall. He looked perfectly normal otherwise, though a bit startled.

"Hey Ramey, that was cool, huh?"

"Yeah! I felt like a balloon getting popped!"

"I know what you mean. Hang on—here we go."

I eased the handle back and the wagon responded, climbing and accelerating at the same time.

We were so small and inconspicuous, we could have easily been mistaken for a bumble bee or a small dragonfly. I noticed, in its smaller form, the wagon was more unstable than before. It bobbed and undulated with the shifting winds, though still it was easily manageable.

Wind surged through our hair as the wagon gathered speed and shot from the clearing like a bullet. Up, up it climbed at a dramatic angle into the sky. We had to hold on tightly to keep from being thrown out the back. But the feeling of flying—actually shooting through the air, free and unfettered—was so exhilarating! All three of us were beaming smiles from ear to ear.

The rim of the canyon peeled away in an instant and within seconds tree tops were green ink spots below us. I leveled out when we were high enough to be clear of obstacles. Looking over the sides at the forest rolling past beneath was a spectacle to behold. The trees all seemed to melt together into various shades of emerald—a multi-textured blanket rising and falling, billowing and angling, interrupted in places by meadows and the occasional creek or pond. I saw deer peacefully grazing in the shadows. Logging roads switch-backed up and down mountainsides like smooth, brown-grey ribbons.

Now to execute my little plan. "Hey," I shouted—I had to shout over the noise of the wind. "Let's go check on mom and dad."

Before anyone could answer, I banked the wagon into a

sweeping U-turn.

This new direction was all right with Ramey. He, more than me, was missing our parents.

I knew mom, especially, would be worried at our disappearance. But how much? And what about dad? He'd been so edgy lately, it seemed neither Ramey nor I could do anything right. Would he even miss us—or care?

I got my answer soon enough. Within a few minutes we approached the Stump and Gorge. The small square log cabin, the barns and outbuildings appeared like game board pieces in the distance. Getting nearer, I recognized every feature: the sheet metal roofs, the barbed wire and board fences, the tractor parked in the shed. Then there were the animals: the pigs rooting through the mire of their pen searching for an unnoticed scrap of last night's meal; cows munching hay; chickens scratching for bugs in the outer coop; and the goats and sheep standing in the rain-beaded grass chewing their cuds. The animals were going about their routines as if this day were an exact copy of yesterday and all the days before.

But to mom and dad, this day was vastly *unlike* any other before. I could see them now.

Oh... my gosh...

It was a painful sight. They were frantically running from building to building, yelling, "Collin... Ramey! Where are you?! Ramey... Collin... stop hiding and come out right now! Collin... Ramey!"

I wanted to stand up and yell back, "Here I am... up here! We're okay—don't worry!" But I knew better. There was no turning back now. I circled. We got a good look at mom hurriedly trotting from the barn. She was dressed only in her pale blue morning gown. Her pencil-thin neck twisted from side to side as she scoured the grounds—searching. In her gown, it was easy to see just how badly the disease had etched away at her body—her arms and legs were mere sticks, her torso looked like a bird cage. There was no color at

all in her face. Tears streaked down her cheeks. She was worried—
real worried.

Now I began to wonder, *Was running away from home
harder on her than the disease itself?* Pangs of guilt stabbed the pit
of my gut.

I couldn't bear to watch any more of this torture.
Completing the last arc of my turn, I aimed for town and fixed my
eyes forward. For some reason, though, I couldn't resist one last
glimpse of my parents. It was a sight I would not forget, a sight I
wished I had missed. Mom was at the end of her strength and had
collapsed to her knees in the mud of the barnyard. She was sobbing.
Dad was at her side stroking her thinning hair, doing his best to
comfort her. But he, too, was weeping. Perhaps the pressures he'd
been shouldering finally became too much and he broke.

I could feel my brother's chest shaking behind me. Ramey
was crying, I knew it, but I didn't want to turn around. The lump in
my own throat was heavy enough that if I looked at him or tried to
say something, I might cry, too. I steered the wagon toward town
and pulled back on the handle. It responded crisply with
acceleration and altitude gain. My resolve to find the Dark Quartz
Mine solidified at that instant. I knew my family's very existence
depended on Ramey and me. We would either find it or die trying.

Chapter Twenty-Five

Lunkhead

There was no talking as the wagon sped across the sky. Each passenger was too busy wrestling with his own dilemmas.

I knew the way to town and steered our speeding red bullet accordingly. Our flight path would, for the most part, follow the winding road our school bus took every morning. Except, of course, we did not have to obey the twists and turns built into the asphalt strip snaking along far below. It would be about six miles as the crow flies before the mountain slopes and conifers gave way to the level river valley and Furry-Pine's residential avenues. I would cut at least two of those miles out by flying directly over Beaver Lake rather than around it.

Unbeknownst to us, we were not the only travelers availing ourselves of the airspace over Tigaks County at that moment. A large dark shape had spied our glinting wagon from his perch atop a distant maple and came flapping swiftly to investigate.

Peering over the wagon's left side, I struggled to wrench my mind from unpleasant thoughts of home by searching for landmarks below. I was looking for the secluded cove where our rope swing hung. *We should be flying over it just about now...*

It would have been an excellent day for swimming. The morning's clouds had fled northward, making way for a brilliant display of dazzling sunshine now bursting forth from above the mountains to the east. The temperature had climbed and the lake's water was still, reflecting hues of deep blue and jade-green. Much of the water's edge was in shadow but in an hour there would be plenty of sunlight for a wonderful swim. I had no intention of actually going swimming, of course.

We could not have been more taken by surprise.

Suddenly, out of nowhere, our wagon was hammered by a tremendous force—*WHAM!*

In the blink of an eye, I was knocked violently sideways—utterly unseated. I fell earthward, spinning and tumbling. It happened so quickly, I didn't even have time to shout.

The last thing I saw before impact was the Red Rocket in the clutches of a very large raven, his great coal-colored wings moving in slow, swoopy flaps.

KERSPLASH! I smacked the lake's surface—the cold water swallowing me whole. Amid a thousand tiny bubbles, I heard two more impacts—*SPLASH...SPLASH!*

Clawing and kicking, I struggled to regain the surface. The other two splashes, I reckoned, were Ramey and Evon. Now treading water, I could see them, bobbing along, unhurt, only a couple yards away. We had landed some thirty feet from the shore, very near our rope swing.

Little did I know, this lagoon was home to a voracious predator. At the very bottom of the deepest part, there was a waterlogged, ages-old cedar snag which had been uprooted during a violent storm and had fallen into the lake and ultimately sank. One end of the trunk still had a few bony roots protruding, which held the log slightly off the muck that was the lake's bottom. It was this gap, this murky lair, that Lunkhead the trout called his home.

Three plunks on the surface reverberated like a dinner bell through the depths and Lunkhead stirred. Swishing his powerful tail he shot forward and set a bead on the nucleus of the largest circular waves above. *Hmmm, very interesting,* he thought. *That's got to be the biggest cricket I've ever seen! And look at him thrash! He shall make a dandy breakfast—a filling one at that.*

Lunkhead owned the distinction of being the oldest, largest

trout in the lake. He was nearly three feet long and as big around as a small log. His diet consisted of insects, worms, small frogs— anything up to two inches in size that moved. On each side of his underbelly were pastel pink, green, and blue rainbow stripes clearly branding his species. He particularly liked the lagoon because it was quite deep, and the tranquility of the protective cove attracted scores of dragonflies, mosquitoes, and other tasty morsels.

But it was also a good spot for attracting fishermen. Lunkhead had discovered this the hard way. There were no fewer than six hooks and lures permanently stuck in his lips and jaw from careless feeding forays of previous years. Somehow though, he

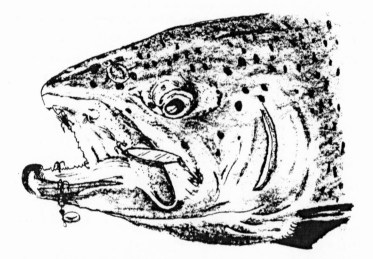

always managed to avoid the net and capture. There was one particular evasive tactic that always worked: When hooked, he would not try to escape by swimming away. Instead, to the inevitable surprise of the fisherman above, he would swim madly and directly at the flashing, spinning thing that hung down a foot or so from the back of most boats. But rather than swim into it and get chopped to death, at the last minute, he would dodge to the left or right—just enough for the spinning thing to miss his body, but close enough that the string would get tangled in it. *Snap!* The string would break, usually only inches from his face, and he would be free. But not without a price. He would dart quickly away, the hook or lure still lodged firmly in his lip. No matter how hard he rubbed on the gravel bottom or submerged logs, the hook never came out. On one hand it was embarrassing to go through life with so much hardware hanging from your face, but on the other, he'd seen many of his kin not so fortunate. Rather, perhaps, not so smart—to be drug upward, flailing and thrashing, ultimately being wrapped in a nylon net and then hoisted from the life-sustaining water. Lunkhead's permanent hooks were an annoyance, to be sure, but at least he was alive, and he had learned to eat around them.

Little doubt the three bugs flaying away on the surface just now were not fisherman's lures or bait. *Too lively for that*, he reasoned. He zeroed in on the largest of the three. *Oh my, but this one is fat! Maybe even too big to take in one gulp, but certainly it's worth a try.* He approached slowly, cunningly, until only a foot or so separated him from his prey. Then he opened his great mouth and with a mighty thrust of his tail, exploded forward for the kill.

Up to that instant, I had been treading water. For some strange reason, swimming while in miniature, even fully clothed, was much easier than when full-sized. Although it would take us a while, I wasn't too worried that we would make it safely back to shore.

But, of course, I hadn't factored in Lunkhead.

"Ramey," I called out. "You and Evon okay?"

"Yeah, we're fine. Maybe a little shook up, but no broken bones or anything."

"Think you can make it all the way to shore?"

"Yep, no problem."

"Evon, how 'bout you? Everything all right?"

"Yes… yeseverything… is fine. I feellike a… a furrybobber! I'llmakeit… to shore… nosweat. ButI'mmuch… much

moreworriedabout… the wagon. Didanyone… see…
noticewherethat… devilish raven…flewoffto? Withoutthewagon…
we could be inrealtrouble. Howarewe… how willwe…
getbigagain?"

I hadn't even considered that. *The wagon!* We had to get it
back or our mission to the Dark Quartz Mine was over before it had
even begun.

"Holy semanigans!" I yelled. "Ramey, we've got to get that
wagon back, or we're… "

But I did not finish my sentence. Suddenly, there was a
terrific yank on both of my legs. Before I had time to breathe or
shout, I was snatched violently from the surface and pulled under.

Instantly, my feet were immobile and I was heading down.
Pressure built on my eardrums. My lips pressed hard together,
straining to keep what little air I had in. Instictively, I began to
thrash, but to no avail. *Slow down—got to keep your cool,* a voice in
my head suddenly penetrated the chaos ringing through my brain.
*You can get out of this if you use your head. But don't take too
long…only have a bit of oxygen left. Now, you know you've been
nabbed by a fish, a big fish. See if you can pry his mouth open.*
Struggling to see through the viscous current streaming past, I
reached down and levered as hard as I could against the fish's jaw.
It only bit down harder. *Okay, that didn't work. But what are those
metal things hanging from his face? Lures? Hooks? Yes! Quick,
grab one and poke him with it—and make it hurt! You're running
out of time.*

My lungs burning, I twisted back into the trout's face. His
left eye, expressionless, perpetually open, staring right back through
me, was so close I could have easily jabbed it with my finger. But I
was after heavier armaments. I grabbed a lure—a double-pronged
spoon. The front set of treble hooks were lodged in Lunkhead's
upper jaw but the second set was swinging free. *This better work or
I'm dead. Got – to – take – a – breath.* I heisted the treble hook

upward then thrust forward with all my might—directly into his face. The air in my lungs had been there too long and was burning like acid vapors.

Thunk!

The hook stuck, embedded midway between eye and nose. Startled, the fish flinched backward, opening his mouth. In a split-second I lashed away, kicking wildly. Memories of the waterfall and the desperate feeling of not being able to surface came flooding back. I closed my mouth and nose as tightly as I could. Would I make it or would my body's automatic breathing mechanism take over and force me to inhale? I looked up—there was the surface only a few feet away! Thrusting mightily, I surged up and broke through just as my mouth flew open. *Sssscccchhhh! Yes! Fresh air!*

No sooner had I breached, I heard my brother shout, "Collin, is that you? What happened? You were under so long—we thought you weren't coming back up!"

"It's a fish," I sputtered. "A huge rainbow trout—must've been three feet long! He had my legs, but I poked him in the face. Get to shore quick—before he comes back!"

Many feet below, Lunkhead spun around. There was a dull pain radiating from his nose. *That foul cricket! That nasty, mean cricket bit me! Well, he shall pay for his insolence. Yes, he shall be sorry, very sorry he ever blundered into my pool. Must get him quickly, however. The others, many others, will be along soon. And I'm in no mood for sharing. No...not this juicy prize.*

The commotion had indeed created a stir in the confines of the lagoon. Other fish were now hurrying to investigate. Within a few seconds, at least four more trout had gathered. It didn't take them long to comprehend that there was a meal in the offing. Each quickly honed in on one of the odd crickets and surged forward with deadly speed.

Chapter Twenty-Six

Gone Fishing

I started shouting orders. "Ramey, take out your pocketknife. You've got to be ready for him. I'm doing the same. How far are we from shore?"

"It's a long way, Collin, especially for you!"

Indeed, Ramey and Evon were still twenty-five feet from shore. But I was even farther, a good fifty feet, having surfaced where Lunkhead spit me out.

Lunkhead closed in again and this time he would take no prisoners. But I was ready. I dipped my head under and strained to see through the hazy green. Here he came, but to my horror, he wasn't alone. There was another fish, not quite as large, but still a good two feet long, shooting toward me like a sleek, olive torpedo.

Lunkhead, still smarting, laid back and let his companion go first. He knew this cricket was too large for the underling. At best, his comrade would grab a leg or two, leaving the juicy part, the body and head, for him.

The new trout shot forward, mouth agape. I lunged at him, thrusting my shiny blade directly into his snout. *Poke!* The blade sunk in just as the mouth clamped shut only millimeters from my legs. My knife, barely an eighth of an inch long, did little more than prick the trout's thick flesh. It was enough, though, to deflect him. I was tossed rudely aside as the trout's tail thrashed a wave over me.

Lunkhead observed this discourse and decided to attack quickly, hopefully catching me before I could regroup. With a powerful flick of his tail, on he came.

I saw what was happening and immediately righted myself. I put my knife hand forward and braced for the impact. Lunkhead opened his mouth as wide as it would go and struck.

Suddenly, everything was dark. Pitch black. I felt the sensation of going down and of being squeezed by something tough but pliable on all sides. An oozy substance gushed upward around my boots. I was in Lunkhead's mouth! Now something prickly and tough was sliding me backward. It was Lunkhead's tongue, shuffling me like a conveyor belt, into his throat and acidy gullet beyond.

"Noooo!" Reacting on pure instinct, I thrust my knife directly upward with all my might. *Shlunk!* The keen steel sunk in. This time though, there wasn't any thick, blubbery layer of outer skin to protect my adversary. Directly into the naked, ribbed roof of Lunkhead's mouth the knife cut. Again, he flinched backward, opening his mouth and spitting me into the water. Again, I swam frantically for daylight.

When I broke surface, I scoured the waters for Ramey and Evon. Had they been chomped yet? A frenzied commotion near our rope swing pulled my attention that way. *Ramey and Evon? Yes!* They had swum together, back to back, and were fighting for their lives. Ramey was slashing the water like a madman and Evon was bobbing his head under and thrusting it forward as if he were trying to bite the attackers with his two sharp front teeth. All around them water roiled and frothed. It was just a matter of time before the fish had their way—they were too many and too brutal.

I dipped my head back under to check my own status. *Oh, my gosh!* Now Lunkhead had two more accomplices and they were closing in. My situation had become grave. *I guess this is it,* I thought. *There's no way Ramey and Evon can hold out long enough to reach shore, and I'm in worse shape than them. What a terrible way to go—to be ripped apart by a fish. Well, at least a few will feel the sting of my knife before their meal.*

I readied myself for the onslaught.

At that moment, just around the bend, where the lagoon gave way to a short stretch of sandy shoreline, my neighbor, Ernie Johnson, grabbed the throttle of his faded turquoise, nine-and-one-half horsepower Evinrude outboard engine and twisted. Gasoline squirted from the carburetor into the combustion chamber, and the engine sped up. *Putt, putt, putt, putt...* The small aluminum craft hunkered down in the back, the nose tilted up, and it gathered speed. Ernie had decided to exercise his retirement privileges this morning for some early autumn fishing. He puffed contentedly at his pipe, its smoke whisking backward just under the brim of his wrinkled Filson hat. His boat cut through the water on its way to his favorite fishing hole. He mused to himself, *Perhaps today will be the day I land that big ol' rainbow...if he's biting, that is.*

Ernie had certainly had his chances in the past. Several of the lures embedded in Lunkhead's face at one time belonged to him. Little did Ernie know at that very moment Lunkhead was indeed out and about—and he was biting.

Lunkhead took aim at me and so did three or four others. The quickest, most aggressive fish would enjoy the spoils of victory. The slow would get only scraps. On they came like an avalanche. I did not know what to do. It was all I could manage to defend myself against one, let alone an entire trout army. Not able to think of any other defense, I began to slap wildly at the water and furiously kick my legs.

An attacker shot in and my right boot connected with its nose. The trout swung wide and circled away, temporarily frustrated. Another advanced, mouth open wide. Luckily his head came under my pumping knife hand which delivered a puncture wound to the top of his nose. He, too, deflected away.

But the exertion was taking a toll on me. I had been treading water for ten minutes now and was tiring. How many more attacks before I was simply too exhausted to defend myself? Still, I kept slapping and thrashing as best I could.

Now Lunkhead slithered up. *Ahh, I see he is tiring. No cricket can thrash forever. The puny underlings have failed. Now, you're mine...* He surged forward.

Suddenly, in the distance, I heard something mechanical, the unmistakable sound of a small outboard motor. *Was it coming this way?* I hollered as loudly as I could, but my voice evaporated into the immensity of the outdoors like a match in a windstorm. I kept flailing, hoping against hope that the boat's occupant would be a fisherman on his way to this lagoon. Lunkhead paused and turned to check on this new development. From his vantage, he could see the straight line of the boat's bright silver keel rounding the corner, slicing the water—coming directly toward him. *Better make this quick...*

Rapidly he gathered himself for one last run. The other trout darted away into the dark depths.

Ernie Johnson plowed on, straight for the middle of the lagoon, completely oblivious to the drama unfolding there. Lunkhead ferociously lanced forward. But in his haste, he slightly miscalculated his chomp, clamping down a fraction too soon. I was so exhausted, there was little I could do. I felt the incline of his nose slam into me, ricocheting me into the air. I was tossed, spinning though the air, several feet. Then I splashed down again—scant inches from the boat's aluminum hull as it slid past.

Frustrated and supremely disappointed, Lunkhead easily evaded the flashing silver thing and slunk down—back to the bottom of the lagoon. Grumpily, he undulated sideways into his shadowy lair. *Darn that cricket anyhow! Next time he shan't be so lucky. I shall not be denied again!*

The boat's wake caught me, and like driftwood on the ocean, sent me surfing away, directly toward Ramey and Evon. But after about ten feet, the wake suddenly gathered itself, rose up, and broke over my head, pounding me under. I held my breath, praying I wouldn't be driven too deeply. I knew I was just about out of gas. Mustering all my strength, I once again kicked for the surface. Up I bobbed, sputtering and gasping. I'd made it!

But I was still a good thirty feet from shore, and almost too tired to even tread water. After surviving the killer trout and the boat's tidal wave, would I be able to even make it back to shore; or would fate be so rude as to have me drown where no other danger existed?

"Ramey!" I called desperately, "Where are you?!"

To my supreme delight, his voice rang out and it was close. "Up here! Collin…we're up here!"

"Where? I can't see you. Ramey, Evon…where are you guys?"

"On the rope swing! We're standing on the knot. You're only a couple feet away. Look up…up here!"

I tilted my head back. Ramey and Evon were on top of the large knot at the end of the rope swing waving their arms wildly. They had climbed up the few dangling threads hanging from the frayed rope end. Thank heavens I had left them when I tied that knot a few years ago! As I doggedly swam towards it, I thanked my lucky stars for Mr. Johnson and his serendipitous excursion.

Chapter Twenty-Seven

Leaf Craft

Ernie Johnson eased his boat to a stop in the center of the lagoon about fifteen feet from the rope swing. He kept the engine idling while he patiently baited a number 10 hook with a squiggly earthworm. Whistling, he then attached a couple of split shot weights and a red and white bobber, then tossed the rig over the side. The worm sank to within a few feet of the bottom, very near Lunkhead's cedar snag home. It hung there squirming out a personal breakfast invitation. Lunkhead casually looked at the bait, smiled smugly and continued treading water. *Not today, Mr. Fisherman. Perhaps one of the younger, more stupid fish will be interested in your treachery.*

Ernie clicked the motor into a slow trolling gear, then putted northward, paralleling the shore. He had no idea he was only feet from his two rambunctious young neighbors. Nor did he know he'd just saved our lives.

Safe on our perch, we quietly watched Mr. Johnson puff at his pipe and slowly motor away. I thought about hailing him but by the time I'd wrestled my way to the ropetop, the drone of the departing motor was far louder than any amount of shouting we could have mustered. Besides that, Mr. Johnson was hard of hearing.

Ramey and Evon bombarded me with questions about the monster trout. Over the next few minutes I recited the high points of my battle.

"Wow," Ramey gasped. "What was it like to be inside a trout's mouth? Was it cool?"

"Well, to tell you the truth," I responded confidently,

soaking up the esteem of my brother and our furry friend, "it was kind of... icky. There was this thick drool coming up around my boots and it really stunk in there. It smelled like, well, kind of like...rotten fish."

"Yeah," responded Ramey. "Proll'y because he'd just wolfed down a big ol' load of perch, and it gave him a bad case of fish-breath!"

I chuckled, looking over at Evon to see if he'd found any mirth in Ramey's fishy comment. If so, he didn't show it—he was not laughing. Nor even smiling. Evon was looking about nervously with a worried expression.

"Fishbreath, Evon, get it?" I said, "Lunkhead is a trout and Ramey was saying...."

"Yesyes... yes I getit." he responded with an edge to his voice. "ButwhatIget... even more...isthatwe're... still... haven'tgot... thewagon back! Andwhat'sworse... wedon'tknow... haven'tthefoggiest... ideawhereit is. Small... we'restillsmall... andwe can'tget... bigagain... without it. That'swhatI... get."

"Yes, yes, you're right, I know," I said, my voice transitioning to concern. "I'm not exactly sure what we should do either. I suppose the only thing for us is to get back to land and start searching. I don't see any other option."

"I know what option I want," Ramey chimed in. "Lunch. I don't know about you two, but all that swimming and battling made me hungry."

We looked at each other. Food. How would we find anything to eat? Our rucksacks were knocked off when we were slammed from the wagon and were now most likely furniture for Lunkhead and his pals at the bottom of the lake.

"Well," I said trying to sound cheerful, "First things first. We won't find any food standing around on this knot. We need to get back to land then we can search for something to eat—while we look for the wagon."

"Okay," Ramey replied. He looked down into the deep pool below. "That sounds okay to me... I guess." Then he looked up, way up, his line of sight following the brown twisting rope as it disappeared into the alder branches overhead. "But, um—how are we gonna get to land?"

"Itssimple... easy boys," Evon piped. "Justclimbthe... rope! Likethis... " He threw himself at the coarse fibers, dug in his claws, and scampered up as easily as climbing stairs. When he got about halfway, he paused, looked back down and shouted, "Well?! Wellaren'tyoucoming?"

"Yeah, yeah, sure we're coming," I shouted back. "You go ahead and we'll be along, right behind you."

I grabbed the rope. It was bigger around than me. I dug my fingers at the tightly wound fibers hoping they would part a little so I could get a handhold. They didn't budge. This would not be easy. Even the rope-climb in my P.E. class was difficult for me; and that was only about ten feet. This rope was at least thirty, and was so big around I couldn't even get a grip on it. I tried the bear-hug approach. The rope pressed hard against my chest, its coarse strands poking through my shirt and pants like a thousand splinters. "Ouch!" This was not working at all.

"That sure was puny, Collin," Ramey observed loudly.

"Well, if you think it's so easy, Mister Monkey Boy, why don't you just show me how it's done."

"Okay, Willy-Weaky, step aside and pay attention." Ramey attacked the rope like a soldier in boot camp. Grunting and straining, he tried the same things I had, and a few more. He made it a little further than me, maybe two inches, but wound up sliding back down in a frustrated heap.

"Now what?" he panted. "I don't think we can make it up this rope and I sure as shootin' don't want to go back into the water with your trout buddies."

Just then, from somewhere up above, a series of high

pitched squeaks came tumbling down. It was Evon. He'd been perched on a limb watching and couldn't contain his laughter. I recognized the sound and felt my face flush with frustration.

"So you think it's funny, Mister… Mister Fur Ball Smarty Pants!" I shouted. "Well, I don't happen to share your opinion. We've got a problem here and it's serious!"

"Itsonlyserious… if you letitbe!" Evon squeaked back. "Youboys… youtwojustwait… there… a minuteandI'llbe… right back."

I followed Evon along the main branch until losing sight of him among the leaves and branches.

"Great," I exclaimed. "Now Evon's taken off, and we're stuck here by ourselves. I'm getting a little worried."

"Yeah, me too," Ramey agreed. "I was hoping ol' Mr. Johnson would turn off his boat motor so we could yell at him, but instead, he trolled right out of the lagoon."

And it was true. The lagoon was now as quiet as a morgue. Ernie Johnson had been gone at least five minutes and the water's surface was as still as a pane of glass.

"I know!" Ramey suddenly shouted. "Let's see if we can get the rope swinging and ride it over to the bank!"

I rolled my eyes and said, "Ramey, that won't work. In fact that's just about as dumb as the time you tried snorkeling with a radiator hose. We don't weigh enough to hardly even move this big knot."

"Yeah, well, it would have worked just fine, the snorkeling, if you hadn't kept plugging the end with road apples. The only problem we've got here is you're too scrawny to get the rope swinging. Lemme show you something…"

Ramey grabbed the rope and began pushing and pulling vigorously. I joined in, trying to synchronize my timing with his.

The rope moved a little, but after a few seconds, it was plain that this attempt was futile. We'd managed to swing the giant pendulum maybe two inches. To get to shore, we'd need to swing it thirty feet.

"Hey... stopshaking... rocking theboat!" a muffled voice squeaked from just above us. Evon was clinging to the rope, struggling to keep his grip. But the reason he was struggling was because he had two giant green leaves hanging from his mouth, each of which were at least three times his size, and probably half his weight.

"Sorry, Evon," I said, looking up with a start. "We didn't see... Hey, what've you got in your mouth?"

He scrambled down onto the knot and spit out the heavy stems. Ramey and I each grabbed one.

"Phew... thatwastough... hardonthe... teeth and... lips!" He said rubbing the sides of his face. "This... these, mymostexcellent... small friends... isa... raft! An origami... boat. Allweneed... todo... nowisassemble... it."

Ramey examined the leaves, comparing their size to himself and me. "Yeah, sure, I get it," he said. "The leaves are big enough and they're waterproof—we just fold them together to make a little raft."

"Exac-a-tac-a-tumundo!" Evon said. "NowwhatIwas... thinking wastousea... double layer... oneleafontop... oftheother, and foldup...theedges a little... to keepwaterfrom... spillingover... intothespace... whereyou sit."

"Very clever, Evon," I said. "Considering our options, I'd even call it a stroke of genius. Here, Ramey, help me out with this."

Ramey grabbed a leaf corner and began folding. "I sure hope this works, Evon," he said. "Because if it doesn't, we may not be as lucky against the trout this time."

I glanced down. Sure enough, the fish had again gathered: dark shadowy missiles circling like sharks before a slaughter. A surge of adrenaline rushed through me and the hairs on the back of my neck stood up straight. *Whoa, boy—here we go again.*

After about ten minutes of shaping and folding, the raft was finished. It was oval-shaped, three inches in the longest dimension.

"Think it'll hold both of us, Collin?" Ramey questioned.

"Um, well, I'm not even sure if it will hold one of us. But I just thought of something else. How will we paddle it? I sure don't want to stick my hands into that water."

"A... paddle?" Evon said suddenly. "Yes... youboyswill... certainlybe needing... must have a... paddle! Youjustleave... that... littledetailup... to me." He turned and scampered back up the rope and again disappeared into the thicket above.

"Um, Collin," Ramey asked tentatively. "Who do you reckon ought to go first?"

"Yeah, I've been thinking about that, too. At first I thought it should be you because you're the lightest. But then I figured it may as well be me. The boat has to hold me one way or another, so we might as well find out right from the get-go. And besides, if someone has to do battle with the trout again, since I've got the most experience, I should be the one."

"Well, if the raft doesn't work and you go in, don't worry, I'll be right beside you—stabbing trout faster than you could say *man overboard*."

Just then Evon scrabbled back down the rope. This time he had a stick in his mouth, a twig actually, about two inches long. "Yourpaddle... boys. Ibringyou... your paddle!"

"Nice work, Evon," I said, smiling, taking the makeshift paddle from his mouth. "This ought to work just fine. I almost hope one of those lunkers tries to take a chomp at me, because if he does, he'll feel this paddle laid upside his face, and I don't mean like a pillow either. Now, Ramey, grab the other side of the raft and let's drop 'er in."

Ramey grabbed the bow and I the stern. We slid our leaf craft sideways and it fell the short distance to the water's surface—*plop*—upside down.

"Oh great…" I groaned. "Upside down—what else can go wrong! Well at least we know it floats. I'll go down and right it, and if I don't get taken out by a trout, I'll give 'er the acid test. Wish me luck."

I grabbed the paddle with one hand, took out my pocketknife, opened it, and clamped down on the blade with my teeth. Ramey and Evon helped me scramble around and under the knot until I had a grip on the dangling threads. Fortunately, there was no wind and the water's surface was still. The raft was floating patiently just beside the threads.

It was no easy task rappelling down having the use of only one hand but somehow I made it. *This better work on the first try or I'm gonna' get wet. I can't hold this rope forever. My hand is killing me.*

With my free hand, I extended the paddle, trying to hook the end of it under the lip of the raft. Now I could see the activity brewing just below me. There must have been five large trout there, all circling like buzzards. But I had no intention of obliging them. *Not today, boys. And just to make sure you don't get any harebrain ideas about taking a leap at me, have a little dose of this!* I raised the paddle, took aim, and smacked it down. *Splash—wham!* The paddle connected with the top of a trout's steely head.

Instantly the water all around boiled as startled trout bolted to escape the fury of the pugnacious cricket!

Now, back to the matter at hand. My fingers were starting to loose their hold; I'd been hanging on about as long as they could grasp. I thrust my paddle under the lip of the raft and lifted. Up came the edge… a quarter inch… half inch… *slip… splash!* The paddle slipped out and the raft slapped back down, still upside down. Panic began to set in. This was harder than I imagined. The raft was heavy, especially from the distant lever end of my paddle. But worse, I didn't have much grip left in my rope hand. Again I thrust at the lip of the raft, and again the paddle sunk in under the edge. Mustering all my strength, I gave a mighty upward thrust.

Instead of flicking the raft back over, my paddle suddenly gave way and came back out, flinging upward. My fingers couldn't hold its momentum and the paddle flew into the air, flipping away as it went.

But worse, the sudden and unexpected jolt unloosened my rope hand... and into the water I plunged—*splash!*

Chapter Twenty-Eight

Red Tail Surprise

Instantly my world was liquid-green and I was kicking to regain the surface—once again. I heard some splashing near by. *Uh-oh. Here come the trout.* By the time I reached the surface, my pocketknife was in hand and I was ready to fight.

But the splashing was not trout. From their vantage on the knot above, Ramey and Evon saw the whole thing. There wasn't a second's hesitation. When I went down, they threw themselves overboard, two swan-dives as near to me as they dared. If the trout were coming back, now they'd have to face three defenders.

I righted myself, quickly wiped away a face full of water and twisted frantically looking for attackers. But instead of hostile trout, I was happily surprised to see my brother and Evon, both paddling nearby. Ramey had the wayward paddle in one hand poised and ready to use it on any assailants.

"Thanks, guys!" I shouted. "I think I spooked the trout when I clubbed that one, but I don't want to wait around. Let's get this raft flipped over, now!"

We converged on our little boat and within a few seconds had it right-side-up. "Hey Ramey," I said. "Since we're here, why don't we see if this thing will take both of us. Climb in."

Evon and I treaded water, steadying the raft while Ramey struggled over the folded edge and plopped himself in the middle. The raft hardly flinched. I did the same and was pleased to see our jerry-rigged vessel would take our weight easily.

"Evon," I said. "I think there's room for you, too! C'mon in."

"That's… notnecessary… no thanksCollin…. " he piped,

paddling back to the threads. "Idon'tmindthe... rope... atall. I'll gobackthat... way. Noneedto... tip... upsettheapple... cart! Andbesides... I'vegot... a littleerrand... to run. Seeyou... back on land. We'llmeetright... near thetrunk... thisalder's... trunk."

"Okay, that's probably the best idea anyway," I called back.

I gave the paddle a few test strokes. It worked. Then Evon's last comment sunk in, *errand?*

"Evon... " I hollered, "What errand?"

There was no reply. Already Evon was out of earshot, clambering quickly up the rope.

It took longer than I reckoned to paddle our leaf-craft back to shore. The paddle, its end being round instead of flat, just didn't push that much water. Fortunately, no trout came snooping. Apparently, they'd had enough of this cagey batch of crickets.

As we approached shore, I steered for the alder's trunk. At the lake's edge there were numerous roots; bony and angular protruding from the dirt bank. I pulled up next to a smallish one. "Okay Ramey, we're here. Grab that root and climb it."

But telling Ramey to climb something was about as necessary as telling a bird to fly. Ramey was already kneeling, hands extended anxiously waiting to grab the root and dock our little boat. In a moment he was out, with his legs wrapped around an angling root steadying the leaf for me.

I crawled out, pushing off slightly as I transferred my weight to the root. I looked back. The empty leaf-boat floated lazily back toward the center of the lagoon. It would soon drift to another shore, wash up, then like all other leaves, rot away. "Thanks for the lift... " I whispered as it drifted.

"What's taking you so long, pokey!" Ramey was hailing me—already standing on land. I crawled up the crooked stalk. Soon, the root broadened allowing me to stand, then walk, and within a minute I was on the soil of the shore next to my brother.

"Whew, solid dirt sure feels good!" I exclaimed loudly.

"Any sign of Evon?"

"Nope, but we're not exactly where we're supposed to meet him yet either."

"Well, let's get going, then. I'm anxious to find out what his errand was all about."

"Yeah, me too. I sure hope it involved food. I'm starvin-marvin."

"I hear you there, little bro. I'm so hungry right now, if a bear came across my path, I'd drop him like a bad habit and barbeque 'im on the spot."

Ramey had already started the steep, ten-yard trek up the hill. He laughed at my bear comment. "Ha! And what would you use to drop him with, Collin—your breath? Or maybe your quarter-inch pocketknife? Or maybe you'd grab a twig and poke his eye out! I think if a bear came along right now, you'd be so scared you'd probably load up your pants, stick your hands in the air, and cry like a spanked baby. That is, if the bear didn't step on you first."

"Yeah, very funny Mister Fearless Freep. Tell me then, just what exactly did *you* have in mind for food?"

There was no reply. Ramey had absolutely nothing in mind and my pointed question brought to his attention just how desperate our situation was. What could we hunt? Of course I was joking about the bear, but in reality we were so small, even the prospect of hunting a mouse was out of the question. About the only thing we'd have a chance against would be insects: ants, gnats, termites—ugh! The very thought of crunching through the exoskeleton of one, feeling and tasting the gruesome colored fluid within, just about made me wretch.

We trudged on in silence. The path between shore and alder trunk was worn smooth. Our own bare feet, the big versions, had seen to that. So it was a relatively easy hike, not having to fight through a tangled jungle of grass, vines, and leaves. But very quickly I realized that our hunt for the wagon would be exceedingly difficult. Every irregularity in the ground—every rock, pebble, and stick was an obstacle to overcome. It was only ten yards to our destination, but it took half an hour. And by the time we got there, I could feel fatigue creeping through my bones and muscles. "Whew," I wheezed, finally leaning against the alder's splotched bark. "That little walk was harder than I expected."

Ramey was breathing hard and for once did not argue the point. I scanned about for Evon but saw nothing to indicate he'd made it yet. This worried me. It had taken us far longer to reach our rendezvous point than it should have taken him. *Maybe he's on the other side of the tree*, I thought. *That could easily be the case and we'd never know it.* From my vantage, the alder trunk was more like a mountain than a tree. *How long will it take us to walk around this thing?* I knew its base was about thirty inches in diameter. *Let's see...area of a circle is pi-r-squared, and circumference is, um—oh yes, 2-pi-r. That's about 2 times 3 times half the diameter—simple.* I had always been pretty good with math and within a few seconds I calculated the base of the alder was about ninety inches in circumference—nearly eight feet around. I had in mind to hike it but that would take another ten minutes.

This simple fact and the growing hollow feeling in my gut started to play on my mind. *How in the world will we ever find a two-inch wagon in the middle of a forest when we don't have the first idea where to even begin looking? And to make matters more impossible, just walking ten yards, over nearly perfect ground takes half an hour. That's twenty yards an hour...one hundred sixty yards in an eight-hour day. At that pace, one mile would take us... twenty days! Oh, my gosh! Our mom doesn't have that long. And even if we somehow miraculously found the wagon, how will we get it back— from the raven? And what if the raven dropped it into the lake or some dark pit or crevasse somewhere? It would be lost forever. Then, how will we get... big... again? Oh, my... gosh.*

I checked Ramey for signs of him having performed the

same gloomy mental gymnastics. He was quiet, looking here and there—up the tree, for Evon no doubt. He showed no indication of the despair now leaching into my mind.

But then I thought, *Wait a minute, what am I thinking? So, maybe we've got some tough going. Fine. In that case it's high time for me to get tough. Only wimps give up. It's like dad says, 'Nothing good in life ever comes easy.'*

I would need all that resolve and then some. There was yet another factor working against us that I hadn't even considered. At an inch-and-a-half tall, we were just the right size to be considered a meal (or at least a snack) for nearly every carnivore in the forest. Hawks, bears, eagles, foxes, coyotes, snakes, wolverines, even raccoons: all were a mortal threat. And being humans, we had virtually no built-in defenses. We couldn't run very fast, we had no network of tunnels to escape in, and we had no real weapons for counterattack. Even the steel of our pocketknives would be of little use against a hawk's talons, or coyote's fangs. We were sitting ducks.

And just at that moment, from his perch high atop an adjacent fir, a predator—a very worthy predator, noticed us. It was a red-tailed hawk who had just landed after a long, fruitless morning's hunt. *Aha,* he thought, *perhaps I won't go hungry this day after all!* Wasting not a second, he took flight, flapping his great wings powerfully over the lake. Circling once, his keen eyesight confirmed it: two mice; odd looking and very slow. Immediately, he calculated a flight path. The shore was too congested with trees for a decent attack from that direction but there was a clear lane if he were to come in from the water's side. The mice had stopped very near the alder's base in the wide open, not even attempting to gain cover. *Not only are these mice sluggish and peculiar looking, they are incredibly stupid as well! But, must be careful—they are so near the tree, it may obstruct my attack. Though I'm hungry enough for them both, perhaps I'd better just try one at a time. They are so slow, I may have time to come back for the other anyway.* Circling again, he chose his target, the larger of the two, tucked his wings and gathered speed.

Not wanting to bring Ramey's attention to the impossibility of our dilemma, I quipped as cheerfully as I could, "Any sign of Evon?"

"Nope, you?"

"No. I hope he's alri... "

Suddenly, there was a great commotion from above. It was a loud, rapid scratching sound and it was getting louder very quickly. I'd heard something like this before—it had a ring of familiarity. I looked up the trunk.

What happened next happened so fast, neither Ramey nor I had time to react. Out the corner of my eye I glimpsed a brown-red blur streaking across the sky, but that was not what was making the noise. Bolting down the tree, directly at us was a huge dark shape with incredibly large fangs. It was brown and hairy and was coming with tremendous speed. In an instant it was on us. There was no time for preparation or counterattack. All we could do was duck and cover our heads as the animal pounced. I braced myself for a gut-ripping mauling. *Well, I guess this is it. We're dead, and I didn't even see it coming.* I opened my mouth to shout a last ditch-effort warning to Ramey, but just that quickly all the breath was violently squeezed from me. Faster than lightning, a large, clawed paw encircled my waist and brutally yanked me inward. I closed my eyes as the pressure increased. *Here it comes...*

Chapter Twenty-Nine

Tunestcha

Something very unexpected happened next. Rather than a bloody disemboweling, I felt my feet leave the earth. The paw hugged me tightly back into the creature's hairy body, and then... *upward acceleration.* Suddenly I was moving—fast.

"Sscccrrreeeeeee!" An ear-splitting scream ripped the air only inches from my head. *Wham!* A tremendous impact rocked my captor and me, knocking us sideways. The grip on me tightened.

But then everything stabilized. I heard pounding thrusts of air nearby and another *"Screeeee!"* And then silence.

Now the familiar scratching sound came back, only a little slower this time, as I felt myself being hauled upward. I opened my eyes but everything was dark. I tried to squirm. No good. I became aware of something else squirming beside me. I decided to conserve my strength and be ready to fight when the paw loosened. Somehow I wasn't dead yet, and as long as I possessed a spark of life, I would fight to my last heartbeat.

But before the paw loosened, before daylight reached my eyes, before I had a chance to even reach for my pocketknife, I heard a voice. A familiar, friendly voice.

"Wellhello there... boys! Gladtosee.... so happytosee... youboth again... alive! Thathawk... that redtail nearly... hadyou. Dredfullysorry... sosorry... itook... so long."

Evon? Yes! Both? Ramey? Hawk? What the...?

All at once I was released then fell several inches to the ground. Blinking furiously, it took a few seconds to take in my new surroundings. "Ramey—where are you?"

"Right here, Collin, behind you. Turn around."

Wherever we were, was very strange. Shadowy, narrow walls surrounded us on all sides. Turning, I realized we were in a tall, round chamber of sorts. The floor was incredibly uneven and lumpy, but the lumps were smooth, not sharp like jagged rocks. Directly in the middle was an object of terrific height and girth that occupied nearly half of the room's space. The object appeared to be supported by two pillars extending upward from the knobbly floor. The only light came from an entrance—a small oval-shaped hole in the far wall. No other doors or windows did the chamber have. And it smelled strange: earthy, somewhat musty, but also strongly of wood. Out of habit, I reached to my back pocket for my comb. Suddenly a deafening "checheche....che" tore through the air.

"Collin... youneedto... mustmoveslowly... until Tunestcha getstoknow...you better. He'snotusedto... humans... yet."

"Tunestcha? Who? Evon? I can hear you, but I can't see you."

"I'muphere... way... up. Look, I'mwaving!"

I looked up, my eyes following the large object in the middle of the room. Suddenly the object moved. The floor seemed to rumble as the pillars uprooted themselves, turning in the blink of an eye, into hairy arms with sharp claw ends. They raised as the entire thing's mass rotated backward. Then the arms began a repetitive twitching motion near the object's top. Now I could make out something else, something startling. An eye... some teeth, and whiskers! The object was... a squirrel... a huge furry squirrel! *Evon?!*

"Evon, is that you?!!!" I shouted. "Have you grown back to your big size?"

"No.. nonono... silly," Evon piped back. "I'mstill... small, I'muphere... ontop... up on topof Tunestcha's head! Seemyhand... er, paw?"

I squinted into the faintly lit domed ceiling. Sure enough, there was a small bit of motion up there. Barely, now, I could see him. Evon was standing on his hind legs on top of the big squirrel's head frantically waving his little paws back and forth. Only about half of Evon's body was visible, the lower portion being obscured by his host's fur.

"Don'tbeafraid... Tunestchawon't...hurt you. Infact... he justsaved... yourbacon... yourlife! Justdon'tmake... anyquick... motions... movementsthough... until he gets... usedtoyou."

From behind, I heard my brother breath an exclamation of astonishment. "Whoaaaa... "

Evon then spoke some unintelligible chatters and the full-sized squirrel lowered himself, allowing Evon to scamper down. He bounded over.

"Well, don'tyouboys... haveanythingto... sayto... Tunestcha? Haveyouno... manners... atall? Don'tyou realize... ifhehadn't... cometoyour... rescue justnow... you'dbothbe... torn... rippedinto... athousand... piecesof... hawk mincemeat?"

"Thank you—pleased to meet you," we both replied mechanically. Tunestcha looked down at us, cocked his head to the side, flicked his tail slightly and resumed twitching.

Slowly, cautiously, I put my comb away. *Oh, my gosh! Saved by a squirrel, riding a squirrel!* "Evon," I whispered. "You need to tell me what just happened out there. What hawk?"

"Well... whileyouwere... waiting... leaning againstthetree... a bigredtailed hawk... spied you, anddecided... to makeyouhis..lunch. Iwastoofar... upinthe... treethen... towarnyou. The hawk... wasonlyabout... tenfeet... away... whenTunestchaandI... cameshooting... down... grabbedyouboth... andranaround... the treetoescape. Thehawkwas... soclose... hecrashed... bangedinto... Tunestcha... withhiswing... butluckily... wasn'tableto... get a hook... intohim. Thenhe... Tunestcha...brought... youback... uphereto... hisden... house. Ofcourse... now... you'resafe."

We stared in awe at Evon, then at Tunestcha. Now that we

understood, many more thank yous and even a few bows poured forth.

"So *that* was your errand, Evon," I finally said. "To enlist the help of your friend here. Great thinking!"

"Yes… " Evon replied modestly. "Iknew… we'dneedsome… helpsooner… or later. Itturnedout… tobesooner! I'mjustglad… Tunestchawashome… andagreeable… to helpacouple… ofhumans. Especiallyhumans… known to… hunt… throwrocksat… andshoot… squirrels."

I felt my face flush with embarrassment. Ramey and I exchanged sheepish glances and swallowed hard.

A muted gurgling suddenly penetrated the space. I pressed my tummy with both hands, embarrassed at its rude growl. It was now late in the afternoon and I'd had nothing to eat since our soggy peanut butter sandwich earlier that morning.

"Evon," I said quietly, not wanting to draw attention to myself and my problem. "You wouldn't happen to know of any food around here would you?"

"Why… howclumsyof… me!" he replied quite loudly, ruining my attempt at discretion. "Yes… yesofcourse… food! Weactually… hadplannedon… alittlesnack… whenwe… caughtupto… you. Doyourealize… know… youare… rightnow…standingona… pileofthe… bestfood… youcanget?"

I looked at the floor. Now I recognized the lumpiness. Nuts! A whole floor full of them. The hollowed out center of the alder tree was filled to some unknown depth below with chestnuts, pine nuts, filberts, and walnuts.

"Wow," Ramey exclaimed. "Where did all these come from? I didn't know there were so many nut trees in this forest."

"Well… Idon'tknowhow… manyofthese… growwild… butIdoknow… wherethereis… an orchard or two... aroundhere. Youmight… be surprised… tolearn… alotof… thesecamefrom… your own… yourdad's… trees!"

"Soooo… that's who's been raiding our nut trees! I didn't know squirrels traveled so far for their food. We must live a good three-quarters of a mile from here! But anyway, right now, I'm awful glad Tunestcha stocked up."

Before Evon could say anything more, Tunestcha stirred, cocked his head sideways, and let out a string of chatters. The chamber got very dark. I became aware of a stirring along the far wall at the entrance hole. Then a new sound reverberated around the confined space—a reply set of chatterings, similar to Tunestcha's but a little more high pitched and faster.

"Excellent!" Evon exclaimed as the darkness gave way to dim light once again. "Retildie… hasreturned… with some… refreshment! Berries… yesblackberries. Iknew… youboys… wouldneedsomething… todrink… wetyourwhistle… alongwith… your nuts."

Indeed, another reddish, fluffy-tailed squirrel had entered the space. Tunestcha scooched to the wall opposite the doorway to make room for his wife, Retildie. She popped in lithely and took a position next to him. In her mouth Retildie held a sprig of blackberry vine with three fragrant ripe berries still attached. She knelt down and gently dropped the vine in front of Ramey. Then both she and Tunestcha sat up and began twitching—watching and waiting to see what we would do next.

Nobody had to tell Ramey what to do. He seized one of the berries in his hands and arms. It was larger than his head, similar in proportion to a watermelon if he'd been normal size. He pulled and the berry popped free. He dropped it to the floor and drove himself into it—face first—like a fat kid at a pie-eating contest. Over the next five minutes he didn't even come up for air.

I was a bit more polite. "Thanks—thank you very much. You'll have to excuse my brother, it's just, well, he's real hungry, and when he gets hungry he forgets his manners. My name is Collin, and my broth…the boy with his head in the blackberry, he's

Ramey. Thank you for allowing us the use of your home and for feeding us. I can't tell you how much it means. Now, if you don't mind, I'm a little hungry too, and—boy, blackberries never looked so good!"

Evon squeaked several cheche-chee passages, translating to our hosts, who chirped back and nodded their heads. I bowed then grabbed a berry, placed it on the floor, and plunged my hands into the soft, juicy flesh. I pulled up great handfuls of sweet, purple berry meat and stuffed them into my salivating mouth. *Ummm, delicious!*

We scarcely noticed Tunestcha shuffling toward the doorway, retrieving a flat dark object that was stowed there. Suddenly an earsplitting *rap-rap-rap* filled the space. Ramey and I snapped up, white-eyed, startled nearly out of our wits. *What in the world... ? Is the tree splitting apart?*

But almost as soon as it started, it stopped. The final sound was an especially loud *crack!* Tunestcha set down his nut-cracking rock, grabbed the chestnut meat he'd just extracted, and inched his way toward us. He set the food down at my feet then resumed his place with his wife.

The chestnut was perfectly seasoned—not too green, not too dry. I again thanked him, took out my pocketknife and carved the head-sized meat into small chips. Then Ramey, Evon, and I feasted. We ate and ate, alternating between chestnut and blackberry, until there wasn't even a small corner of room left in anyone's stomach. Oh, it felt so good to taste such delicious food! Simple to be sure, but when you are that hungry, wholesome food always tastes best.

Ramey, now sitting, arms folded over his bulging belly, suddenly let fly—*"bbrrrrappppppp!"*—a colossal belch.

"Ramey!" I exclaimed, looking over at my yahoo-brother. "Excuse *you!*"

Suddenly embarrassed, he put a hand to his mouth and said quietly, "Sorry. Um, excuse me."

But it really didn't matter. Evon chittered in mirth, and aside from an eye-blinking gawk, the other two squirrels didn't care because they didn't know good human behavior from bad.

"Glad… nicetosee… youenjoyed… yourmeal… Ramey," Evon said after his squirrel-giggles subsided.

Then his demeanor visibly changed to a more serious mode. "But soonerorlater… boys, we… needtoplan… makeaplan… toget… retrieve… thewagon."

Chapter Thirty

Squirrel's Den

Now that my belly was full I was able to switch my thoughts to other pressing matters. We, indeed, needed to find the wagon—but how? "You're right, Evon," I said. "I've been giving our situation a lot of thought, but to tell you the truth, I don't have the first idea what to do. Finding the wagon will be like looking for a needle in a haystack."

"More like a thousand haystacks," Ramey quipped.

"And even if we somehow find it," I continued, "how will we get it back from the raven? Compared to him, or her, we're about as threatening as a few thimblefuls of fresh meat."

"Yeah," Ramey said. "For all we know, that Raven may take one look at us and think, *Yep, Frosted Kiddie Bits, hold the milk.* He'll probably grab us in his big ol' claws, peck our eyes out, and gouge... "

"Ramey, that's enough of that kind of talk," I scolded. "Our only chance is to keep a positive mind—and thoughts like those out."

"YesCollin... you'reabsolutely... positivelyright... rightonthemoney," Evon said, throwing Ramey a squirrel-scowel. "Nowlistenup... boys, I'vegot... Ibelieve... Ihave... atleastsome... of the puzzle... figuredout. Ialready... think... Iknowwhere... thewagon... is."

"What?—How?" I stammered. "Evon, how on earth could you possibly know where the wagon is? A raven—a strange, completely unknown bird—there's got to be hundreds of them around here."

"Iknow... whatyoumean, Collin... andyou'recorrect... we

probably… shouldn'tgetour… hopesup. But… beforeI…
cametoget… resscue… youandRamey, Ihadatalk….
withTunestchaandRetildie. That'swhat… took… mesolong.
Tunstchatoldme…. saidheknows… ofaparticular… raven…
thathasan… extraordinarylust foranything… shiny. Waymore…
thanother… ravens… or crows. Thisparticular… ravenlives…
intheattic… ofthetop… floorof… old man… Johnson's…
thesameman… intheboat… thefishingboat…his pumphouse."

"Whoaaa… " My mind whirred with a hundred new
possibilities. "That is too good to be true. I wonder how Tunestcha
can be sure about this particular raven—I mean, how does he know
there aren't other ravens that like shiny things too?"

"That'sjust… exactlywhat… Iaskedtoo. But hesaid…
toldme… that ofcourseall… ravensare… scavengers…
raidingcampgrounds… garbagecans… andlittertossed…
alongsidethe road, but thereis… onlyone… he's everseen…
carrying awaythings… notfood, butshiny… glitterystuff backto…
hishouse. AndTunestcha… knowswhere… hishouseis…
becauseitis… sonear… Mister Johnsons's… orchard. Whereall… his
nuttrees… are."

"So, we can't be one-hundred-percent guaranteed this is our
raven, but it seems like the chances are pretty good. And at this
point, it's all we have."

"Yeah," Ramey said dourly. "All that is good and fine, but
it's a half-mile to Mister and Mrs. Johnson's place. Judging by how
long it took us to walk from the shore to the alder's trunk, I'd guess
it'll take us at least a week, maybe two to get there. And that is *if* a
hawk or eagle or coyote doesn't snare us first. I'm worried we won't
even make it, and if we do, it might take more time than our mom
has."

I didn't reply. Ramey couldn't have been more right. I
pursed my lips in frustration and stared at the floor.

Night was falling, and outside it was nearly dark. There was just a faint bluish-purple haze filtering into the chamber from the opening in the far wall. Tunestcha and Retildie had curled up together, their faces nestled in the soft fur of each other's tummies. They were still, except for the occasional random twitch of a foot or tail. Their breathing was heavy—apparently they'd turned in for the evening.

Evon finally broke the silence. "Yes... yesIknow... we'vestillgot... ourselvesabit... ofaproblem. Butdon't... despair! I'mworkingon... a plan. Ineedtogive... itsomemore... thought. Say, it'slate... andwe'veall... had abigday. Whydon'tyou... two... fellas... dolikeour... hosts... andturn in... for the... evening. Wecan... takethisup... again... inthemorning... whenwe're... fresh."

Even as Evon spoke, I felt the day's fatigue creeping through my bones. What a day, indeed. *Need a bed. These nuts just won't do.* I rousted myself and walked to the blackberry sprig. The three leaves were still attached to the vine. I bent over and carefully touched one. I was surprised to feel the fine stubbles covering the leaf were actually rather soft, sort of like peach fuzz. I climbed over the lip edge and lay down. *Not as comfy as my bed at home, but this will definitely do. Second time today a leaf has come in handy.*

"Ramey, Evon," I called out in a loud whisper. "This blackberry leaf seems like it'll make a decent bed and there's one each."

Soon we were all bedded down for a good night's sleep. It was cozy inside the alder's trunk—plenty warm even without blankets. *Now I see how a squirrel can snooze all winter when they hibernate, it... sure... is...*

I didn't finish that thought. Sleep snuck up and stole me away to fantasy dream lands where, for the first time in many days, my troubles and predicaments did not follow.

The next morning dawned bright. There was a crisp, autumn

chill in the air. Ramey and I slept right through everyone else getting up and bustling about. Finally, Evon rousted us.

"Say… lazybones! Areyou… twogoing… tosleep… allday? We'vegota… wagon… tofind. Betterget… up… upandat'em!"

After wiping the sleep from my eyes and yawning gigantically, I was surprised and delighted to see breakfast was ready. Our hosts had already been out and back, bringing a couple of dew-covered blueberries, a salmonberry, and a blackberry. Tunestcha cracked open a walnut and again we feasted. And how delicious it was! Each food item seemed to burst forth with tingling flavor and scrumptious aroma.

"Wellboys… Ihavesomegood… newsforyou… thismorning! I'vebeen… talkingwith… Tunestcha and Retildie… aboutourdilemma… of gettingto… MisterJohnson's… place. They… haveagreed… to… bear… carryus… there!"

I gaped at Evon in astonishment. Ramey perked up, too. This was incredibly good news! Being transported by squirrel-back would cut our time from days to minutes. *Yes!*

"But," Evon said, his expression turning more serious. "They… TunestchaandRetildie… will go… nonearer… than… theold… mapletree… inMisterJohnson's… frontyard. Toorisky… dangerous… forthem… to gofurther. Dogs… youknow. MisterJohnson… hassomehounds… thatwould probably… love… freshsquirrel… forbreakfast. Can'thave…mustn'thave… that!"

"No, of course not," I quickly agreed. "But what great luck that they'll take us that far. The maple tree is only about twenty or thirty yards from the pumphouse. We can cover that distance in a snap."

"Okaythen… it's settled. Assoonas… you'reready… Isay… wesaddleup… andride! Ofcourse… withoutthe… saddles… just ajoke… thesaddleup part."

"I'm ready!" Ramey and I exclaimed in unison.

Evon chattered something to our hosts, who responded by

hopping out of the den. "Okaythen... fellas... let'sgetgoing. We... mount... upoutside... onthebranch."

We climbed out through the knothole doorway into the brisk morning air. Sunlight amid cloudless blue filtered through goldening leaves, making me squint. We stepped onto a fairly large branch, some six inches in diameter. It was not quite level, but close, and thus was relatively safe and easy to stand on. Looking down, I was surprised at how far above the water we were. I could see the rope-swing below and to the right—it was probably fifty feet down. *That means we're a good eighty feet above the water! Whoa...better not fall. Wouldn't want to wind up trout-kibble this morning!*

"Okayboys... " Evon instructed. "Collin... Ramey... youtwoget... on Retildie, I'llgowith Tunestcha. Nowthebest... waytoget... on... istoclimbup... theback... thenstraddle... theneck. Like... this."

Evon motioned to Tunestcha, who lowered himself, to allow Evon to bound up his backbone and into position. "Youguys... ready?"

We nodded. Although I was ready, butterflies swirled in my stomach. I was keenly aware that one false move would prove disastrous.

Tunestcha moved out of the way by climbing onto the main trunk, allowing Retildie to back into position. I went first. Starting at her tail, grabbing handfuls of fur, I scaled Retildie's backbone like a mountain climber. Her fur was so soft and deep! I was careful not to yank too hard—I certainly didn't want to make this any more uncomfortable than it had to be. Over the hump in the middle, then back down her neck I slid. I felt just like a cowboy slipping into the saddle of a fine, strong quarter horse. Then I turned to call for Ramey but was shocked to feel him slide into place just as I started to twist my head.

"Yeee-haaa!" Ramey hollered, directly into my ear, as his

legs got their grip and he took hold of my belt.

"Ahem—Cowboy Bob," I said over my shoulder. "Nice to see you're enjoying yourself, but if you must 'yee-ha' could you please not do it in my ear."

"Okay... Sensitive Sam. Soooo, what're we waiting for? Let's ride!"

Retildie moved forward. Following Tunestcha, she walked to the main trunk, then without hesitation headed down. I felt my weight shift as Retildie went from horizontal to vertical. It was the same scary feeling you get on a roller coaster—that jolt of adrenaline as your stomach lifts into your throat when your car tips over the first big hump. As soon as Retildie got vertical I realized there was a problem—a major problem.

At once, Ramey's weight slid forward and pressed hard on my back. Were it not for my legs wrapped so tightly around Retildie's neck, we both would have come off and somersaulted over her head. "Ramey!" I yelled. "Back up! You're too heavy pressing on me. My legs are slipping!"

"I would if I could! But there's nothing to stop me...except you!"

Retildie took a few steps down, but now, sensing our dilemma, stopped. We were momentarily held in suspension, gripping for our lives. Retildie moved sideways then rotated her body 180-degrees to point back up the tree. As she did, my weight shifted. Now I slid backward against Ramey, who slid backward from Retildie's neck to her back. But fortunately her shoulder blades were there acting like wheel-stops.

Retildie stayed motionless for a moment as if testing. Nothing happened. "Ramey, you okay?"

"Yeah, other than these shoulder blades poking up my backside. Let's get on with it!"

Retildie slowly descended, backwards, down the great leaning alder. She used her bushy tail as a feeler, adjusting herself sideways as necessary to avoid the branches. Within a couple minutes we were on the ground, side-by-side with Tunestcha and Evon.

After a moment of comparing notes and making sure everyone was okay, Evon chattered something to Tunestcha, and the squirrels bounded away.

Chapter Thirty-One

Bareback

The trip from the leaning alder to the Johnson's place was relatively uneventful, except for the first few minutes. Neither Ramey nor I had ever ridden a horse, let alone a squirrel, let alone bareback! No stirrups for the feet, no saddlehorn for the hands—it was scary to say the least. After a few hair-raising minutes of nearly sliding over sideways, we finally got the knack. The trick was to go with the motion fluidly, letting your body absorb the up and down rolling movements.

The squirrels kept to well-used paths. Some were deer trails, some used only by rodents, but they were all easily passable. Knolls and vales—a few grassy, most brushy—slipped past. Our path took us over fallen logs, gnarly roots, and the shoulders of sandstone and granite rock outcrops. We even had to ford a couple of small creeks, but fortunately, Tunestcha's local knowledge told him the location of well-positioned fallen log bridges, so no one got wet.

I noticed the aroma of the forest was particularly pungent from such a low position. All the familiar smells were there: the conifers and the occasional blackberry of course, but now other smells were dominant too. Ferns, rye grass, skunk cabbage, and a host of other low growing vegetation gave off their spicy odors. Even the earth itself, rich with the mulch and humus of decaying conifer and hardwood emitted a very distinct odor. It reminded me of my dad's clothes after a hard day's logging.

The squirrel's path took us from water's edge at Beaver Lake to the intersection of the Johnson's driveway with the main asphalt road. Then, not wanting to risk the clear open drive, we paralleled the long gravel lane, staying well to the right, in the ubiquitous, untamed fern and briar thickets. About halfway up the driveway, the undergrowth gave way to grass—short and well-mowed. This was where the Johnson's orchard started. The orchard covered several acres, completely surrounding the cluster of buildings that was the Johnson's home. There were fruit and nut trees of every description: apples, apricots, pears, plums, cherries, walnuts, filberts, chestnuts, and more.

Looking beyond the trees and expansive lawn, the buildings were just as I remembered them. In front was the house: white, of modest size with steep gabled roofs. It had two red brick chimneys and two dormer windows facing the driveway. Behind and to the right was the garage. It was a white, rectangular box, big enough for two vehicles, detached from the house by about ten feet, with its double doors facing us just now.

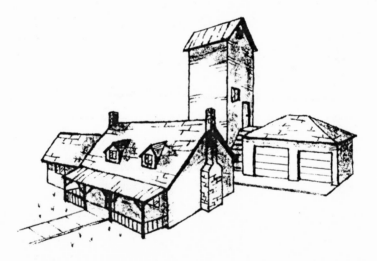

Next to the garage, separated by about five feet, and directly behind the house, was the three-story pumphouse. There was a covered breezeway connecting the back door of the house with the only entrance to the lower level of the pumphouse. Several times a day, Mrs. Johnson would travel this way fetching home-canned jars of fruits or vegetables, or meat from their big freezer chest located out there. The pumphouse itself was tall, at least 50 feet high. It was so tall in fact, Mr. Johnson never had the courage to repaint it. And so, of the three buildings, it was the only one gray and barren-looking, long since devoid of its original white paint. The purpose for its height, of course, was to harness gravity. The top floor housed a great, galvanized metal water tank that stored the Johnson's drinking water. The structure seemed skinny—about thirteen feet to each side. Access to the second floor was by way of stairs routed up the space between garage and pumphouse. The top floor was accessible only by a permanent ladder nailed to a second floor wall, extending up through and into a corner of the third floor.

It was in the attic of that lofty place that Tetrink the raven made his home. There was a round, wooden-spoked air vent on each gable. But on the south side, the side facing the weather, the vent had long ago rotted and several of the spokes had fallen away. This provided easy access to any flying animal. It was about three years ago, while on a picnic raiding mission, that Tetrink noticed a sparrow fluttering from there. Curious, he investigated and quickly decided the accommodations were much too spacious for such a small bird and barged right in. The displaced sparrow family was never invited back.

We were now some two hundred feet from the house, but I sensed that Retildie was nervous. She was exposed and she knew it. Following Tunestcha, she bounded quickly from tree to tree, pausing at each, looking all around for predators. *What if one of the Johnson's dogs happens to notice us?* I wondered. *Retildie would have to bolt up a tree. Would Ramey and I get tossed off? Would we be able to hide from a dog—a hound that can sniff out a rabbit at a hundred yards? Not likely.*

Fortunately, no dogs or other predators came. When we got to the giant maple the squirrels knelt as low as possible, allowing us to slide off into the dew-covered grass. Ramey and I whispered many thanks and Evon chattered his own gratitude. The squirrels cocked their heads and flicked their tails. Then they turned and gracefully bounded away.

"Well... wesurewere... fortunate... luckythatTunestcha... and Retildie... weresokind... tous," Evon said. "Itwouldhave... beenacompletely... different story... hadthey... refused. I havemy... doubts... we'devenstill... bealive... now."

"Yeah," I replied. "I sure hope that someday I can do something nice for them—you know, return the favor."

"Me, too," whispered Ramey, nodding his agreement. "But in the meantime, I'm getting a little nervous... about... um, dogs... or hawks... or something."

"I hear you there, little bro," I said, glancing all around. "In fact, just standing here gives me the willies. It feels so... naked. Like we could be snared any minute."

"And that reminds me," Ramey said. "Not only do the Johnsons have a couple of hounds, they also have a cat, a big yellow tom. I think they call him Gunner. Best mouser in the county, according to Mister Johnson. And I doubt that cat could tell the difference between us and a mouse, even though we've been here before and petted him."

"Wellthen, we... betterget... going," Evon said. "Let's... see. Youboyshave... been herebefore... right? So... youknow... how... thebestway... to getinto... the pumphouse... theattic... of the pumphouse, right?"

"Yes, we have been here before," I responded. "Several times to visit. But we've never gone into the pumphouse. I know where the stairs are, though. They're on the outside, between it and the garage. But, um, how are we, uh, going to climb them?"

As I spoke, it occurred to me that a set of stairs posed a very sticky problem indeed. There would be no way we could reach from one tread to the next even if we jumped.

"Well... " Evon quipped, trying to sound cheerful. "Wewon'tknow... howbad... thisproblem... is untilwe... investigate... lookintoit. So... let'sgo."

"You ready, Ramey?" I asked.

But there was no answer. Evon and I turned to see what Ramey was doing. To our surprise, he had completely ignored our last dialogue and was getting himself a drink of water. He'd turned his head sideways and was slurping along the shaft of a blade of grass with his tongue, harvesting the dew that hung there in rope-droplets.

"Hey, Ramey," I exclaimed. "Great idea. Think I'll join you."

"Mmm... sure," Ramey said, not bothering to look up. "There's plenty."

True enough, every blade of grass had a tremendous supply of delicious dew clinging to it. We were verily standing in a grass forest, each of the blades a little taller than ourselves. This would be good camouflage as we worked our way to the pumphouse.

And so we spent the next hour doing just that. It was an easy go. The ground was flat with minimal obstructions, except for the grass itself. The blades were not that dense and were flexible, allowing easy passage. Ramey pretended he was on an African safari, hacking and judo-chopping his way through the tropical jungle.

We approached from the garage side. The grass ended at a sidewalk, which ran all the way along the back of the house. To get to the pumphouse we would have to risk being seen crossing this walkway.

We were now directly in front of the pumphouse stairs and could see the challenge they posed. It wasn't as bad as it could have been, however. Nailed to both the pumphouse and the garage walls were boards, 2x12's I reckoned, that formed the jacks for the stairs. They ran up to a small wood-framed landing at the door to the second floor. The actual stair treads were nailed between these jacks. Though they were never meant to provide a footpath themselves, the top of the jack boards would do just that, if only we could get up on the first step.

But the first step was a doozie. It was about eight inches up from the concrete walkway and there was no direct method for a one-and-a-half-inch boy to get to its top.

"Getting to the second floor will be a cinch," I said encouragingly, "if we can just make the first step. Anyone got any ideas?"

"I've got an idea," Ramey quipped. "Follow me."

Without waiting for discussion, he bolted across the concrete walk directly to the garage. There was a narrow gap between the left door and its jamb, through which he scurried. I couldn't help noticing how much like a mouse he would have looked to Gunner had he been within eyeshot.

Evon and I hurriedly followed.

Chapter Thirty-Two

In Search of a Hook

"Hey there, Brave Bolt," I whispered to my intrepid brother once we were all inside the garage. "Next time you decide what you want to do, how about talking it over first? You'd be cat chow right now if Gunner would have seen you."

"Oh, relax, Scaredy Sally. I checked before I ran."

Evon sniggered.

The garage was fairly dark. There was only one window and it was located on the same wall as the pumphouse stairs so the adjacent pumphouse blocked most of the natural light that would have come through. The place smelled of oil and grease, and engines. Mister Johnson had a long workbench against the far wall over which was scattered many tools, nuts, bolts, small engine parts and the like. He was a tinkerer. The garage's center space was clear. This was where the car and small boat trailer were normally parked. Since they weren't here now, I assumed Mister Johnson was out on the lake again trying his skills against Lunkhead. Lining the garage walls was all manner of stuff: paint cans, boxes, shelves with various hardware and small jars, a couple of old bicycles, a shovel, two hoes, a metal rake, a wheelbarrow and so on.

"Look for fishing tackle," Ramey said quietly.

"What?" I questioned. "Why in the world would you possibly want to go fishing at a time like this?

"I don't want to go fishing—for fish, nincompoop. I want to go fishing for... a board. I mean, use a hook and rope to help us climb the first step. Get it?"

"Ohhh, yeah. I get it," I said as comprehension clicked in my mind. "Pretty good idea. I think I see Mister Johnson's spare fishing tackle and a couple of rods and reels over there on the other side, by the paints."

"Well, let's go then," Ramey said. "But I'd feel more comfortable if we stayed to the edges. No sense in giving ol' Gunner an open invitation."

"Sounds good to me. And if you want to lead, Mister Daring Dingus, go right ahead."

Ramey struck out. Slowly we crept, all senses alert, winding our way through the maze of stuff cluttering the floor. When we got to the workbench Ramey stopped, stiffened, and sniffed the air. "Hey, you guys smell that?"

Thinking my rambunctious brother was on the verge of another prank, I said, "What's that, Wally Wiseguy, my bad breath again, or did you just let fly with some filbert-cheese?"

Evon, from his position at the back, stifled a giggle.

"No, I'm not joking. I smell something rotten. And I don't like it."

Now that I could see he wasn't kidding, I sniffed. Sure enough, there was a definite stink—a rancid odor faintly wafting our way. "Okay, I smell it too, Ramey. It smells like something died."

"Yeah, that's what I was thinking. Remember the time we found that deer carcass out in the woods and the stench it gave off? That's what this reminds me of."

Ramey inched forward. It was tough going because this was where Mister Johnson's power tools were stashed. Circular saws, a jig saw, a couple of drills, sanders, a router, an air compressor—all were stored on the floor below the workbench. There were cords snaking everywhere which had to be climbed or jumped, and the tools themselves were placed in a jumble. With every step the putrid odor got stronger.

Suddenly Ramey stumbled. I was following so closely I banged into his backside.

"Hey, watch where you're going, Clumsy Claude!" he

hissed.

"Sorry. I didn't expect you to stop so suddenly. Phew... I can hardly breathe. Hey, what's that? Is that what you just tripped on?"

I was pointing to a small round cord laying on the dusty concrete. But this cord did not look like normal wire or rope. It was tapered, and it only extended about two inches beyond the edge of a worm-drive saw laying there. *What the...?*

"I see it Collin," Ramey said, blinking hard, as if the fetid reek was attacking his face. "I'll follow it and see... *AAaaughhh!*"

I leaped forward. Then I saw it too. "Oh, my gosh... that is—sick."

It was a mouse. Or what was left of one. Its head was slammed under the trip mechanism of a mousetrap. Its small beady eyes were still open, bulging outward. But what was most gruesome was that it had been there too long. It was rotten, literally. There were maggots, blind, white and voracious, crawling in and out of the festering carcass. I could even hear them—the sickening *schloop-shlop* they made oozing through the jellified entrails.

I gaped in shock and disgust for a moment, then feeling the contents of my stomach starting to turn, spun and hustled away, holding my mouth shut with my hands. Ramey did likewise.

Over cords and machinery we jumped, not bothering to look back. Finally we rounded the corner at the end of the back wall, leaving the workbench and its grizzly trappings behind.

"Yucchhh... that was the most repulsive thing I've ever seen," I said, gasping for breath.

"Yeah, I think I'll agree with you there." Ramey consented.

"Wassa... matter, boys?" Evon quipped evenly, as if nothing unusual had happened. "Haven'tyou... everwitnessed... theagony... of defeat... before? That'showit... isinnature you know. Maybe... I'vegota... betterappreciation... foritthan... youdo, though, because... I'vebeen... livingitfor... the lastsix... years.

You'vejust… gotto… getusedto… getoverit! Now, Ithink…
Iseefishingpoles… dead, ahem, ahead."

I didn't really appreciate Evon's pun, but was glad to move
on, glad we were indeed standing very close to our phase-one
destination.

Leaning against the unfinished wall studs were a couple of
fishing rods and at their base was what Ramey was looking for: the
spare tackle box. "There it is, boys," he said, somewhat
triumphantly. "We just open 'er up, grab a spare hook and some
string and we're outta here!"

But there was one small problem. The box was closed and
the big hoop latch mechanism was snapped shut. Undaunted, Ramey
strode forward. "Step aside, wannabes, while I pop open the latch."

He reached as high as he could and pushed at the bottom of
the snap-mechanism with all his might. It didn't budge. "Uh, say, I
could use a little help here."

I positioned myself to help. Evon eyed the latch then said,
"Ihope… surehope… youtwo can… openthat… thing because…
Ican'teven… reach it."

"Don't worry, Evon," Ramey said. "We'll pop this sucker,
no problem. Ready now, Collin? One – two – three – push!"

Nothing.

With all our might, the latch was too stiff for us to even
budge.

"Great," I muttered, "So much for your brilliant idea, Mister
Einstein Egghead. Now what?"

Ramey harrumphed then plopped down to the concrete, chin
in his hands. "I dunno. I need to think about this for a minute."

"Boys…" Evon spoke up. "What'sthe… matterwith…
thehookandstring… upthere? Uponthe… rod… attachedto… the…
reel."

Sure enough, each rod was rigged with string and hook. The
hook hung around one of the rod's mid-shaft eyelets and the reel

was cranked tightly, causing the tip of the rod to bow a little.

"Duh… !" I exclaimed. "How stupid can we be? There're two treble hooks, one on each rod, already with string attached. Can you climb up and get one, Evon?"

"Icansure… try," he replied, bounding over to the closest rod.

Getting up the cork handle past the reel was easy, but suddenly where the cork ended and the smooth fiberglass rod started, Evon's paws slipped and he nearly toppled off. "Unh… oh," he said looking down at our two anxious faces below. "Mypaws… don'tgrip… this… thisfiberglass… atall. Idon'tthink… Ican't… climb this thing."

"Wait a minute Evon," Ramey called back up. "Can you chew through the string right where you're standing? That'll loosen up the whole rig, including the hook, and maybe it'll just fall down… right into our laps."

Evon scanned up and down the rod, following the path of the string and saw that, of course, Ramey was right. He reached out a paw, grabbed the string, and with one chomp, cut it in two.

Poing! The string sung out as the rod unflexed. Loose string whipped back through the eyelets as the weight of the falling hook drew it down. *Bonk!* The hook and its string-tail landed on the concrete a few inches from me.

"Yes!" Ramey exclaimed. "You did it, Evon, way to go! Evon, Evon?"

Ramey was looking at the place on the rod handle where Evon was moments previously, but he wasn't there now.

"Unh… over… overherefellas," came a weak voice from several feet away.

Ramey and I rushed to our fallen comrade, who was lying prostrate in a dusty nook among some old paint cans. "Evon, are you okay… what happened?" I asked. "How did you get way over here?"

"Well... I'mnot... sure. WhenIbit... throughthestring, therod... unflexed sofast... justlike a bowand... arrow... onlyIbecame... the arrow. Itlaunched... melike... arocket... straightintothese... paint cans. Ithink... Imayhave... dented one... withmyhead... noggin."

Evon collected himself and wobbled to his feet. He was so coated in dust, he looked like a breaded lump of meat ready for the deep fat fryer. "You sure you're okay?" I asked.

"Isuppose... I'llbefine. Nothingbroken... justbruised. ButIfeelmore... likea... dust bunny... thana... human squirrel."

"Or Rocky and Bullwinkle," Ramey said, grinning. "Remember Rocky the Flying Squirrel from Saturday morning cartoons?"

"Yes... yesyes... Iremember... veryfunny... Ramey. Now, who'sgot... thehook... thestring... and hook?"

"It's right here." I had already coiled up the string and cut off the excess with my pocketknife. "Here you go, Ramey. I coiled 'er, you pack 'er."

I tossed our makeshift mountain climbing gear to my brother who caught it and said, "No sweat. If you're okay, Evon, I say we go climb us a pumphouse."

"Let'sgo... getonwith... it then."

We turned and headed for the door, only this time taking the other way around the garage.

Chapter Thirty-Three

The Pumphouse

Ten minutes later we were at the base of the stairs. "All we have to do," Ramey explained, eyeballing the steps, "is get on this first step here and then walk on that board there, straight to the second floor landing. Lemme show you how it's done. Step aside, amateurs." He grabbed the hook and string, got himself into position, and with a couple of pre-toss circles, let the gold-colored treble hook fly. It arced through the air, landing out of sight, well onto the first stair tread above. As he reeled the string in, the hook grabbed—then slipped, then grabbed again. He jerked a couple of times to set it. Satisfied that the hook had a good bite, he started his climb by walking his feet up the butt-end of the stair jack while pulling his body up with his hands.

Suddenly, without warning, the hook pulled free, the string slackened, and Ramey fell—*wham!*— directly onto his back. *"Ooofff!"*

I rushed over. "Ramey, you all right?!"

"Yeah… I think… so. But why… are there two of you?"

"There's only one of me. That must've rung your bell pretty good. Your head smacked the concrete as square as a homerun. Good thing you were only a couple inches off the ground."

Ramey shook the cobwebs from his brain then slowly regained his feet. Evon spoke up, "Boys whydon't… youletme… carrythehook… up andsetit… solidly… for you. Thenyouwon't… thiswon't happen… again."

"Duhhh..!" I groaned. "Great idea, Evon. Help yourself."

Evon clamped his teeth on the shaft of the hook, scaled the rough stair jack, took the hook to the back of the first stair tread, then lifting it over his head, sunk it as deeply as he could. "There... thatshould... hold... boys. Give 'erarip!"

This time I went first, repeating Ramey's climbing maneuver—except for the falling part, and soon heisted myself over the edge. Ramey followed, though a little unsteadily.

Soon we were all together, standing on the first step. I re-coiled the string, handed it to Ramey and set off. We ascended the angled stair jack in single file as effortlessly as three mountain mice.

"Anybody see any signs of Gunner?" I asked, looking about anxiously. "I feel pretty exposed right now."

Ramey and Evon scanned left and right. "No...I haven't," Ramey replied. "But let's hustle. No need to tempt fate."

We gained the landing at the top, turned left and easily crawled under the door. Now we were standing in the small room which was the pumphouse's second floor—a place we'd never been before.

It was another workshop. It smelled strongly of Mister Johnson's pipe and tobacco, and of solder and flux. There was a workbench along two of the walls and a putty-gray shop chair toward the middle. Old cords hung down in several places and TVs and radios in various stages of disassembly cluttered the bench. Soldering irons, screwdrivers, and pliers lay among the electronic gear.

"There's the third floor's stairs," Ramey said, pointing to the wall on our left. "But I don't like the look of them."

What he was pointing to was much more a ladder than stairs. There were seven, rough 2x4 rungs nailed directly to the wall studs, the top one located about six inches from the third floor above. At that point there was a two-foot-square framed opening through the floor with a trap-door. It was the only way up. For one-and-a-half-inch-tall boys, this ladder and trap-door posed a very difficult obstacle indeed.

Keeping warily to the wall, we walked over and looked up

214

the ladder. The trap-door was shut. "Now what?" I said disappointedly. "We might be able to climb this ladder with our hook and string but we'll never push open that trap-door."

Ramey looked around the room for other options. There was a window on each opposing wall, but they were closed and would be of no use. The room was unfinished; no covering over studs or joists. A naked light bulb hung in the middle of the ceiling with faded-white Romex wire trailing from the ceramic socket across a joist, then down a stud to a light switch near the door. There was another Romex wire going up the side of the same stud, disappearing through a hole in the top plate, presumably to provide power to the third floor.

Ramey walked back to the door and looked up, tracking the wire to the point where it disappeared eight feet overhead. "Hey guys, c'mere. I see something."

Evon and I hustled over. Anxiety was building in us—we were so close to the end of our search for the Red Rocket. At least, so we were hoping.

"I can't tell for sure, its pretty dark up there, but see this Romex, the one starting at the light switch. It goes up the stud then disappears through that hole in the top plate. A hole, guys—get it? A way through the third floor."

Without so much as a "Yep," Evon sprang into action. In the blink of an eye, he jumped onto the stud and scaled it. A moment later he was in the shadows of its upper reaches. Then, just that quickly, he descended and was standing next to us again, breathing heavily.

"Ithink… thismight… justmight… work, boys. Handme… yourhook."

"Okay," Collin said. "But remember Evon, the string is only about four feet long."

"Yes…yesIknow. We'll… haveto… dothisin… stages… twostages. Andit's… goingtobe… dangerous… abit risky."

Chapter Thirty-Three

Evon grabbed the hook in his teeth and rescaled the stud, though this time stopping at the light switch. He found a hole in the top of the electrical box where the switch's wire protruded, and hung one prong of the hook from its edge. Then he tossed the string down. It reached us easily.

I looked up the string. This would be a challenge. It was four feet straight up, with no chance to rest or pause. If anything happened, the climber would be in trouble. What was most worrisome, though, were our hands. The string was fishing string—smooth and bare. Would our hands have the strength for this? What if one of us slipped? He'd slide back down, being rope-burned all the way. The string could easily cut into the flesh of our hands if that happened. But there was no other option. "I'll go first," I said grimly, stepping forward, grabbing the string.

Ramey, who was still a little woozy from his earlier fall, didn't argue.

Hand over hand I pulled myself up. I wrapped my feet and legs around the string, also using them to help push. I made good progress until I was about three-quarters of the way up. Then my fingers started getting tired and sore. The string felt like it was cutting in. I paused for just a moment and looked down. Mistake. Suddenly my fear of heights kicked in and a small wave of vertigo washed over me. It was so far down, a free fall right now would probably be fatal. *Got to keep going.* Slowly I continued, putting one hand above the other, pushing off as much as I could with my legs. Now my shoulders were aching and so were my forearms. *Only a few more inches.* I made it to the bottom of the electrical box. I looked up and saw that Evon was laying on it, his paw extended over the edge waiting to grab me. *Got… to… keep… going…*

As I scaled the side of the box, I noted a few small dings and dents in the metal. *Footholds—handholds… yes!* I scaled the final few inches, grabbed Evon's paw and levered myself over the edge. Onto the top I plopped, exhausted, gasping for breath.

"Iwasn'tsure… youlooked… so tired… Iwas… worriedthatlast… foot… ifyouweregoing… tomake it. Whew!"

"Yeah, that was tough. But now Ramey's got to do it. And not only that, when he gets up here, we're still only halfway. Hey, wait, I've got an idea that may make it a little easier."

Ramey was staring up at us, a tremendously worried expression on his face. His earlier fall had him spooked.

"Ramey," I called out. "Wait a sec. I'm going to try something."

I hauled the string back up. Finding its midpoint, I made a loop and tied it off with a knot. "A foothold—a place to rest," I said to Evon, who was looking on with great interest. Then I dropped the string back down. Having been shortened a couple inches, it now barely reached Ramey's outstretched hands—but it reached.

Ramey looked at the loop and smiled. He knew exactly what it was for and was glad for my ingenuity. He stepped forward and climbed to the loop with ease. He rested a minute then made the remainder of the climb with very little difficulty. Now we were all together again contemplating the next phase.

"Theonly… thingI'm… notsure of… is whetherornot… youboys… you… fatsos… will fit throughthe… hole… atthetop. Icanmake… it… noproblem. Butyou… especiallyyou… Collin… Ican't tell."

"Great," I groaned. "Not only are my hands killing me, I may not even fit when I get there. I'd give anything right now for some axle grease and a pair of gloves."

I turned my hands out for Evon and Ramey to see. There was a fine pink line across my palms where the string had cut in. There was no blood yet, but the skin was so thin, I had little doubt the next climb would produce some. Ramey looked at his own hands and was relieved to see he wasn't in as bad a shape.

"Collin, I'll go first this time," he said solemnly. "My hands don't look as likely to bleed, and blood on the string could be disastrous, if you know what I mean. Evon, are you ready to move the hook up?"

Evon nodded, gripped the hook in his teeth and scaled the splintery stud into the shadows above. A few grunts and skritching noises followed, then the string swayed into place and hung there, its bottom end resting on the metal switch box. "Here I go," Ramey said, grabbing the line. A few minutes later he disappeared from view into the dark shadows above.

"It's a tight fit, but I think you can make it," Ramey called down. "Evon and I are both on the third floor and its cool!"

"Okay, here I go." Struggling to keep my mind from the consequences of failure, I gripped the string. Immediately pain shot through my hands as the string fell precisely into the sensitive ruts it had cut moments before.

Chapter Thirty-Four

Tight Squeeze

I adjusted the string a little so as to use different parts of my hands. *Better. Now, get on with it.*

Slowly, I ascended, hand over hand, carefully placing the string in the good parts of my palms. *Say, this isn't so bad—almost to the loop—halfway.*

When I got to the loop, I put a foot into it, stood up straight and rested. Now I looked down. *Geeze, I feel like spider-man up here. It sure is a long way. If I fell, I'd be...*

I tried not to finish that grisly thought. After a couple minutes of hanging in mid air, my heavy breathing causing me to sway slightly, I gritted my teeth and resumed climbing. "Here I come, guys," I hollered up. "Wish me luck!"

"Good luck, Collin!" came the echo from above.

Up, up, I climbed. Again my arms, shoulders, and fingers ached, but so far, I'd managed to keep the string out of the ruts in my hands. *This is it—do or die time. There's no turning around now—only a few... more... inches...*

Now I could see the final challenge. The Romex wire I'd been paralleling bent horizontally at the top of the stud then jutted several inches sideways before bending upward again into the hole in the top plate. The hole, by itself, would have been plenty big for me to fit through. But, unfortunately, I had to share it with the fat strand of Romex, too. *Well, if Ramey made it, so can I. Once I get my shoulders in, I can wedge myself and, hopefully, worm on through. By then Ramey and Evon can grab my hands and pull, too. Just another half inch, and...*

But then, disaster struck.

I was thinking so much about how to fit through the hole, I forgot to pay attention to my handholds. The string came to rest in the pink rut of my right hand just as I applied force. *Slice*. It bit in, cutting through the last protective layers of epidermis. Blood seeped from the wound.

"Owwww!" I screeched, jerking my stricken hand backward. Suddenly, my left hand was all that was holding my weight, but it was too tired and weak for the task. *Slip!* It too failed. I felt myself falling, unfurling—my head swinging a downward arc.

Oh, my gosh—what have I done! Adrenaline blasted my heart. *This is it—I'm dead. In one second my brains will be spattered all over the floor...* I closed my eyes and tensed, waiting for the life-extinguishing blow.

The thing that saved me was my foot—my left foot. Fortunately, just before that fatefully bad grip, I had wedged my left boot in a small triangular gap between the Romex and the top plate. When my hands failed, my body fell, but my boot jammed in and twisted, locking it in place, I was now dangling upside down—from one leg.

Gunner the cat suddenly pricked up his ears. *What was that?* he thought. *It was high pitched and squeaky—coming from upstairs.* Standing up from his napping spot on top of the dusty extra refrigerator in the corner of the pumphouse's lowest level, he stretched his arms, then his back, then his claws, and wondered, *Could that have been a mouse? Odd, if so. It would be most unusual for mice to be stirring at this hour in broad daylight. Better go investigate, just to be sure.*

He jumped lightly from the refrigerator to the window sill, then to the floor. Out the door he quickly trotted, across the concrete walkway, and under the stairs to his well-used path between the garage and pumphouse. The path led to a great old maple tree in the back yard, some twenty feet from the two buildings.

Now that Gunner was getting up in years, it was becoming more difficult for him to climb the thirty-five feet up the maple's trunk in order to slink his way out one particular branch that reached across the south face of the pumphouse just below the broken gable vent. He would then jump about two feet through the air, aiming his body perfectly to fit through the missing spokes of the vent. The slightest mishap would certainly result in disaster—lethal disaster. But he had made this trip hundreds of times and was very good at each dodgy aspect of it despite his age. And, it almost always yielded booty—a meal of some sort.

"Collin, COLLIN!" Ramey yelled down through the hole in the floor. "Are you all right?! I can't see you…" He had just been ready to grab my hand when instead he witnessed the disastrous mishap through the tunnel-vision of the one-inch hole.

I finally opened my eyes and looked around. *Upside-down? Everything is upside-down and there is tremendous pressure on my left ankle. What the…? Am I dead? I can hear Ramey calling, but he sounds so far away.* I looked at my trapped foot and the realization of what had just happened sunk in. "I'm here, Ramey! I'm hanging from the electrical wire!"

"Okay… my gosh, Collin, I—we thought you were a goner! Can you reach the string again?"

Already I was calculating a plan. *No one can help me now— but me.* I looked down to the wood floor eight feet below. Vertigo slammed me. *One slip now and it's all over.* I tried to crunch up and grab the cord, but was too tired and weak. *No good. And I can't reach the fishing string either. I've got to try again and somehow grab the Romex. If I can do that, maybe I can hang from it and shimmy my way to the hole. Need to swing a little—get some momentum…*

Using my arms like pendulums, I got myself swaying. *One… two… three!* I thrust as hard as I could, jerking my arms up like a trapeze aerialist.

Slip!

My boot! As my body rotated, my left foot aligned itself to back out of its wedge and in one heart-stopping moment, gave way. But luckily, not all the way. I groped wildly for the cord. *Clamp!* My arms grasped it, just as my boot came free. *Swoosh!* My legs fell toward the earth.

But I felt it coming and was ready. With both arms encircling the cord like a vise, I let my body rotate down. Then just at the furthest point in the arc, I reversed momentum, thrusting forward with all my might. Now my torso and legs came snapping back up and I clamped both feet around the cord. *Yes! Got it!*

Without wasting a second, I inched, upside down like a sloth, along the cord. My cut hand stung like fire, but there was no time to even consider that. Like a wounded soldier, I blinked back dizziness and pain and dragged myself forward. In a few heartbeats I was at the hole. I stuck my head and shoulders in, following the cord around the edge.

Up above, Ramey, refusing to believe the worst, positioned himself over the hole, face-down, his head and arms poised to grab me should I somehow get there. Suddenly a patch of brown hair, then a forehead, then two fiercely determined eyes skirted into view. "Collin!" he shouted, joy and relief bubbling through his voice. "You're alive—you made it! Here, give me your hands, I'll pull you up."

I thrust one hand up and Ramey gripped it—hard. There was no way he was letting go.

Now I shimmied the upper half of my body into the hole and with a little squirming and grunting and a lot of pulling and levering, I finally emerged topside. With a gigantic sigh of relief, I rolled over, sucking for wind. Immediately Ramey and Evon pounced with pats on the back, "Way to go's", and questions as to what had happened.

How good it felt simply to be alive! I smiled, telling them all they wanted to know.

Meanwhile, Gunner was just approaching the trunk of the giant maple tree. He stopped short and cocked his head slightly, listening. *No doubt about it this time. There is definitely activity up there!* Licking his chops, he quickened his pace. In two bounds he was on the trunk, scaling hastily upward.

Still lying on the floor, I looked up to the ceiling. Aside from Ramey and Evon's grinning faces, I saw roof rafters. No ceiling, just open space from floor to the corrugated metal roofing. *Interesting. No ceiling. That means there's no attic. Then, if this is where the raven's lair is... where does he stay? Where's his nest?*

Looking about further, I saw that nearly the entire floor space was occupied by a huge galvanized metal water tank. There was just enough space between it and the walls for a man to walk. In the corner, leaning against the top of the tank, was also an old, hand-made ladder.

The tank had a lid, of sorts, consisting of boards, unevenly spaced and warped. From my vantage point I could only see their jagged ends extending several inches over the tank's edge. *Aha! If there's a nest up here, it's got to be on top of the tank, on those boards.* Suddenly the desire to complete our quest—to find the wagon and reclaim it—took over. *Forget my cut hand and any further congratulations. We are too close now to dawdle another minute.*

"Collin, you sure you're okay?" Ramey asked for the umpteenth time. "What about your hand, it's ... "

"Yep! I'm fine," I cut in, springing to my feet. Ramey and Evon jumped back, startled.

"Yes, there's a cut on my hand, but it's not too bad. My ankle is a tad sore, but it'll be fine. I tell you guys, I'm tired of messing around. I bet the Red Rocket is up there and we need to get it—right now!"

"Ww... well, okay, Collin," Ramey stammered. "If you say so. What do you have in mind? I mean, how do we get up there to get it?"

"I think I've got it figured out," I replied. "Probably the only way up is that ladder in the corner there. But it's too steep for you and me, Ramey. So I say Evon goes up by himself. He can scale the ladder, get the wagon and fly it back down. Then we shoot off through the vent, in the gable, up there."

Suddenly all eyes were on Evon. He squirmed a little under the pressure then said tentatively, "Um… okay. I s'pose… that'sokay. Buttotell… youthetruth,boys, I'venever… driven… flown… thewagon."

Chapter Thirty-Five

Gunner and Tetrink

Suddenly Evon was twitching. A lot. Just like he'd done when we first saw him. He was up on his hind legs, paws to face, rubbing. His nose and whiskers were flinching and whipping around wildly. Even the whites of his eyes showed a little.

"Evon," I said. "I haven't seen you do that—that twitching, since the cave. Is everything all right?"

"Ohyes... yes, yes... everything'sfine... justfine. Itsjust... youknow... thethoughtof... flying... meflying thatdoggoned... wagon... makesme uneasy... a trifle... nervous. Yes... nervous, youknow."

"Well, can you do it? I mean, if not, then we're—Ramey and I—will have to climb the ladder using our hook and string. And that'll take for ever especially with my cut hand. And not only that, I'm assuming the raven isn't in just now but there's no telling when he'll be back. The longer we're here the greater our risk of another bad encounter—right?"

"Yes... ohyesright... mostdefinitely... correct." Evon's already rapid speech had ramped up a full notch and even his bushy tail was now thrashing violently. "Youcouldn't... be moreright, Collin."

At that instant I couldn't help thinking Evon looked a lot like the Cowardly Lion when he was forced to confront the great and powerful Wizard of Oz.

Trying my best not to grin, I said, "Okay then, it's settled. Off you go. We'll be right here. Holler if you need us and we'll get up there as fast as we can."

"Allrightthen... hereIgo." He blinked hard a few times then

turned and sprang for the ladder.

Ramey and I watched him effortlessly scale it, leap onto one of the overhanging boards and disappear. In a moment he reappeared, a smile beaming radiantly all over his face. "It's… it's…. boys, it's… "

"What? What is it?!" I yelled back, my impatience boiling over.

"It's… *here!*" he squeaked at the top of his lungs. "Thewagon… it'sup… here… alongwith… aton… ofotherjunk. Yes, it's definn… effinately… right here!"

"Well, then, go get it!"

"Yes… ofcourse… I'llget it. I'lljust… walkright… onup, climbin, andfly… away… backdown… to…"

"Evon! Go now! Right now!"

"O. K.!!!"

Again he disappeared over the edge. Ramey and I waited, hardly daring to breathe. But the next sound to reach our ears was not Evon's "Lift!" command. A sudden deep, banging commotion near the top of the wall on the other side of the tank froze my heart. There was no way Evon could make that much noise. *What the…?*

Before Ramey or I could speak, Evon's face reappeared at the top edge of the tank, shrieking at the top of his lungs, "A CAT!… it'sa… CAT… run!"

I felt my face blanch in absolute terror. *Gunner! Where can we run? Are there even any hiding places to be had?* Before any decent plan had time to materialize in my brain, Evon was standing beside us, panting ferociously and twitching so violently it looked like he might explode.

Then I heard a sound that curdled my blood. It was a hiss— so loud it made my eardrums rattle. I jerked my head up. There was Gunner, crouched at the edge of the tank's lid, his mouth open wide, back arched high, and ears pinned. His gleaming white fangs looked like daggers ready to plunge.

Without the first hint of a plan, I yelled, "Run!" and took off. We sprinted away from the ladder, around the tank. I frantically searched the walls and floor for any hiding place whatsoever—a nook, a chink, a narrow gap—anywhere large enough for us, but small enough to keep a cat's paw out. What I saw as we fled was disheartening. If the whole way around was like this, we were dead meat.

Gunner watched from above, slowly circling with us. Had he gone for the ladder right then, there is little doubt he would have had his meal. But for some reason, he opted to watch and wait—to see what these queer mice would do. He knew we could neither escape nor hide. Others of his victims had been in the same predicament, only to run chaotically until exhaustion slowed them sufficiently for an easy pounce. But today, Gunner's decision to wait would be the very thing that denied him. For at that moment, Tetrink the raven approached the pumphouse, flapping slowly, with a tawdry new treasure dangling from one claw.

With a deep, clunking commotion up above, Tetrink's huge dark shape entered, landing on top of the tank. A terrific hissing and cawing rang out immediately. Then scuffling. Then Gunner's screeching and screaming, along with more scrabbling, flapping, and scraping. We huddled in terror, covering our ears. Suddenly Gunner leapt from the top of the tank, back out through the vent, with the raven in hot pursuit.

We crouched, waiting, against the wall, our hearts hammering like drums. Two minutes, three minutes—five. Nothing.

"Evon," I finally whispered. "You've got to go back and get the wagon. I think you may as well go now, before we have any more visitors."

Poor Evon was mortally frightened. He had wedged himself into a corner, huddled into the smallest possible ball, and was shivering uncontrollably.

"Evon!" I whispered again, more urgently this time.

"You've got to go—*now!*"

Evon unfurled himself and nervously glanced around. "O... oke... okay," he stammered.

We watched him go, our own nerves jangling, praying neither Tetrink nor Gunner would choose that moment to return.

Finally, we heard the sound we'd been waiting for: a barely audible, "Lift." I held my breath, when suddenly, a red movement flashed through the air over the tank's edge. "Evon! Yes!"

Sure enough, here came Evon flying the Red Rocket! His furry little face was jerking and dodging, straining to see over the wagon's sides. His paws had a white-knuckled grip on the handle and he was bobbing and weaving erratically. Rather than bring it in for a quick landing—*zoom!* like a jet over our heads he flew! He circled the tank once, then on his second pass brought it in low, but still slightly out of control. Finally, three feet from crashing into the wall, he managed to screech, "Down," at the same time thrusting the handle forward. Obeying the commands precisely, the wagon immediately dropped to its wheels. But its forward momentum kept it rolling—directly at Ramey and me. We put our arms out to brace for the collision. *Wham!* It slammed into us with so much force it pushed us backward, skidding, across the floor toward the wall. Somehow, through gritting teeth and smoking shoe soles, we held on and the wagon stopped mere inches from the solid wood wall.

"Evon!," I shouted. "You did it—you made it! I knew you could!" Ramey and I exploded with joy and congratulations.

But Evon didn't move. He was catatonic—staring like a marble statue straight ahead, his hands still welded to the handle.

"Evon, Evon? *Evon?!*" I said, extending a hand and gently jiggling him. Suddenly he snapped out of his temporary state, shook his head a few times and said, "Ithink... Ilikeit... betterwhen... youdrive... Collin."

Ramey and I had to chuckle. Then I said, "Okay, little buddy, then let's go.

We pushed the wagon back, turned and rolled it into position for an easy takeoff. Then we hopped in and I gave the command, "Lift." The wagon responded smoothly. I eased back on the handle, circling the tank once to gain altitude, then crested the rim and made a bee-line for the vent.

As we flew over the tank, Ramey looked down at Tetrink's nest. He was shocked at the bizarre collection of junk and trinkets scattered about: foil gum wrappers; irregular pieces of cellophane; thumbtacks; arms, heads, legs, and other odd parts and pieces of dolls; dimes and nickels; marbles; keys; matchbox cars; spools of thread; beads of many colors and sizes; and much more. *Holy cow, what a junkyard! Here—you can add this to your collection.* He tossed over our hook and string. It landed in the middle of the only clear space. *Just be sure you don't sit on THAT tonight when you lay down to sleep!* Ramey chuckled to himself as I guided the Red Rocket through the gap of broken spokes and out into the bright blue sky.

Chapter Thirty-Six

Strange Flight

Whoosh! I flew straight over the Johnson's orchards then banked right, all the while gaining altitude. The house, garage, and pumphouse fell away behind us and gave way to forests and, once again, Beaver Lake. The fertile farm fields of the Tigaks Flats lay in the distance, creating a checkerboard of tans, browns, greens, and golds.

It was about noon and the sun was out. Fluffy white clouds glided lazily across an azure sky. The smell of autumn; cool, fresh, and crisp, was in the air. A brisk wind chilled our noses and tousled back our hair. How wonderful it felt to be flying! Safe, we were, for the moment at least, with the sure knowledge that in a few minutes we would again be big. Ramey and Evon kept an eagle-eye out for ravens or any other flying menace. But no intruders came.

Cruising over the toe of the mountains, I, feeling exuberant indeed, eased back on the handle. *Think I'll open 'er up a bit—test this thing's speed.* The wagon seemed more than happy to oblige. It gathered speed readily, springing forward with firm acceleration. The thrust reminded me of a speedy carnival ride. In a second the wind in my ears increased to a low howl and my hair was fluttering so violently, it stung my face and neck. A nervous shot of adrenaline coursed through me and anxiety sprang up in my brain. *Whoa, this thing really moves—almost too fast. I barely pulled the handle at all.* The Rocket's acceleration had pushed me back slightly, and as before, this made it difficult to move the handle forward again. Our speed increased.

Fear began to grip me. Something bizarre was happening. It almost felt as if the wagon now was hurtling forward of its own will—ever wanting to go faster. Scary thoughts of losing all control—the Rocket suddenly rolling and tumbling through the air, spilling us recklessly over the countryside—reeled through my head. Velocity still increased.

An eerie feeling built in my gut. It seemed we were gravitating toward something—something imperceptible, but strangely powerful, as if a force, unearthly and mysterious, was sucking us forward.

Faster yet we zoomed. Through either fear or the constant backward acceleration, I was frozen; for the moment unable to react. A strange sensation came over me—a sort of tingling, and at the same time small dots and flashes of light encircled my field of vision. Though we were now a bullet-streak across the sky, strangely, the wind in my face and ears suddenly went dead. And then, in an instant, distant trees, farm fields, houses, barns, everything blurred and became smaller…and smaller. It felt like the earth was stretching away from me—as if I were entering some bizarre, invisible passageway in the sky.

Mustering all my strength and will, I thrust forward on the handle. Instantly the wagon slowed and lost altitude, and the weird sensation abated. The wind again rushed over my face and objects in the distance locked back into sharp focus.

"What was that?" I shouted over my shoulder. "Did you guys feel—see that?"

"Whoa, yes, and I didn't like it," Ramey replied, a worried edge to his voice. "But it seemed to stop when you slowed down. Maybe we should just take it easy until we have this thing all the way figured out."

"Yeah. I'll ease up—just cruise."

Evon didn't say anything but he, too, sensed it and it unnerved him. He'd witnessed enough of Peter's magic to know how unpredictable it could be. But what he'd just experienced was way beyond anything he'd ever felt or witnessed in the past. This was overpoweringly strong—unfathomable—supernatural. Did Peter even comprend the magnitude of this creation? Evon kept these troubling thoughts to himself. *No need to rattle the boys,* he thought, *especially after what they've just been through.*

I made a mental note and tucked it away in a particular corner of my brain with all the other little tricks and nuances about the Red Rocket. How could I have known that we were within a few scant miles per hour of discovering an astonishing new piece of the Red Rocket's sensational power? Peter Kringle had designed it to fly and shrink, but it could do more—much, much more.

There were no more surprises or mishaps for the remainder of our flight. Now flying at a much relaxed pace, within a few minutes the first buildings on the outskirts of Furry-Pine sprang up before us.

Evon broke the silence as we began our descent toward the center of town. "Okay... okaynowboys... we havetoland... this contraption... andgetinto... enterthe building...withoutbeingseen... or heard. Bytheway... beforeour... tripbackto... towngot... waylaid... interrupted, Imeantto... say sorry... I'm... realsorryabout... your folks. Whenwe... sawthem... inthebarnyard... Icould...tellforsure... definitely... theyreally... really love... youguys."

Genuine sorrow permeated Evon's voice. He understood only too well the heartache of separating from one's parents. His own mother and father had abandoned him when he was but a small child.

The memory of my mom and dad rushing around, looking in vain for us came flooding back. "Thanks for caring, Evon," I said. "I know you're right, our parents do love us. It's just, lately they've had a hard time showing it. I can't even remember the last time my dad gave Ramey or me a hug."

"Well, justbehappy... behappy you've... gotparents. Notallboys... no... certainlynotall... childreneven... have a

momanddad. Trynotto... pleasedon't... worrytoomuch.
Oncewetakecareof... getridof... well, completeour mission... you
boyswill have... allthemoney... you need tohelpyourmom... and
dad. Then... won'tthey... both...bepleasedwith... you! So... let's
getonwith... it. Now, weshouldfly... land aroundback...
aroundinthe... alley. This way."

We were cruising over Metcalf Street, twenty or so feet
above the tallest buildings. Metcalf, the main street, was lined
mostly with brick and board, three-story-high, old-west looking
structures. A few people were milling around below, but of course
none had the faintest idea there was a pint-sized adventure party
plying the airspace above them. Evon pointed to a planter-box-lined
walkway between Kringle's and a brick building next door. I swung
down into the walkway, then turned right into the back alley and
began looking for a secure landing spot.

"There... set'erdown... over there," Evon piped.

He was pointing to an ivy-covered trellis extending from the
orange-red clay brick wall which was the back of Kringle's shop.
The trellis formed a small alcove veiled on three sides providing a
semi-private means of access to the back door. I swung the wagon
into the alcove and gave the command, "Stop."

Of course, this had no effect because it was the wrong
command. The wagon continued forward and plowed into the trellis.
Wham! It struck a vine and all three of us tumbled headlong into the
ivy. *Ooof! Ooofffff! Clang!*

We fell into a human-squirrel dog-pile, the wagon coming
down last and clonking me squarely on the top of my head.

"Owww!"

"That's what you get, you nincompoop!" growled Ramey.
"Can't you remember the command is 'DOWN'?"

"Sorry about that, guys." I picked myself from the dog-pile,
and brushing off, noticed a crumpled brown ball of fur still lying on
the concrete. "Unh oh—Evon, are you okay?"

Poor Evon, being in the front of the wagon, had been discharged first, so had landed at the bottom of the stack. His small frame was certainly not made for such abuse. He levered himself up, checking for broken bones. Finding none, he scolded, "I'mwith… countmeinwith… Ramey. Thatwassure… mostdefinitely a… bone… a knuckleheaded move… Collin! Luckywedidn't… hurt… killourselves! Nowlet'sget… bigagain… andgo on inside… beforesomeone… hears… seesus."

The wagon, fortunately, was fine. My head had cushioned its fall. We piled back in, then I gave the command, "Grow." *Pop!* The wagon and its contents instantly transformed to normal size. "Phew!" I exclaimed. "That sure feels good!"

Ramey and Evon checked themselves to be sure all their parts and pieces were accounted for and in the right places at the right proportions. "Yep!" Ramey finally said. "It's all here. Evon, is the door locked?"

"Yes… yesit is. But, there'sakey… hidden… underthedoor… underthe door mat."

Ramey lifted the mat and retrieved the key. I touched the wagon's handle and gave the command, "Shrink." Instantly it popped back to its small size and I placed it in my front pants pocket.

Ramey slid the key into the lock and twisted. *Click.* The door opened with almost no effort, though it creaked noisily. We entered and crept slowly and quietly down a narrow hallway that had several closed doors on either side. There was a musty smell and a thick covering of dust everywhere.

I almost felt like a burglar. A surge of adrenaline quickened my pulse. *Will someone see us? How many other children only dream of being where we are right now?* With each softly placed step, my heart beat a little quicker. At the end of the hallway there was a short, louvered, two-way swinging door. Beyond it I could see… *the toyshop!*

Chapter Thirty-Seven

The Toyshop

My eyes grew large as I headed for the door and the toyshop beyond. It almost felt as if the mystical place was drawing me forward. I could see the potbelly stove's black tin stack, the airplanes and the model train clearly above the top of the doors. Nothing was moving, of course—all the fascinating apparatus and mechanisms were eerily silent, like Sleeping Beauty's spellbound castle. *Wow! Kringle's famous toyshop, right here, just footsteps away!*

But before my hand touched the door to open it, I was stopped in my tracks by Evon.

"NO!... nonono... " he hissed as loudly as he dared without it being a shout. "Youcan'tgointhere... notnow... yet... anyway. Areyou... crazy... outofyour... mind? Youwouldbe... someone walking past wouldseeyou... forsure. Wecan't... mustn'tgothat... way. Follow... comewithme."

I knew he was right. Even though I wanted like crazy to continue straight, I turned and followed him and Ramey to the last door on the left before the end of the hallway. Evon sat on his hind legs at the door as Ramey and I waited for him to open it.

"Well," I finally said after a few seconds. "Aren't you going in?"

"Yes... yesofcouse... I'mgoing in. ButIcan'treach... I'mnottall... enoughto... toreach the doorknob. Won'tyou... pleasehelpme... open it."

I felt pretty silly not intuitively knowing this, so quickly I shot my hand forward and turned the knob. The door opened into a dark, downward stairwell. The first few steps were illuminated by the light of the hallway, but beyond that was pitch black. The stale smell of an old kitchen mixed with other aromas: paints, heating oil, wood, and more, wafted out.

"Pullthe… string… thelightswitch… stringto… your left."

I gave the fly-speckled string dangling near my head a tug and light emanated from the depths. "Follow… followme," Evon said cheerfully, bounding down the stairs.

At the bottom of the L-shaped staircase one look around told me this basement served many functions.

"Thisiswhere… thisismy… place!" Evon chirped with enthusiasm. "Peterlives… hisroomis… upstairs… mineisdown… here. Whatdoyou… boys… think? I hope… trustthatyoulike… it, because… thisiswhere… you'lllivetoo… where you'llbe… staying… foralittlewhile."

My initial impression was not at all in line with Evon's excitement. The basement was one huge open space, probably 5,000 square feet or more, but almost every inch of floor was occupied with something. There were boxes, crates, and antique wooden trunks stacked to the ceiling. Over much of the middle were spare wooden toy parts and pieces on oak racks and shelves: doll arms and heads, chess pieces, castle turrets, wheels, axles, and so on. There was a section devoted entirely to paints. Shelves and shelves of them—large cans and small, perhaps a thousand in all. Most had been previously opened; bright colors of every hue, now dry, in dribbles down the sides.

Way in the back was the sooty, cast-iron boiler with its myriad pipes, gauges, and valves. It sat there like a massive, dead robot, patiently waiting for someone to flip its switch. Against another wall was a long workbench littered with dusty tools and half-finished projects. And nestled right in the middle of it all was a studio apartment—of sorts.

By winding around the boxes at the base of the stairs to the left, then right, then left again, you would come to a small bed and a dresser. There was also a stand-alone sink and a stove toward one side—a makeshift kitchen. A few sturdy wooden fruit crates, with the colorful brand-name stickers still visible, were arranged between the dresser and stove to form a dining table and chairs. I wondered where the restroom was but thought better than to ask—at least not now.

Looking over the expansive and cluttered basement, I thought, *On one hand it's kind of interesting down here, but on the other it's a little spooky. The way all this stuff is cluttered around, a kid could easily get lost. The walkways branch out all over the place, almost like tunnels, and most are dead ends. It's like a rat's maze. There aren't even any windows. But, at least there're a lot of light bulbs.*

Indeed, many ceramic light sockets dotted the naked ceiling boards, though most were dim with age and dust. Frayed electrical wires drooped between them causing me to wonder whether the place might go up in an electrical fireball at any second.

"Well… whatdoyou… whatdoyou… think?" Evon chirped, obviously excited to be home again. "Pretty… prettyneat, huh?"

"Neat" was not the adjective I would have chosen but I didn't want to disappoint him. So I responded with the most appropriate, non-insulting word I could think of. "Yeah, Evon, it's—um, well it's… *busy.*"

"Gladyou… happyyoulikeit! Well, whydon't we… go onin… andhave… whipup some… lunch."

He hopped off the steps and scampered through the maze to his kitchen. "Howaboutsome… porkandbeans? Youboys like… porkandbeans… don't you?"

Our breakfast of nuts and fruit had long ago worn off, so anything sounded good. "I'm so hungry, I wouldn't mind pork and *brains* right now!" exclaimed Ramey.

"Good… goodgood… nicetosee… gladyou'vegot… your appetite. And,mymost… excellentyoung… friend… MisterRamey, you're inluck! I think I might... mayhavesome... cannedhog brains... and snouts... way intheback... ofthat... thatcupboard... overthere."

Ramey shot me a quick glance and I gulped hard. *Hog snouts and brains?*

"Just... onlykidding... you two! Cheche!... Youlookedlike... like you'dseena... ghost... for a secondthere. Don'tworry... youwon'tfind... anybrains in the... cupboard. Butyoumight... comeacrosss... findacan... offruitcocktail... for... dessert."

The look of relief on the Ramey's face was palpable. This basement was scary enough without having to worry about weird food.

We ate a hearty lunch. I prepared it since I was the only one tall enough to reach things and strong enough to operate the old-fashioned can opener. Then we tidied up and sat back on the fruit crate chairs to consider our next course of action.

"Well, nowthatyou... boyshavea... place... a home base... we'vegotto... mustgetdown to business." Evon's light-hearted demeanor was giving way to bonafide seriousness. "We'rerunningout... running outoftime... actually. Yousee... neitherPeter nor Torry... hasmuchtime left... before... before Malcrook... beforethey're... well, inthemines... disastercan... strikeatany... time. We'vegotto... infiltrate... andrescue them... somehow...andquick."

Up to that moment, I was just beginning to relax. Evon's last comment, however, cut my respite short. Now my mind switched back to the dangerous job ahead.

For the first time, it occurred to me that Evon's goals and ours were somewhat different. *Wait a minute,* I thought. *We're not here to rescue people, just to find the Dark Quartz Mine and get a little gold. We don't even need much—a handful or two should do it. Might only take one quick trip in and out. But rescuing people—*

that's a whole different story. A dangerous one at that.

"Um, Evon," I remarked. "I don't mean to seem rude, but Ramey and I, um… well, we didn't plan on rescuing anyone. We just want to find the Dark Quartz Mine and get some gold."

I knew instantly my comment did not go over well with Evon. He turned, narrowed his eyebrows and shot me a steely glare. The basement fell deathly silent.

I squirmed uneasily. Finally Evon spoke. "Nowlisten… webothwant… need something. The onlywaywe're… goingtoget… whatwe… needisto… work… worktogether. Youcan't…won'tlivetwo… minutes… in thetunnels… without… me. TheTommyknockers… or worse… Malcrookwillhave… you beforeyoucan… say… goldnugget. Andif… when… thathappens… you'redead… dead meat. Ontheotherhand… Ican'trescue… save… mymaster… withoutyou. I… needhelp… andyou're… myonly…hope. I'vewaited… nearlysix longyears… forsomeone… tocomealong… whocanhelp… me… and youtwoboys… arethe ones. Theonly… ones. Weneed… musthave… eachother. Together… we're a force… tobereckoned… with. Apart… we're… nothing. Iknow I… haven'treally… toldyouthis… yet… butI *really… really… need you.*"

Although our intentions were divergent, I understood the wisdom in Evon's words. I hadn't fully considered being captured—of the horrible consequences that went along with it. Also, Ramey and I *didn't* really know the first thing about the cave or tunnels or Tommyknockers for that matter. And who really was this Malcrook?

You could have heard a pin drop as I wrestled with my thoughts. *Do we help Evon rescue Torry and Peter—risk our necks for a couple of total strangers? Or go for the gold alone?* The boxes and crates seemed to press inward, adding pressure to the already thick air. For the first time since we'd met, I noticed Evon was not moving a muscle—not even a slight twitch of the paw or nose. His

240

attention was focused on me like a lighthouse beacon. The ball was in my court and my next play was crucial.

After several tense moments, I came to my conclusion. *Evon is right. We must join forces if we're to even have a hope of being successful. Malcrook's underground world is simply too foreign and too dangerous to go alone.* One reassuring nod from Ramey told me that he was thinking the same thing.

"Okay, you're right, Evon," I said. "We're in. And actually, I kind of feel bad for thinking otherwise, but I was so bent on helping my mom, I just got, well—maybe I got a little selfish. Sorry. Ramey and I, we're with you—with you all the way. Right Ramey?

"Right."

"Just like the Three Musketeers," I continued. "One for all, and all for one!"

The look of relief and gladness on Evon's face radiated like a full moon. "Yes!" he squeaked, erupting into a full-body twitching spasm.

I stood, walked over to him, called for Ramey, and extended my hand, palm down. "Put your hand, er, paw on mine, Evon; and Ramey, put yours on Evon's. This will be the signal of our pact. Any time we're in doubt or trouble, remember our hands cemented together and this saying: Our Team of Three—Will Succeed!"

Two hands and a paw came together like a fur sandwich and each voice repeated our new pact, "Our Team of Three—Will Succeed!" We looked at each other with grim smiles. I wondered just what the consequences of this new bond might be. Maybe we would succeed, maybe not, but whatever the outcome, we were in it together.

"Thank… thankyou," said Evon. "Now, weneed… musthave… a plan. Butbeforethat… there're afewcritical… someimportantthings… you needtounderstand… mustknow. Gatherround… fellas… I'vegota… story… ataleto tell… you."

Chapter Thirty-Seven

We scooted our crates closely around the small table. With twilight's shadows lengthening outside the basement's brick walls, Evon told us the wondrous but frightening *true* story of Malcrook the Dark Quartz Mine.

Chapter Thirty-Eight

Malcrook

It was well over a century ago, when Furry-Pine was little more than a main street of dirt and a few log buildings, that a scraggly, gray-haired loner wandered into town. He looked to be a prospector, judging by the gold pans, picks, and shovels dangling and clanking from his burro. Of course, there were many other prospectors in those days, so no one gave him much notice. But the few people who had any dealings with this man quickly learned that he was extraordinarily mean. He called himself Malcrook—no first name, just Malcrook. Locals recounted that he was so cruel and stingy, even to his own animals, one day his burro and flea-bitten dog both up and left him.

Nobody knew where he stayed. He would come to town only occasionally for supplies. And he always paid with gold, pure gold.

Malcrook was by trade a geologist. His journey to Furry-Pine had started in his home state of North Carolina. He owned a consulting business there for many years, but ultimately became so impatient and angry with his ever-pestering clients that he sold the business. He was never married, had few, if any, real friends, and was essentially unhappy. He decided that his problems could be solved if he were to become rich. And being a geologist, finding gold seemed the most logical means to that end.

So for many sleepless nights he studied his geological maps and textbooks, searching, probing to determine the most probable place to find gold—where no one else had yet uncovered it. Ultimately he chose the area of Furry-Pine, Washington, bought himself a burro, lured a mongrel dog to join him, and struck out on foot.

It was an arduous journey. He braved fierce snowstorms, was perpetually wet and miserable, climbed up and down mountains where no trails existed, swam raging rivers, and ate whatever he could gather or catch. Once, while wading across a seemingly placid stream, a flash-flood came thundering down and washed away all his provisions and supplies—and nearly his burro and dog, too. He escaped death only by clinging to a fortuitously positioned low-hanging willow branch.

A few kind souls along the way offered him help, but his mean disposition offended or alienated every one of them. He drove his burro so hard it nearly died, and he meted out food so stingily, both animals soon became creaking bone bags. He prospected and panned for gold along the way with just enough success to purchase the supplies he could not gather, catch, or trap.

Finally he made it to Furry-Pine and began panning the outlying creeks. At first his success was very limited indeed. But one day he found a particular creek which yielded a few yellow flakes. He panned his way upstream, finding more and more gold. Before long, he came to a magnificent waterfall. At the edge of the splash pool, he found some nuggets. "Eureka!" he cried.

Though it was difficult, he discovered a way around the waterfall and continued his search upstream. More and more yellow flakes swirled in his pan! Further on he went, until the gold petered out—which, in fact, was exactly what he expected. He knew this gold had washed there from a rich vein somewhere in the creek's walls. He reasoned the point where he stopped finding flakes would be very near the vein itself.

Redirecting his hunt from the creek bed to the broken rock of the creek's steep canyon, for days and weeks he chipped away with his miner's axe searching, searching.

Then, finally he found it—the very thing for which he'd traveled three thousand miles. On this particular day, he had chopped his way through a grimy cluster of maple roots to get at what appeared to be a vein—a quartz vein. At first he couldn't tell if the darkish, fractured layer was quartz at all because there was such shadow in this deep cleft of the gorge. As he chipped away, though, it occurred to him that this unusual looking, murky mineral could perhaps be what miners called 'dark quartz': shadowy, vaguely translucent gray crystals, in contrast to the bright, clear-whitish quartz so common in textbooks and museums. After a few more blows with his mining axe, several bright yellow nuggets abruptly fell from the pulverized rock. Suddenly Malcrook was trembling. He bent down, picked up one of the gleaming, pea-sized chunks and bit it. His teeth sunk in a little; the nugget did not shatter. *Yes! Gold!* Jubilation coursed through every artery and muscle. This was it— his mother lode! And, it was all *his*—no one else had even the first inkling it existed!

Suddenly, gold nuggets were literally falling from the side of the mountain into his small leather pouch. He dubbed his find *The Dark Quartz Mine*. Within a few days, he'd excavated a small tunnel and had several pounds of pure gold. It was easily enough for him to retire on and be wealthy for the rest of his days.

But, that is not the nature of gold. No, if you are inclined to greed, once you have a bit of gold, you always lust for more. And once you have more, you need yet more. And so it goes—forever. A person of the highest moral fiber might possibly avoid gold's potent infection, but that characteristic could not have been further from describing Malcrook. He was probably the greediest, not to mention cruelest, most callous, despicable human on the face of the earth. As easily as slipping on a banana peel, he fell headlong into gold's relentless grip. To make matters worse, his disposition became even more unbearable with every new nugget. Suddenly, now he was filthy rich, which he took to mean that he was better than everyone else. His gold mine became his single-minded obsession and soon he viewed himself the most powerful person alive.

Malcrook made more and more trips to town to spend his newfound wealth. He was buying anything and everything he'd ever wanted: fancy clothes, gold watches, snakeskin shoes, the finest cigars, and guns—lots of guns: shotguns, rifles, revolvers, pistols, even a few small cannons. He had more firearms and ammunition than he could possibly shoot in a hundred years.

All of this, of course, did not go unnoticed by the townsfolk, especially since he always paid with gold.

A few of the less desirables around Furry-Pine tried to befriend the suddenly rich Malcrook with thinly veiled overtures of flattery. Of course, Malcrook wouldn't trust his own dog, let alone another human, so none of the ingratiating suitors succeeded. But one shifty fellow did get Malcrook to brag over one too many whisky shots at the Button Ram Tavern, that he had discovered a rich vein he called the Dark Quartz Mine.

That was all it took. Rumors of Malcrook's find, embellished with every new telling, swept through the town and through neighboring towns like wildfire. Now every whisky-soaked saloon and speakeasy in the county was abuzz with talk of the Dark Quartz Mine. People ran to hardware stores and bought up every pick, pan, and rocker slough on the shelves. Then they hauled these tools and other belongings up the mountain to stake their own claims. But when they got to the waterfall they met with a surprise. Malcrook, ever cunning and crafty, was expecting them. He had put up razor-sharp barbed wire fences everywhere, and signs that read,

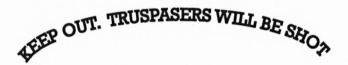

KEEP OUT. TRUSPASERS WILL BE SHOT

Though his spelling was suspect, his intentions were not. Indeed, he had already staked government claims encompassing nearly the entire mountainside. He'd also purchased as much land surrounding his mine as he could. Only a few stubborn homesteaders would not sell. So, by and large, he was lawfully entitled to his fences and his signs.

But when gold and greed come together, neither fences nor signs will keep some people away. A few foolhardy souls clipped the barbed wire and ventured forth. Most were never seen nor heard from again.

One unfortunate wretch, a homeless man with only two teeth, managed to sneak his way into the mine. He was one of the lucky ones—he made it back alive. But *lucky* can be a subjective term. It was speculated that Malcrook allowed him to escape as evidence of what might happen to trespassers. This poor man came straggling back to town, limping and mumbling. He was missing three fingers and part of his left hand. For several days, he would do nothing but mumble and cower, as if being assaulted by imaginary demons. Finally, he regained a small bit of sanity and told horrifying tales of being captured and tortured; of dungeons and small mean people called Tommyknockers; and of a mysterious liquid he called *yecrim*. A few days later, he lapsed back into a state of dementia and was taken, twitching and incoherent, into custody at the State Mental Institution.

The townsfolk were shocked—torn between horror and rage. But Malcrook's ploy worked. No one was motivated to action. In fact, just the opposite occurred. Not even the sheriff would intercede. "Got no proof o' no law-breaking. Every man's entitled to his own property—even ol' Malcrook," was his stock response. The gold rush was snuffed out nearly as quickly as it had started.

But now, when Malcrook came to town, people shunned him. They were openly frightened of him. Shop keepers served him, but without conversation. People avoided eye contact. Women would duck into alleys and side streets to avoid passing him by. Malcrook had assumed that finding wealth would bring happiness but it did not. It seemed just the opposite. Now, with more money than he could spend in several lifetimes, he was more miserable than ever. He couldn't trust anyone—they were only interested in his gold. He had to resort to dastardly means to protect what was his. He knew that people would steal from him at their first opportunity. He even started to fear for his own safety. Townsfolk glared at him angrily, clenching their fists. One growl and a sneer was all it usually took to turn them away, but he came to realize it was just a matter of time before someone would muster the courage to take a potshot.

Gradually, his trips to town became fewer and fewer. Over the course of several years, he reduced his visits from several a week, to one or two a year. How was he surviving? What was he doing for food? The locals wondered, but none ventured up the mountain to find out. Soon, the town returned to normal and the Dark Quartz Mine faded away to local legend.

Chapter Thirty-Nine

The Mine

Ramey and I were on the edge of our crate-chairs. So many questions now swirled in our minds. Ramey couldn't restrain himself and asked, "So, it *is* true about Malcrook and the Dark Quartz Mine? I knew it—I just knew it! But what about the kids? You know, the boys who work his mine? Is it true about them too? And how does he capture... er, kidnap them?"

Welllwasn't sureifyou... wereupto... wantedto... hearanymore. Butbythelook... onyour... facesIguess... Isuppose you do. Okay... that'sfinewithme. ButI'vegot... needto... warn you. Thisnextpart... ofthestory... isalittle... frightening, gruesome... scary. Areyyousure... youwant... meto... go on?"

"Sure as shootin'," quipped Ramey.

"I do, too," I said evenly. "If there's any chance we'll run into Malcrook, we should have an idea of what we'll be up against. Please continue."

And so Evon did, and this is the rest of his tale.

The townsfolk left Malcrook alone and over the years the Dark Quartz Mine was all but forgotten. But Malcrook was not idle. He continued mining—all by himself.

As greed entrenched itself deeper and deeper into his soul, he found he would need help to extract more gold, faster. There was a problem though. He didn't trust anyone enough to allow them into his mine. So how could he get the labor he needed? One day, by accident, he found his answer. He was in town on a rare supply-purchasing trip. A young mercantile employee, a boy no more than 13, assisted him in rustling up equipment and provisions. The boy was adolescent and foolish. He did not understand fear and was fascinated by this person—a man seemingly with all the money in the world. Because Malcrook needed the boy's assistance, he treated him with a small shred of niceness. The lad waited on him hand and foot, ever eager to fill the order. Then it hit Malcrook: *Young boys! Why of course. If the mercantile can employ children, so can I!*

And employ them he did. Malcrook began searching alleys, riverbanks, and out-of-the-way places for young boys, especially those running away from home or otherwise unhappy with their parents. They were the easiest prey. He would simply show them a bulging handful of glittering gold and promise them generous portions if they would come work for him in his mine. Dollar signs verily rang up in their eyes and greedy smiles spread across their faces. They were only too eager to follow Malcrook, like the pied piper, up the mountainside, through the razor wire and into the Dark Quartz Mine. But once they went in, they never came back out.

Within a few years, the mine was well-stocked with child laborers. To feed and house them, Malcrook created a nearly self-sufficient mining city. He planted gardens and grew livestock. He devised an elaborate water supply and irrigation system—which also powered an electrical generating turbine. But what made this most incredible was that it all occurred *underground!*

Malcrook knew if his camp operated in the open, it would be just a matter of time before either his workers escaped or intruders barged in. To foil these eventualities, he blasted out vast underground caverns, tunnels, and vaults. In the garden areas, he cored out expertly positioned holes in the rock ceilings and installed an ingenious system of mirrors to direct and focus sunlight on his plants and livestock. He brought in wagonload after wagonload of fertile topsoil from the surrounding plateaus and terraces. Of course, he did very little of this infrastructure building himself. It was all accomplished by children. Child slaves.

But how did Malcrook keep the children from running back

to town? Naturally, after a few days of hard labor, any kid would realize his folly and want to flee. But escaping was much easier said than done. The razor wire fences were only a minor obstacle. A more serious deterrent was Malcrook's Doberman Pincers.

Although Malcrook was mean beyond comprehension, he was not stupid. He knew he'd have to utilize animals to help maintain his workers—he certainly could not patrol the vast expanses of his underground operation by himself. So he bought dogs. To ensure he did not make the same mistake as with his burro and original mongrel, these he actually kept fed, though sparingly. He wanted them lean and agitated. He found Doberman Pincers the best suited for his task. They could be trained to hunt down an escaping boy and bring him back relatively unharmed, save a few puncture wounds and minor slashes. Certainly, if the injuries sustained in the capture were too serious, the boy would be useless as a worker, so he took extra care in the training of his beasts.

The dogs were still not the worst deterrent, though. It was what happened after the dogs brought you back that was the real nightmare. A captured escapee would be subjected to a dose of *yecrim*. Yecrim was the ultimate punishment for a boy trying to flee his underground prison.

Malcrook had invented this peculiar substance to assist in the processing of gold. It was a silver-colored, mercury-like liquid with the favorable property of binding with gold particles, making them easy to separate from rock and crystal ore. Most miners used quicksilver for this purpose, and of course Malcrook started with quicksilver, too. But in his greed and lust, he became frustrated with quicksilver's slow reaction rate and inefficiency. He wanted a substance that would react with gold instantly and completely; and was also simple to then unbind, leaving only pure, sparkling gold. So he went to work in his laboratory and ultimately devised the perfect gold amalgamation chemical: yecrim.

But yecrim had one serious drawback. It was extremely

hazardous to use. Malcrook found this out the hard way.

One day he spilled a drop onto the tip of his ring finger. Immediately, excruciating pain—as if a blowtorch was trained on the spot, shot up his arm. The pain spread, directing itself straight at his heart. Then a red streak appeared, beginning at the stricken fingertip and slowly working its way up. With each millimeter of the streak's advance, the pain grew more intense. He ran to the sink and thrust his finger under a stream of cold water. But this only intensified the pain. Minute by minute, the red streak advanced. But now something else—something awful was happening. The infected spot turned purple then it darkened to black. Malcrook raced around his laboratory, applying anything and everything that might sooth it—salves, lotions, elixirs, anything. But nothing worked. As he applied the last possible ointment to the spot, his fingertip literally crumbled away to nothing. There was no blood, just a black stump at the knuckle. It was a nightmare—and it wasn't stopping. The purple-black progression continued morosely up the finger stump and into his hand.

He was truly panicked now. The red streak was visible all the way to his armpit—making its way apparently to his heart. His entire hand was beet red, swollen to twice its normal size, and his entire ring finger was nearly gone. There was only one thing to do. He raced into his kitchen, directly to his butcher block full of knives. He grabbed a cleaver, ran to the cutting block and slammed his swollen, crimson hand on it. The cleaver raised and fell.

Thankfully… instantly, relief surged from the wound and flowed through his veins. The red streak dissipated and turned back to skin color. The throbbing subsided. His hand, though bloody and now missing a ring finger and a pinky, ceased its tormented burning. That was close. How much longer until the infection reached his heart and killed him?

Then a horrible thought—a terrible, dastardly, hideous thought came to him. *This stuff, this yecrim, will be the perfect escape deterrent for my children! Yes! I will catch one of them trying to escape, and make an example of yecrim's tremendous power while the others are forced to watch. Oh, yes! Now I won't have to worry about my precious workers ever leaving me again!*

And sure enough, he carried out this ghastly plan. Several times. That was why, if anyone would have come to the mine, they would have noticed a few of the children limping, or struggling to perform their tasks. Some were missing a finger, some were missing toes. But all of them lived in fear. Fear of Malcrook, and fear of yecrim.

So between the razor wire, Doberman Pincers, and yecrim, no child of the mines would ever escape.

But there was another ominous thing about the Dark Quartz Mine. As the years and decades rolled past, Malcrook's stockpiles of gold multiplied and grew. He continued raiding neighboring towns for new child slaves. But there was a peculiarity every single new boy noticed upon entering the mine. None of the other children were more than seventeen years of age. How was that possible? Where were the children from twenty years ago? Did they not age, or was there another, more sinister ploy? Unfortunately for the children, the latter was the case.

Chapter Forty

Intruders in the Dark

Ramey and I sat riveted to our seats, eyes wide as goose eggs as Evon finished his tale. My imagination was running wild with visions of Ramey and myself being captured by a Doberman and being hauled, kicking and screaming, to the evil Malcrook. And of Malcrook hissing, "So, we have a couple of intruders, do we? Well, here in the mines we have methods of dealing with *truspasers*! Let's get the yecrim and teach these boys some manners shall we…aha ha ha…yessss, these rude boys need to learn proper etiquette if they wish to come calling on Mister Malcrook!"

But before the grisly vision could play out, Evon exclaimed, "Wellboys… it's getting… itmustbe very late. There'salittle… moreto…thestory, anotherdetail or two… I needtogo… overwithyou. But, we'll havetofinish… wrapitup… tomorrow."

I blinked hard, snapping back to the present and Peter Kringle's cluttered basement. "Okay," I replied, checking my fingers and toes just to be sure they were all still there.

"Nowthere'sblankets… lotsofblankets… inthatbox… over there… and pillowsinthatboxthere. Findyourselfaplace… aspotonthe… floor andlet's… getsomesleep. I'll tellyouabout Torry… andthedungeons… tomorrow. Then… we'll puttogether… hatch… aplan."

Ramey and I exchanged glances, our eyes growing wide again. I spoke up. "Dungeons? Evon, what dungeons?"

"Never… neveryoumind… about that! I'lltellyou… allaboutit… tomorrow. No needtoworry… your littleminds. Mightcause… baddreams… nightmares. Oh, thedungeons… deepdark… horribleplace… butdon't… nevermind… aboutthem…

now! Let'sgetsome… sleep. We'll beneedingallwe… can get."

Great, I thought. *Razor wire, Doberman Pincers, yecrim, Tommyknockers, and now dungeons! How in the world will we ever get out of there alive?* I looked at Ramey, who was arranging his blankets and pillow over a clear spot right next to mine. He was scared. His face was sheet-white and he trembled slightly as he went about his task. He was only ten years old—this was a lot for him to take in.

"Ramey," I whispered. "Remember our pact. We've got to do this for mom. Our Team of Three Will Succeed!"

Right now Ramey wasn't feeling nearly as brave as when we'd forged the pact. But he didn't want to say anything—didn't want anyone to think he was scared. "Yeah," was his only reply as he curled up and waited for someone to turn off the lights.

Evon fluffed up the blankets on his bed then nuzzled down into them.

"Um, Evon," I said, "…you going to turn out the lights?"

"No… no of coursenot, silly. Icouldn't reach the string… iflhad… to. Fromnowon… that's… it'syour… job, Collin."

Double-great, I thought, hauling myself from my covers and winding through the maze toward the stairs. *This'll be easy until the lights are out and I've got to find my way back. Probably trip over a Doberman or two.*

I climbed the stairs and pulled the light switch string. *Click.* Darkness. *Terrific. This is really dark. I can't even see the first stair step.* And it was true. There was not a shard of light penetrating the basement anywhere. I groped my way down the steps, reached the floor and put my hands out to feel my way along. *Now, do I turn right or left at the first corner?* Suddenly, visions of being lost in the gigantic maze filled my mind. *Oof!* I bumped into a stack of something. Now my imagination sped up. *What if someone was hiding down here? It certainly would not be difficult, with all the clutter and dead-end walkways. A blind boy groping around in the pitch dark would be easy prey.* Being scared was quickly turning to being frightened.

"Evon!" I called in a whisper-shout. "Where are you guys? I can't see a thing and I'm afraid I took a wrong turn!"

"We're right here, ninny," came Ramey's reply from approximately two feet away. "If you take one more step, you'll squish me like a slug!"

Whew, I thought, reeling my fear back in.

Everybody settled into their bedrolls and waited for sleep. The basement was as quiet as a cemetery.

Then, a noise. It started over by the paints—a faint scratching sound. But very rapidly, it got louder, and spread to other parts of the basement. Ramey levered himself up, straining to listen. The noises were coming in short bursts: scritching and shuffling; starting and stopping—as if the perpetrators were scuffling forward with great speed, then pausing. Now, more noises were coming from the boiler area and several other locations too—and getting louder by the second. Whatever it was, was making its way toward us!

I felt my heart speed up. *Tommyknockers!* I thought. *They've tunneled their way into the basement!* "Evon!" I hissed. "Do you hear that? What—or who is making all those noises?"

Evon did not answer. The only sound coming from him was heavy breathing.

"I hear it, too!" Ramey replied with obvious fright in his voice. "I think Evon is asleep. Whatever it is, there's a bunch of 'em… coming from four or five different directions. I don't know about you, but if we're going to get ambushed, I'd like to see who we're fighting. Go turn on the light!"

I bolted up and hustled back through the labyrinth toward the stairs. I was in a crouched stance groping my way among the boxes and crates, readying myself for unseen hands to take a grab. I made it to the stairs and climbed them as fast as I dared.

Click. Light.

Ramey was out of his bed with the nearest weapon he could find in the dark, a dessert plate, ready to do battle. When light flooded the basement, he was blinded at first, but as his eyes adjusted, he saw a flurry of movement.

Mice. It was only mice. There were probably twenty of them scurrying back to their hiding places—running along the ceiling joists and electrical wires. *Whew!*

I, with a wild look on my face and expecting the worst, bounded down the stairs in time to see the last of the mice disappear into cracks and holes in the walls and ceiling. My war face gave way to a relieved smile.

"Whatonearth… what's goingonhere?!" Evon squeaked as

he sat upright. "Can'tasquirrel... afellow... getanypeace... anysleep... around here?!"

"Um... well," Ramey stammered. "False alarm, Evon. We heard a noise and thought we were being attacked."

"By mice?!!!" Evon squeak-yelled. Ramey's embarrassment was obvious in the crimson hue of his face as he slid quietly back into bed. "Sorry about that, Evon."

Click. Off went the lights.

No sooner had we all settled back down, the scritching and scratching returned. But this time we did our best to ignore it. Even though it was only mice, and we knew it, it was still a little unnerving wondering if any would come to investigate two strange boys lying on the floor. And if one did, how would his little claws feel running across your face... and what if one crawled up a leg?

These were the thoughts Ramey and I struggled with as we waited for sleep to relieve our troubled minds.

Then we heard it.

And this time it wasn't mice. It was unmistakable. Suddenly the scritching stopped; the mice heard it too. The basement was silent again except for the intermittent creaking and groaning of floor boards above, and the soft *plip...plip* of someone's footsteps. Footsteps! There was someone in the building and they were walking around upstairs!

I sat bolt upright and turned my head toward the stairs. *Creak...creak...*the floor boards groaned under the weight. It was someone or something very large. I immediately thought the worst: *Malcrook! He's somehow heard about us and wants to take us to his mine—to become slaves!*

"Ramey! Evon!" I hissed. "There's someone upstairs!"

"Nowdon't... panic... worry," Evon responded in a panicked, worried voice. He had heard it too, and was alert. "Everyone... grabaweapon... and follow... comewithme."

Ramey found his dessert plate. I groped around and found a

spatula. Evon grabbed a coffee mug. We huddled together then made our way to the stairs. "No way we're letting him ambush us," I whispered. "We're a lot better off taking the offensive. *Shhhh.* Our best hope is to take him by surprise."

As quietly as we could, we climbed the stairs. The door at the top was slightly ajar. We could see the flitting beam of a flashlight. *Plip – plop – plip.* The footsteps got louder; they were coming our way! We held our breath and waited on the top stair. *PLIP – PLOP – PLOP.* Now the flashlight was trained on the door. *PLIP...*

Click. Light.

"ATTACK!" I gave a battle cry and all three of us tore into Malcrook.

But it wasn't Malcrook at all. Artimus Hawkwelts, the attorney, flinched backward in astonishment as the basement door flew open and three small persons (actually two persons and a large squirrel) began to flail away at his legs with kitchen utensils. "Whoa, wait a minute you guys! Wait a minute! WHOA! HOLD ON THERE!"

At the sound of his voice, I realized this was not anyone to be afraid of. We held our fire. I took a step back and examined the face of the intruder.

He was a kind-looking man, probably in his sixties, thinning gray hair, with a broad smile. He was staring back down at this diminutive resistive force with arms crossed and a look of curiosity.

"Hello... hi there... Hawkwelts," Evon said evenly.

Ramey and I shot a puzzled glance at Evon. Apparently he knew this person. Curiously, though, I noted a small amount of impatience or perhaps even mild resentment in Evon's voice.

"Well, hello, Evon," the man responded. "I see you've got some company. You should probably let me know these things so I don't call the police. I saw light coming from the building."

"No... nononono... don't call... thepolice!" Evon

squeaked. "Everythingisokay… fine. These… boysarefriends…
friendsofmine. They're… okay. We'rehatching… makingaplan…
torescue… Peterand… Torry."

"Oh, is that right? You're thinking of waltzing right in to
the mine and plucking Peter from the dungeons like a loaf of bread
from a grocery shelf? Well, I wish you luck, and plenty of it. You'll
need more than that if you and these boys aim to come out alive.
And by the way, I hope you've got a few weapons more dangerous
than your spatula and dessert plate there. Malcrook just might be
able to defend himself from those. Ha ha. But, it is quite late now.
I'm going back home. I'll be making my rounds again in a couple of
weeks. See you later, Evon. Nice to meet you boys. Oh, I didn't
catch your names?"

"I'm Collin and this is my brother, Ramey. Nice to meet
you too, Mister, er…Hawkwelts."

"Charmed. And do you boys have a last name? One never
knows who'll pop up on the missing children's roster next."

"Miller."

"Got it. Sleep well, now." He turned and walked down the
hall and out through the back door which he closed and locked with
a loud *click*.

"Missing children's roster?" I asked. "What was that all
about, Evon?"

"Oh, thatwas… that wasjust… Artimus…
ArtieHawkwelts… theattorney… nextdoor. Iwouldn't…
worrytoomuch… about any… missingchildren's… rosterthough.
Hewasjust… blowing smoke… tryingtomake… youboysnervous…
scaredthat he'll callthepolice… orsomething. Don'tworry…
hewont'dothat. Allhewants… allhe'sinterested in… is this
buildinghere. See… beforewe… PeterandI… wentintothemine…
Peterasked…. him… ifhewould'nt… mindchecking ontheplace…
from… timetotime… incasewe… didn't come rightback. Ithink…
Peter… hadsomearrangement… withhim… topaythe… bills

andtaxes... and he's beendoingit... forlotsof... manyyearsnow."

"I see," I said. "I could tell, Evon, from your voice that Mister Hawkwelts isn't exactly your favorite person. But it seems like he's helping Peter, right? Why don't you like him?"

"Well, Idon't... hate... him... ifthat'swhat... you mean. ButI... don'tlikehim... much either. Yousee... whenPetergotcaptured... andIgot... turnedinto... a squirrel... he was... Hawkweltswasthe onlyoneI... couldgoto. Anddoyouknow... whathedid? Thefirstthing... he did... was... laugh... atme. Ididn'tlike... thatdidn'tsitwell... withme. Andthen... he refused... wouldn'thelp rescue... Peter. Saiditwastoo... waytoodangerous. ButIthink... he really... doesn'tmind... ifPeterlives... or dies. Infact... he'dprobably... preferit... ifPeterdied! Because... I think... Petermighthave... lefthimin... charge... ofthebuilding. Andthisbuilding... isworth... a lot... abunch... ofmoney."

"Oh, I get it—he wants to inherit this building so he can sell it off and keep the profit," I said. "He seemed nice enough, but now that you mention it, there was a certain creepiness to him. Does he know about the Red Rocket?"

"No... nohedoesn't. Anddon'tlet... hisbigsmile... fool you. He's niceallright... aslongas... his interestsaretaken... careof. But... I think... he'sreally... acoward... anda greedy one... atthat. Theonly... reason... he doesn'tmarchinhere... andsell... everythingrightnow... isthat he'safraid... Imight... report... turnhimin to... the authorities. Yousee... hecan'tlegally... sell anything... withouteither... Peter'sor... my signature. He'snotsure... whetherPeter... isreally... alive... ornot. But... aslongas... I'm around... he'safraidto do... anything. Ithink... he'd justassoon... killme... but... he's toofraidy... too... chicken! BAWK!"

Ramey laughed at Evon's feeble chicken mimic. "No, Evon," he said tucking up his arms and bulging his eyes. "It's more like this, Baaawwkkk... BOK BOK... Beegauwkkkk!"

We all broke into peals of laughter. Then we erupted into a chicken impressionist contest—with arms flapping, necks thrusting, feet marching, and of course lots of Bawwkkkk... BOK... Bawking. Ramey and I laughed until our faces hurt at the sight of our squirrel friend jerking and thrusting about in his own peculiar brand of chicken mimicry.

Finally, realizing our ruckus could easily attract more unwanted attention, we collected ourselves and headed back down the stairs. I waited for Evon and Ramey to pile into bed before turning out the lights then stumbled to my own. Just like clockwork, the scritching and scratching started up, announcing the arrival of the mice. But this time, we hardly gave them any notice. Within minutes we had drifted into peaceful sleep.

Chapter Forty-One

Dungeons and Heroes

The next day dawned cloudy and overcast, but Ramey, Evon, and I wouldn't have known it. The basement was utterly impervious to daylight. We awoke feeling fairly refreshed—as refreshed as you could feel after having just spent the night on a floor of cold, hard wood. Evon suggested a breakfast of canned peaches and canned corned beef hash, which I was happy to prepare. We spent the next hour sitting around the fruit-crate table discussing what lay ahead.

"Well… to…todayistheday!" Evon exclaimed, trying his best to sound cheerful. He was, in truth, a bit nervous concerning what the day had in store and it showed in the slight quaver of his voice. "Rr… reallyallwehaveto… dddo… issetPeter… and Torryfree… andgetyouboys… get youalittle… gold. Couldn'tbeeasier… rr… right?"

Evon's one-sentence description of our mission sounded simple enough but both Ramey and I wrinkled our foreheads in doubt. It wouldn't be that easy and we knew it.

"You keep talking about this Torry," I said. "Who is he and what does he have to do with anything?"

Evon looked up, his little face twisted incredulously. "Ihaven't told… youabout… Torry? Goodnessme… goodnessgracious… me! Firstofall… Torryisn'taboy… a *he* at all… she'sa… *she*. Andsecond… Torry… isthereason… thecauseof… Peterbeing captured… inthefirst… place. Isuppose… it'simportantyou… knowaboutTorry… beforewe… beforewego… intothe mines. Yesthat'sgood… critical information. Wouldyouboys… like… tohearwhat… reallyhappened…

aboutsix… fiveandahalf… years ago? It'sthereason… it's
alsowhy… I'ma squirrel… today."

I was anxious enough to get cracking, but on the other hand,
I was a little nervous too. I had no real idea what would happen
once we entered the mine. Would we succeed? Would we be
captured, only to rot away in a dungeon? Would we become
Doberman kibble? Would we wind up black, flaking piles of yecrim
powder? A slight delay for a bit more background would probably
be a good thing—yes, probably so. And now that I thought about it,
Evon had not yet explained how it was that he became a squirrel, or
how Peter got captured, or what Torry had to do with any of it. I
glanced at Ramey, who was biting absentmindedly at a fingernail. I
could tell he was in no gigantic hurry either. "Okay, go ahead
Evon," I said, "I think I'd like to hear about Torry."

Ramey and I listened attentively as Evon told the story of
how Torry was lured to the mines by Malcrook, and how the Red
Rocket came to be made. Then he related the dreadful details of
Peter's capture and of the magical squirrel transformation.

"Iwasabout… to giveup… boys," Evon concluded.
"Throwinthe… towel… hoistthewhite… flag. Seeingmy… kind
mastertreated… that waywastoomuch… justaboutmore…
thanIcould… bear."

"But you didn't, right, Evon?" Ramey piped up. "You
didn't give up on your master. You went back, right? Found him—
made sure he was okay?"

"Yes… that'sright… Ramey. I didgoback… but… okayisn't
the… wordI'duseto… describewhatI… found."

"What, then?" Ramey persisted. "What did you find? And
how did you find it?"

"Doyouboys… wanttohear… the rest… havemefinish…
thestory?"

We responded with an enthusiastic, "Yes, please!" and
Evon took a deep breath and continued his tale.

The scene of the Doberman Pincers on top of Peter, ripping savagely at him, was Evon's last memory of the cave and of Malcrook. He tore out of that place in a blind panic and did not stop running until he was halfway back to town. But then he did stop alongside Bartelt Creek in a heavily wooded section where the stream slowed to form a large, wide pool. He bent over the pool and from his reflection got his first glimpse at what he had become. A squirrel. He was a large gray squirrel. All humanity had been stripped away: no clothes; paws instead of hands; a long bushy tail; and his mouth was dominated by yellowish, sharp, gnawing incisors instead of even, white human teeth.

And to make matters worse, his best friend and employer had been captured, probably was dead. He'd watched the entire episode but did nothing to help. Maybe this whole thing was his fault. After all, it was he who'd gotten attached to Torry in the first place. How could he carry on with that kind of guilt forever pressing on him? All these things entered and exited his brain over and over again like the incessant crashing of ocean waves on a rocky shore. Before long he was sobbing—crying uncontrollably. He was alive, but so what? What would his life be worth as a squirrel—and without the one person he cared most deeply for?

Evon spent the next several days in the forest in a daze—a personal fog. He moped around doing nothing—not eating, nor even making an effort to gather food. He found himself hoping a large bear or cougar would come, see him and give chase. But he wouldn't even run. He would just stand there, arms flung wide and shriek, "Come and get me—I'm all yours!"

But no bear came, nor a coyote, nor any other predator. He lost so much weight, he was scarcely more than a hide-covered skeleton sack. After about five days, he dragged himself to the wide spot in the creek to stare at his reflection again. He wanted one more look at what he'd become before dieing of starvation.

But when he stared into the quiet pool of crisp, cold water, it was not himself that he saw staring back. No, the reflection on the pool's mirror surface was someone else! An older man with a week's growth of graying stubble. And the man was in trouble—it was obvious from the frightened look on his gentle face. He, too, was thin, gaunt in fact; as if he hadn't eaten anything in days. And he was saying something or trying to say something, but there was no sound. Evon strained to read his lips; he was speaking slowly, weakly, as if near his last breath.

H-e-l-p m-e... h-e-l-p m-e, E-v-o-n. Y-o-u m-u-s-t c-o-m-e n-o-w. I'm d-y-i-n-g. H-e-l-p m-e... p-l-e-a-s-e... E-v-o-n.

Oh my goodness!

Evon's mind reeled. It was Peter—now barely recognizable. It was as if he'd aged 50 years in the last week. He was still alive, barely, after beingcaptured and being held prisoner somewhere—the dungeons no doubt. And he needed help, *now*. He'd somehow sent a magical message. Thank goodness Evon had gone to the pool for one last look!

This was the inspiration Evon needed to snap him from his despair. His master was in dire trouble and there was no one to help but himself. He'd failed once. He would not fail again.

Evon stooped to the pool and took a big drink. The rejuvenating liquid soaked into his body. Suddenly he had energy and purpose. He looked around. Food. His master needed food. Quickly he found some berry bushes and picked as many as he could carry, which wasn't much, but maybe it would be enough to buy Peter a little more time until he could bring something more substantial.

Off he raced for the waterfall. Down into the box canyon, across the spring boards, through the tunnel and into the cave he ran. In no time, he located the tunnel at the far end and scrambled in. Fear didn't even enter his mind.

The tunnel was virtually straight, gradually gaining

elevation. Soon he reached a fork. The left branch continued its upward gradient and from its depths came loud banging and grinding noises. *The mines,* he reasoned. The right fork headed downward and a bad odor came from that direction. *This must be— has to be the way to the dungeons.* He bounded down as fast as he could.

Tunnels branched on either side but he kept straight, always heading down. There were noises, angry mean noises, coming from the darkness of some of the tunnel branches, but he paid no attention.

After what seemed like an hour, the tunnel leveled and abruptly opened into a large hall. There was a single, small torch mounted on the angular rock wall adjacent to the hall's entrance. It barely shed enough light to see, but at least it was something. Along one side were heavy wooden doors, probably ten of them, each with a small opening in the middle covered with closely spaced heavy iron bars. An incredibly fetid odor filled the air. It was a foul reek of things rotten, and of excrement.

Blinking hard through the wall of stench, Evon squeaked in a wildly panicked voice, "Peter! Peterwhereare… whereareyou!"

From the second to last cell door, a hand slowly protruded. "Ev… Evon," came the weak reply.

"Peter!" It was Evon's master, still alive!

Evon scrambled to the door and leaped up to the bars. The berries he was carrying fell to the floor but he didn't care. He just wanted to see his friend. He grabbed the bars with his paws and held tight. There, not more than six inches away, staring back through narrow gaps in the cold iron was the kind face of Peter Kringle.

"Hello, Evon," he said. His voice was weak and frail. There was no color at all in his gaunt, gray-stubbled face. "Quite glad you noticed my call for help. I also see my little squirrel escape spell worked for you. I wish I could've conjured one up for myself, but they were too fast…too strong…too vicious. Caught me off guard, you know. Tossed me about a bit, then brought me here. Malcrook didn't think I'd make it three days without food or water. But he was wrong about that! ha ha... *cough cough... cough...* "

Just making this small conversation was taking a toll on Peter. "Rough treatment" was probably the understatement of the century. There were dark spots and slashes all over his arms, hands, and face—dried blood from the Doberman Pincer's attack. Several patches of hair were missing, ripped out at the roots. His clothes were shredded, torn, and tattered... and filthy. Not only was he severely injured, he was desperately weak from lack of water and nutrition.

But he continued speaking. "Yes, my little friend, you don't travel the world like I've done and not pick up a few survival tips along the way! It's true, I didn't fare too well against the dogs, but once I got here, why, I had it made! You know, rat isn't as bad as you might think. It's the catching them that's the hard part, ha... ha.—*cough!* And did you know, Evon, that a patient man with a dexterous tongue can harvest quite a bit of water from the weeping cracks and fissures in most underground cave walls—like these here."

Rats, Evon thought, *He's been eating rats, probably not even cooked, to survive. How absolutely repulsive. But... at least he's eating...and he's joking about it. He hasn't given up... hope... like... I... did.*

As this thought registered, guilt hit him like a sledgehammer. Here was his master: beaten and bitten—who should've been dead three days ago—with virtually nothing to eat or drink. And still he had hope—the will to survive.

But he himself had spent the past week in a forest of plenty doing...nothing. Waiting, hoping to die. It was at that moment his resolve solidified. He was the only one on the face of the planet in a position to help his master. He made up his mind he would do anything and everything he could; risk life and limb to keep Peter alive. He'd make fifty trips a day into the tunnel carrying only three berries at a time for fifty years if he had to. He would not give up. Not now. Not ever.

"Andthatwas… nearly six… almost… sixyearsago," Evon said, finishing his story. "I'vebeenmaking… severaltrips… aweekever… since. Oh atfirst, Iwent… twoorthree… timesaday, but the Tommyknockers… gotwise. Mean… nastythings! I'vehadto… severelylimitmy… comingsandgoings. It'ssorisky… everytimeI… go. They're laying… waitingforme. Andifthey… catch me… Peter'sfinished… done for. Ijustgo… enough… to bring the… essentials. Youknow… freshfruit… and nuts… whatIcan… gatherfromthe… forest… andthelocal… orchards. He'sgotmeat: rats… mice… and water. I carrythefood… in a smallleather… pouch… slipitunder… the door. ButIcan't… take…toomuchat… a time. Tooheavy… too hardtoavoid… the Tommyknockers. They'rewaiting… alwayswaiting… for me… lurkinginthe… darkness. Itsamiracle… amazing I've notbeen… captured… caughtyet."

Evon stopped speaking and waited for a reaction from Ramey and me. He was afraid his story might have scared us into reconsidering our purpose and our pact. And why wouldn't we? How appropriate or right would it be to take two innocent young boys, children actually, into the treachery of the Dark Quartz Mine? He would not have blamed us had we decided to simply go back home to our parents right then and there.

After a few moments of tense silence, Ramey spoke up with a question. "Evon, if Peter has so much magic, why doesn't he use it to escape?"

Whew, Evon thought. *Maybe they're still in.* He answered, "Verygoodquestion! I'm…notsureI…have that…good ananswerfor…youthough. Ithinkthere… mightbe… couldbe… several reasonsactually. First, Idon'tbelieve… Peter'smagicis… anygoodat… other than… constructive andcreative… things.

Itworks... wonderfully... withtoys... butnot tobreakdown... dungeondoors. Second... ittakes... alotof... atremendous... amount of energy... to workmagic. Justimagine... tryingtodo... somethingthat... goesagainst... theverylaws... of nature. It'shardto... evenvisualize. But Peterhasa... gift... hecan... doit. Butitsnot... withoutaprice. Everytime... he works... somemagic... ittakessomething... significant outofhim. Ordinarily... itsnotthat... bigofa... deal... because... he'ssostrong... andhealthy... normally. Butnow... eversincebeing... captured... he'sliterally... beenjust surviving... neardeath... allthetime. I'mnotsure... hecould... even... workanymagic... now. Tooweak... justtooweak. Probablyhas... somethingtodo... with... whyhe was... soeasilycaptured... inthefirstplace. Ithinkafter... heturnedme... intoasquirrel... hewas... drained... weakenedfora... moment. Thenthedogs..."

Evon's voice trailed away as the horrible memory replayed itself in his mind.

Shortly, I spoke up, "Thank you, Evon, for telling your story. If ever I had doubts about our mission, I don't any more. If I could be just half as brave as you and Peter, I mean risking your hides for someone... someone not even in your own family. Now that's what I call brave. But it even goes further than that. You've been risking your neck several times a week for the past six years for your master, hoping against hope something or someone would come along and help out. Evon, I may only be twelve-and-a-half years old, but I know a hero when I see one, and sure as I'm sitting on this fruit crate, I'm looking square at one right now. It would be an honor for Ramey and me to help you and I can't wait to give it my best shot."

Ramey stared at me, pride welling up in his chest like never before. Suddenly, his fear was gone. How in the world could he even think of being afraid after hearing Evon's tale? It was the most inspiring story to ever reach his ears. "Yep, Evon," he said squarely.

"I'm proud to be on your team, too."

Evon could tell we were sincere. He felt his eyes moisten and a lump welled up in his throat. "Thank... thankyou... boys. Youdon'tknow... can'timaginehow... muchthat... means... to... me."

"Thank *you*, Evon," I replied. "Now that I understand what we're up against, I can see it won't be easy. But, heck, nothing good in life ever comes easy. My dad always says that. And he's right most of the time. I think there are a few things we can learn from yours and Peter's first experience with Malcrook. I know one thing for sure. I'm not about to go into the mines half-cocked, without an escape plan. I mean, I'm pretty sure we'll be okay, you know, succeed in there, but just in case, I want a bail-out strategy."

Ramey and Evon looked at each other, then at me, and said, "Me, too!"

We gathered around the fruit-crate table and began hatching our plans.

Chapter Forty-Two

George Miller

There had been a lot on my dad's mind lately and his short-tempered behavior showed it. As he lay in bed staring wide-eyed at the ceiling after sending Ramey and me to bed without supper, he wondered if maybe he'd over-reacted.

Dang it, he thought. *All they did wrong was come home a little late. But this is twice in two weeks. Then again, they really weren't misbehaving—they could have been off with the bad gang of boys stealing, or vandalizing, or beating up on other kids. But they weren't. No, Collin and Ramey are good kids. So why do I have to be so hard on 'em all the time? They're just children, for Pete's sake. Isn't it a kid's job to sometimes forget about the time clock?*

He didn't have a good answer to his own fundamental question and that bothered him. There were times, like tonight, when he secretly wished he could undo his punishment, rush up and give us a big hug—for no reason at all. But he never could do such a thing. His decisions had to be final; like an umpire whose face is hidden behind the steel bars of his mask. Reverse a call? No way—might show weakness. Sometimes he hated himself for that.

Earlier that evening during supper, he and mom sat at the table in silence. She didn't always agree with his strict disciplinarian rule and tonight was one of those occasions. She truly wanted to sit at the table and listen to us spew excited stories of our adventures of the day. It didn't matter what the story or adventure was about, all that mattered was that we were excited and happy. She was dying. There wasn't much in her life that brought her gladness any more except her two boys.

As she lay in bed wrestling with these thoughts, the urge to give Ramey and me a hug and kiss came to her. Unlike her husband, she didn't have to be a faceless umpire. Her rules allowed her to be a mother, anytime. Without speaking, she slid from bed and shuffled slowly down the hall to our room. We were both asleep. As she bent down, she noticed we didn't have our usual half-smile and peaceful demeanor. Were she and dad such bad parents? Gently, she brushed back Ramey's hair and kissed his forehead. Then she did the same to me. Walking away, she felt a lump form in her throat and a tear trickle down her cheek. Had she known this would be her last kiss for a long, long time—perhaps ever, she would not have left the room.

The pitter-patter of rain on the cabin's metal roof woke mom and dad at about 7:45 the next morning. They got up and mechanically made the bed. Dad went directly to the kitchen but mom headed for Ramey's and my room. She was planning to make a special breakfast for us, our favorite: cinnamon rolls and fruit salad. "Guess what we're having for breakfast boys!" she announced, easing the door open. "Cinnamon rolls and fr…." Her words drifted away to silence as the empty beds registered in her mind. *What the…?* she thought, startled. *They always sleep in on the weekends, why in the world would they get up early this morning? They're probably in the kitchen making something to eat. They've got to be hungry.*

She exited the room and called down the hall, "Collin? Ramey? Guess what I'm making for breakfast? Cinnamon rolls!"

But there was no answer.

"George, have you seen the boys?"

"No, weren't they in bed?"

"No." She could feel panic building in her gut.

"That's strange," dad responded, his brow wrinkling. "Maybe they're feeling guilty about last night and got up early to tend to their chores. I'll go outside and have a look around."

"I'm coming with you."

Still in their pajamas, they headed for the barns calling our names. The rain had turned to a steady drizzle and within a few minutes they both were wet. With each empty place they checked, worry and panic gripped them a little harder. Neither wanted to admit the unthinkable—that we'd run away from home—but that very thought was the one building in their minds.

Now dad was running. Dashing from building to building, pen to pen, shouting for us. But no answer. Mom was doing the same. She had started to cry.

Finally, after searching all the buildings and pens in vain, they met in the mud of the barnyard. Dad's face was stark white, drenched in worry. Mom, her thin hair clinging to her wet scalp like twigs, collapsed in his arms, sobbing.

The same thoughts dad had struggled with last night came screaming back as the reality of what was happening sunk in. It was too much. His world was coming apart at the hinges and he was powerless to stop it. Grief overcame him. Tears filled his eyes. He couldn't remember the last time he had cried.

Far overhead, unseen and unheard, a tiny bright red speck circled. Ramey and I watched our parents below. The sight struck grief into our hearts. Tears silently streamed down our faces as we made our last arc and flew away.

After searching and re-searching the grounds, hollering our names into every cobwebbed and out-of-the-way place he could think of, dad accepted the fact that we had run away. He'd finally pushed us to our limit and we'd reacted in the only way we knew how.

Later that morning, over a lukewarm cup of coffee, he managed to gather himself and level out his emotions. *Now, what to do?* he thought. *I've got to find those boys but where do I look first? Town? Probably not. They're smart enough to know they'll be seen and brought back here quick. Beaver Lake? Maybe—but if they went there, my chances of finding them are needle-in-a-haystack*

slim, especially if they don't want to be found. No, gotta start searching places I've got at least a fighting chance, like, like...

Then it hit him. *The mine.*

The Dark Quartz Mine. That's the most likely place. Those boys are spellbound by the prospect of finding gold. And not only that, since I laid down the law about not going there, it could help explain why they run away. Yep, I'll start my searching there.

Mom was stiffly ambling about the kitchen, head down, jaw set. Dad knew better than to try conversation; she would have none of that. One word right now would more than likely result in an explosive fit of screaming. She was beside herself, and she blamed him. Dad walked out without discussion. He had a job to do. There was no sense putting it off.

The screen door banged shut behind him. He knew from

Ramey's and my recount of our adventure with the waterfall and fool's gold where to go and how to get there.

From the kitchen window, mom watched him walk away. He didn't pause or turn around. She did not know it but he would not be back that night or the night after. Like her two sons, now her husband, too, would be gone for an undetermined amount of time— most likely forever.

Within 30 minutes, dad reached the box canyon. He had little trouble negotiating the moss-covered steps and the spring boards—he was a logger by trade, used to treacherous footing. Five minutes later he found himself in the cave. Suddenly, amid the quietness and the dim light, the first pang of fear announced itself from deep within him. He instinctively felt for his pocketknife. *Shoot!* he thought, as his hands brushed the flat right-front pocket where the knife should have been. *Must've forgotten it in my rush.* It was an error he would come to regret many times.

His eyes scanned the rough, shadowy walls of the cave for an outlet. Shortly, he noticed the dark hole that was the exit tunnel at the far end, and carefully picked his way across the jagged rock floor. With a quick, deft jump and a little scrambling, he was in the tunnel. The opening was circular, about five feet in diameter, which meant he had to stoop. There was a cool breeze and a stale odor coming from the darkness ahead. He took a few steps. Quite suddenly the dim light of the cave was at his back and he was utterly in the dark. *Shoot*, he thought again. *Should've brought a flashlight. I can't even see my own shoes. Maybe I should go back— get some proper supplies.* His mind wrestled with his options. *Nope. Not now. There's no going back now. I've got to find my boys.*

And so he started his traverse into the Dark Quartz Mine. Like a hobbled blind man, he put his hands out and clumsily stepped forward. It wasn't as bad going as he imagined. Although the tunnel was narrow and squatty, the floor was relatively smooth and the cool breeze guided him. It was uphill and relatively straight.

After about half an hour of painstakingly slow progress, he began to hear noises in the distance. Banging, clanking, and grinding noises. *Must be getting close to the mine*, he thought. A branch of the tunnel opened to his right. It went downward and a foul odor emanated from there. *Better stay left. If my kids are in here, they wouldn't have taken that fork.*

Inching his way forward, the industrial sounds got louder. Soon, the tunnel grew brighter, illuminated by a light source ahead. He flattened himself against the wall and crept like a burglar. A tunnel branch opened on his left. It was dark and breezeless. *Nope, not that way either.* Adrenaline was now coursing through him, his heart thumping in his chest. The banging and grinding noises had become loud—really loud, dead ahead. What would happen next? He hadn't the first idea. Bloody scenarios of hand-to-hand battle with pick-wielding mine workers flashed across his brain.

The tunnel took a mild turn to the left just before coming to its end at a gigantic underground room. Dad stopped and gawked, awestruck.

The room was huge, probably one hundred feet or more across. It appeared circular with a high, domed ceiling. It was definitely not formed by nature, as was the entrance cave behind. No, this was made by men—many men. All the walls, ceiling, and floor, were cut into granite rock. The surfaces were unbelievably smooth. Someone had gone to enormous effort to create this place.

But the contents were even more impressive. Pinning himself to the tunnel wall, dad took it all in.. What an incredible, unbelievable scene it was.

Chapter Forty-Three

The Stamp Mill

Dad gaped in absolute amazement at this underground colossus. He struggled to absorb it all, scanning the room from his left.

Spanning about one-third of the cavern's perimeter were anterooms, each with dusty wood plank walls connected to the rock ceiling and floor, and several windows in their walls. The first appeared to be a laboratory of some sort, containing equipment in glass-doored cabinets and scattered on many work tables—scales, sieves, mullers, crucibles, ingot forms, apothecary jars and the like. There was a small smelting furnace in one corner. A girl, not more than 17, dressed literally in rags and dirty from head to foot, was standing over a bench, working at something. She was intent on her task, as if driven by someone at her back with a whip.

Adjacent to the laboratory was another room, with several windows and a door to the main cavern, but no glass or wood in the rough openings. Inside it was fairly dark, the only light coming from a single, naked bulb in the ceiling. In one corner was a metal forging furnace with a jumbled pile of black coal at its base. In the middle was a giant anvil bolted to an immense cedar stump. A large hand-operated bellows hung from a hook near the furnace. The walls were covered with rough wooden shelves, cubbies, and cabinets, all open-faced. Well-worn hand tools littered the place; some scattered on the workbenches, others half-protruding from cubbies. There were wrenches of every description, screwdrivers and hammers—from sledges to ball-peens. In another corner stood a four-foot-tall cast iron apparatus dad guessed to be a drill-sharpening machine. This room was undoubtedly the blacksmith's shop. Someone was working in there, veiled in the shadow of a corner.

Past the blacksmith's shop was the opening of a large tunnel. From it issued a set of narrow-gage railroad tracks which entered the cavern, then forked: one branch going to the middle of the room, the other staying left, winding around to the far side. There were several old, banged-up ore cars sitting on the tracks. Alongside the right branch, clamped directly to the rock floor, was a cast-iron pipe, probably six inches in diameter.

Beyond that tunnel and further around to the left were three more tunnel openings. These, however, were not as large, nor did they have railroad tracks or piping entering them.

Directly in front of dad, occupying more than half the space of the expansive cavern floor, were huge machines: the ones making all the dust and racket—the heart of the gold mining operation. Dad knew a little about mining; he had friends who dabbled in it. He recognized this machinery. It was an amalgamation-concentration stamp mill. But it was old, very old, like the kind used in the early 1900s.

The ceiling sloped up steeply from the offices to accommodate the great height of the apparatus. Dad gaped, awestruck at the vast complexity of gear wheels, conveyor belts, steam lines, ore-crushing pistons, and even a suspended tramway. It was all in full operation. The sonic assault on his ears was nearly painful. The ground literally shook from the pounding of the seven-stamp battery. Dust was flying and steam hissing. Dad had always been interested in things mechanical and after a few moments of study had a decent idea of the basic concept. It went something like this.

In the exact center of the cavern was a giant, A-frame tower, some 40-feet tall, hewn from huge timber poles and diagonal struts. At its top was the steel head frame of a hoisting winch. Cables, drawn tight by a three-foot diameter electric motor mounted near the frame's front legs, were routed up and over a tremendous sheave wheel pulley, probably eight feet across at the very top. The cables extended downward through the A-frame's heavy timber latticework into a vertical mine shaft. Wooden ladders were built into the A-frame to allow workers access to the sheave wheel and landing platform at the top. Several teenage boys were scrambling around tugging at the latch of a huge ore bucket which had just been winched up from the depths. They meant to dump the ore into a waiting tram car.

The tram was suspended on cables high overhead. It traveled between the A-frame and the top of the stamp mill immediately to the right.

A lone boy stood at the stamp mill's landing, pulling levers and pushing buttons at a tremendous control panel. Tangled, heavy, electrical cables, lights, siren horns and transformers gave the panel a creepy appearance. Off in the shadows was a huge electric motor, even bigger than the one on the A-frame, which drove a series of belts. These belts stretched away in various directions, providing power to the tram as well as to the myriad individual pieces of machinery.

The mill itself was tall, at least three stories, and was arranged to take advantage of gravity. Ore arrived at the top via the tram then worked its way through from right to left, back toward the A-frame tower, by sliding or dropping from one process to the next. The cave floor stair-stepped underneath it. Various pieces of machinery were arranged at different elevations so the overall appearance was angled, as if the mill were on a sloping hillside.

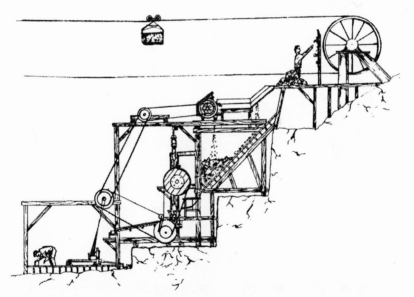

Ore was dumped from the tram at the very top, to a sloped series of vibrating grates that dad recognized as a grizzly. Smaller chunks of ore fell through the grates to a hopper bin below. The larger pieces slid over the grizzly to a crusher.

The rock crusher was the loudest machine in the mill. Its

great cast-iron crushing jaw, probably three feet high and one foot wide, *opened-and-closed, opened-and-closed* smashing the human head-sized chunks of rock ore into pebbles. Dust and rock chips flew like exploding fireworks with each menacing thrust of the jaw. Pulverized rock fell through the crusher's open bottom into the same hopper bin the grizzly tailings emptied into.

Then the ore was hammered some more. To facilitate extraction of the fine gold laced within its granite and quartz, it had to be reduced to rock powder. The stamp mill performed this task. Pebble-sized ore was discharged from the bottom of the hopper bin into the base of a vertical stamp mill. The machine had seven pounding pistons that rose and fell several times a second. Chunks of rock were finely crushed to tiny pebbles and then to powder under the tremendous force of the hammering pistons.

The next step involved separating gold from the rock powder. Most of the gold particles leaving the stamp mill were so small and so dispersed within rock dust, a person couldn't even see them, let alone pick them out. Chemicals were needed to separate the gold. Amalgamating plates and Malcrook's evil substance, yecrim, were used for this purpose—though of course dad knew nothing about yecrim. He was familiar with other chemicals, like mercury and quicksilver, typically used for the process. A flat, copper-faced plate, about 5 feet by 8 feet, was located just below and to the left of the stamp mill. It was placed horizontally, but one end was driven to rise and fall by an eccentric pulley. Only Malcrook's most trusted worker was allowed to operate the amalgamating plate because with each batch of ore, a thin layer of yecrim was applied to the plate's copper surface. And only Malcrook himself would apply the substance. No one else had access to yecrim. It was kept securely in a bank vault in the office rooms.

As the rock powder, now combined with a spray of water to make a slurry, was discharged to the yecrim-coated amalgamating plate, the yecrim would selectively search for gold particles. It ignored all other materials. As soon as even a molecule of gold-touched yecrim, they would bind together. The worthless rock materials would vibrate over the table to be discharged to the final process, the concentration table.

Once the amalgamating table was cleared of everything but amalgamated yecrim and gold, the worker, wearing thick rubber gloves, carefully scraped the mixture to one corner with a large copper-plated wooden paddle. He would then pull a plug in that low corner, allowing the yecrim mixture to trickle through into a large apothecary jar underneath. The jar was then carefully taken to the offices to divide the gold from the yecrim—a multi-step process involving the blast furnace that only Malcrook himself would perform.

Because yecrim would bind only with molecular-sized particles of gold, the larger chunks and nuggets had to be separated by another procedure. This was the last step in the process—a concentration table. It was located adjacent to, and looked very similar to, the amalgamating table except its surface was covered with angled wooden slats spaced at intervals. It was mounted on a slight tilt, and was gently vibrated via belt and pulley. Water was continuously sprayed over the table. Gold nuggets and flakes, being heavier than rock, would be trapped in the upper riffles, while the lighter rock materials washed down to an ore car waiting at the low end. This same principle was the one employed by sluices in Placer-style mining.

A worker was hunched over this table, sifting, ever sifting through the pebbles trapped in the upper riffles. He wore rubber gloves to protect his hands from the traces of yecrim still clinging to the ore. Occasionally he would pluck a yellow nugget from one of the riffle dams. This would go into a small jar that Malcrook personally collected every hour or so. Spoils washing from the low end—worthless dust and rock—would be towed out of the mine on rails and dumped somewhere, probably over the mountainside.

As dad took all this in, he was particularly shocked to witness the entire operation was being run by…children. At each station on the mill there was a boy, or several boys. None were more than 16 or 17, some looked no older than 10. But there was no boyish activity here; no laughing, no goofing around. Just expressionless faces, grim and hard-set. They were filthy, covered from hair to boot in a fine coating of rock-ore dust. And they worked. Constantly, without looking up. Some had a slight limp or were missing a finger. The boy working the amalgamating table was missing most of his left arm; it was gone up past the elbow.

Dad was aghast. This was torture—child abuse; it made him sick to his stomach. *What kind of monster runs this place?* he thought. *Who in their right mind could steal children and turn them into slaves? I sure hope my boys ain't come here. But what to do next? I know what I'd like to do—find the man responsible and give him a great big piece of my mind and maybe my knuckles. Then again, if the old stories are true, there's been others before me, probably standing in this exact spot, who never come back out. And that surely ain't what I'm after. Could be I'm better off just finding my boys and leaving other men's business alone. Let someone else be the hero. I've got a wife and family to tend to.*

He glanced quickly about. None of the children seemed to have noticed him. Certainly, they wouldn't have heard him amid the din of the machinery. *The girl. Maybe she can tell me whether or not any new boys have showed up recently. But what're my chances of sneaking over to the office where she's working without no one noticing?*

He looked again at the mill and hoist. There were probably ten boys at various stations there, scrambling about, pulling levers, shoving ore through the machines. They worked like mules, never looking up, concentrating intently on their tasks.

Dad's heart was pounding. He wasn't a burglar, didn't have

the first notion of how to be sneaky. So he did what he'd done all his life. He gathered himself, stood up straight, put one foot in front of the other and simply walked forward.

Directly to the office door he strode. It was slightly ajar. He entered and walked over to the girl. Amazingly, no one noticed.

Chapter Forty-Four

Torry

The girl was so intent on her work that she did not hear or sense dad enter the room. He stopped five feet from the table where she was working. She was preparing an ore sample for assaying using an odd-looking hammer with a heavy cast iron head. The hammer, a muller, had a platelike face, but rounded. With one hand she was pushing down on the backside of the head while the other hand rocked the handle up and down. In this manner she was crushing to powder a small sample of pebble-sized rock ore. It was hard, dusty work.

"S'cuse me, Ma'am. Name's George Miller. I'm looking for my two boys—they're age 10 and 12. You haven't seen any new kids around here this morning have you?"

Torry snapped her head up. What man's voice was this? She had only heard one in the last five-plus years—and it certainly didn't sound like this. There, standing not five feet away, was a stranger. He was a big man, strong—dressed in work clothes, with a day's growth of stubble on his face. He looked worried, but his eyes were kind, like a father's eyes. She couldn't remember the last time she'd seen a grown-up's face with that expression. And he had called her "ma'am." Ma'am? No one had ever called her that. Instinctively she took a step back.

Dad stared at the girl. She was dusty, her hair messy, and her clothes were loose-fitting, faded rags. But her face—it was a complex mixture of beauty and tragedy. Her eyes were strikingly green under dark, thick lashes and her skin, where she'd wiped the sweat and dust away, was smooth olive. She was tall, probably five feet seven or eight, slender, with a woman's figure. But the eyes, beautiful as they were, spoke of hardship. Her mouth opened to speak, but no words came out.

Dad sensed her fear. "I ain't gonna hurt you," he said, taking a half-step backward and putting his hands up, palms out. "I was just wondering if you'd seen any strange, um…new boys around here today. Y'see, my two sons, well, they decided to run away from home and I figured they'd probably head here. I'm kind of in a hurry and just a little worried about barging in unannounced, trespassing and all. Have you seen 'em?"

Torry's mind reeled. She had not seen a grown-up from the "outside" for so long. Finally words came to her and she responded in a voice so low he could hardly hear it. She was uncomfortable looking him in the eyes, so she looked at the floor as she spoke. "Ma'am? You called me ma'am. My name is Torry. You are in danger, serious danger here. You should go…now."

Dad's urgency welled up. He knew he was on borrowed time but was not getting the answer he needed. He asked again: "I want to go, believe me, there's nothin' I want more, and for that matter, you can go with me, too, if you'd like. But I need to know if my children are here…and if they are, where?"

Torry's mind spun. His words confused her. "…you can go

with me…" he'd said. The prospect of leaving this place, this slave's den, was an impossible fairy tale. *No one leaves here*, she thought. Her mind drifted back in time. She remembered being a ten-year-old kid living with her mother in a small travel-trailer on the outskirts of Furry Pine. They didn't have any money and her mom wasn't always home. But at least she was free. Free to play in the streets, free to visit the nice man at Kringle's. Free to…

Clank… bang!

Loud noises from the blacksmith's shop in the next room jarred her back to the present. She blinked hard. *Who is this man… and why is he being nice to me? Master would be angry if he knew this nice man was here.* "I'd love to go with you," she said softly. "But I can't leave. I can never leave… Master won't let me, or any of the others, go."

Dad fidgeted in his logger's boots. He could see the girl's torment and felt sorry for her. But she wasn't answering his question and his time had to be running short. How many more minutes, or seconds, did he have before Malcrook came rounding the corner and found him standing there?

"Look, you *can* leave with me, if you'll just tell me whether or not any new boys showed up yesterday or today. As soon as I'm done with my business here, I'm surely turning heel and heading back out. But, dogonnit, right now I need to know about my two boys. If you haven't seen 'em, that's fine, just say so. A simple yes or no's all I need, ma'am."

Torry's mind continued to twist. "…you can leave…with me," he'd said. But she knew—it was ingrained in her—that, in fact, she could *not* leave. There was no escape from this place. And even if there was, it wasn't worth the risk, the punishment was too severe. Yecrim. She'd seen it with her own eyes many times. The evidence was everywhere you looked.

"No… no new boys. But you must leave now, mister. Mustn't let him… Master can't catch you here. He'll put yecrim on you… cut you… take you to the dungeons to…"

But Torry did not finish her sentence. Even as she spoke, the sound of heavy footsteps reverberated in the room and another man's voice rang out. Malcrook. Prancing at his side was a dog—a Doberman Pincer. "What's all the talking going on?" he barked, entering the lab. "I sure hope none of the boys have come sneaking…." Looking up, digesting the sight before him stopped him in his tracks. At first he seemed confused. Then a smile, an evil grin spread across his lips.

"Soooo, we have a visitor today do we, Torry? A tourist come to inspect our mine - how quaint!" He glanced at his dog then continued. "We hardly ever get visitors these days, do we now, Cleaver?" The dog at his side looked back up at his master, then at dad. Growling, he bared a glistening set of white incisors, hair prickling in a perfect swath down his backbone.

"Oh, so you like him too, Cleaver!" Malcrook cackled. "That's very nice of you, boy. I'm sure your brothers and sisters will find him a wonderful playtoy as well! It's been so long since you've had a playmate. Some six years if memory serves correctly. Perhaps this one will give you a bit more challenge than the last!"

Malcrook gave a shrill whistle. Within seconds, five more Dobermans came running from various directions and gathered at his feet. Seeing the stranger, they, too, began growling and slavering.

"You look here, mister," dad said in a firm voice, trying to disguise the adrenaline now zinging through his veins. "I'm not here for any other reason than to fetch my two boys—if they wandered here in the first place. Now, I can't say I agree with your use of kids to run your operation here, but I suppose that ain't none of my business. I just came to get my boys and leave. And if they ain't here, I'll be happy to walk out the way I come. But if they are here, I'd like 'em back."

"Well, well," Malcrook replied in sarcastic falsetto. "So you don't like how I'm running *my* mine! Isn't that special! Can't stand to see children do a little WORK, eh? I suppose while you're after your own kids, you might also like to take Torry, here, out with you as well? And while you're at it, maybe you'd be happy to kidnap some of the others working on the stamp mill and take them, too!"

Suddenly, as if a switch had been thrown in his brain, Malcrook's demeanor went from fake pleasantness to venomous hostility. As he spoke, drool began forming at the edges of his swollen purple lips, and he spat with the pronunciation of each "s." At the same time, the dogs' snarling became louder and more menacing.

"Well you can FORGET it! And for that matter, you can FORGET ever leaving thisss place alive yoursssself! NO ONE truspasssses on my property and getsss away with it! And I don't happen to have your two preciousss boys. But by the look of you—sssuch a big, sssstrong logger man—I wish I did! They'd be good workersss, oh YESSSS! I'd make them work hard, REAL HARD in the deep minesss… where no other boys like to go. *But watch out!* My little friendsss the Tommyknockerssss essssspecially like it down there. You say you have TWO boyss? Probably only lose one of them to the Tommyknockers, at mosst. But if they're sssstrong and fasst, it's possible they both might live. And if they did, I bet they'd be good for a couple of ouncesss of gold a day—APIECE!"

Dad just stood there. Who did this man think he was? Nobody talked to him that way, and certainly not about his children. Those were fighting words. Generally, dad was a peaceable man, but if you pushed him hard enough, he would fight. He could feel the blood beginning to boil deep in his veins.

"Mister, I don't know who you think you are and I really don't care. But you don't talk about my boys that a-way, unless you're lookin' for a fight. Now you apologize for what you just said or I'll be forced to teach you a lesson in proper behavior."

"So, the big logger man thinkss he's BRAVE doesss he?"

Malcrook's voice had escalated to nearly a scream. The Dobermans were now pawing the floor and growling savagely. "Well letss see how BRAVE you are againssst a few of my puppiesss! Cleaver, Scimitar, Cutlass, Switchblade, Scythe, Pegleg... SIC 'EM!"

The dogs leaped forward like they'd been fired from a cannon. But dad was ready. He crouched into a defensive position with both hands out.

Cleaver was the first victim. He jumped from where he'd been sitting and flew nearly the entire distance through the air, feet extended, mouth agape. With lightning reflexes, dad caught him in midair by the roof of his opened mouth and by a front leg. With a quick flip, Cleaver found himself hurtling at great velocity in a different direction. He crashed into a glass-doored cabinet. The door exploded, spewing shards everywhere.

Cutlass was next. He'd chosen a route on the floor and was quickly closing in for a chomp of dad's leg. But instead, he was greeted rudely by dad's logging boot. It drove him, spinning like a top, sideways into the mulling table.

Switchblade started by Cutlass' side, also taking the floor route, and managed to escape the boot. He struck, sinking his teeth into dad's calf muscle. At the same instant Scimitar jumped for dad's neck, but misjudged his leap slightly and instead clamped down on dad's nose and cheek. Dad yelled in pain and reflexively grabbed Scimitar by the waist and yanked. The force of his mighty pull was enough to dislodge the dog, but Scimitar did not let loose his grasp, and as he slid away, his teeth cut deeply. Like Cleaver, in the next instant he found himself hurtling through the air, spinning as he went, into the bank of glass-doored cabinets. *Kaboom!* Hitting like a bomb, glass, apothecary jars, and rock samples exploded back into the room.

Scythe and Pegleg hung back for a second waiting for the first wave to strike, then on they came at full force. Switchblade was still attached to dad's leg, and now dad reached for him. As his hands came down, Scythe and Pegleg zeroed in on an arm. Their teeth sunk in. Dad cried out, reeling backward, staggering as he went. He slammed into a workbench, stopping his momentum. But that was all he needed to regain himself. With a dog hanging on each arm, he managed to wrap his great hand around Scythe's neck. He squeezed and in the next instant the dog went limp, dropping to the floor.

Pegleg tightened his grip, but now dad had one free hand. Pegleg felt the hand encircle the narrow part of his waist and squeeze. In the next instant his hind legs went numb then his teeth were torn loose of the arm and he was airborne. He hit the front office window with such force that glass exploded into the main mining chamber, chards flying everywhere. Pegleg continued on this trajectory until one of the log legs of the A-frame winch stopped him.

Now the only dog left was Switchblade. He still had a deathgrip on dad's calf muscle and was wrenching his head back and forth with a terrific tearing motion. Dad reached down and with both hands grabbed Switchblade by the neck. Switchblade went limp and slumped to the floor. Dad kicked him aside like a ragdoll.

Chapter Forty-Five

Coldcocked

Dad, his face and arms bleeding profusely, leveled a laser glare on Malcrook.

"Now, mister… " he panted, spitting blood from the corners of his mouth, "I don't normally believe in beating up on innocent animals, and I'm real sorry about your dogs—mostly sorry they got stuck with a cull like you for a master. Seein's you ain't got my boys, I'll be leaving. I'd advise you to step aside or some of what just happened to them dogs'll be happening to you next."

Malcrook gaped around his ruined laboratory and at his precious dogs lying about like carrion after a war. He certainly had not expected this outcome, but worse, was not prepared for any further action. All the boys on the stamp mill had stopped their work and were gawking at the office in amazement. Malcrook had no choice but to acquiesce. As effortlessly as flicking a light switch, he changed his manner to that of humble subservience. "Yes, yes of course you may leave. Sorry…so sorry for the misunderstanding. I'm sure your children are at home waiting for you by now. Good luck, sir."

But as he spoke and shuffled aside, he made a slight gesture to Torry. It was so subtle that dad did not notice it. But Torry, who had watched the whole fight with emotions somewhere between horror and ecstasy saw it. The gesture was intended for her. Malcrook was staring intently at the muller she'd been using to crush the ore sample, and with one hand he made a slight pounding motion. She saw the gesture and knew what it meant. He wanted her to club this man on the head with the muller. *No*, she instantly thought, *I can't do that. I don't want to hurt him. I don't want to hurt anyone.*

Dad started for the door, limping. His wounds were numerous and deep.

Malcrook made the gesture again, only more urgently this time. And this time, he had an evil look in his eyes. Torry knew that look. It was the same one he always had when he punished someone for trying to run away.

Mechanically, she reached for the muller. She watched her fingers close around the heavy wooden handle. Now she felt herself walking, following the stranger. How was this happening? She did not want to hit him. Was Malcrook willing her hands and legs to move?

Now she was standing behind the man and the muller was rising in her hands. She felt her eyelids close. The hammer fell— and connected... *thud...* directly on the back of the man's head. Her eyes opened in time to see him slump to the floor. She stood there motionless, arms at her side.

Malcrook erupted into fit of delight. He clapped his hands in glee and shouted, "YESSS! TORRY, I knew you'd come through for your Massster! You love your massster, don't you Torry? Yesss... Torry, you will make a fine wife for me one day...one day sssoon."

Torry stood there like a zombie. She had heard what Malcrook just said, but had no reaction at all. She knew what she had just done and abhorred it. She hated herself, her life, and what her future held. It was so awful, so terrible.

"TORRY!"

A new voice rang out across the wreckage of the laboratory. But it wasn't a strange voice. Torry knew the voice; it was the only bright sound to be heard anywhere in the mines. "Gertrude," Torry sputtered, surprised. "I didn't see you come in. We've had a bit of a disturbance here. I think... I just killed a man."

Gertrude, the elderly wife of Malcrook, one hand covering

her gaping mouth, looked on in horror and bewilderment at the bizarre scene. Then she looked up at Torry, who was standing stone-still and expressionless with the three-pound muller dangling from her limp arm. "Oh, my gosh… my goodness, Torry. What have you done?"

But before she could answer, Malcrook spoke out loudly. "She just killed that intruder—that mean, nasty man who stole in here and brutalized my precious puppies. She was protecting her beloved massster! Yessss, Torry-girl loves her master. Doesn't she Torry? Torry?"

Torry said nothing. She felt paralyzed, like someone had just thrown a 2x4 into her spinning mind-spokes. She knew better than to answer Malcrook with the truth. She despised him. Couldn't stand the sight or smell of him. "Yes, Master," she finally replied blankly.

Gertrude rushed over and hugged Torry, pulling her dusty-haired head onto her shoulder. The muller dropped to the floor. Suddenly Torry found she was weeping—tears streaming down her face like a rain-streaked window. The old woman hugged her tighter, rocking back and forth comfortingly. "There now, Torry, it's over with. You're okay, everything will be fine. Don't you worry."

Still Torry wept. The sobs and tears would not stop. Was she crying out of grief for having just killed a perfectly innocent man? Or were her tears due to the fact that this episode had just foiled her own plans—her and Gertrude's well-thought-out strategy to dispense with Malcrook once and for all? Why had this stranger chosen this day of all days to come looking for his lost sons? His timing could not have been worse. At exactly 5:00 this afternoon she and Gertrude were to carry out their life's mission: to mutiny against their captor, Malcrook. To incapacitate him and set everyone free. To finally bring an end to the Dark Quartz Mine. But George Miller had blundered in and now the plan would have to be waylaid or perhaps scrapped altogether. There was simply too much disruption and confusion now to ensure their complicated plan would succeed. Certainly, if it did not, the consequences to Gertrude and herself would be grave indeed.

Several of the Doberman Pincers were now whimpering from where they'd come to rest. All but Scythe and Switchblade were stirring. Those two would not move again. The four surviving Dobermans limped and dragged themselves back to Malcrook's side. Cleaver, as he hobbled past dad, squatted and urinated on his hand.

Suddenly, dad stirred and moaned. Torry looked down at him, astonished. He wasn't dead after all! *But the muller—it had connected squarely. Or had it?* Malcrook noticed dad's movements too. Quicker than lightening, he sprang forward and without breaking stride, reared back with his steel-toed miner's boot and delivered a sharp kick. Dad's head snapped sideways. He was silent once more. Without hesitation, Malcrook darted into the main chamber and gave a shrill whistle. Instantly, five boys sprang from their stations at the whirring machinery and were by his side, standing in rapt attention. "Yes *sir!*" the oldest one said loudly.

"Quallor," Malcrook instructed. "Will you and Rothie and your other friends assist me here? Seems we have a *truspaser* in our midst. Oh, look, there he is now." Malcrook spat at dad's lifeless shape. "Would you mind collecting this wretched intruder into a hand cart and take him to the dungeons—before he recovers from the love pat my boot just placed on his miserable head? Oh, yes, and please be sure *not* to lock his dungeon cell door. I wouldn't want to spoil the fun for our little friends, the Tommyknockers!"

"Yes sir," Quallor responded without emotion. Immediately two of the boys hustled off for an iron-wheeled wheelbarrow. Within minutes they had dad loaded and were hauling him away, bumping along the same tunnel from which he'd entered.

Several hours later dad came to. He was lying face-down on

a cold, uneven stone floor. He opened his eyes.

Nothing.

He couldn't see a thing. He shook his head slightly. Immediately, pain stabbed through his face, particularly the right side where the jaw bone connects to the skull. As his head turned, he felt a loose rattle and could hear bones grinding together. "Augghhh!" He wanted to cry out, but the pain prohibited it. Instead, all that came was a small yelp in a half-whisper.

"I'm... I'm blind... can't see a thing," he muttered as he blinked furiously, trying to invent vision from blackness.

"Hello there, neighbor!" came a cheery, loudly whispering voice from a few feet away. "Not to worry, you're not blind. Well, probably not anyway. No telling what Malcrook's done to your eyes, I suppose. More likely it's just that there's no light to be had here in the dungeons. Can't see without light you know! But that's all right, you'll get used to it. Now, you'd better swing your dungeon door closed, and quick. No telling how long before they arrive."

What the...? dad wondered. *Who in the sam hill is that? And where in the dickens am I? Dungeons... what dungeons?* Mustering all his strength, he croaked, "They? Who're *they*? And who're you?"

"Oh, you'll find out soon enough! We've got lots of time to swap stories, that's for sure. By the way, I'm quite glad to see you. Been by myself down here going on six years now. It'll be good to have a little company! Not that you're glad about it, I don't mean it that way, oh no! Anywho, if you don't do as I say and shut your door, it will be too late, especially with your great big voice. They'll hear you from far away and come running. *They* are the Tommyknockers. And in your condition, it won't take them long to finish the job Malcrook started. So if you know what's good for you, you'll limp over to the door and shut yourself in."

Utter darkness pressed inward as dad struggled to shake the

cobwebs from his mind and process this bizarre information.

But the quiet was abruptly broken by a shuffling in the distance and the murmur of gravelly voices. Darting fragments of dim light bounced randomly off the rough rock walls announcing the arrival of someone with a small flashlight or candle.

"Too late!" the kind voice yelled. "Shut your door *now*, or you're done for! Shut it, I say!"

Dad pushed himself up to his knees. *I'd be glad to shut the door if I only knew where it was.* He looked around. Every now and then a flash raced over a surface of rock. *At least I ain't blind.*

Now the sound of boots tramping on rock was clearly audible…and getting louder. He could make out a word or two, and they weren't kind. His head was throbbing and the right side of his face felt icy numb and on fire at the same time. Dad crawled forward with hands extended. Nothing but empty space. As the voices got louder, he thought he could tell from which direction they were coming. *Darnit, goin' the wrong way; gotta turn around.* He crawled back to where he'd started and already the light source was nearly there. It was clear now where the door was—the light was shining through the opening. He crawled as fast as he could, but his injuries were so severe, he teetered and shambled like a drunk. Finally, he reached the opening and put his hand up to the door.

But what he touched wasn't hard and cold—it was warm and soft, and dirty. It was greasy fabric covering a person's belly. Dad looked up, directly into a beacon of candle light. He snatched his hand back in disgust. Looking him almost straight in the eye was a man—a short, thick, filthy midget of a human. With a leering smile, bulging wart-covered nose, and an odd felt hat, the man asked menacingly, "Going somewhere? And so soon?"

Chapter Forty-Six

Door Jambs and Dilemmas

Dad could see five of them, all dressed similarly, crowding in the opening of the doorway. Several held candle-lanterns. All were sizing him up, rubbing their hands together in anticipation of something—something evil.

"So, it looks like our good friend Mr. Malcrook already had some fun with you!" the largest one said. As he spoke, dad could see the small man had only about four teeth and the stench pouring from his mouth was like sewage. "Well, perhaps he's just got you warmed up for us! What do you say, boys, why don't we show this stranger a little good, old-fashioned Tommyknocker hospitality! Just like his granddaddy's granddaddy before him showed us once upon a time!"

He and the four others stepped forward. All this time, dad had been desperately searching his brain for his best course of action. He knew he wouldn't stand a chance if they got in the room with him—he was far too weak and bleary to be any good in a fight. There was only one chance—shut the door, with them on the outside.

As the first one strode through dad made his move. Balancing precariously on his knees and one hand, he lashed forward with his best effort at a punch. He would only have one shot so it had to be dead on.

Smack! It was.

His fist connected squarely with the leader's knobbly nose and drove him backward, shrieking. Three of the others were directly behind, and so were swept backward also. But as they surged back, the fifth Tommyknocker, who was standing off to the side, dashed through the door and landed a boot to dad's ribs. Dad hunched in pain and instantly the little man leaped onto his back, screaming and tugging at dad's hair.

White-hot pain shot through dad's head as the Tommyknocker rocked his fist back and forth on the spot the muller had previously connected.

Fortunately, dad's skull had not been shattered by the muller's blow. Neither he, nor Torry for that matter, knew she had not actually let the muller free fall. No, if she had, he wouldn't be alive now. Subconsciously, Torry had slowed it just enough that it knocked him out and bruised his skull but did not crack it. Torry simply was not a murderer no matter what malevolent pressures Malcrook might apply.

But this was not the thought in dad's mind at the moment. The little wild man on his back and the laser-pain in his head consumed his full attention. Now the other Tommyknockers had regained their feet and were striding angrily forward for their revenge.

"That's twice this month I've had my nose mashed," the leader cursed. "The boy who did it the first time got away—lucky for him. But you, mister big strapping logger man, you shall pay for *both* assaults. You shan't be so lucky." Dad, of course couldn't have known it was me who delivered the first broken nose—I never had a chance to tell him that evening we were sent to bed without supper.

Summoning all his strength, dad reached backward and grabbed at the Tommyknocker straddling his back. His great hand found a stubby leg. Dad yanked. The man slid off like snow from a hot tin roof and went flying through the air like a Frisbee. Straight back through the door he shot. In a continuous motion, dad reached for the door, grabbed an edge of it, and heaved-to with all his might.

The Tommyknocker leader managed to dodge his projectile friend then lunged at dad. But too late. Just at that moment, the heavy wood and iron door slammed shut with a mighty clang. An ear-piercing shriek lacerated the air.

"My hand… you horrible man, you've cut my hand! Aaauggghhhh!"

And it was true. The unfortunate Tommyknocker had not pulled his hand from the door's path quickly enough. The great iron rim bit into his wrist like a knife, severing it.

Suddenly dad felt sick. He wretched; the contents of his stomach pouring forth onto the rock floor.

Outside, the commotion quickly died down. The Tommyknockers, though violently angry and bent on retribution, knew once the impervious dungeon door was shut, they were done. Again, flecks of light danced and darted across random surfaces as they turned about, cursing and hissing angrily. Then they were gone. Dad dragged himself to the center of his cell and collapsed. The intensity of his pain and exhaustion overcame him, and he fell into a deep and troubled sleep with dreams full of knives and teeth and wickedness. He was searching for his sons in dark, dangerous places. But all his yells and calls echoed back empty.

It was many hours later before he awoke, and as the last of his troubled dreams sifted away, he recalled that someone else was down here, too: the kind-sounding man who had told him to close his door. *Probably saved my life,* he thought. *But who—who's the man behind the voice? Also, now that the door is shut, how'll I get out? Got to find my boys—get back to Marge. She'll be worried, real worried.*

Dad sat up. Blind. Utter and complete blackness pressed in on him. He felt himself for injuries. The cloth of his pant legs and shirt sleeves were hard, encrusted with dried blood. But his limbs seemed okay with the exception of the few rips and puncture wounds. Then he felt his face. *Oh… my… Gosh.* His mind couldn't believe what his fingers were relaying. The left side of his face felt normal for the most part, perhaps some swelling and puffiness.

But the right side—it felt like a horror story. What was once his nose, was now only about half there. His right nostril had been caught by one of the Doberman's teeth and was ripped, badly. As his fingers ran across the line of his jawbone they sent impossible, confusing information to his brain. The jawbone was supposed to be straight, but it wasn't. Somewhere near his molars, there was an abrupt angle, sideways. The skin stretched hideously over the broken bone. Beyond the break, there was no bone left, or rather what bone was there had been shattered to splinters. *Must be where Malcrook's boot connected,* he thought. He tried to open his mouth. Instant searing pain rocketed through his mandible causing his face to contort. *Owww! How'm I gonna eat? For that matter, what am I gonna eat? I need to get out of here—and quick. Got to see a doctor.*

Dad stood and stumbled toward the door. Groping clumsily, he found the bar-covered opening. Setting his lower jaw as best he could, he called into the darkness, "Pssst, 'skuse me. Are you there? Mister?"

From the darkness came a jovial reply. "G'morning neighbor! Top o' the morning to you! If it is morning. Never know down here. Don't get a whole lot of sunlight here in the dungeons, ha ha! Little joke there to help brighten your day! But anywho, now that you're safe, what's your name, mister? And what's your story? And don't be too quick in the telling! We've got lots of time, nothing but time way down here underground. You know, it's great to finally have a little company, and I don't mean the Tommyknockers either. Not great for you, of course—I didn't mean it that way, no. By the way, nice piece of handiwork against that small band of the buggers! I wasn't sure you'd be able to close your door in time. I imagine one of them will be smarting for quite a while!"

That voice, dad thought, *it's familiar. I know I've heard it before. But where? And what's with the cheery tone? How could anyone be anything but depressed here?* Dad spoke, enduring pain blasts with every word. "Name's George Miller—and thanks… thanks for warning me about those Tommyknockers. I owe you one there. My story's simple. I'm looking for my two boys. Seems they run off somewheres and I aim to find 'em. Nice to meet you, mister—mister… Say, I never got your name."

"Name? My name? Of course! How clumsy of me! It's been so long since I've had company, seems I've forgotten my manners! My name is Kringle. Peter Kringle. And so you are George… Miller. Hmmmm… I thought you looked familiar when the boys brought you here in that wheelbarrow. They always bring torches with them so I could see you through the gaps in the bars don't you know. Nasty mess Malcrook's made of your face, but it looks like with time it will heal. You must set your jawbone back into place though—can't let it fuse the way it is now. Oh no, that would never do! Anyway, where was I? Hmmm, let me rake the cobwebs from my feeble old memory a bit—hoommm. Yess. Didn't you used to go by Georgey when you were a young lad? And you had a couple of friends, I believe. Yesss, hmmm, let me see… Oh yes! That would have been Brett Lunt and Ronnie Williams, if I'm not mistaken. I recall you three boys used to pal around quite a bit, and mischief had an uncanny way of finding you—especially that Williams boy! Wasn't he the one who got in trouble with Sheriff Cooper for throwing firecrackers at Old-Lady Parker's mangy old blind dog? And didn't he also get expelled from third grade for calling Miss Nichols "The Beak" a little too loudly once? Ha ha ha—too bad about that one! Everybody knew she had a generous chimney, but, if anyone was going to get in trouble for bringing it up, it would have been Ronnie."

What the…? How in the world could he know that? Dad's mind whirred in amazement. *How could he know any of it? And he said his name was Peter Kringle…THE Peter Kringle? The missing toymaker? So, this is where he's been all these years.* Powerful memories of his childhood came flooding back. Memories of himself at age 10, side by side with his two best buddies, staring in awe through green-trimmed, gigantic plate-glass windows at all those wondrous toys!

For a moment, dad was able to nearly forget the stabbing pain in his face. He asked, "How'd you know all that stuff? Nobody's called me Georgey for twenty years or better. And yes, Brett and Ronnie were my best friends. Ronnie finally married Linda Nichols, The Beak's daughter. Now there's one for you! But Brett...sad to say he died in a logging accident."

"So sorry about Brett. He was a good kid. Had moxie, common sense."

"Yeah, he was my best buddy. Still have dreams about him. But anyway, how do you know those things? And more important, how do we get out of here?"

"It's funny how I know those things," came the merry reply. "Seems I know all the kids. I know who's been naughty, and who's been nice. Just a little gift I have. Can't really explain it. As far as leaving the dungeons, there's no escaping—sorry to say. Malcrook made sure of that when he built this place. Been here five plus years myself and haven't figured a way out yet. Fact is, ol' Malcrook thinks I'm dead. Some of his boys know better, but they don't tell him. Do you know, Malcrook's such a coward, he never comes here himself? Gets his boys and the Tommyknockers to do it for him. That's the only reason I'm still alive. Well, that and Evon... how I miss Evon! But anyway... boy-oh-boy! If ol' Malcrook knew I was still alive, why he'd probably blow a gasket! And wouldn't that be fun...the gasket part, of course."

Chapter Forty-Seven

Gertrude

Dad listened to Peter rattle on. If there was anything at all good about his predicament, at least his dungeonmate would be interesting.

Peter continued his cheerily-told account of despair. "You know, most folks, kids that is, who come here don't last a week. Of course I do what I can to help, but sadly, they don't have the mental fortitude to stick it out here in the dark. Oh, I understand the accommodations aren't all that cushy. Beds are a bit hard, sanitation facilities don't work that well, and the menu's a tad on the lean side. Not exactly the Taj Mahal! Ha ha! no sir. Rat…that's all there is to eat. And what's worse, you have to eat them raw. No fires to be had down here—can't cook them. But they're not as bad as you might think, after you get used to them, that is."

Rats… ughhh, dad thought, struggling between revulsion and admiration of Peter's pluck and ingenuity. "Wellsir," dad responded, pain once again raging through his face and neck, "I appreciate your neighborly tone and all. And I have to tell you, it sure is an honor to finally meet you, but I'm gonna have to disagree on one point, in a friendly way, you understand. I don't mean anything by it, but there's *got* to be a way of escaping. I aim to get out of here no matter what you or anyone else says. I've got two boys to rustle up and a sick wife to tend to. Now, how thick are these doors?"

"Sir, no offense taken! If you manage to find a means of escape, I certainly hope you'll be kind enough to share that knowledge with me. Heavens to Betsy, I've tried all I can, but this place is a fortress! The doors are a good twelve inches thick, cedar heartwood posts bolted together with a steel rim around the periphery. The hinges are massive iron things, sunk deeply into the rock. And the walls, well, if you have any means of breaking solid bedrock with your fingers, you are a stronger man than I!"

The reality of just how hopeless the situation was began to set in. Out of frustration and anger, dad gripped the steel bars in the center hole of the door and shook. Pain flared through his jaw and the back of his skull, but there wasn't any give in the door, not even a fraction. It was impenetrable.

"I'm sorry, sir, terribly sorry," Peter said sadly. "It is truly a bleak existence down here, but perhaps with two of us, we can buoy each other's spirits. My hope is that someday Evon finds someone to help rescue me, or rather, us. But more about that later. In the meantime, I'd be happy to share with you the survival tips I've learned—if you're interested in hearing them. But first, can you tell me why the Tommyknocker shrieked when you slammed your door?"

"The door done chopped his hand off," dad said flatly. Suddenly the gravity of his doom hit him. Now it seemed the very rock walls were pressing in on him, squeezing away his will to survive. He understood what it felt like to be a caged zoo animal, only this was worse. At least zoo animals got sunlight and proper food. Without food, and especially without water, he was a dead man.

"Ohhh... now that's an interesting development!" Peter exclaimed. "And what happened to the hand? Did it, perchance, land on the *inside* of your cell?"

"Yeah. It's right here... " He kicked it, sending it skidding across the floor into some distant corner.

"Oh, you mustn't lose it!" Peter called out. "With a little luck and good care, that hand will keep you fed for several weeks!"

Dad just about retched again. The very thought of eating... It was too barbaric to fathom. "That's disgusting," he breathed, holding back another volume of vomit.

"Oh, no... no, no, no, no! I don't mean you should eat the hand! Gadfry, that would be cannibalistic... oh no... that's not at all what I intended! What I mean is, you use the hand for bait! Rat bait! The rats will smell it from hundreds of yards away and they'll come running by the score! You must be ready for them. It will be your means of survival for a good long time! But first, you've got to drink. You'll get nowhere quick if you dehydrate. But know what? This is your lucky day! There is a veritable gushing fountain of the clearest, purest spring water you ever tasted oozing from the rock walls of your very cell. Now pay attention and I'll tell you how to use your tongue to harvest drabbles and dribbles from the nooks and crannies... "

Meanwhile, back in the laboratory, after the boys had removed dad from the room, Gertrude finally let go the hug she and Torry were sharing. Torry didn't want the hug to end, not now...not ever. As long as she was in Gertrude's gentle arms everything seemed okay. But as soon as an inch's distance came between them, she was fair game for Malcrook all over again.

Gertrude stood back from Torry and looked at Malcrook. If

looks could kill, right then she would have lanced his forehead with a laser beam intense enough to bring down missiles. But she knew better than to say anything. If she did, she'd pay. And at her advanced age, one more such payment could be her last. He was brutally ruthless, even to his own wife.

"There now, Torry, honey," she said. "That strange man from the outside is gone and you're fine, right? Say, it'll be suppertime soon and the boys will be back from the deep tunnels with a big appetite. Tell you what. That ore sample you were crushing can wait. Come with me and help prepare dinner. Mister Malcrook will have one of the other kids clean this mess up. Isn't that right Mister Malcrook?"

He glowered back at her, anger festering under his skin. It absolutely enraged him when Gertrude came between him and Torry. *Curse that old blister*, he thought. *Why must she always meddle—come racing like a mother hen to Torry's side when things get a little difficult? I shall be so relieved when the old hag is gone! And that day draws near. Yes, it is only a couple weeks until Torry's seventeenth birthday! The day when Gertrude will be out—gone for good. And Torry, my lovely young flower, will be in. My new wife! Oh, yes... that will be a good day indeed! But, in the meantime, must keep cool. Torry has been through enough for one day. I can be nice, bide my time a little longer. Oh, yes.*

He smiled and replied mock-sweetly to Gertrude, "If you insist, dear. That would be fine."

****

So ends Book 1

The story continues in Book 2, *The Dark Quartz Mine*